To request permissions, contact the publisher at
ScharaReevesPress@gmail.com

Paperback: 978-1-7362987-2-5

First paperback edition December 2021.

Edited by Alyson Montione
Proofread by ScribeCat (ScribeCat.ca)
Cover art by Jake Bartok

Schara Reeves Press

ScharaReevesPress.com

ACKNOWLEDGEMENTS

Editor:

Alyson Montione

Proofreader:

ScribeCat (ScribeCat.ca)

Cover Artist:

Image by Jake Bartok

Text by Ashley Harris (The Modern Jane)

General Support:

Jesus Christ

Family

Friends

Schoharie Library Writing Club

Beta readers:

Heather Heckman

Emma Panzera

Jubilee Schmid

NYTHRIL

PRONUNCIATIONS

Aelor Ven (AY•lor vehn)
Adyne (ah•DINE)
Alarune (al•uh•ROON)
Alenor (ah•len•NOR)
Ameri (uh•MAYR•ee)
Ascriot (AS•kree•ot)
Asher (ASH•er)
Astra (AS•trah)

Baeno (BAE•no)
Bandilarian (ban•duh•LAYR•ee•un)
Bandon (BAN•dun)

Cithan (SIGH•than)
Coryn (COR•in)
Cyl (SILL)

Dannsair (Dan•SAYR)
Delnor (DEHL•nor)
Destrin (DES•trin)
Dia (DYA)
Drogan (DROH•gan)

Eatris (EE•tris)
Entrais (ENT•rays)
Eren (eh•REN)
Ethian (EE•thee•uhn)

Faizos (FY•zohs)
Farian (FAIR•ee•un)

Gavin (GAH•vin)

Graece (GRACE)
Grenedil (GREN•uh•dill)

Havirax (HAVE•uh•racks)

Ithynian Gasper (eye•THIN•ee•un GAS•pur)
Ivinon (IHV•ih•nohn)

Jahng (J pronounced like *ge* in *beige*: JAHNG)
Julyn (JOO•lin)

Kaeden (KAY•den)
Karja (car•ZHA)
Kassander (CAS•and•dur)
Kayliene (kay•lee•EN)
Keeshiff (KEE•shiff)
Kelosthmane (kell•LOSTH•man)
Killyan (KILL•ee•an)
Kryso (CRY•so)
Kythdexlentu-Orsha (KITH•de•len•ta-OR•shah

Lieris (LEER•ys)
Litash (lih•TASH)
Louko (LOO•co)
Lucian (LOO•shee•un)
Lusan (LOO•san)

Macridean (MACK•rih•dee•un)
Mariah (mah•RY•uh)
Matthes (MATH•es)
Melye (MEL•yay)
Merimeethia (mer•eh•MEETH•ee•ah)
Merym (MER•im)
Miadoris (mee•ah•DOR•is)
Mitheau (MITH•eeyou)

Nythril (NITH•ril)

Omath (OH•math)
Orshian (OR•shee•un)
Ovok (OH•vok)

Qura (COO•rah)

Ravyen (rah•VEE•en)
Ren Dhag (REN DAHG)
Rhioa (rye•OH•uh)
Rhumir (rue•MEER)
Rufio (ROO•fee•oh)
Rusie (ROO•see)

Silbyr (SILL•beer)
Soletuph (SOUL•tuff)

Tallaman (TAW•lah•mahn)
Tehng (TENG)
Tirzah (TEER•zah)
Tuloi (TOO•loi)
Tyron (TIE•ron)
Tzaro (TSAH•row)

Verzaer (Ver•ZAYR)
Vheil Esr (VEIL es•EER)

Xyrilcylduin (zy•rill•SILL•doo•inn)

Zhahn (ZAHN)

A Synopsis of The Exiled: Of Shade and Shadow
Book I of A Daughter's Ransom

Less than a year after The Great War, Princess Astra Verzaer is exiled from her home country of Litash. She is sent to Merimeethia by her brother in the hopes of finding proof that her enemy, Tyron, is still alive. Instead she finds that her unwilling companion, Prince Louko, is only cold and withdrawn as a result of dealing with his abusive father.

In a dramatic turn of events, the king of Merimeethia is murdered by Steward Kaedan, and Louko and his brother Keeshiff are blamed and forced to flee. They, along with their sister Mariah, a small group of palace knights, and Astra, all head for the country of Nythril where Louko's uncle might give them refuge. Their journey is plagued by close calls with soldiers, animals, infighting, and Mariah's increasingly antagonistic behavior towards Louko.

However, the obstacles they face bring Astra and Louko closer together, allowing them to learn more about each other and eventually develop a friendship. Louko learns that Astra believes Tyron to be alive, while Astra discovers Tyron was once a father-figure to Louko. Through their combined information, the two begin to suspect that Kaeden is actually Tyron in disguise.

However, right before they reach Nythril, Mariah betrays Astra, who is captured and taken to the capitol. Louko goes after her alone, believing that he can talk Tyron into releasing her. But upon arrival, Tyron assures Louko that Astra is safe and offers him the chance to rule Merimeethia. Louko finds himself at a crossroads: does he help the only person that showed him kindness as a child, or try and find the new friend who has already sacrificed so much on his behalf?

This book is dedicated to our sister, Jubilee, who has been our biggest fan since before anyone else knew Louko and Astra even existed.

THE EXILED:

A GAME OF WITS

A DAUGHTER'S RANSOM: BOOK III

BY NIAMH SCHMID

AND REBECCA SCHMID

CHAPTER I

Asher:

Asher was worried. When Prince Louko had ridden off to rescue Astra, he'd told Keeshiff only to come after them if they weren't back in three weeks. It had been a month.

Keeshiff had been in a frenzy when they hadn't returned after two weeks and hadn't even waited for the agreed-upon third before stubbornly insisting on setting out with a few of his knights. No amount of arguing dissuaded Keeshiff's determination to come, and Asher gave up after even Bandon could not convince him of the risks. Lord Aelor Ven, Louko's uncle, had at least outfitted them with supplies. The lord had been worried to the point of hostility when they had arrived without his nephew. Hopefully he wouldn't kill anyone before they got back.

Now, Keeshiff, Rufio, Ivinon, and Asher were one day away from Melye, the capital of Merimeethia, where they assumed Astra had been taken. But the impending storm had made for a moonless night, forcing the small party to stop until first light and set up the tents. The last near-encounter they'd had with a patrol had been too close for them to dare continue in such pitch dark. Rufio and Ivinon had settled down in their shared tent, though Keeshiff was no doubt lying sleepless in his. Asher had been able to talk the prince out of taking a watch only because Keeshiff had taken it almost every night for the last week.

And so here Asher was, kneeling by the fire and prodding the coals gently as he tried not to think of worst-case scenarios. Staying clear of villages had kept them from being seen, but it had also kept them away from any source of news. For all they knew, they could slip into Melye tomorrow and find that Louko had been executed days ago.

Shying away from that dark thought, Asher nudged a log nearer to the flames. It would have to dry out before he added it. At least the rain and overcast sky meant that the smoke was unlikely to be seen, and they were able to risk the fire. It was cold enough to be miserable even with this meager warmth.

A sound like a branch cracking made Asher's gaze jerk upwards. Nothing. Then, just as he was beginning to relax again, he caught the sound of distant footsteps sloughing through the mud. Too heavy for a person; it had to be a horse. Hand on the hilt of his sword, Asher silently got to his feet and crept over to the tents. Rufio was nearest the entrance so he shook him awake, held a finger to his lips to signal for quiet, then returned to the fire.

The lone hoofsteps grew closer, and then there was a muted thud and a grunt.

"Who's there?" Asher asked, voice low. He gripped his sword hilt.

"Asher? It's you? She needs help," a raspy, desperate voice replied even as a figure came into view. He held a limp bundle in his arms.

Behind him, Asher heard Rufio draw his blade.

But Asher only stared at the intruder. He was muddy, bedraggled, and was clearly underweight.

And...was that a *person* he was holding?

"Hurry! She needs help!" the young man half-shouted as he struggled to keep the form in his arms.

Suddenly, Asher recognized the voice. The shock was like a punch to the gut. *Prince Louko.*

Asher stepped forward, reaching out to take whoever it was Louko held.

"She got sick…she—I don't know if she'll wake up. I tried to—" Louko sputtered out half-finished sentences in a frenzy. However, staggering though he was, he wasn't letting Asher take the bundle. He wasn't even letting Asher near him.

Trying to calm the panicked Louko down, he said, "Louko, you're safe now. Let me see her and we will try to help."

That's when it clicked. *Her.* Louko was holding Princess Astra.

"Louko?" The voice came from Keeshiff's tent, and Asher looked up to see the prince emerge. He stopped, staring in slack-jawed shock at the thin figure before him.

"Keeshiff, get as many blankets as you can find and put them in my tent, *now.* Have Rufio start a pot of hot water. Louko, give her to me." Asher spoke with authority, though his mind did not process fully what he was saying. The instinct that came from years of practice had taken over. Louko looked as if he was about to fall over, and yet, when Asher moved forward to take Astra from him, he recoiled again with unnatural swiftness.

"I'm not leaving her!" His rasping voice might have been a shout had it not been so clear he was in dire need of water.

Asher automatically raised his hands to show he meant no harm. "No one will try to make you," he assured in a deep, calm voice. "But if you don't let me help her now, we only ruin her chances."

3

Louko's breathing quickened and he flinched when Asher moved closer, but this time he allowed the physician to take the small burden. Even with the heavy blankets, Asher could feel her shivering. A look down revealed a deathly white face. They had to move fast...but even fast could be inadequate. With as much swiftness as he dared, Asher carried her to the tent that he and Keeshiff had shared. Shallow, uneven breathing gave Louko away as he followed right behind.

Ignoring the stricken Keeshiff, Asher ducked inside and laid Astra on the makeshift bed. The physician began pulling back the layers of blanket so that he could assess what was going on.

"Louko, where are you hurt?" Keeshiff's question still held his shock.

Asher realized that Louko's clothing was bloodstained. Whether it was his or Astra's, Asher couldn't tell. But it looked old enough that he decided it could wait.

"Is she going to be alright?" It was as if Louko hadn't even heard Keeshiff.

Not daring to answer the question, Asher pointed at one of his cases in the corner of the tent. "There are strips of cloth in there. Bring them here, along with the dark blue vial." Astra was malnourished, dehydrated, and dangerously fevered. It was hard to tell if there was anything more beneath all the mud she was caked with. "And Keeshiff, go check on Rufio and bring me water if it's ready."

Both princes acted without a word.

It seemed Louko hadn't missed Asher's lack of reply, for as his shaky hands offered the blue vial, he said, "She's going to die, isn't she," with a hollow conviction.

"I can give no diagnosis without first assessing the patient," Asher replied in as professional of a manner as he could. It would be the best way to keep Louko calm.

And yet, already, he understood Louko's doubt. They did not have the proper supplies to take care of someone so sick. Even if they did, they couldn't afford to stay in one place long enough to nurse her back to health. "How long since she was last awake?" he asked without looking up.

Keeshiff re-entered silently with a pot of water and Asher pointed towards a spot where he could set it down. "Louko, are *you* alright?" The older prince's voice was barely calm.

Louko's eyes were fixated on Astra; Asher could feel it. "She hasn't woken up since...um..." He appeared to be concentrating. "Yesterday night, maybe? Yesterday night...I took the one cuff off yesterday morning...but I couldn't get the other one...."

Asher noted both Louko's total avoidance of Keeshiff's question, and the repetition of his speech.

"Alright." The physician poured several drops from the vial into the water. "Are you wounded at all?" he asked as he stirred the mixture and then began to soak two cloths.

"No. He didn't touch me. I told you he wouldn't." The answer was a void. "Taking off the cuffs should help, but I couldn't get the last cuff off...."

His distracted thought pattern was disconcerting. But Asher would have to trust Louko's statement for now. "Use this and start cleaning her face and neck. It has a mild disinfectant." He wrung out a cloth and handed it to Louko. Best to keep him busy.

"What can I do?" Keeshiff's strained question broke through.

"Get more water," Asher said, barely glancing at the already reddened pot by his side.

With some of the blood and grime removed, the physician was better able to evaluate Astra's condition. She bore all sorts of marks: bruises, burns, gashes, fractures—all clearly recent and yet in different stages of healing. Some of the lacerations were even fully scarred over. But how? They hadn't been missing long enough for...Asher refocused. Her high fever and the fluid in her lungs were far more pressing matters. He needed to start with cleaning the wounds and getting them bandaged.

"Try and get some of the mud out of her hair," he instructed Louko. The princess's hair had apparently been chopped short, likely in an attempt to control the filth of it. The bright red color was completely hidden by layers of dirt and damp.

"I tried to cut it...but all I had was a knife," he mumbled as he obeyed, taking the water from Keeshiff and fulfilling the next task.

"That was a good decision," Asher responded with what reassurance he could.

For a time, no words passed between the three besides the physician's orders. Astra did not wake and only time would tell if she would—and then, only if given the chance. It would be foolhardy not to assume Louko had been followed. Even now, soldiers might be on their tail.

"Is she going to be alright?" Keeshiff asked quietly, though still staring at his brother with painful concern.

Asher phrased his reply carefully. "It is too early to say for certain, but she has proven remarkably resilient in the past." He gently examined her wrist again where the copper-colored manacle still wrapped around it. He thought of the various pins and picks in his medical supplies, mentally matching their size to the lock.

He got to his feet, picking up the water and soiled cloths. Until Astra woke, there was no way to administer medicine. He would have to see if he could scavenge up enough ingredients for a poultice. He motioned to Keeshiff, and the prince quickly copied him. Then Asher's assessment turned towards Louko, who still knelt by his unconscious friend. The boy was thin and nearly as dirty as Astra had been. His sunken eyes spoke of dehydration and his sluggish movements gave away his exhaustion.

"Let's get you cleaned up," he said. "And get you some food."

"I'm fine. *She's* the one who needs help." His breathing had already picked up its pace.

"Louko…" Keeshiff's voice was soft. "You look half dead. Please, let him just make sure you're alright."

Louko's head shook violently as he replied, "I'm fine. She can't die. Please."

Asher raised his hands again, both to calm Louko and silence Keeshiff. "Nevertheless, you are covered in dirt, Louko," the physician pointed out gently. "It is not good to have all of that so close to Astra. If you could clean yourself up, your brother could see to getting you a change of clothes."

"Alright...alright…." Louko ran his hand through his hair, and that's when Asher noticed it. The hair. There was white in it. Louko's once jet-black hair was peppered with white.

The realization took Asher aback. For a moment, he could say nothing. What had *happened* to them?

"I will fetch you more water. Find a clean cloth for yourself in the satchel," he finally managed. "Keeshiff, go find him new clothes."

The prince nodded and ducked out of the tent.

Asher glanced once at Astra then at Louko. They would be alright for a few seconds. Asher took the dirty water and exited.

"One more pot, Rufio," Asher called quietly, emptying the other one beyond the camp. "And heat some rocks to wrap up in the blankets. She'll need the warmth."

Rufio obeyed in a hurry. Only when Asher came closer did the knight ask, "What happened?" His face was pale.

"I can't tell yet. Something bad," was Asher's quiet reply. "I know nothing beyond that."

Rufio, who had been emptying the cooking pot of hot water into Asher's basin, stopped midway. "Are they alright?"

Asher gave an impatient motion for the knight to hurry. "I don't know, and now is not the time to ask."

The reply was enough to head off any further questions. Rufio finished his task and Asher took the basin of clean water back to the tent.

"It's me, Asher," he announced in a soft tone before entering, hoping it would keep Louko from startling. Then he slipped through the entrance. "You can use this to clean up."

Louko obeyed without a sound. Every noise—even made by him splashing the water as he cleaned his own hands—startled him. "She still hasn't woken up," he stated as soon as he had finished, even though the fact was an obvious one.

Asher took the proffered cloth and gathered it up with the other dirty ones. They would need to be washed before reuse.

"We'll have to get that cuff off first and then give her some time to rest," the physician said, quickly surveying Louko. There was no sign of physical illness beyond hunger and dehydration.

"I've got the clothes." Keeshiff's breathless entrance startled even Asher.

Louko jumped, taking out the sword that was still strapped to his belt and looking like a cornered animal for a moment. Recognition flashed across his face as he realized it was Keeshiff, but the sword didn't lower— only trembled with his hand.

"Woah, woah, easy." Asher spoke as if to a spooked horse. Slowly, he took a step back. Keeshiff followed his lead. "It is just your brother. No one is going to harm you."

Slowly, he lowered the blade, shaking his head as if fighting against himself as he did so. He did not resheath it.

"Why don't you put that away for now?" Asher made it a suggestion. "It will not help Astra."

The fierceness with which the younger prince shook his head was not encouraging; neither was the fact that he gave no other response.

"Alright. Then what would you like us to do?" The question was calm. Asher was not going to try and argue with the one holding a sword.

Louko ran his hand through his hair with his free hand, clearly unsteady on his feet. "They're going to find her...we're too close. Tyron is going to find her...."

Tyron? Asher hadn't heard that name in years.... What in Eatris did a dead man have to do with all this? *Focus. Get Louko to sit down.* "Yes, we are close. But we need to give Astra a little more time. It is going to be difficult to move her and we will all have to gather our strength. Including you."

"I am *fine*." Louko's harsh words were only combated by the fact that he did, thankfully, put away the sword.

Keeshiff remained silent, clearly afraid to do any further damage to his shattered brother.

Asher did not try to argue the obviously false point, instead reasoning, "Why don't you sit by Astra? Hearing you nearby may help her wake up."

The younger prince swallowed hard, but seemed to like this idea much better, slowly making his way over to Astra. "I kept talking to her...Killyan said it might help keep her awake...but she stopped responding..." he mumbled.

Killyan? As in, the patrol captain who had captured Astra? Asher exchanged a glance with Keeshiff. It was becoming clearer and clearer that they needed to know what happened. Did Asher dare ask? He didn't want to with Louko being so skittish. But did he dare wait?

"When did you speak to him?" Asher asked cautiously.

"Right before we escaped. He gave me the door keys and Rhumir got us out...Astra was already sick, and then it wouldn't stop raining...." Louko half-fell onto the mat near Astra. He took her hand and began rubbing it as if he hoped life would return.

That went alright. Now for the more difficult question: "Who was it who kept you there?"

Louko's hand froze mid-motion, as did his entire body. Every muscle went visibly rigid. "Tyron." The name came out hoarsely, as if it was nearly physically impossible to say it out loud.

Asher remembered the man from when he had come to Merimeethia. Tyron had been quiet, respectful, and fond enough of Louko to protect him from Omath. Asher had thought him a good man. But that had been nearly fifteen years ago. Tyron had only stayed for two years and then gone off with his brother. Though Asher had heard plenty of rumors about the Litashian prince during The War, he had never met Tyron again. And he didn't expect to, considering that everyone said Astra had killed him.

Asher chanced a look towards Keeshiff. The prince seemed equally baffled. But while any such questions might be valid, Asher had no intention of challenging Louko's sanity. "Alright. We will make sure he does not find us."

The laugh that came from Louko's mouth was startling. "Right. Just like that…." He returned to rubbing Astra's hand.

Asher saw Keeshiff's wide-eyed concern as he looked his way. The physician had no idea how to respond.

"I have to wash these," he finally said. "Will you be alright to stay with Astra?"

The only response he got from Louko was a nod.

"Keeshiff, grab that basin and follow me." Asher gave the order and turned away.

Keeshiff finally wrenched his gaze from his brother and the motionless form of Astra, obeying without a word and grabbing the water bowl. The two walked out the tent in silence and back into the rain.

It was Asher who asked in a hushed voice, "Is his claim about Tyron possible?" Keeshiff had been more involved in the war than Asher.

"I..." Keeshiff stumbled over his words. "I mean...I don't...she killed him...but Louko, before he left...he said something—he was convinced Kaedan wouldn't kill him...but I suppose...."

Asher processed this all silently. His mind was swirling with the events of the night. "I think she was hurt and then healed with Gifting. Would he be capable of that?"

"I don't know...." Keeshiff was quiet, and Asher realized it was in part because Ivinon and Rufio were now standing there, waiting for any word.

"Boil these and then hang them under a tent to dry," Asher instructed, dropping the cloths near the cauldron. "And then use what basins we have to catch rain; we will need water to replace our stores."

They both looked as if they wanted to ask at least one of the many questions spinning in their heads but thought better of it. They went off to their work, leaving Asher and Keeshiff alone again.

"I never should have let him go alone," Keeshiff said, with guilt lining every word.

"As if that would have helped," Asher grunted. "Then I would just have three of you to treat."

Keeshiff didn't say anything further on the subject, but it was clear he didn't believe it. "We have to get her back, obviously, but how are we going to do it? We're right outside Melye: We could be found any minute."

Asher sighed at the reminder, rubbing the back of his neck. "I don't know," he admitted. "She needs to be kept as dry, safe, and stationary as possible. There's no way of doing that while traveling in Merimeethia." How were they going to get her all the way to Nythril in this condition? "We could put her in front of another rider, potentially, or maybe find a way to hang a sort of sling on the side of a horse."

"Alright," Keeshiff replied simply, chewing the bottom of his lip. "Let's see what we have."

A GAME OF WITS

CHAPTER II

Louko:

Louko couldn't sleep. He wouldn't sleep. Not while Astra was so sick. He had watched helplessly as she had deteriorated; Tyron trying to get who knew what out of her. He couldn't watch anymore, but neither could he do anything to help her. She had to make it. She just had to.

And so, he refused to leave her side, nearly oblivious to those around him, and yet at the same moment panicking at every noise. Everything sounded like Tyron coming down the hall...or the keys jingling against the lock, or Astra being chained up. It was as if every nerve was frayed to its end, and the only thing that reminded him Astra was safe was the fact that she was right in front of him. He rubbed her hand again, hoping she would awaken with the movement.

"Louko, it's just me, Asher. May I come in?" The frighteningly gentle voice made Louko jump.

With an attempt at a deep breath, Louko replied, "Yes," as he forced himself to calm down.

Asher entered bearing a plate and cup. "Here," he said. "This will help."

Louko looked at him, confused. "She's unconscious…."

The physician, now closer, shook his head. "It's not for her—it's for you." He held out the bread and water.

He didn't make any move to take it. "I'm fine," he murmured, thoughts wandering back to Astra and wondering how long they would have to wait before they knew if she would die.

"You need to keep up your strength if you are going to fully be able to help her," Asher countered.

Nerves again threatened to break as he ran his free hand through his hair. He gave no answer.

Asher seemed to roll his words around in his mouth before saying them. "What would Astra want you to do?"

Louko did not answer immediately, but he slowly let go of her hand and took the food.

"Thank you," Asher said, crossing to the other side of the tent and beginning to sort through one of his cases. He pulled something out and set it aside.

"Yeah," Louko managed to say, forcing himself to eat what he'd been given.

Asher must have been watching him as, once Louko finished, the physician collected the dishes and thanked him again. He went to leave but stopped and regarded Louko carefully.

"Astra has never been one to give up. I do not think she will start now," was his sincere statement.

Louko certainly hoped so. He didn't think he would be able to live with himself if she died.

The physician exited the tent and returned minutes later, stopping to pick up whatever it was he'd taken out of his pack earlier. "I'm going to see if I can get that last cuff off, alright?"

"Wait. No, it'll hurt her. She can't slip it off. It's too tight." He stiffened, already fighting the urge to put himself between Astra's clammy figure and Asher.

"I know it's too tight," Asher said calmly. "I'm going to pick the lock, see?" He held up two metal pins that were bent at the ends.

"I...you'll be careful?" he asked, tapping his finger nervously against his lap as he eyed the lock picks in Asher's hand.

He nodded, kneeling next to Astra. "Very careful," he promised.

Slowly, Asher took Astra's chained wrist and laid it by her side. The heavy chain that once bound her hands together had been sawn through. Louko watched as the physician positioned the manacle so that the lock was facing up before picking up the metal pins and setting to work.

Every click or scrape invoked a "careful" or a flinch from Louko, and once or twice he actually started to get up from his seat.

A metallic snap made him jump.

"Got it," Asher breathed, setting his pins aside and pulling the red bronze away from Astra's wrist.

Louko jumped up. "Is she okay, is she any better? Is she worse?" He had no self-control, nor focus enough to even think of stopping long enough for Asher to answer. Louko just fretted and panicked and ran his hand through his hair as he babbled on. He needed to shut up. He needed to shut up. But was Astra going to be alright?

"It may take time to tell," Asher cut in, now stowing the manacle away. "But having the cuff off should help. For now, the best thing is to simply let her rest." The physician poured something from a vial onto a cloth and came back, swabbing Astra's raw, blistered wrist. "You should rest, too, while you have the chance."

Louko stared at Astra for a long time. He didn't want to fall asleep. He needed to watch her—to make sure she was alright. "I'm fine," he mumbled at last. No. He couldn't sleep.

Asher moved Astra's arm so it was back under the blankets. "It is a long way back to Nythril," he said softly. "You will need all your strength to get her back to safety."

It was hard, but the prince took a deep breath, trying to remain calm. "But what if she wakes up while I'm asleep? She'll panic."

"If you try to stay up simply because she might wake, you'll probably collapse within a few days." Asher spoke more bluntly now. "And I think Astra would be more panicked to find you dead from exhaustion than she would to find you resting."

Louko stilled, realizing that Asher was right. Again, he looked at Astra, then back at Asher, though only holding his gaze for a moment before looking away. "Alright."

Apparently satisfied, Asher turned away and took the last blanket that sat folded next to the cases. "Use this."

Louko took it with stiff fingers.

"Would you prefer that I stay in here or just outside?" he asked.

"Stay here. In case she wakes up," Louko mumbled, looking over to a corner in the tent and slowly going over to it. He didn't want to sleep. He didn't. Astra needed him...but his eyes ached with weariness and his head throbbed. Perhaps a little sleep wouldn't hurt....

"But then what? How long? A few weeks? What if that's not long enough? Years?" Louko hardly knew the words that were coming out of his mouth, let alone processing their outrageousness.

"Three weeks," Tyron replied firmly. "I promise. And then you will be in charge and you can do what you think best. Even bring back Keeshiff after a little while. Merimeethians have short enough memories."

Louko hesitated. "And what will you do then?"

Tyron bowed his head ever so slightly. "You will be in charge. I will do whatever you ask."

"And if I ask you to stay?"

"Your word is my command."

Doubt seeped deeply, and Louko shook his head. "No...no, this isn't right." It felt...wrong. And then he remembered Astra. Even if she had gotten away—where would she be going? She was his best friend, and he'd promised—promised they'd do this together. And here he was, facing Tyron alone, and just leaving her. Even if Tyron had simply been misunderstood, it wasn't right to just leave Astra in the dust when Louko had been so distraught at the thought of her doing the same to him. No. There had to be another way.

Any hurt that flashed in Tyron's expression was quickly and masterfully hidden. "What do you mean? How so?"

"I don't want to rule, I shouldn't rule...and I can't just turn my back on Astra." Why had he opened his stupid mouth in the first place? Compulsive idiot. But he was still conflicted. There had to be a resolution to this.... He couldn't turn his back on Astra but neither on Tyron.

"Ah." Realization dawned with sobriety and Tyron let out a pent-up breath. "I understand now. You cannot be with me and still be with her."

"What? No. We need to figure this out. You still did...that...to her." Louko stumbled at the reminder of what had happened in The War, the haunted look Astra had always worn from it.

"Louko, you are no fool. You know why Astra came to Melye in the first place," Tyron said, shaking his head gently. *"Do you think she will be able to rest while she knows I am alive? What happened...."* His voice faded and he cleared his throat in an effort to hide it. *"What happened to her was too much for anyone to forget, much less forgive—even if Astra wanted to. I know that, no matter what my reasons were, I cannot escape my actions."*

Louko was confused. "What are you saying?"

"I'm saying that you cannot have us both," Tyron answered as if wishing he did not have to. *"And that the answer to this choice is obvious—I don't hold it against you."* He squared his shoulders and folded his hands behind his back in a sad sort of resolve.

The prince felt as if the very floor had been taken out from under him, "What? You're making me choose?" Tyron was...running away? Again?

Tyron's attempt at a smile only made him look more sorrowful. "Could you really ask Astra to be anywhere near me? You saw how she reacted to Kaeden even before she made the connection."

"The Tyron I knew would at least have the guts to explain—and apologize." Louko only realized this as he said it, and the knowledge gave doubt a further hold. Something definitely wasn't right.

"Yes, he would have," Tyron's voice was faraway, his head bowed. *"And in the same stroke, would have forced Astra to pick between her only friend and the justice she seeks."*

"So instead, you make me choose between you and the only friend I have?"

With his head bowed, it was impossible to see Tyron's face. That's why the sudden, slow laugh didn't even register at first. Only when the unearthly sound echoed in the vaulted ceiling did Louko catch his breath.

"You really got to him, didn't you?" Tyron looked up with a smile that made Louko's skin crawl. The man shook his head, laughing again. "I have to give you credit—I didn't think he would give in to you so easily. But then, you always were a stubborn thing." Tyron turned and walked back to the map-covered table; any sign of conflict wiped from his entire posture.

Louko's blood ran cold, "Who are you talking to?"

"Oh, yes, how rude of me," Tyron's smile tipped to one side. "I haven't introduced my other guest." He gave a twirl of his fingers and the wall to Louko's left flickered.

There, covered from head to toe in chains, was Astra. Her eyes were wild, her whole body strained as she fought the cruel metal.

Louko's very life's breath was stifled in his lungs, and it was all he could do to manage to say, "What have you done, Tyron?"

"Nothing yet. Don't worry—I wouldn't dream of starting without you."

Louko jerked awake to voices beyond his range of sight. Oh, no. Tyron. He was coming for Astra again. Immediately, he stopped and listened for his friend's soft breathing, unable to see her through the dark. He heard her just a short distance to his left. Louko crawled on hands and knees to get back beside where she was lying, feeling her hand to make sure it still had life in it and then holding it tight.

But then his mind began taking in other details. He was not sitting on cold, damp stone. No, he had been on a mat of some kind, and Astra lay on blankets. As his eyes adjusted to the dark, the prince realized he was not surrounded by bars but by canvas. The pieces all clicked together and triggered a flood of memories. The escape, their flight through the woods, and at last finding Keeshiff and the others.

As if on cue, the voices clicked into focus, and he recognized one as Asher.

"While it will not be good for her, I'm afraid you're right," the physician said in undertones. "We can't risk staying here and getting all of us caught. We will have to move on and hope she wakes anyway."

They were talking about Astra. Louko felt very cold, grasping his friend's hand even tighter and rubbing it.

"Please, Astra, please wake up," he murmured, wishing she could hear him.

But there was no motion. No flicker of movement nor change in breathing. The only sounds were the voices of those outside who were already losing hope.

Louko lay there for long minutes, just listening and rubbing Astra's hand. Finally, they decided on a plan and the prince heard them all disperse to begin packing. Louko didn't move. He began murmuring, using what voice he had to quietly talk to his friend.

Then he felt it. The movement in her hand.

Louko froze, second-guessing himself and wanting to be sure he hadn't caused it. But then it came again, that subtle shift, now accompanied by more shallow breathing.

"Astra?" he whispered.

Her eyes opened suddenly. Before Louko could even register the miracle, she was pulling frantically to take her hand from his.

Oh wonderful, here they went….

"Astra, Astra, it's alright, we're out. Keeshiff is here—Asher's taking care of you." Louko was feverish as he tried desperately to get something to catch hold of Astra's attention.

"L-Louk-ko?" Astra's voice came out in an awful, scraping whisper, barely audible between her gasps for breath.

"Yes, yes. I'm here. We did it, we got out. You're going to be safe, don't worry." He wasn't sure who he was trying to convince: her or himself.

It was hard to tell if Astra understood him or not. Her gaze still fluttered around the tent, unable to focus on anything, and her shoulders still heaved with the effort it took to breathe. Whether it was his assurances or the inability to keep it up any longer, Astra let her head sink back onto the pillow.

There was a noise from outside the tent and, to Louko's relief, in came Asher. "Is she aw—"

The movement that followed was explosive. Louko barely registered that Astra was the source of it.

"Stay away from us," she hissed, somehow upright as she put herself between Louko and the physician. In one hand she brandished Asher's lock picks like a weapon. He must have left them out…. "Get back!"

"Woah," Asher had both hands up as he took a step back.

"Astra, it's okay, it's Asher. We're out, remember? We're safe. Astra, calm down," Louko said very calmly, slowly reaching out for her hands. "Just give the lock picks to me. I won't let anyone hurt you," he pleaded.

For as much as her hands were trembling, Astra's grip was like iron. "W-where are we?" came the gravelly whisper. She still kept between Louko and Asher.

"On our way to Nythril. In Asher's tent. We'll be far away soon." Louko continued to try and ease the picks from her. The last thing she would want to do was hurt Asher.

Astra glanced towards him, face still full of that wild fear.

"Louko, perhaps you should step back," Asher's voice was hushed. "She may hurt you without meaning to."

"Stay *away*," Astra growled again, sparks of blue now flickering at the end of her improvised weapons.

"Asher, I've got this under control. If she's going to hurt anyone, it will be you." Louko's jaw was clenched now, even as he put his hands again on Astra's. "We're alright, Astra. Please believe me. Trust me, we're fine. It's just Asher. He'll stay away."

The silence stretched long and taut, ready to snap. Louko could see the way fear and trust warred out in Astra's wavering hands. He knew she was trying desperately to believe him. The blue glow faded slowly, and after another slow minute, Astra surrendered the metal pins.

"Thank you," he whispered as he slowly took the pins, stowing them in his pocket. He knew better than to give them back to Asher in front of his feverish friend.

Astra did not say anything, exhaustion now showing where before there had only been panic. She was still on her knees, half upright, wavering with the effort it took to remain so.

"Get her to sit. I'll get food and water," Asher said, and slipped out of the tent.

"How are you feeling?" Louko asked. "Do you understand where we are yet? You're rather feverish...you know it's me, though, right? I should stop pelting you with questions...that isn't going to help...." He trailed off as he looked her up and down repeatedly.

Astra finally stopped looking at the tent's entrance and down at herself. Her brow furrowed and one hand went to the loosened piece of bandaging that dangled from her wrist. Louko saw comprehension break through the fog of her fever as she picked her head up. Her eyes fastened on him. "L-Louko...we're out...how are we out?"

"I got us out. Rhumir and Killyan helped. Remember them? Rhumir was that one servant who was always trying to get fired. And Killyan was the captain who found us. They're leading any pursuers off our scent," he reassured. "You're going to be fine."

Astra's shoulders were drooping with fatigue. "And, and you? Y-you're alright?" Her voice was still so hoarse.

He nodded quickly. "Yes. Yes, I'm fine. And you will be, too." She had to be. "But Asher is going to need to be able to help you. I promise, he's going to make you better. And I'll be here. You remember Asher? We can trust him." He hoped he wasn't about to trigger another major fit...Astra was hanging on by a thread.

He could see Astra's lips pressing together and her eyes focusing on nothing in particular—signs that she was trying to process.

"I'm coming back in," Asher's call came from outside the tent.

Astra was instantly rigid, but she was looking at Louko now as if gauging his reaction.

"Trust me," he whispered one last time before only slightly raising his voice to address Asher. "Come in." He knew shouting would only raise Astra's panic further.

Asher did so slowly, bearing a wooden bowl in one hand and a battered metal cup in the other. Steam emanated from the bowl and filled the tent with the soft scent of meat and herbs.

Astra remained frozen.

Louko just kept talking to her, reassuring her they were safe and that Asher was not going to do anything but help. But inwardly he was already thinking about what they would need to do next. Bringing up Killyan and Rhumir brought with it the reminder that they needed to get moving—they needed to get out of Merimeethia. Far away from Tyron.

Asher looked from Astra to Louko and set the bowl and cup down on the ground. "Why don't you give it to her? I'll just sit down over here." He stepped back and sat himself down near his medical cases.

Louko nodded. Yes. That was a good idea. He gingerly picked up the cup and made eye contact with Astra. "Thirsty?"

Her attention was torn from Asher and pulled towards the cup. He saw her falter. "What about you? Is th-there enough?"

"I already had some, while you were sleeping. Promise," he coaxed gently as he slowly moved the cup closer to her.

A deep suspicion flashed across her face, but the draw of water proved too much. Astra glanced once more towards Asher then took the cup with both hands.

"There we go. Slowly though. Don't make yourself sick," Louko slowly coached her, taking away the water eventually so that she would not gulp it all at once.

Her frail hands were still cupped as if trying to hold on to the cup, but she let him take it.

"There is broth in the bowl," Asher said, not moving at all.

"Here. Let's have some food." Louko took the cue and traded the cup for the broth. "Sip slowly. It's broth."

She took the bowl with the utmost care, now less preoccupied with Asher. "You ate, too?" Astra asked, fervid in her scrutiny.

"Yes, don't worry. Asher is taking care of me." He tried to again put in anything that might help her both remember where they were, as well as solidify her trust in Asher. In her right mind, she would of course not have hesitated, but she was sick and hurt....

Astra still seemed so uncertain, but trust won out again, and she held the bowl up to drink.

As always, Louko talked her through it. "There you go, nice and slow. We won't run out this time—there is as much as we need." It was hard to judge when she had enough but not so much that she would get sick from it. She had drained most of the bowl before he noticed her slowing down. He pulled it away, saying, "Don't worry—it won't go to waste. I'll set it aside and you can have some more in a bit, alright?"

Astra's nod was slow, and her head drooped with the motion. Though she still stole glances back towards Asher, her adrenaline had run low enough that fatigue was winning out.

"Let her rest," was Asher's quiet instruction.

Louko set the bowl with the cup before asking Astra, "Do you want to lay back down?"

She began shaking her head.

"I'll be right here," Louko reassured. "But you are still very sick and need to rest."

"No, no," Astra was still shaking her head, that panic bringing tension back into her movements. "Not if y-you're keeping watch."

"I'm not," Louko promised. "I've been sleeping, too. See? My blanket is right over there." He pointed to the opposite end of the tent.

Astra stilled, apparently taking this in. Louko watched as she scanned the rest of the interior, catching on Asher and the tent's exit. Finally, she swallowed and whispered, "Alright."

Louko helped her lay back, trying to do so without hurting her further. Then he pulled her scattered blankets back over her.

"Are you warm enough?"

"Mmhm." The murmur was already fading.

It was only a few minutes before Louko heard her breathing even out. She always fell asleep quickly after her panicked moments.

Louko ran his free hand through his hair, feeling like the tent was falling down around him. He should have seen it! Should have known Tyron had been lying about her escape. But he'd realized too late.

"That was a good start." The physician spoke quietly from his spot in the corner. "The fact that she could move and process so much is good."

"Oh. It was?" Louko asked, struggling to keep himself still. His chest ached and he couldn't tell if it was from panic, fear, or something else.

Asher came forward, looking as if he was going to check Astra's forehead before thinking better of it. "I wasn't sure she'd be able to move at all. So, while her reaction was extreme, it's a good sign that we'll be able to move her." He looked up at Louko. "We can't stay here much longer."

Louko felt his breath catch. "How are we going to move her?" He knew they had to leave—and quickly. But how? Astra was on edge, and Louko had hardly been able to get her on the horse the first time.

"Our only option is to put her on a horse with another rider," the physician explained, somehow unerringly calm. "We can't risk riding on the main road, and a stretcher would never make it through the woods. Ivinon's horse is the best trained, so we will put her with him."

"I'll take her," Louko said quickly. Right now, she knew only two people: him and Tyron. If she wasn't sure who she was with, she would assume the latter.

Asher let out a breath as if this confirmed some old worry. "Are you sure that you are strong enough to manage both her and a mount?"

"Yes." It was the first time Louko had been certain of something in a long time. "I got her this far."

Rubbing the back of his neck, Asher looked him over. It took every ounce of Louko's fractured will just to look him in the eyes. But finally, the physician gave in. "Alright. I will let your brother know." He got to his feet.

Louko did not respond, eyes floating back to Astra's near motionless body as she slept feverishly. What would he do if she died?

CHAPTER III

Keeshiff:

The packing was going quickly, despite the heavy humidity of the early morning. The urgency of the incoming storm, however, was nothing to the frantic despair clouding everyone's thoughts.

At least, clouding Keeshiff's.

It was all he could do to remain focused: one task at a time. Astra barely even *looked* like Astra. Every time Keeshiff had to go into the tent where she was lying, he was sure she wasn't breathing. And that wasn't even mentioning the haunted remnant of his brother.

How had Keeshiff not seen Mariah's betrayal? How had he let this happen?

Asher's emergence from the improvised medical tent was enough to make everyone stop what they were doing. The physician skirted the fire to meet Keeshiff, motioning to Rufio and Ivinon.

"She woke up," he said quietly. "Tried to stab me. I guess we should be heartened that she has that much spirit left."

Keeshiff blinked. "Oh...I...see. Can we move her?" It was a good thing she'd been awake enough to fight...right? But Astra had to be in bad shape to outright attack Asher—the very one who had treated her before.

Asher rubbed his neck, giving a helpless shrug. "We have no choice but to try." He let out a deep breath. "But Louko insists she rides with him. I think they'll both panic if we put her with anyone else."

31

Keeshiff forced himself to remain still. "What do we do?" Asher was the only one that could really know. But did he even have an answer?

"I would recommend still using Ivinon's horse," the physician replied, each word heavier than the last. "But we'll just have to hope that Louko has the strength to hold her in place."

"Alright. And is Louko capable of keeping steady with her?" Keeshiff asked quietly. He couldn't get his brother's frailty out of his head.

"He brought her this far," was all Asher said.

Keeshiff didn't have the strength to pursue the subject further. "When can we leave?"

Asher looked up, eyeing the clouds. "As soon as we're packed. We will just have to hope that this storm skirts us."

"Yes...." Keeshiff trailed off. "Let's get to it, then."

The knights returned to their work, and Asher to his tent.

Knowing he needed to set an example, Keeshiff promptly went back to his packing. There wasn't much left to do, but he knew the others were just as shocked as he was, and he needed to at least *pretend* he was calm. But Keeshiff wasn't sure he could do that anymore. Pretending had cost Louko enough already.

Everyone worked in silence. Rufio finished first and set to burying the fire. Ivinon prepared the horse for Louko and Astra. Keeshiff took the palace horse that Louko had arrived on and led it a few yards south of the camp. He cut the reins and then pulled at the raw edges until it looked like they'd torn off. Then he released the animal with a slap on the hindquarters. Hopefully it would run for a bit before getting its bearings and returning home, leaving a trail of false footprints behind it.

That done, Keeshiff returned to the camp and sat down near the knights, who had apparently finished all there was to do. Each one fiddled with something, clearly wishing there was something more to be done— something more to keep them all busy. But there was nothing to do but wait. It felt like hours slid by in the growing, grey dawn while they waited for Asher.

And as they waited, Keeshiff wrestled again with his guilt. He should have gone with Louko—or at least sent someone with him. Perhaps then they would have been able to get Astra out. But that was not the worst of it. The worst thing was that Keeshiff was losing his only brother, and his brother was losing his only friend...his *only* friend. The friend Keeshiff perhaps could have been. Every moment of him stepping aside surfaced—every time he had been silent in the wake of Mariah or his father's cruelty.

Keeshiff winced. Mariah. He should have left her to the mercy of Kaed—*whoever* was currently running Merimeethia. He never wanted to see that backstabber again. She could stay and rot in Melye, for all he cared. Whether or not she'd known who Kaeden really was hardly mattered to Keeshiff, and he wondered if it would even have made a difference to her.

The unpleasant thought was interrupted by the more unpleasant reminder of reality as Asher came out of the tent. Everyone again jumped to their feet, quiet as they watched him stand to the side and hold the tent flap open for Louko to step out.

Keeshiff could hardly breathe as he stared at what was left of his brother, unable to get used to the sight no matter how many times he was forced to behold it. True, Louko held no physical wounds, but he was skin and bone, and his hair was knotted, grown out, and speckled with white and grey. Dark circles made themselves at home in deep rings under his eyes. And his eyes...oh, his eyes would not allow themselves to settle on any other living soul.

Louko hovered near the tent while Asher crossed to Keeshiff.

"We have to get him on the horse before we can put Astra with him. Which means someone will have to carry Astra," Asher explained in an undertone. "He has relented so long as you are the one who does it."

Oh.

Keeshiff again remained still. "Alright," he replied, feeling Louko's trust in him was deeply misplaced. Louko had always given him more credit than he was due, and now Keeshiff only hoped he would finally come through; he couldn't bear it if he hurt Astra.

They walked back to the tent and Keeshiff's younger brother immediately started in on some nervous rambling. "Be careful. Don't move suddenly. She may panic, so I will go with you and try to reassure her. You don't look as much like him as Asher does, so it should be okay...maybe...be careful...." Louko went on as he ran his hand through his hair over and over again.

"Alright," Keeshiff said softly, wondering how badly this would go. Asher had said something about almost getting stabbed, after all....

"I'll...I'll go try and explain it to her...again...." Louko dodged back into the tent, leaving Keeshiff to wait awkwardly outside, apprehensive and beyond concerned for his brother and Astra. He didn't think he could handle them not making it, and yet was too afraid to really ask Asher.

Louko reappeared. "I have done my best. Walk slowly. Let me go first."

Knowing he was definitely not equipped for this, Keeshiff again nodded and followed his brother inside, hoping that he wouldn't let Louko down for once. Astra's life could depend on it.

"See? It's Keeshiff. Remember him?" Louko was kneeling on the ground as he spoke in gentle tones to his friend.

It took Keeshiff's mind a moment to identify the figure next to him as Astra. She was awake, sitting up, and much cleaner than she'd been last night. But even with this and the full daylight, Keeshiff recognized her even less than before. Not only was she deathly pale, she was so much thinner than he remembered her—even under the heavy layers they'd bundled her in. Her sunken eyes, still that chilling blue, eyed him the same way a cornered animal watched its hunter.

"He's my brother—he came to help you and Ent during The War," Louko went on. "And then he came to get us. He's going to help us get to Nythril."

Astra's gaze stayed on Keeshiff for several long seconds. Then she turned her head and said in a whisper, "He's the one that didn't want you tied up."

Louko's brow furrowed. "Hm?"

"When I found you." Astra seemed more persistent now, even if her raspy voice was weak. "All the knights and Mariah wanted you tied up, but he didn't."

She really *was* delirious. But still, she was awake, and talking. That had to be good, right? That being said, the seeming distance between her and reality at the moment was beyond frightening, and it was clear the fever was not helping. He'd never seen Astra like this, and for the first time in a long time it made him realize how young she was. Not even twenty. A kid. But war had long made her older.

Or had forced her to pretend to be.

"Yes, that's right." Louko's quiet reply sounded thunderous in comparison to Astra's thin and rasping tones.

Astra looked back at Keeshiff and he saw her swallow hard. "Alright," she acquiesced.

Keeshiff looked to Asher. "Is there a particular way to do this?" he asked hopelessly.

"With slow, deliberate motions," the physician answered with reassuring calm. "One arm under the shoulders and another under the legs."

"Don't restrict her arms," Louko added hoarsely. "And she has a deep cut on her left side, so be careful of that, too."

Keeshiff wasn't sure he could do this. But he had to. He *had* to.

And so, with a near-frantic younger brother and a worry-worn physician to guide him, the elder prince gingerly knelt and gathered Astra in his arms. He could feel her stiffen and shiver, but she made no sound. He made his way outside and to the side of Ivinon's horse with a precarious slowness a dead man would have envied.

Once there, Louko mounted unaided and with surprising swiftness, only to have to take a moment to steady himself. Then he reached out for Astra. It wasn't that lifting her up was difficult—she weighed so little. But Keeshiff was so afraid of causing further harm. Besides his men, he had never been responsible for the care of another—or had never allowed it. Not unless it meant protecting them with a sword. So, as gently as he knew how, Keeshiff helped situate her in the saddle in front of Louko.

"Thank you." Silence would have been louder than his younger brother's whisper, and the stormy breeze hid it almost entirely.

Not knowing how to respond, Keeshiff only tried to lock eyes with Louko. But his brother quickly looked away, fussing over his friend like a mother over an empty nest.

Keeshiff turned around and made his way quickly over to where Rufio was holding his horse.

"We need to make as much progress as possible. We can't risk the extra time going south to the Forest of Riddles. We'll have to take a direct path through the Adyne Forest and hope that it offers enough shelter," he announced. It wasn't exactly inspirational...but what else could he possibly say?

Of course, Rufio didn't help, only nodding mutely in response. Asher and Ivinon made quick work of the makeshift medical tent and attached it to Rufio's saddle. Then everyone mounted, and Keeshiff was grateful again that they'd thought to bring an extra horse. Of course, it had been intended for Astra....

They hadn't thought *this* was what they would find. Keeshiff at worst had thought maybe Astra would be sent back to Litash or something—but Louko had been so worried when he'd taken off. Scared to death, even. At the time Keeshiff had thought his little brother was overreacting. Astra had always been able to take care of herself, and Louko...he'd always figured something out. To see them both so vulnerable was unsettling. To think Astra could die was even worse.

Riding soon proved as stressful as staying; the threat of Astra or Louko falling off the horse was ever imminent in everyone's mind. Only worse was the storm that broke out less than an hour after they started.

As if the winds weren't enough, the storm also brought pelting drops of rain that found every crack in his clothing, no matter how closely Keeshiff drew it around himself. As miserable as it was, all he could think of was what it was doing to Louko and Astra.

The single good thing about the storm was the cover it brought. Not only was it severe enough to keep any sane person indoors, it also brought down enough water to hide the tracks they left in the mud. Of course, the lack of visibility made Keeshiff nervous. He knew well enough that patrols didn't always keep to the roads. So even as he kept looking over his shoulder to check on Louko, he made sure to be listening for the tell-tale clanking of armor.

There was the sound of a horse being spurred slightly faster, and Asher joined Keeshiff at the fore. He didn't have to say a word.

"At the next level place, we will be stopping," Keeshiff called back to the rest. Hopefully there was somewhere that offered some semblance of dryness as well as protection from the storm—and prying eyes. But at this point, Keeshiff was willing to stop even without proper shelter.

And he would have given up, if they hadn't rounded a gentle hill and found a nice little hollow.

There was a scramble as Keeshiff and the two knights set up the medical tent first. Asher remained with Louko and Astra, trying to keep the former calm. As Keeshiff approached to help them down, he could hear his brother sputtering, "She's shivering. Her blanket is getting soaked."

Keeshiff noticed Louko wasn't looking too stellar, either. Soaked to the bone, he was making a valiant effort of not convulsing with shudders.

He must have been too busy trying to keep Astra dry to do anything for himself.

"Here, take this." Keeshiff took off his waterproofed coat and waited for approval from Louko before taking Astra's oilcloth blanket off and quickly, but gently, putting his coat over her. He had really wanted to put it around Louko's shoulders, but Astra was in the most imminent danger.

That done, Keeshiff took Astra from his brother's arms and carried her into the waiting tent. Louko had been right—she was shivering. Badly. He wasn't even sure if she was awake. As soon as he laid her down, Asher was by her side.

"We need to get her warm," the physician said, with a calm he could not possibly feel. "If there is any bandaging or blankets or *anything* that is still dry, bring it in."

Keeshiff ran outside the tent, shouting, "We need anything that is dry!" It was all he could do to be heard above the rain.

"Take this!" Ivinon came quickly over, carrying one of the waterproof satchels Aelor Ven had provided them with. "It's our blankets. I'll see what else we have."

He wasted no time in getting them to Asher, and soon Astra was being piled with as much as they could find. Keeshiff had never been so glad for Louko's uncle.

Asher paused in his work only once, and that was to hand one of the mostly dry blankets to Louko.

"Get yourself dry," he ordered.

"But she needs them," Louko croaked.

Keeshiff didn't think, only said, "And she needs you. Get dry."

Louko did not argue further, and so Keeshiff managed to tear his eyes from him and ask Asher, "What else do you need?"

"My cases," came the immediate reply. "The big, black, leather one first."

Apparently Rufio had been one step ahead, as he practically burst into the room with them before Asher even had time to finish his sentence. The triumph his quick thinking would have brought was diminished by the fact that Louko looked like he was about to die of a heart attack from the sudden and unannounced entry.

"Your medicine, Asher," Rufio mumbled upon realizing his mistake.

Asher didn't even take the time to comment, opening the trunk with haste and pulling out several dark-tinted vials. "Get me a cup," he said without looking up.

Rufio darted out, returning more discreetly this time.

Asher began to pour and stir in sure, short motions. "Louko, we need to try and wake her enough to swallow this."

Louko was quicker than a loyal dog to his master's heels as he instantly knelt by Astra's side, startling Keeshiff again when his brother took the princess's hand. He'd never seen his brother so much as allow someone six feet near him—unless it was his father or Mariah, who forced their way in.

"Astra," Keeshiff heard his brother mumble. "Astra, please wake up. I have something to make you feel better." His voice was thinner than he was, and weaker than even this morning as he softly called his friend's name.

Astra did not move.

Keeshiff could only watch, helpless and unwilling to leave. He desperately wanted to do *something* for them, anything to aid...but his wish had come too late, too late.

"The fact that she is shivering means her body is fighting to stay warm," Asher encouraged quietly. "She is not too far gone."

"Astra, it's safe to wake up," Louko's voice rose only slightly. "Please, please wake up."

It was so hard to look at this pale figure, wrapped in blankets and bandages, and remember the strange, fierce, redheaded princess who had always come so hotly to his brother's defense.

"Astra, please," Louko begged.

A soft moan filled the tent, and Keeshiff saw her turn her head.

"There you are." Louko's relief sounded so burdened and soulful that it was difficult to listen to. "Astra, please, can you hear me? I'm giving you something to help. Please. It's just me, just me," he said, very slowly putting his hand behind her head to lift it ever so slightly up. It was clear even to Keeshiff that this had been a process he had practiced and perfected.

Another moan, but no words from the princess—at least, none that Keeshiff could understand. But when Louko put the cup to her lips, Astra suddenly resisted, pulling back as she sat up and coughed up whatever he had managed to make her drink.

Realizing Louko was about to fall backwards, Keeshiff stepped forward instinctively, grabbing his brother gently by the shoulders to help steady him.

"Who are you?" Astra's voice demanded. Before anyone could even answer, she growled, *"Let go of him."*

41

"Woah, Astra, calm dow—"

Keeshiff didn't catch the rest of what Asher was trying to say. Something slammed into Keeshiff's chest and knocked him to the ground, driving the wind from his lungs.

"Astra, relax, please?" He heard his brother's voice through the ringing in his ears. Oh, ugh, had he hit his head?

Keeshiff pushed himself upright, dazed. Wait, he was wet, why was he wet? How was it raining? Keeshiff realized all at once that the tent was gone and that he was sitting inside a square of ash. He looked over and saw that Asher was sitting up, too, looking just as bewildered.

Louko, meanwhile, was the only one standing, looking up at the sky and holding out...the empty cup? "How thoughtful to help me refill the cup. I knew you were thirsty."

"What happened? Are you alright?" Keeshiff turned and saw Rufio and Ivinon running towards them.

"Woah, stay back," he said, staggering to his feet and raising both hands. "We're okay, we're just...." He looked over his shoulder at where his brother now sat next to Astra, chatting away in what seemed to be an attempt to calm her. Keeshiff turned back to Rufio. "I think we're going to need another tent."

<u>Asher:</u>

After he was sure that both Astra and Louko were in a deep enough sleep—in the tent that Ivinon had generously given up—Asher sent Keeshiff off to see about food. Then he set to making another poultice for

42

Astra. As he worked, Asher couldn't help but face the fact that Louko had been right about one thing: They did not have enough medical supplies. Not for this.

Disheartened, the physician wondered how they could possibly make it all the way to Nythril. They would be traveling daily in the cold and the wet, with only minimal treatment, trying to move fast enough to escape Astra and Louko's captors, but not too fast for their condition to bear. How could they get her through the mountains and all the way back to Nythril without letting her recover first? With a deep breath, Asher finished applying the poultice and drew the blankets carefully back over Astra's sleeping form.

That's when Keeshiff re-entered, bearing two steaming bowls of stew. "Here," he said.

Asher, wiping his hands clean, only gave a pointed look to the stool in the corner.

Keeshiff set one bowl there before sitting down cross-legged in the other corner. Asher was acutely aware that the prince was watching, not eating. And he didn't blame him. Asher hardly had any appetite, himself.

"So...is this blowing up tents thing going to be a recurring...issue?" Keeshiff's question came slowly.

Asher sighed. "I hope not. But Louko wasn't very confident when I asked. He said that, apparently, she doesn't have very good control over her Gifting and always wore red bronze to keep anything from, well, blowing up."

Keeshiff's brow furrowed as he seemed to process the information. At last, he murmured, "So that's what it was for."

If he hadn't had the same realization, Asher might have been confused. But he remembered back to their first escape and how Astra had always worn a copper-colored bracelet. And how, when Asher had taken it off of her to help her heal after the mudslide, she had immediately demanded it back.

He was about to say more when there came a commotion from outside, and suddenly Ivinon poked his head through the tent flap, startling Asher and Keeshiff half to death. "You will never guess who just showed up...."

Asher would have guessed bad news if it weren't for the fact that Ivinon's expression was void of any sort of sign of danger.

"Who?" It was Keeshiff who asked, now getting stiffly to his feet.

"Rhumir."

Rhumir? Julyn's son? Rufio's brother? That's when Asher recalled Louko trying to explain their escape to Astra. He had mentioned Rhumir and something about locks.

Keeshiff was already halfway out of the tent. Asher took one last look at his sleeping patients, then followed.

"Where are they?" Rhumir was standing in the center of their camp, wetter than a fish and moodier than even his brother. But Asher's eyes were almost instantly drawn to the horse whose reins he was holding, and the clearly full saddlebags that she carried. It was Astra's painted mare, the one she called Dannsair.

"They are in the tent, sleeping." Asher took the lead, only because he knew from Graece that the last thing Rhumir would do was listen to Keeshiff. He did not like stepping in front of his prince, but neither did he want an argument started.

They'd all had quite enough of those.

There was a pause. "Is she still alive?"

Asher gave a terse nod.

Rhumir's sour expression lightened. "Good." He immediately went on, "I'm guessing you need supplies? I brought as much as I could fit. Medicine, bandages, and food."

Asher felt nearly dizzy with relief.

Rufio and Keeshiff were already unbuckling the saddlebags, bringing them towards the tent. Asher was right behind them. He dared not hope until he had sorted through and seen what Rhumir had brought.

The boy passed Dannsair off to Ivinon and caught up to Asher. Wiping his face with an already soaked sleeve, he said, "I want to see him."

"He is sleeping," was Asher's simple reply. "And it's not easy to get him *to* sleep."

Disgruntled, Rhumir stayed outside when Asher went in.

Rufio and Keeshiff had carefully set the bags in the corner so as not to disturb the patients. Asher opened the first one, finding a folded blanket over well-wrapped food. The physician only looked in one package and noted with satisfaction that it was meat stock for making broth. Probably Graece's idea.

Not allowing himself to dwell on the thought of his wife, Asher moved to the next bag. There, wrapped in clean bandaging to keep them from breaking, lay scores of glass vials. Tinctures, sleep inducers, salves, auminar tonic—everything he could have hoped for. And enough to last two weeks. Only Graece could have known to pack with such precision. Asher found it hard not to linger on each item he unpacked. It was the closest he had gotten to seeing her in months, and now, after seeing Astra and Louko, he couldn't help but wonder if she, too, was in danger.

His worries for Graece were traded for more immediate ones when he heard the raised voices over the roar of the rain.

Oh, no.

Stepping outside, he saw Rhumir jabbing a finger at his brother, nearly poking him in the chest. "You're going to yell at me? Oh, that's rich, Rufio. What have you ever done for Louko?" His hand gestured towards the tent, sending more droplets flying as he turned on Keeshiff. "*I* helped get them out. And I didn't dawdle around on my way, either. What took you so long, exactly?"

"Would you *all* be quiet?" Asher kept his voice as harsh as possible while still not matching their obnoxiously loud ones. "You are going to wake up one of my patients and send them into hysterics."

Rufio and Keeshiff both looked contrite, even if still flustered. Beyond that, they looked exhausted.

Rhumir, on the other hand, seemed totally unapologetic. But he kept his anger to himself, and that was all Asher needed. With a last stern look at the nettlesome boy, the physician returned to the tent.

He was disheartened to see Louko sitting upright, tense to the point of bursting as his eyes riveted on Asher with a cornered wildness. Fortunately, he seemed to recognize him, and then turned his attention to Astra. There was a silent sort of panic that passed as he stared at her, followed by a deep breath. Then his gaze turned upwards, and he said, "We still have a tent, I see."

"Yes," the physician replied. "And now we have proper medicine— Rhumir showed up on Dannsair with supplies." And an extra tent—a point which had made Ivinon very happy. Though, Asher suddenly realized that if a castle serving-boy could find them so easily, that did not bode well concerning those who would be searching for Louko and Astra.

Louko got to his feet swiftly—in fact, too quickly, for he almost fell back down—and said, "Rhumir's here? He's alright?"

Asher was instantly at his side to steady him. "Yes, yes, he is alright. And he brought Astra's mare."

"And he brought medicine," Louko murmured, now setting eyes on the supplies that had been unpacked. "Is it enough?"

"Yes." Asher nodded. "All she needs, and enough of it for the journey back."

"And it's enough?" Louko's repeated question was disconcerting.

Asher knew better than to let that worry show through. Louko would misconstrue it. "Yes. Enough."

Louko didn't even look like he'd heard Asher, coughing a couple times before asking, "Are her chances better?"

As a personal rule, Asher never lied to the friends and loved ones of a patient. Hope proven false was so much worse than despair turned to joy. But at this point, hope was all Louko had—it was all any of them had. Asher could not take it away from him. "Yes. Much better. All we have to do now is get her to safety."

"Alright," Louko croaked, eyes again on Astra.

Asher said nothing else. He only prayed that they could get them both to Nythril in time.

The next day found everyone mounted up and riding again. This time, Louko and Astra were on Dannsair, and Rhumir rode the spare horse. Ivinon's mount had been returned to him. Keeshiff led the way with Rufio, Asher stayed by Louko, and Ivinon and Rhumir rode behind to listen for any unwelcome guests. And listen they did. Without the gloom and rain to hide them, everyone felt uncomfortably visible.

But Asher couldn't help but be glad for the milder weather. Keeping Astra and Louko dry was worth the risk, in his opinion. The former was still unconscious most of the time, and the latter still coughed more than Asher was comfortable with. Nonetheless, the day's ride was spent in a strained quiet that took its toll on everyone. Even when they did stop, no one could keep from constantly checking over their shoulders.

Camp was much easier to set when it wasn't pouring. Within half an hour, Astra and Louko were both resting in the medical tent, and stew was bubbling over the fire. Asher pulled out two bowls and approached Ivinon, who was cooking.

"Just broth in this one," Asher instructed. He mentally decided to add something for Astra's pain and see if the broth would mask the bitterness enough for her to take it.

Ivinon began ladling out broth. In the background, Rufio was hobbling horses and Keeshiff was gathering up wood. Only Rhumir sat, watching.

"Wow, thanks. Don't worry, we have it covered, go right ahead and make yourself at home...as usual," Rufio grumbled from where he was working on the horses.

Rhumir's head snapped in his brother's direction, and his eyes narrowed. But when he opened his mouth to reply, Asher interrupted.

"So, how exactly did they escape?" he asked, hoping it would be enough to sidetrack the oncoming argument.

Apparently, it worked. Rhumir's glower turned into something more grim as he faced the fire again. "It was the captain who found them. Killyan, I think his name is. He had become suspicious when he didn't hear anything about Astra around the castle. He said he went down to the dungeons under the pretense of talking to one of the prisoners but couldn't find them. Then he saw the guards delivering a meal to that back isolation cell that no one ever uses."

Rhumir shuddered. "He told me only because he knew Rufio was with the rest of you. I told Graece. So, she packed the bags, Killyan distracted the guards, and I stole the door keys. We set Louko out with Astra, and I took Dannsalr to leave some false tracks. Killyan was tasked with the largest patrol and so led them all down my trail." Rhumir thumbed towards Dannsair, grazing outside the little ring of tents. "I was supposed to double back and meet Louko at a set mark, but he wasn't there. That mare, though…she started sniffing like she was some hound on a rabbit's trail. I didn't have any other ideas, so I let her have her head. She came straight here."

"What of Killyan?" Keeshiff's concern was evident. "Surely his acts won't go unnoticed…."

Rhumir's frown deepened. "That's what Graece said. Killyan wouldn't say what exactly his plans were—probably because he didn't have any for sure."

"I hope so…" Keeshiff trailed off. "Though, we will have to make sure Aelor Ven knows. Seeing as he has not yet brought our problem to his king…."

"Let's just hope Tyron hasn't thought that far ahead," Rhumir muttered darkly.

The camp went quiet, and Asher and Keeshiff exchanged glances.

"Tyron?" Asher echoed. Louko had mentioned it when they'd first arrived, but he had been half hoping the prince was merely delusional.

"Yes, Tyron," Rhumir replied tersely. "He was Kaeden this whole time. I don't know what he wants, except maybe revenge on Astra...."

"I...I still can't believe it. Tyron was *Kaeden*?" Keeshiff gaped.

"That's what I said, didn't I?" Rhumir snapped. "He's one of those shape-shifters from Litash. Must've been maintaining it all these years to keep an eye on Omath."

The silence was deafening.

"I still can't believe it." Keeshiff's mouth was hanging loose in disbelieving shock. "How could I have missed it—and he was there, while Tyron was in Alarune of all things."

"Well, apparently you didn't notice, because he was here and he was the one who arranged Astra's capture," Rhumir said, only further irritated. "If you don't believe me, ask Louko—he's the one who told us."

"Ah." Keeshiff's voice faltered.

"What in Eatris does a dead man like Tyron want?" Ivinon's conflicting statement would have perhaps been amusing...but it fell heavy on everyone in the light of the situation. Asher knew Ivinon had meant it in all seriousness.

With a frustrated sort of shrug, Rhumir admitted, "I don't know. I don't even know if Louko knows. I guess Astra is the only one who does...."

Even though the boy trailed off, everyone knew exactly what was left unsaid: that Astra might never get the chance to tell anyone.

Now thoroughly unsettled, Asher remembered his waiting patients. He picked up the now full bowls, nodded to the others, and returned to the medical tent.

A GAME OF WITS

CHAPTER IV

Louko:

Louko had given up trying to decide if he was too cold or too warm. As the days wore on, Astra grew even worse, and worse brought, well...destruction in various degrees. They were now down to two tents: one tent for the sick, and one...for everyone else. Or rather, everyone else besides Rhumir; he usually got booted from the tent before the night was out. If Louko *did* sleep, it ended up being on the floor in the sick tent. He couldn't leave his friend, not when she was fighting for her life in a miserable country far from a home that didn't want her anymore.

They were almost through the mountains when Astra's fever spiked again and she became completely delirious. Half of the time, she didn't even recognize him and called him Ent. She would go into hysterics, refusing any food or drink and insisting that no one was helping Ent. These fits would escalate her Gifting until Asher used the mangled remains of her red-bronze manacle to quell the storm. But using it always left Astra unconscious for hours at a time.

Louko found himself talking to her, alternating from making awful jokes to trying to soothe her—anything to keep her from leaving. Anything that would convince her to stay. Asher told him that the more temperate air in Nythril might lessen her fever. But when they descended from the

Merym Pass and into the steppes of Nythril, Astra fell asleep and would not wake up. Not for all of Louko's begging.

"It should be close, right?" Keeshiff's voice came out of nowhere, startling Louko.

Keeshiff tried again, pointing to the carved rock monument on their left. It was hard to make out through the dimness of the setting sun. "Doesn't that mean we're close to Aelor Ven's manor?"

"Yes." But Keeshiff should know that.

Louko turned back to Astra, who was so limp he was almost sure she was dead. Only the puffs her breath made in the cool evening air gave him hope.

"Alright. Then we can make it," Keeshiff reassured. "She can make it."

Louko said nothing.

The fading light lent even more urgency—as if they needed any more—and the desperate group pushed their horses as fast as they dared. Just when it seemed it was getting too dark to risk continuing, Louko saw the lights in the distance.

"See, Astra? We're here. Please, don't die. It's *right* there," he pleaded with all he had left in his aching soul, hoping that what little will he had was enough to keep her from slipping away.

In another few minutes, the lights began to outline the shadow of a walled house, and that shadow grew into a large manor that Louko only vaguely recognized from his childhood.

"Help! We need help!" Keeshiff shouted, throwing decorum to the wind and startling Louko. Yet Louko would have shouted, too, if he'd had any strength left in him.

The heavy gates swung open, and they rode into the open courtyard. The doors of the manor let out a stream of servants and exclamations of surprise, but Louko was either too tired or too focused on Astra to really understand what was going on. Soon, they were surrounded by people, and hands reached to try and take his friend.

Instinct and panic overwhelmed Louko's logic, and he would have done something drastic if Asher had not broken in.

"Please, step back, we'll get her down. She's very sick."

But the servants didn't back off until a deeper, more authoritative voice ordered, "Do as he says."

Louko didn't take the time to see who spoke. He was too busy with trying to get Astra safely down from Dannsair and into Keeshiff's waiting arms.

"Alright. I have her. She's steady," his brother said.

Louko forced himself to let go, and even then, only so that he could dismount and follow.

And by dismount, apparently he really meant fall. For that is what he did, Asher fortunately being right next to Dannsair to catch him.

Louko only registered it enough to mumble a hurried thanks before staggering off to catch up with Astra and her entourage.

They made their way inside the mansion, and Louko was at least cognizant enough to recognize the other knights who were standing in the large foyer. But no one said a word unless it was the servants or Asher, all flurry and rush as they tried to get Astra upstairs and into a warm, dry bed. All Louko could do was follow, hardly even with it enough to register how strangely low to the ground the bed was.

"Is she still alive?" Louko did not realize he had spoken. The only reason he came to that conclusion was because the man who had ordered everyone around outside turned and looked at him—noticing his presence for the first time.

"Louko?" The deep tenor of the man's voice broke in before anyone could say a word. His eyes widened and he took a step forward. Well. Louko had a feeling this was his uncle. Apparently, over a decade could change a lot...or perhaps the memory of a child was not a precise one.

"Yes, she is alive." Asher's voice came briefly from next to the bed as he carefully unwrapped the travel blanket from Astra's limp shoulders. He nearly interrupted himself giving orders to the servants that bustled around him.

"Louko, you look half dead. What happened? Here. Let me get you a room so you can rest." His uncle took yet another step forward, forcing Louko to take one back—which almost resulted in him tripping.

"N-no, I'm fine. I can't leave her again," he stuttered out, barely processing what was going on.

"Let him stay." It was Asher who spoke, though he did not look away from whatever fluid he was measuring out. "It's best for both of them."

"Fine. I'll have one of the servants fetch a chair—Etai!" Louko's uncle passed by and poked his head out the doorway, stopping a servant as he passed. "Fetch a chair for Louko to rest in. Quick now." He had a commanding, though not cold, manner about him. Not that Louko really cared right now.

"Is there anything I can do?" Louko asked Asher softly, unsure whether talking would distract him too much. He just couldn't bear the thought of sitting here uselessly any longer.

Asher still did not look up, but Louko saw him thinking this request through. Finally, he said, "Fetch that bowl of water. Pour some of that green vial in it and use a cloth to wet her forehead."

Louko had not really expected to actually get a task but did not complain in the least. He jumped to action, following Asher's instructions to the letter and then quietly coming up to the bed where Astra's head was. Her face was flushed and feverish, but everything else about her was deathly pale.

Ever so gently, he placed the cloth on her forehead. He was careful to avoid the half-moon cut around her eye. Louko's teeth grit as he thought of the sort of scar it would leave. Assuming she lived long enough for it to heal….

Louko didn't know how long Asher worked to try and bring Astra's fever down. A woman, some sort of healer, had joined the efforts at some point along the way. The lamps had been lit, and it was well into the night before the physician stopped. He was quiet for a moment, only looking at the still figure in the bed.

Then Asher said, "There is nothing else we can do," and stepped back.

Louko didn't move.

"Louko, sit." His uncle's voice came from behind him, and Louko turned to see the empty chair that had long since been brought in for him.

"I'm fine."

Uncle Ven turned to Asher. "Are those the only words he knows? Truly he had more vocabulary at the age of seven."

Asher looked grim. "I know little of his education, but those are the only two words he will abide to use of himself," he said. "If you wish for his well-being, you will have to force it upon him."

Well, this was awkward.

"Ah, I see." Uncle Ven then turned to Louko, pointing to the chair and saying, "Sit" with raised eyebrows.

Completely lost, too tired to care, and not really wanting to argue with an uncle he hadn't met since he was seven, Louko sat down. He felt very dizzy.

"You need rest," he heard his uncle say. After that, there wasn't much else. Louko couldn't help his eyelids drooping, nor the darkness that overcame him.

Keeshiff:

Keeshiff stood at the top of the wooden stairs, knowing better than to enter the room but not having the heart to go any further away. He wanted so desperately to offer some sort of comfort, some sort of help for his brother. Something more than simply carrying his broken friend inside to be hurried away by physicians. There had been a time when he'd thought he'd had his brother's back, but only now did he realize how long ago that dream had died. How long ago he'd quenched it.

With that thought all too present, he watched as servants dashed in and out of the guest bedroom that Aelor Ven had ushered the group into. Keeshiff hated waiting, and yet he supposed he had put himself here, not even close enough to his brother to be wanted in this nightmare. Was he really that different from Mariah? The very thought put a bitter taste in his mouth, and yet he didn't allow himself to push it away. It seemed Aelor Ven thought so. Honestly, he didn't blame the man. Right now, the only one that could comfort Louko was in there, dying...and Keeshiff had let it happen. His own *sister* had done it to them.

Keeshiff leaned against the wall in an attempt to relax, but when met with the plaster wall he instantly remembered he wasn't in the stone houses of Merimeethia, and once more stood upright. Was plaster fragile? Keeshiff was not mentally capable of taking another catastrophe on his shoulders, even one as small as a hole in the wall.

Minutes passed and tension rose as people stopped coming out of Astra's room. All the servants had exited, and no more went in. Stress grew, and Keeshiff did his best to keep from pounding on the wall. In a hopeful attempt to curb the temptation, he came close to the wooden door, which backfired nearly instantly when it opened without warning.

Aelor Ven strode out, almost slamming the door right into Keeshiff's face.

"Oh. You." The lord's face twisted into unmasked disgust as he straightened his intricately embroidered jacket. "Hello."

Keeshiff supposed he deserved the greeting. Nonetheless, he swallowed his reaction to ask, "How are they?"

"Next question?" The lord raised both his eyebrows, but the expression he was hiding was all too clear to Keeshiff.

"That bad?" he mumbled, disheartened.

Before Aelor Ven could say anything more, Asher joined them in the hall. He looked exhausted.

"Your physician said that she will watch them until we return," Asher reported to Aelor Ven.

Keeshiff didn't say a word but waited to be told to leave. Would Asher want to talk to Aelor Ven alone? It was fully evident the lord had made more of an effort to help Louko than Keeshiff had through the years. But still, he hoped Asher, whom he considered advisor and friend, would not make him leave.

Aelor Ven nodded acknowledgement. "Alright. Now tell me what you know." He did not so much as glance towards Keeshiff.

"Our guess is that they were held for about three weeks," Asher began. "They were rescued by some within Melye who discovered them there. As far as we know, Astra was the only one physically harmed, but the time in captivity has taken its toll on Louko."

The lord's face was like stone. "And who, exactly, is responsible for this?"

Here, Asher looked to Keeshiff before answering. "According to Louko, it was Tyron. He claimed that the man has been masquerading as the advisor Kaeden all these years."

"*What*?" The word was emphatic in its disbelief. "*Tyron*? But...you realize...." He trailed off. "Never mind. Apparently I was mistaken." His whole body was rigid, even more so than Keeshiff's.

"We know no more than you," Asher admitted. "Louko has not been in a state for these sorts of questions; we decided such things could wait until after everyone was safe." With a sigh, the physician rubbed the back of his neck and went on. "I can't give you any answers concerning their health. To be honest, I don't even know how Astra is still alive—she has been delirious since we reached the Merym Pass and comatose since we reached the steppes. If she doesn't wake up in a few days, my guess is that she never will."

And if Astra died, then Louko...Keeshiff felt like he was choking.

"Currently, Louko is mostly running on adrenaline. That can only last for so long. It will be hard to tell the extent of his illness until that runs out." Another deep sigh. Asher's voice dropped as he finally said: "I believe his survival depends on Astra's."

"I see." Aelor Ven's shoulders sagged, weighed with this great knowledge.

Keeshiff was beyond burdened, feeling crushed by it. He had never been so scared in his life.

For a long moment, none of them had the strength to break the silence. In the end, it was Aelor Ven who said, "Come. You must be exhausted and in need of a meal. That is at least one area I can help in."

Asher definitely did look exhausted, and Keeshiff—though he doubted the comment was directed at him—would be lying if he didn't admit he was feeling almost ill with the stress, fatigue, and hunger the swift journey had involved.

And so, they followed the lord through the corridor and down the stairs, taking a right to go down yet another hallway. They came out to a large dining room where all of the other knights—Rufio and Ivinon included—now sat, picking at their food in an odd mixture of starvation and half-heartedness. The room must have been Aelor Ven's official dining hall, as the sense of minimalism that the corridors had offered was nowhere to be seen, leaving instead the overwhelming sight of a thousand details, from the broad panels lining the walls and depicting scenes of nature to the gilded trim that reflected the light of the odd, paper-covered chandeliers. Columns of dark, polished wood stood like soldiers in their rows on either side of the room. But in all of this splendor, all Keeshiff could think about was how much Louko would have loved this, and how instead he was half-starved and stuck in a room with a possibly dying Astra.

But that thought was shoved away as he faced his men, who upon seeing the older prince all got to their feet.

Keeshiff immediately waved the gesture away. "As you were," he murmured, too tired for formalities. Or was it tired *of* formalities? Besides, he wasn't really even the prince of anything anymore.

Wordlessly, he sat down at the table, Asher following suit. A servant brought out some broth, and they were left to stir and poke and finally eat just like the rest of the men. Well, at least Keeshiff was. It was hard to miss all the hopeful and apprehensive glances that were cast Asher's way.

Finally, the physician said, "It is too early to tell."

And that was about when Aelor Ven took the floor. He was still standing at the end of the table, hands folded neatly behind his back and showing every sign of being ready to give them a good, long lecture. Keeshiff didn't blame him. He probably would be as disappointed as the Nythrilian lord was...in fact, he was. In the lord's eyes, this was their fault.

"Before I begin, let me please just note that the only reason I am tolerating any of your miserable presences is because of my nephew. If it were up to me, I'd throw you all out quicker than you'd come. But he seems to *like* you." Keeshiff almost flinched at the word just as much as Aelor Ven. It only pointed out Louko's almost faulty sense of loyalty. "So, you will stay. But under no circumstance are you to set eyes upon, vocalize to, or attempt to make contact with, my nephew. Unless he tells *me* that he desires to, or unless you come to me with a *very* valid reason for needing to do so, you are to stay in the section of the house I have sacrificed for your shallow little selves. Is that understood?"

All of the knights nodded.

But for Keeshiff, the answer took longer. Not see Louko at all? But he had only just gotten him back. How would he know how he was doing? Who would be with him if Astra...if Astra.... He was suddenly aware of Aelor Ven staring pointedly at him. Swallowing hard, Keeshiff nodded. Louko would probably not want to see him anyway.

"Good. Obviously, the exception lies with you." He nodded to Asher. "Now. Enjoy your meal. I will be figuring out how to address this *mess* I've been so beautifully shoved into." And without so much as another remark, the man swiveled around and left with a flourish.

The door to the hall clicked shut, and silence descended. Anyone who had been attempting to eat gave up entirely now.

"I will do my best to keep you all updated," Asher sighed. "Until then, it is best to follow his orders anyway. The last thing Louko and Astra need is to be overwhelmed by guests."

This did not seem to ease many consciences. At least, it did nothing to ease Keeshiff's.

But he still had a job to do, and he would make sure that it was done. "Thank you, Grandfather," Keeshiff said sincerely, using Asher's nickname. Then he turned to the rest of his men. "Eat what you can," he told them all. "And then maybe we can find some parchment. I'm sure that many of you are eager to write home."

This seemed to provide some sort of encouragement. Many of the men had family still left behind in Merimeethia, and Keeshiff knew how eager they'd been to contact them. It was a wish that the prince finally truly understood. Only, his family was on the other side of the same house from him—and yet still out of reach. Maybe nothing had really changed since Omath died.

CHAPTER V

Asher:

Two days. It had been two days, and Astra had not so much as moved her head. Not a single movement. Not a single sound. If she didn't wake up soon, the lack of food and water would mean she never would.

It seemed that Louko was all too aware of this. He was glued to the chair that they'd left by Astra's bed. Day and night he stayed, and no one could coax him elsewhere. After the second day, they couldn't even get him to eat. All he did was watch. Wait.

And then it happened.

Louko was in his usual place, holding Astra's hand as always, and, of course, trained almost unnaturally on her breathing. It was clear he expected it to stop at any moment.

Astra's groan made Asher swivel around, and Louko nearly hit the ceiling. The prince recovered first and began rubbing her hand, calling her name, begging her to wake up. Asher rushed to join him at the bedside.

Louko didn't seem to notice, still fixated on his friend. "Astra? Can you hear me? Oh, please, please, please, wake up."

Her eyes opened suddenly, piercingly blue and fever bright. They fixed instantly on Louko.

"E-Ent?" The name left her lips like a gasp. "N-no, no, y-you have...have t-to...." Her chest heaved with effort of breathing and her voice was ragged beyond recognition. "Run...p-please, go...."

"Shh. Shhh. Astra. Listen, it's me—Louko. You're in my uncle's house. See? You're in a bed, with blankets. Asher is here. We're safe. You're going to be alright." Louko was quick and precise, using his free hand to try and gently rub an end of a blanket on her hand so that she could feel it.

"B-but...." The girl was frantic, writhing beneath the sheets. Asher had to hold her down. "T-T-Tyron, he'll...he'll f-find...."

"No. No, he won't. We are far, far away. I won't let him get you, again, you hear?" Louko's voice was almost stern.

Astra's thrashing movements stilled, though Asher suspected more from her condition than any coaxing. For a long moment she lay there, laboring just to breathe.

Asher used the chance to add water to the tonic and then hand it to Louko.

"P-please," the word was more of a whimper.

Louko was beyond distressed, and Asher was afraid the boy would break at any moment. But no, he just kept coaxing and reassuring, just like he had been doing for weeks. It was hard to watch, and the more Asher witnessed it, the harder it got.

Somehow, Louko calmed Astra enough that she let him put the cup to her lips.

"Easy, easy," he said, pulling it away when she reached for it. "It's alright. It won't go away. There is a lot of water here—you don't have to be thirsty anymore. We'll just take it slow."

"A-alright," came the rasping whisper.

"That's it," Louko encouraged. "Nice and slow."

Asher turned away, telling himself it was only to fetch the bowl of broth that had been waiting on the hearth since that morning.

Astra's waking proved to be a crucial sign of her survival, as it yielded more days of her slowly growing cognition. This meant that Louko was able to give her regular food and water. But it also meant that she had enough strength to do something in those frequent moments of panic. Anytime anyone entered that she didn't recognize, or anytime there was any sudden sound, or anytime that she was simply disoriented from having just woken up, it resulted in her Gifting lashing out.

Sometimes it was something as small as a singed blanket. Other times, the wide window shutters burst into flames. After one occasion where Astra had somehow made the entire manor begin to shake, Keeshiff had come up with the idea of going through her things to see if she'd had any spare red bronze. The effort had yielded several bracelets identical to the one Astra had used to wear. Asher kept two on her bed stand to use when needed.

Yet, as difficult as it was to control her errant powers, Asher held more hope than he'd had since Louko had staggered into their camp that first night. Over the course of a week, Astra's fever had lessened, then lingered, and now finally broken. She was still very weak and very frightened, but Astra would survive.

That being said, Asher knew better than to tell Louko right away. Oh, yes, the prince would be glad, but Asher also knew that Louko was running almost entirely off of the adrenaline that stress provided. To take away that stress would take away all of that nervous energy. That would likely mean collapse. So, with permission of the Lord Aelor Ven, Asher had brought Keeshiff up to the improvised medical room.

"Is everything alright?" Keeshiff asked.

"Yes," Asher assured as they climbed the stairs. "Astra's fever has broken and, so long as she has enough strength left to recover, she will survive."

Keeshiff nearly stopped, letting out a long breath in relief. It had been weeks since Asher had seen him look so at ease.

"I want to tell Louko, but I suspect he may, well, pass out," the physician explained.

"*What?*"

"He has been running on minimal sleep, food, and a lot of adrenaline." Asher kept his voice calm. "When we take that adrenaline away, we will take what he is currently running on. I suspect he will sleep for a day or two and then wake up very tired."

Keeshiff swallowed hard. "But he'll be alright after that?"

"There may be some lingering effects, but he'll be alright," Asher replied, hoping he was correct.

The prince asked no more questions after that.

They reached the room, entering only after Asher had given a subtle knock of warning. Louko was, as always, sitting by Astra's bed and waiting for her to wake up. He glanced their way only briefly before turning back to his friend.

"What is it?" he asked quietly, fear stirring at the end of the question.

It concerned Asher that Louko barely seemed to notice his brother's presence. He waited until Keeshiff was nearer to his brother before answering, "I believe that Astra's condition has stabilized. So long as no major bout of infection or fever returns, I believe she will survive this."

The abruptness with which Louko stood up was startling for one in as poor condition as he. "What?" he whispered.

"I believe the worst has passed," Asher said more slowly. "If she continues this way, she will survive."

"She's...she's going to make it?" Already, Louko was swaying in relief. Keeshiff stepped forward to steady him.

"Yes," Asher confirmed. "She'll be alright."

Louko's swaying became more precarious as a guarded relief took over, and Keeshiff was just quick enough to catch him as he fell over.

Asher immediately examined the unconscious prince, checking his pulse and breathing rate. "He's alright—just asleep," he reported to the already anxious Keeshiff. "Let's just get him to the other room. Aelor Ven had a bed prepared."

Keeshiff's eyes were wide as he tried to get a better hold on his brother. Clearly, as much as Asher had explained this would happen, the elder prince still had not been prepared. But Louko was much shorter and thinner than his brother; it was not hard for Keeshiff to scoop him up and carry him into the other room.

Asher and Keeshiff worked together to get Louko settled in the other room. The physician conducted a more thorough examination, since this was the first time Louko had been still enough to do so in weeks. Keeshiff kept himself busy by checking the fire, the blankets, and pretty much anything else he could think of. His fretting was nearly motherly. Asher had never seen him so tender, even if it was stumblingly so.

"Why don't you stay with him for a bit?" Asher suggested.

Keeshiff looked down at his pale, motionless brother. Then he nodded rapidly. "Yes, good idea," he said, finding himself a chair and pulling it over to the bed.

With one last glance at the brothers, Asher returned to his other patient.

Asher was exhausted. Splitting his time between two uncooperative patients for what was now weeks had left him utterly drained. Even though Aelor Ven's personal physician had started taking shifts so that Asher could rest, he often found himself too worried to stay away for long.

It didn't help that Astra was not compliant without Louko there. It seemed that Louko was the only one with enough of her trust to be able to calm her down. While the amount of trauma she had endured made this understandable, it had also made keeping the girl fed and hydrated nearly impossible. And since it had been almost two days, this was becoming a problem. Asher had resorted to putting the red-bronze cuff on her immediately after she woke up simply to keep her from burning the whole manor to the ground. Even with her powers aside, Astra kept wearing herself out with her violent reactions—a habit she was too weak to maintain. Asher didn't know what to do.

The physician had just settled down in the chair by Astra's bed for some much-needed rest when there was frantic knocking on the door. By the time Asher was on his feet, the servant had already entered.

"Your friend in other room say he need you," the man said in stumbling Merimeethian.

"Stay with her," Asher ordered even as he rushed into the hall. "Get me if she stirs." He didn't wait for a reply.

"Where is she? She's probably panicking right now!" Louko sounded almost hostile, his voice echoing out into the hallway.

Once in, he found Keeshiff distraught as he tried to calm Louko down. The latter was on his feet, teetering, and trying to make for the door that Asher had just entered.

"Woah." The physician grabbed the runaway patient by the shoulders and forced him back down onto the bed. It was surprisingly hard, considering how frail Louko appeared. "Settle down. She's just fine—she's resting. You don't want to wake her, do you?"

"But she'll wake up alone—she won't understand—she'll hurt herself." His ragged breathing became progressively worse.

"Louko, I need you to take deep breaths," Asher said with practiced calm. "If you panic now, it won't be good for you *or* Astra."

The prince at least seemed to react to this, as his quickening gasps slowly stuttered to reveal more controlled ones. But the look in his eyes remained, as well as the way they darted about the room.

It was better than before. "There you go," Asher tried to comfort. "That's an improvement. Now why don't we see about something to drink? You've been asleep awhile and I'm betting that you are thirsty." The physician motioned to Keeshiff to pour a glass of water from the pitcher in the corner.

"No. No. I'm fine. Is Astra alone?" Louko looked beyond him to the door before focusing on the pitcher Keeshiff was pouring, clearly wincing at every sound it made.

"No, there is someone with her," Asher replied. "They will come get us if she stirs." Keeshiff held out the glass and Asher took it, pressing it into Louko's cold and shaking hands. "Now drink."

"*Who*? She's in there with *strangers*?" He dropped the ceramic cup as if to make for the door, but the thing shattered on the wooden floor. Louko jumped in surprise and then just stared at the shards of pottery before apparently remembering what he had so frantically been trying to do.

Asher was beginning to wonder if it was a good idea for the two patients to be separated. But Louko really ought to be lying down.... The physician pressed him back onto the bed with gentle firmness. "I'll make you a deal: If you drink and eat everything I give you, we can go see her. Alright?"

Louko nodded vigorously. "Alright. Yes. Alright."

From there, it was nearly easy to get Louko to drink a full glass of water, half a bowl of broth, and every last drop of the auminar tonic Asher gave him. It was more than the physician had gotten him to do in the last week.

As soon as he was done, Louko staggered to her feet. "Now where is she?" came the disoriented demand.

"This way." Asher motioned, nodding to Keeshiff. The elder prince took the hint and steadied his brother.

Louko would not be calmed until they at last set foot inside Astra's room. It worked like a charm, the prince was suddenly quiet and careful as he entered. The servant that had called Asher earlier was still there, looking awkward and out of place. He gladly exited when Asher dismissed him.

"Why don't you sit down?" Asher prompted. It would at least be better than letting the boy stand.

Louko nodded quietly, accepting the chair that was offered without a sound. He didn't even take Astra's hand, most likely out of fear of waking her, and instead settled his elbows on his knees, resting his head on his hands.

Asher suppressed a sigh. Now what? How was he going to get Louko to rest? He didn't dare drug him into sleep—Louko barely trusted anyone as it was. Besides, if his reaction had been so drastic when waking up normally, then an induced sleep would be even worse to come out of. For now, Asher pulled the spare blanket from the foot of Astra's bed and held it out to Louko.

"Here. Make sure you stay warm."

There was a look on his face that showed he wanted to argue, but then he glanced again at Astra and took the blanket.

"Thank you," Asher said, then turned back to the pensive Keeshiff. Rubbing the back of his neck, he murmured, "I think we may have to talk to Aelor Ven about some better arrangements."

<u>Astra:</u>

"Astraaa, wake up," I drag the words out, patting her cheek. "Do you intend to sleep the day away? Come, it's past noon already."

She wakes up with a jolt, scrambling as far back as the cell wall allows. Her chains scrape across the stone.

I smile widely. "There you are. So glad you could join us. We still have much to learn and only so much time. Are you ready to continue?"

Voices tugged at Astra's consciousness, trying to drag her back to the waking world. She didn't want to go. The dark was much safer. It was cold, and silent, and completely numb. She tried to wrap herself in it, but the voices were persistent, rising and falling like ocean waves that lapped at her ankles. They pulled her further in, dousing her in pain with each measure. She couldn't get out. She couldn't get away. She was in over her head….

"You have not slept properly in days! You cannot keep this up," one of the voices said.

Whoever they were talking to gave no response.

Another voice spoke. "Really, Louko, do you plan to kill yourself?"

*Louko...*Astra opened her eyes.

"I'm not the one you need to worry about," came a thin defense. The voice was unmistakably his.

Astra bolted upright.

"Oh, you're awake! You're awake. Um. Please don't blow anything up." Astra felt Louko's hand almost before she heard his voice.

"Yes. Please. I've already lost my grandmother's urn...." A deep and unfamiliar voice sounded from somewhere else in the room.

Astra tensed, gripping her friend's hand.

"Don't worry," he immediately assured. "It's my uncle—Aelor Ven. Remember? We were trying to get to him, and we finally made it."

Though her vision was still blurry, not yet adjusted to the overbright lighting of the room, Astra's gaze fixed on this stranger. "I remember," she heard herself say.

"Good. That's a start." Louko squeezed her hand back in reassurance. "You were very hurt, but you're getting better now. We're in Nythril...obviously. I mean, Uncle Ven would never set foot in Merimeethia." There was a snort from both Louko and where Aelor Ven was standing.

Nythril.... They'd really made it? Or was this another dream? Astra didn't think everything would hurt this much if she was just dreaming.

"How are you feeling?" Louko asked.

Astra looked back to him, unable to process. He looked so...normal. He was dressed in day clothes, face and hair clean, sitting in a chair in the well-lit room. It was a jarring contrast to the mental image she had of him in chains.

"Astra?" Louko asked, notes of concern now coloring his voice.

She recalled the conversation that she had woken up to and asked, "W-why aren't you sleeping?" Her mouth felt like it was full of sand.

Louko blinked. "Um...I do not think that is an answer...."

"But it is a valid question," Asher grumbled from off to the side.

75

Astra glanced at the physician and back to her friend, fear doubling. "You are sick, too—you have to let them take care of you."

Louko let go of her hand and made a confused open palm gesture as his brow furrowed. "What—?" His eyes narrowed. "Are you still mad about the hair? Is this revenge?"

...*Hair?* Astra's brow furrowed, causing the scar at her temple to sting. What was he talking about?

"I've never cut hair before, let alone a girl's hair...I mean, it would be rather odd if I *did* cut hair...I'll leave that to Rufio...except that I *did* cut your hair and now it's gone and I am pretty sure I did a horrible job." He breathed deeply—a ragged sound. "Oh. You didn't realize it was short. I should have shut up."

Shoulder protesting the movement, Astra reached up and felt for her hair. How had she not noticed how short it was? Where it had once hung to her waist, now it barely brushed her jawline.

"I do not approve of knives for cutting hair," Louko said nervously. "It is not as easy as it sounds. But I probably would have done even worse with shears. So. Yeah. Sorry."

"We can discuss this all after you rest, Louko. If you so desire to continue your career in...fashion." Aelor Ven's dry tone again entered the conversation.

Astra's hand returned to her lap, but her attention remained on her friend. *Please rest...please.*

"I'm sitting down. That's resting." Louko's reply was indignant.

This only prompted a scoff from Aelor Ven, followed by, "I'm going to put that on your tombstone. Now if you don't rest, that pyromaniac over there is probably going to burn my great grandfather's bureau at the end of the bed. So please. Be considerate."

Wait, pyromaniac? Astra's frazzled mind couldn't process if Aelor Ven was talking about her or Asher. Neither seemed to make much sense. She gave up and refocused on Louko. "Please," was the only word she added to his uncle's little speech.

Louko's entire demeanor changed from obstinate to something between desperation and pleading as he looked back to her.

"I'll even set aside my sense of propriety for once and bring in another mat for the other side of the room, if that will change your mind," Aelor Ven said in clear exasperation.

Louko's brow furrowed, but the tension in his shoulders released and he gave a quiet, "Alright."

Relief made Astra feel the slightest bit dizzy. "Thank you."

"I hope this means you plan to set an example," Asher said, stepping forward. "Starting with eating when you're supposed to."

"Ha!" Louko pointed a finger at Astra in triumph.

Astra tried to glare at him but had the feeling it came off more as a feeble sort of squint.

"Careful, Louko," was Asher's dry admonition. "If you spite her into doing what she's told, you'll be my next target."

Sighing, Louko got unsteadily to his feet, "True. But it would be worth it," he said as Asher helped him regain footing.

"Sleep well," she called softly.

The next few days blurred together in Astra's mind. It was all the same; she would wake in panic and by nightmare, Louko would calm her and help her to eat and drink, and then she would fall back into heavy sleep. Astra did not know how many days passed in such a manner before she could sit up alone and hold any real conversation. But as her strength began to return and her mind grew sharper, her memories returned.

Astra continued to suffer from vivid nightmares: glimpses of what had happened; terrors of what could have been; or, worst of all, twisted snatches as if she was in Tyron's mind. She relived walking into that cold, dark cell as if she was the one who held the key. She watched herself faint dead away with no more emotion than a thoughtful frown. Though these nightmares made her wake up shivering and sweating, Astra said nothing of them. Who could she tell? Certainly not Asher. And she could not bring herself to tell Louko.

Louko...while not as thin as Astra remembered him being during their capture, he was still a little underweight, so much paler, and he almost looked...older. His smile was rarer, too, and worry marked his brow constantly.

It had been around two weeks since they had arrived at Aelor Ven's manor—or so Astra was told. She could only recall the last half of that. The few people she had gotten to see were Louko, Asher, and the occasional servant that came to the door. Now and then, she would also spot the lord of the house observing things from the background. He stayed in the hall or—if he entered—the back of the room, rarely speaking.

Louko, on the other hand, did enough talking for the both of them. Well. It wasn't the amount of talking so much as the fact that he constantly seemed to describe what was happening all the time. When Asher came in, he would tell her who it was—even though she could tell. When any noise was made, he explained where it was coming from. Even when people talked, he would sometimes tell her what they meant. It was as if Louko was just as nervous and jumpy as she was, but took the time to reassure her before calming himself.

Today was no different, with Louko narrating Asher's usual afternoon routine: check her temperature, ask a few questions, make her drink her tonic, then send for a servant to fetch their lunch.

"Do either of you need anything else?" Asher asked, giving them their bowls.

The smell of broth made Astra's stomach twist.

Only after looking her way did Louko reply, "No, thank you."

"Alright." The physician stooped to add a log to the hearth, then straightened. "I'll go take my own lunch, then. There is a servant by the door if you need anything—just have him fetch me." He was halfway out the door before he stopped and leaned back in to say, "And don't get any ideas: The fire does not need feeding." He gave a very specific look towards Astra and she looked away, face red.

The door closed, and she and Louko were alone again.

"Feed the fire, eh?" The prince raised an eyebrow, but she saw worry beneath.

"I can't even reach the fire," Astra mumbled, stirring the contents of her bowl.

Louko's hands fidgeted in his lap before seeming to strangle each other into stillness. "I think it was just an expression. Though you wouldn't need to be near the fire to get to it."

Astra paused, allowing herself to be distracted enough to ask, "What does that mean?"

"You're just...very...capable of making fire, is all. Or transporting food *into* the fire. Or just making your food...evaporate. I suppose it depends on the mood?" He said this all very innocently.

Astra's distraction became a little more genuine. "What? Wait, have I...." Suddenly, she remembered the two red-bronze bracelets she'd noticed on the bed stand and it all clicked. *Oh no....* "Did I hurt anyone?"

His hands quickly went forward. "No, no. You didn't. We just got...wet. but I think you're alright now."

"I can lose control very quickly," she said, words tripping over each other. Fire laced around her ribs in a reminder that she wasn't used to talking much. "It will seem fine for weeks on end and then suddenly snap. I should be wearing one of the bracelets—that's what Ent had them made for." She recalled that day when she'd gone before the Court and thought she could nearly taste the burnt air.

"I see." Louko's lips were pressed firmly together, his hands white in what almost appeared to be tension.

Turning her head, Astra spotted the copper-colored cuffs only a little out of reach. She moved to set down her still-full bowl. "Can you reach them? Could you hand me one?"

Louko went very still, looking from the cuff to Astra. "Is that...a good idea?" His voice was very soft, and as he asked the question, his hands subtly rubbed his wrists.

His distress was the only thing that could have halted hers in its tracks. But the idea of being helpless to suppress her Gifting while Louko was there was too terrifying to push aside. "I nearly leveled an entire palace wing. It's too dangerous—I'm too dangerous."

It seemed to take great effort for Louko to stop rubbing his wrists, but he did. "I don't know," he mumbled, eyes averted to the cuffs beyond Astra's reach.

"I could hurt someone: you, or your uncle, or Asher." *Calm down. If you don't calm down, you'll only make it worse.* Astra found herself gripping her wooden bowl and biting her tongue just to stay quiet.

"It's alright." Louko slowly took the hand that was gripping the bowl. "I didn't mean to upset you. I just...." His eyes wandered back to the bracelets, and his sentence remained unfinished.

Astra didn't move. She wasn't sure she could.

Louko added, "Why don't you ask Asher?"

Trying to swallow, Astra nodded. "Sorry," she whispered without looking up.

"It's alright."

Her chest hurt with the force of everything pent up in it. *Breathe. Take a deep breath.* She tried to refocus on her meal, but the thought of eating only made it worse. "I-I don't think I'm hungry yet."

Louko's brow furrowed. "Sorry, I didn't mean to upset you. Are you alright? Does something hurt? Do I need to get Asher?"

"No, no." Astra's chest constricted. "I-I just...." Her hands were shaking, threatening to spill broth everywhere. She tried to tame it.

Louko did not say anything. He didn't prod, he didn't try and finish her sentence. He just waited, dark eyes watching her with concern even as he so patiently sat in silence.

Breathe, idiot. She attempted to deepen her own rapid breathing. That took a few minutes. And then she tried to summon up the courage to speak again. That took a few minutes more. But Louko never pressed.

When the pressure on her lungs had finally lifted enough for the words to get out, Astra said, "I just want to lay back down." She didn't want to be awake anymore.

"Alright," he said, voice quiet. "I won't argue with rest, I suppose." But his eyes pierced her with worry, all the more.

Neither said anything as he took her bowl and set it aside on a nearby table. At least Astra was able to lay down by herself—a new freedom. She didn't know what Tyron had done to her to make her heal so slowly, but her recovery had never taken this long before.

"Thank you," she murmured from beneath her blanket as Louko drew the window shutters.

When there was no reply, Astra pulled the blanket over her head and shut her eyes, wishing she could shut out her thoughts, too.

The next morning, Astra had just woken up when Louko came in. He had his own room across the hall but almost always managed to be back in her room before she knew he was gone. Their routine played out as usual: Asher did his daily check, made sure Astra was sitting up comfortably, then waited until Astra and Louko had eaten before going to get his own breakfast; Louko would gather the empty dishes and leave them on the tray by the door, then open the shutters on the other side of the room to let the light in.

It was in this morning light that Astra suddenly noticed a difference.

She summoned the courage to ask, "What happened to your hair?"

Louko cocked his head, confused enough to look her in the eye. "What do you mean?" A hand went to it, as if he was afraid it was suddenly gone.

"It has white in it," Astra pointed out, voice still raspy.

He gave a weak sort of scoffing sound "What? I think you might be delirious, Astra." The faint comment held a half-hearted jest.

"Not this time," she returned, shifting slightly on the pillows that held her upright and reaching out a hand towards him. "Look—it really does have...white in it."

His brow furrowed. "Er...alright. I'll...have to get a mirror, I suppose." The remark was somewhere between amused and worried.

Astra didn't have the time to think of a reply before a knock startled them both. Their heads both snapped towards the doorway in time to see a servant enter.

"Sorry," he said in heavily accented Merimeethian. "But I have a parcel here, sent for the Princess Astra."

Astra stared at the man in bewilderment. A parcel? How could someone have sent her a parcel? How would they have known her title? Her blood ran suddenly cold: *How did they know she was here?*

She turned in panic to Louko, only to find him looking equally frightened.

The prince stepped forward. "Um. Thank you," he said, voice distant and suspicious. The servant left, and Louko stared at the package in his hands. After another moment, he inspected it as if it might be something dangerous. Only after close examination did his expression ease. "I think...it might be from Entrais...."

Astra said nothing, trying to comprehend how that would be possible. Had Louko's uncle contacted Ent? Or had he figured out where she was from the last letter she'd sent? "What makes you say that?"

Louko held up a piece of folded parchment that was attached to the parcel strings. "There is a note. It's coded and translated like the letters you send to your brother."

"May I see?"

Crossing the room, Louko gave her the note.

Astra took it and quickly translated, deciphering what it said.

At first, she could not move. Then she began to tremble so that she could barely hold the parchment.

Since you would not give me what I wanted, I have decided to add a couple more players to The Game.
Your move.

Looking up in terror, Astra saw Louko had opened the wooden carry-box. A deep frown marked his face as he picked up the three boards made for TetraChess. "Why would...." He looked over at Astra and immediately set down the game, getting to his feet. "What is it—what's wrong?"

Astra felt wretchedly sick to her stomach. What should she say? What *could* she say? Louko would know if she tried to lie. She forced herself to swallow and whisper the paralyzing words: "It's from T-Tyron."

Louko was by her side in an instant, and all but wrenched the note from her, staring at it himself—even though he couldn't read what was written. "What? How?" he asked breathlessly.

"He must have known, must've known we were going to come here," Astra murmured, suddenly aware of how loudly her own pulse drummed in her ears.

Louko's hands shook slightly. "But...what does it say? What does it mean, Astra?" He locked eyes with her, and Astra saw the war of fear and anger within.

Trying to suppress her own fear, Astra told him. What if Tyron was coming? What if he already had someone here?

The prince's jaw set, and his whole face became suddenly expressionless.

"Please, help me get up." Astra was already trying to move, adrenaline helping her ignore the pain that seared across her skin with the motion. "I need to see the boards." Maybe there was some clue, some hint, some evidence of what would come next.

"What?! No."

Astra flinched.

Even Louko seemed surprised at how loud that had been and added more softly, "Stay there. I'll bring it to you if you must see it." His voice was barely audible now, and he looked back at the boards. He ran his hand through his prematurely peppered hair, face creased in worried lines as some inner battle raged within him.

Louko brought each board over and Astra took them, searching them everywhere for anything that would help her understand. But there was nothing.

"Are there pieces?" She asked, desperate.

He hesitated then nodded.

"Please, let me see."

"Astra...."

"Please!" Her still-healing voice cracked. "I h-have to find out. I have to know."

Fists clenched, Louko knelt down, carefully picking up the case and bringing it over to Astra. He set it next to her so that she would not have to move much in order to see it.

Astra reached over and began picking up each piece, searching them over one by one, but she found nothing in the beautifully carved marble. Then, picking up a white pawn, Astra found a single word inscribed on the base. *Mariah*. Astra paused, looking at it. Then she kept searching. Only one other piece revealed anything else; it was the black bishop, which also bore Mariah's name.

The two labeled pieces in each hand, Astra's mind worked rapidly to try and decipher this riddle. She didn't understand. She set the pieces aside and searched the case itself over, even pulling up the piece of cloth that rested at the bottom. That's where she saw it. It was another piece of folded parchment, this one bearing a black wax seal in the shape of a king chess piece. She opened it carefully, preserving the seal. Inside, written in neat, flowing script, was a sort of log.

Princess Astra rides to Merimeethia—White Queen moves forward three

Kaeden kills King Omath—Black King forward one

Prince Keeshiff flees to Nythril—White Knight No. 2 forward three, left two

Mariah's betrayal—Black Bishop No. 2 forward/right eight, takes White Castle No. 1

Prince Louko escapes with Princess Astra to Nythril—White Queen back two

Black Bishop No. 1 forward three, right two

White Bishop No. 1 forward/right four

Black Castle No. 2 forward six

"What is going on in here?" Asher's concerned tenor made both Astra and Louko jump.

There was a long pause before Louko and Astra simultaneously began stammering some half explanation. They realized they were interrupting each other and stopped as suddenly as they had started.

"It's my fault," Louko sputtered out. "I shouldn't have let her see it."

"It's not his fault," Astra argued hoarsely. "I asked to see it."

Asher had stepped forward to examine the package and its contents. He held up a hand to silence them both. "Don't worry—it's alright," he said. "It's good for Astra to have something to do while she recovers." He turned to Louko. "Really, it was a good idea. Perhaps it will actually keep her in bed for as long as she ought to be."

"But—" Louko began.

Astra interrupted. "Yes. Thank you."

Louko gave her a long, hard glare. "Yes. Thank you." The way he emphasized the last words were less than pleasant.

Astra felt sick for having cut Louko off and gone against his wishes. But she could not let Louko try to spare her when so much was at stake.

However, she was all too aware of Asher's keen observation, and was relieved when the physician announced, "I will run these dishes back down. Do either of you need anything more?"

Both shook their heads mutely.

"Alright. I'll be right back." He picked up the tray and left.

Immediately, Astra picked up the note that logged the chess moves.

"You should be resting." Louko's statement was simple and Astra could not read the emotion behind it.

"Asher will be back soon," she murmured in reply. She picked up one of the pieces with Mariah's name on it, trying to think. What did it mean? Was it saying that the piece represented Mariah? How?

Louko said nothing, and only sat there as Astra continued to go through the board game and its pieces.

She wanted to apologize. Over and over, the words formed on her tongue only to die away. Why did she only ever seem capable of hurting him?

When she did speak, it was only to wonder aloud, "Why a game? What does he want that he would send a game and not some letter or threat?" She went back to the note. "If he knows where we are, he...he could have just come himself." She knew that Tyron was powerful enough that he could walk in, take them, and leave without anyone being able to stop him.

Running his hand through his hair, Louko replied, "I don't know. But whatever it is, he wants to control it. That's the reason for The Game, at least. It gives us rules; rules he dictates. And a certain amount of predictability. This has to do with why he wanted you in the first place...." His words wandered off.

"So...." Astra tried to remember the days she'd spent in Melye's library as Louko taught her chess. It seemed a lifetime ago. "If all of these pieces represent people, then each move represents an action. And if we can find out what the winning action represents, we can find out what he wants."

Silence. Louko's eyes were riveted on the boards, unmoving and with an only-slightly hidden panic. Then, quietly, he murmured, "Yes. We're at war now...only, it's a very different kind of war."

CHAPTER VI

Louko:

Louko sat by Astra's bed while she slowly settled in and fell into a restless sleep. It had taken the better part of an hour to coax the chess pieces away from her, and then to get her to relax enough to rest. This newest play by Tyron was just one more nail in the coffin, at this point. What in Eatris were they going to do? What did it all even *mean*? Surely, Tyron wouldn't just give away information, so what was it really for? Some trap to lead Astra back to that nightmare?

Hadn't Tyron done enough?

Get a grip, Louko. In an attempt to distract himself, Louko got up from his seat, pacing about the room and letting his eyes settle on anything they could find; the patterns on the wall, the mantlepiece.... He froze as his gaze landed on the image in the corner of the room. It took him a moment to register the thing as a mirror, and even longer to register the person he was looking at was himself. He'd been so trained on how horribly different Astra looked that he had somehow not fathomed that he, too, might be changed. Who he saw in the mirror was a complete stranger. Another casualty of Tyron and his sick game. Whatever it *was.*

The gauntness, the wear and tear of the last few weeks...he couldn't have cared less about that. Instead, he was drawn to the grey and white now sprinkled throughout his once jet-black hair, a marking that was supposed to mean age and wisdom. But Louko felt young and stupid. Too stupid to see Kaeden was Tyron. Too stupid to have kept Astra safe. And now, too stupid to figure out what Tyron was doing through the note and the TetraChess.

With a sigh, he looked back over at Astra as her ragged breaths barely disturbed the silence. She needed rest...and him being in here pondering all of his life's bad decisions would only heighten the chances of her waking again. Besides, he couldn't hide forever. He needed to get up and do things and try and keep himself together so that whatever Tyron was planning could be stopped. So that this nightmare could just end.

Reluctantly, he quietly left the room...only to find his uncle was awkwardly waiting outside.

"I was just coming to see if you would eat." Ven had both hands folded behind his back, but it did not make him look any more relaxed.

Louko sighed, taking a moment to process that his uncle was speaking Nythrilian. He was suddenly glad Kaeden had always pushed him to be fluent in the language.

There was a sour taste in his mouth. Not Kaeden.

With an unfortunate amount of effort, Louko returned to the conversation with his uncle. "It won't really matter what I say, will it?" he asked, tired.

His uncle cocked an eyebrow. "Reading minds now, are we?"

"Well, will it make a difference?"

The man sighed. "Not one bit."

Louko smiled slightly. "Then yes, I am reading minds."

"Why don't we go to my study, then?"

Louko gave his best unimpressed expression. He was well aware that Uncle Ven had purposefully kept him away from the knights. More importantly, he had been keeping Louko away from his brother. And that wasn't fair to Keeshiff. Louko had seen the fear in his eyes whenever he *was* allowed to see him. This whole ordeal had probably scared his brother half to death. It certainly had done so to Louko.

"Why don't we go to the dining room? Your study is so dusty," he suggested with a forced hint of amusement.

Uncle Ven scoffed. "There is no need to insult my study when all you wish is to see your brother. Though in my opinion, both actions are foolish."

"What? Dusting?" Louko chose to ignore what his uncle really meant.

Now his uncle laughed. It was a deep, contagious thing. If it had been a couple octaves higher, it was much how Louko had imagined his mother's laugh would have sounded.

"When you put it that way, yes. To do the work when I pay others so much to do it for me," Uncle Ven replied, shaking his head.

"Nythrilians are so lazy." Louko rolled his eyes, beginning the journey down to the stairs and trying not to panic at the fact that he was leaving his best friend alone. But he couldn't keep hiding.

The comment elicited another chuckle from his uncle, but this time, no reply. The two fell into a companionable silence until they reached the door to the dining hall.

Then Uncle Ven stopped and asked, "Are you sure you are ready?" Concern was written clearly in his face.

"Of course." Louko kept his voice light.

His uncle did not seem to believe him, frowning as he said, "I don't see why you would bother. I am personally ready to throw the lot of them out into the cold and watch them freeze."

Louko rolled his eyes. "Uncle, in their defense, you wanted to do that before you even met them."

His uncle gave a grunt. "True." With that, he motioned for two servants to open up the dining room doors.

In walked the uncle and nephew, greeted by the sight of a dining table full of knights...and Keeshiff. Someone stood and raised a hand in greeting. Oh, Rhumir.

The movement from the former servant proved enough to gain everyone else's attention, and Louko flinched as Keeshiff's chair was pushed back with a scraping noise.

Keeshiff looked like he wanted to say something—and badly. But either he thought better of it, or he lost the words. Louko realized he was staring at his brother and quickly diverted his gaze.

Keeshiff cleared his throat. "Um. You, uh, must be hungry."

Louko's tired brain was a little slow to switch from Nythrilian to Merimeethian in time to reply.

"What an astute observation. Maybe that is why he is in the *dining* room," Ven muttered darkly.

While Louko completely understood his uncle's less-than-stellar opinion of Keeshiff and the others, it was not helping.

"Why don't you sit here?" It was Asher who came to the rescue. He had been sitting by Keeshiff, close to the end of the table. He stood up, picked up his plate, and nudged Farian next to him. The young knight followed suit and so left two cleared places for Louko and his uncle.

Louko's uncle, of course, replied dryly, "Charmed. What great hospitality to offer me my own seat in my own house."

"Uncle, please," Louko whispered, relieved when his uncle gave a relenting sigh and simply led the way to the two seats.

No sooner had they sat than servants tended to them, giving them each a bowl of soup along with a warm piece of bread.

"Funny how Nythrilian food choices change," Louko mumbled, trying his luck at a joke. It was very clear that Ven—for all of his grumbling and show of force—was catering to the Merimeethians as best he could.

The comment was received with an unintelligible grunt from Ven, who simply continued sipping his soup.

Louko supposed he should do the same but found himself toying with the silverware instead. He was all too aware of Keeshiff's constant sideways glances and attempts at conversation that never got beyond a slightly opened mouth.

In the end, it was Rhumir who broke the silence, ignoring Asher's looks of warning as he did so. "What comes next?"

Louko's fiddling subsided, but his eyes remained on the silverware. He thought again of the note and the package that had arrived only hours ago, and suddenly wondered if Astra was still asleep or if she had woken, unable to resist the panic any longer. What if she was alone, trying desperately to figure out what Tyron had sent the game for?

"We finish dinner," Keeshiff broke in, sounding almost stern.

While it didn't keep Rhumir from muttering something under his breath, it seemed enough to keep him from asking anything else.

That's when Ivinon spoke up. "You should let Astra know that big mare of hers misses her," he said in his usual quiet way. Then he nearly smiled as he added, "But maybe leave out the fact that she's taking it out on your uncle's poor grooms."

"Yes, it has been...an adventure," Ven huffed, apparently more pleased with this conversation than the last. Louko didn't disagree.

"Perhaps if I go see her, she will settle," Louko offered.

Ven set down his bowl and pulled a chunk off of his bread. "Or give you a black eye. Poor Xel—he'll be out for a week."

Louko winced. Yes, he would definitely need to see the mare. Or better yet.... He turned and looked beyond his uncle to Asher. "When do you think Astra would be well enough to see her?"

The entire dining room went still.

"Well," the physician spoke slowly. "It is hard to say. Her rate of recovery has been remarkable, but...there was much to recover from. I think it is best to take it one day at a time." He had reverted to that calm tone he always adopted while in Astra's room. "But your idea is a good one. Maybe we can at least arrange getting her over to the window in order to see her mare." The proposal hung in the air like a question as Asher looked to Ven.

"Well, perhaps if the mare would stop insisting on murdering my household, then yes, it could be arranged." Ven's reply was no less than expected.

Louko piped up, "I could do it."

He felt more than saw everyone look at him.

"I'm not sure that that would be the best idea," his uncle said in a diplomatic, albeit rather strained, fashion. He sounded like he had more to say but didn't get the chance.

"What if he visited her first?" Keeshiff suggested. "See how she reacts, and move on from there."

Uncle Ven appeared a bit annoyed at Keeshiff speaking up, but Louko couldn't have felt any more opposite. He was almost...touched? And so, before his uncle could list reasons against the idea, the younger prince added, "Keeshiff would go with me, of course. That way I wouldn't be alone."

Louko hoped his uncle would be willing. While having seemed trustworthy so far, it was difficult to think anyone could be when his family's track record was smeared with...well, stunts like Mariah's. But perhaps people could be better. Astra had not been like the others. And Keeshiff...Keeshiff had shown himself to be different. At least, Keeshiff *could* be different. He could be more, and Louko was so hungry for that.

There was a pause before his uncle finally huffed, "Fine. But I want that fire-breathing dragon of a mare in a stall when you visit. And you are not to go in. Not unless my head groomsman deems it safe. Which he will not."

"Thank you, Uncle," Louko said sincerely.

Ven's countenance softened then, and he gave a small show of amusement as he replied with an equally sincere, "You're welcome. Now, don't make me regret it."

Both Keeshiff and Louko replied with, "Yes, sir."

"I'm concerned already...." Ven's eyes were a little wider now. "And please, stop calling me 'sir'; it only makes me feel old. I like to live in denial."

Louko raised an eyebrow and gingerly asked, "How is that going, *Uncle*?" Instinct warned against such behavior, and yet Louko actually pushed past the feeling, holding in a wince.

"Better than my groomsman trying to teach that Litashian mare manners," Ven returned to the subject, feigning a sour mood. "I should have guessed Litash would have animals so uncivilized as that *thing*."

Louko's shoulders relaxed, and he gave a small smile of amusement at his uncle's...interesting opinions.

Keeshiff was the one who replied, giving an uncharacteristic snort as he said, "Oh no, Dannsair is quite a novelty."

A few chuckles went around the table. Louko, however, was busy thinking that they had seen nothing until they had seen Entrais's talking horse: Now *there* was a novelty.

Keeshiff was having second thoughts—that much was clear. As Louko walked with him to the barn, his brother's stiff movements signaled his nervousness.

"I rode her all the way to Melye, you know," Louko offered.

Keeshiff grunted in acknowledgement. "Maybe the problem is that she hasn't been ridden," he said as they crossed the tree-lined courtyard. "I doubt cooping her up has helped the issue. Your uncle said she's already broken out of two stalls."

As they entered the stable, the very first stall was evidence of this. The door was gone—evidently taken off for repair—and deep gashes decorated the wooden walls inside. Great. As they got closer to the end of the first barn, Louko could already hear the shrill neighing of a horse in the other building.

"Prince Louko, I presume?" An anxious-looking man addressed him in Nythrilian as soon as they entered the second section of the stable.

It was hard to hear him over the noise in the background. "Er. Yes." Louko was already distracted, not quite having expected *this* level of chaos. He'd seen Dannsair cooped up before, but this was the worst he'd ever seen her. He wondered if it had to do with the mare not knowing how Astra was.

He hadn't thought of that.

The groomsman turned to where Dannsair craned out over a stall door, trying to snap at one of the poor stablehands. The mare's ears were pinned flat against her neck and her teeth were bared.

"Maybe it would be better to try this another day," he suggested slowly.

"No...somehow, I get the feeling the longer she's in there, the worse she'll get," Louko murmured in reply. He took a step forward, gathering himself and forcing a chiding tone. "Dannsair, what in Eatris are you doing? Do you think Astra is going to be *pleased* when she is allowed to come down to the stables and see you? Why, she'll be mortified—you could have killed someone. How would that make her feel, eh?" Yes. Yes...he was talking to a horse.... Something was very wrong with him.

The horse stopped suddenly, picking up her head and staring at him with ears forward. Her nostrils flared as if verifying his scent. Then she dropped her head, whickering and nodding and reaching towards him as far as she could.

"Oh don't you give me that—I heard what you did," Louko continued to address the mare sternly. "You know Astra's going to want to be allowed to ride as soon as possible. How is my uncle ever going to allow *that* if all he sees is you thrashing around?"

Louko was suddenly aware of all the grooms staring at him with dropped jaws. He supposed it was extremely odd how he was addressing the mare...but he wasn't sure that was what they were so "jaw-dropped" about. He only folded his arms in front of him, glaring with a fierceness at Dannsair. "Well?" he asked.

There was a snort and a fierce shake of the horse's large, black-and-white head. Then she blew out a big breath like a sigh and looked towards him again.

Louko raised an eyebrow. "You'll have to do better than that."

Dannsair only pawed the ground inside her stall, banging the stall door in the process.

A few of the grooms jumped.

"She's doing fine—sitting up and eating and everything," he reassured. "And in fact, we want to get you out so she can see you from her window. But we can't do that if you keep kicking people in the face." He took a few steps forward, hand outstretched and palm facing upwards.

Dannsair huffed again, but this time her ears flicked forward and back before resting in the middle. She reached out, pressing her warm muzzle to Louko's hand. Her jaw worked gently as if chewing something—a sure sign of relaxation.

"Thank you," the prince whispered. He hesitantly used his other hand to stroke her neck and show his appreciation.

The mare leaned into his touch, even pressing her heavy forehead to his chest in the manner she'd often done to Astra.

"Well," the word came like an exhale from the head groom. Disbelief was painted on every face in the room.

And Louko was equally shocked. While he had expected to be able to calm the mare, he had not expected...this. He continued to run his hand along her neck, the warmth of her body and the press of her forehead a foreign sort of comfort.

In response, the mare nibbled at the edge of his coat.

Behind him, Keeshiff chuckled and said in Merimeethian, "Just wait until Aelor Ven sees this."

Louko couldn't help but find Keeshiff's chuckle contagious. Smiling, the younger prince replied, "Think he'll be jealous?"

"I was thinking 'livid', but sure, 'jealous' works." Keeshiff shook his head, returning the smile with a grin of his own.

It struck Louko very suddenly that he hadn't seen his brother smile like that since...well, a long time ago.

Uncle Ven was glaring down at Dannsair from the second-story window. He had been the one to go in with Asher to help Astra to the window. Meanwhile, the mare next to Louko was impatient. She pawed the cobblestone and tossed her head—all without so much as pulling on the lead line that Louko held. Then she went rigid, lifting her head with fixed attention. The high-pitched neigh that followed vibrated through Louko's entire body and left his ears ringing.

And yet, in that moment, it was all worth it. For there in the window, outlined by nearly chin-length red hair, was Astra. And she was wearing the closest thing to a smile that Louko had seen since their escape. She lifted a pale hand to wave, and Dannsair responded by pounding both front hooves on the ground.

Louko couldn't help but smile, as well.

He had only just put Dannsair away—a long and dubious task which involved several threats—and was heading for the house when Ven came to meet him. His uncle no doubt had been wondering where he was, as getting Dannsair settled had taken at least half an hour. But no. There was something in his hand. It was an open letter, the seal freshly cut. Tension shot with renewed force through Louko's body, and his eyes searched his uncle for any sign of what the letter held. Was it something from Tyron? He didn't like the deep creases of worry that were settled on his uncle's forehead.

"Uncle, what is it?" Louko forced the words from his mouth as Ven finally joined him, motioning for them to continue walking to the house.

"A letter just arrived." The reply was taut. "From King Dia Tzaro," he added in an undertone.

Louko was not really sure whether he should be relieved. "What does he want?" At least it wasn't Tyron.

His uncle held it out to Louko. "I suppose you ought to read for yourself."

Louko again noted his uncle's expression and took the letter quickly, scanning it with growing horror.

To Prince Louko of Merimeethia:

Greetings. It has come to my attention that you are currently residing with your uncle, the Lord Aelor Ven. I am pleased to know that you are safely within our borders, away from that dreadful country which seeks you so unjustly. I hope you may find our country more hospitable.

Indeed, I would like to show you the hospitality of Nythril myself. I would be delighted if you would join me at my palace for a ball, which is being held in celebration of the fiftieth year of my reign. You ought to, of course, bring along your brother, High Prince Keeshiff, and that famed companion of yours, the Lady of the Stars. Their presence would very much enhance the celebration.

I understand that it may take some time to move all of your effects. Therefore, I shall look forward to seeing you in one week's time.

—Ezai Ru Dia Tzaro Kado
High King of Nythril
High Seat on the Council Ezai
Conqueror of the Lower Lands

Transcribed by Scribe Folwyn Bast

This was a disaster. Lady of the Stars...Louko remembered the inscription on Astra's bow and how she had come by her name.

"How...how did he know she was here?" the prince asked, hands now shaking. If it was discovered that Astra was helping the exiled princes, that could get Entrais involved in a war with Merimeethia—with Tyron. That was the last thing Astra needed.

Ven frowned in thought. "The package," he said suddenly. "It was addressed to Princess Astra."

Louko didn't even notice how hard he was gripping the letter until the sound of crumpling paper startled him. "That stupid package," he growled.

With an arched eyebrow, his uncle calmly replied, "At least it seems that the king does not know of the knights." He came to a stop before the doors. "But what will he want from Astra?"

Louko stopped with him, pensive. "You said that Tyron has let the rumor of Astra's exile spread since we were..." His words failed for a moment. "...detained in Melye. The king could want absolutely anything. An ally. Or a bargaining chip." The last option was said quietly as the paper began to tear between Louko's hands.

"Is there any possibility of Tyron being in contact with the king?"

"Only if Kaedan tried to make any contact," Louko replied. What would Tyron gain from it? Did he want a war with Nythril? Or a war with Litash? Did he want a war at all?

Uncle Ven seemed to force himself back into motion, and he gave a double tap on the doors of the mansion. As a servant allowed them in, his uncle looked at Louko and said, "There have been ongoing negotiations since Omath died."

Oh, no. No, no, no. All the same, Louko waited until the servant was out of earshot before asking, "Is he going to be at the ball?" Panic wrenched his gut like a vicious monster, and Louko could only picture trying to pretend...Astra being forced to pretend.

"I don't think Kaedan has yet to dare setting foot across the border," his uncle replied. "He didn't win much admiration by targeting you."

Trying to slow his unsteady breathing, Louko nodded slowly. "Al—alright. That's good, then." His worry for Astra grew; would she be well enough to travel to the capital?

Uncle Ven nodded. "Yes." He began pacing in the vestibule of the manor. "I will accompany you. *Obviously*, I cannot miss a celebration of the king's reign."

Louko did not understand. "Obviously?" The way he'd said that....

Ven did not even look at him. "Well, as the king's chosen heir, it would look very bad for me to not celebrate his reign," he explained, a cough right before the word "reign."

"Um...I'm...sorry?" was all Louko could get out. He was what?

Now Uncle Ven glanced at him. "What?"

"I just thought you said you'd been chosen as heir," Louko said, hoping he'd just been hearing things. It was entirely possible. In fact, it was likely, because clearly that would be something Uncle Ven would have told him about before.

His uncle stopped, cocking his head slightly. "You...didn't know?" he asked. Then his expression soured. "Of course, they didn't tell you."

Oh dear, he wasn't kidding. He really wasn't. "Wait—how long has this been in effect? You're going to be *king* of Nythril?" While Louko could definitely picture his uncle sitting on the throne, never once had it crossed his mind. If he had known this, he might not have been so eager to bring Keeshiff or the knights to Nythril...as Uncle Ven had never been very fond of Omath...or his son...or Merimeethians...or Litashians.... At this point, Louko was about ready to jot it down as 'people in general.'

"It happened shortly after you left for Litash," Uncle Ven explained, voice still acidic. "You were going to come here, remember?"

The failure of that endeavor had been long lost to the past, and Louko focused on trying to wrap his head around this. He winced. "Sorry."

105

Ven waved his hand as he shook his head. "Yes. Please apologize for being the undyingly noble nephew I thought you were. How dare you."

Was that a...joke? More so, a compliment? Louko was afraid to take it as such.

Then Ven added, very quietly, "The failure was not on your part."

Unsure what to say to this, Louko tried instead to return to the subject at hand. "But why didn't you tell me?" He still should have found out some way. The Nythrilian heir choosing was always a great event.

It almost sounded as if his uncle sighed. "I thought that you would know," Ven explained. "It caused such an uproar in Merimeethia that I assumed you would surely hear of it. It didn't even cross my mind that they would keep it from you. But I suppose now it does make sense...because I would have had some power to protect you." This last sentence held years of bitterness and regret in them that were all too evident to Louko.

"Ah," was all the young prince could manage to get out. Well...that would explain why his father had been suddenly all for a war with Nythril. Louko remembered very clearly Omath's dislike for Uncle Ven—hence why Louko had not seen him in over a decade.

"Well, I suppose we ought to inform your brother of the invitation," Ven said. "He had better be prepared if he plans to walk into the capital of Nythril, with his reputation." He turned to leave then paused. "What will you tell Astra?"

Louko sighed heavily. He hadn't really noticed he'd been holding his breath. Whoops. "Um. I'm not really sure." His chest tightened as he wondered if this counted as a move in the TetraChess game. Did Tyron already know? What else were they in the dark about?

"Will she be able to travel?"

Running his hand through his hair, Louko took a moment in replying, "If she has a little while more to rest...and if we can use a carriage. Perhaps." Perhaps....

"Alright." Ven gave a short nod. "That will be easy enough. We have one week."

With that, the man turned and began to leave the room. That's when Louko realized the worst problem of all.

"Um...Uncle Ven?"

"Yes?" He turned around, already visibly worried by the perplexity in Louko's voice.

"I can't dance."

A GAME OF WITS

CHAPTER VII

Astra:

The closer the day of Dia Tzaro's ball drew, the more Astra's head swirled with nauseating anxiety. There was so much that could go wrong! Louko had told her of the letter two days ago and how, despite its cordial tone, Aelor Ven had said it was little more than a thinly veiled order. Astra had felt an immediate prick of terror. Now, it had dulled and twisted into something like a knot in her stomach. The last thing she wanted was to go to another castle.

It was a sentiment that Louko seemed to share. He couldn't seem to sit still, even when sitting at her bedside. And then there had been something clearly bugging him. Something other than the evident threat of Tyron and what he could do. Even now, his fingers drummed on the arm of his chair. Then he opened his mouth as if to speak, only to close it.

Finally, Astra could take the strain no longer. "What?" she asked.

"Um. It's just...." He trailed off as if trying to gather strength. "It's a *ball*."

Astra was not put off. "What's wrong?"

"I can't...." He paused, letting out a sigh. "I can't dance. You remember, don't you? Only, there I only had to dance with you, and you didn't really seem to care—we were both so angry at Entrais...but...now it would reflect on us...and I have to look dignified and able to actually hold a negotiation—with a king...and...well...I can't...dance."

Astra stared at Louko. Was...was he serious? Was that all? A shadow of a smile spread across her lips. "That's all you are worried about?" she asked in relief.

"Dancing is very important to Nythrilians," Louko muttered, pale face actually a little pink with embarrassment.

The semblance of a smile stayed. "Well, in that case, I suppose I can teach you."

His brow furrowed. "You can—well...I suppose that makes sense. You danced better than me, at least."

"Ent taught me to help with my footwork when he was teaching me swordsmanship," Astra explained. She wasn't sure if dancing would be the same in Nythril, but surely this wouldn't hurt.

Louko's mouth formed a silent "oh," and he shifted uncomfortably. "Well. We're leaving in a couple days...and I'm not sure you should really be standing. I know Asher let you stand a little bit yesterday afternoon, but I'm not sure that would be a good idea."

Between the game and the inactivity, Astra had grown restless. She was no longer so weak as to keep willingly bedridden. "Asher said this morning that it was alright for me to walk a little each day if you helped me," she said. "You were asleep when he came in."

Louko's eyes narrowed. "I don't think dancing quite qualifies...."

"Why not?"

The pink returned to Louko's cheeks with a vengeance. "I might step on you."

His embarrassment gave her the confidence to try and persuade him. "We'll start slow and be careful."

"This isn't a good idea...."

Encouraged by the fact that Louko did not say 'no' outright, Astra added, "It might help me get some coordination back."

He ran his hand through his hair as his expression grew more perplexed, but he did not shake his head. After a very long sigh, he gave in. "Alright."

"Can we start now?" Astra asked, eager to be out of the bed and finally doing something.

"I...suppose. But carefully."

All by herself, Astra was able to push aside the blankets and swing her legs off the side of the bed. Then, ever so gently, Louko took her hands and helped pull her up. She stood still for a moment, trying to steady her shaking legs. Astra was no longer used to the feeling of her own two feet.

"You may have to help me stay upright," she whispered, a little embarrassed.

In response, he kept one hand under her arm so that she could brace against him for support. "Are you alright? Does it hurt too much? Do you need to sit back down?"

She was sore and stiff, but the only real pain was the sharp ache in her left side. "No, no, it will be fine," she assured. "Just, um, not used to standing, is all." Then, before Louko could argue, she started giving slow instructions. "Before you begin, you bow to each other. I don't think we have to practice that. Then, you take one hand and hold mine, and your other hand goes around my back."

"Alright," Louko said softly and then stayed silent, allowing her to continue.

"First, you take a step back with your left foot. I follow you."

And so, their lesson began. Astra realized they must be an awkward looking pair, him with his mixed-up steps and her in her long, plain dress that one of the servants had lent her. They were both so out of place in the elegantly decorated room.

"Don't look at your feet," Astra instructed, a little more sure of her words now. "Focus on how it feels."

Louko muttered something unintelligent and tried to look up, proceeding to step on her foot. "Ugh, I'm sorry. I told you I can't dance. Sorry, are you alright?"

Astra just nodded. "Don't worry—it didn't hurt." She paused, trying to think of what was causing Louko to struggle so much. Perhaps it was because he had to hold her up. Then Astra remembered why Ent had taught her and decided to try the process in reverse.

"Maybe...think of it as footwork for sword fighting," Astra said. "You give ground, and I take it. You thrust, I pull back. You sidestep, and I turn to keep you in front of me."

Louko made a face. "An...interesting description."

"Just try it."

He did not argue with words, but his face gave away his skepticism. They started again, this time with Astra naming footwork steps with each movement. Louko looked down at his feet the entire time.

"Louko," Astra called his name sharply

He looked up, sheepish.

"Look at me. Don't look down," she said. "Just listen, and feel, and really try it."

This seemed to get Louko to swallow his pride, and he mumbled a 'sorry,' and promptly looked down at his feet.

Astra used one hand to lift his chin until she was looking him in the eyes. "Keep your eyes on me."

"Vain, are we?" Something tugged at Louko's lips, and it took Astra a moment to realize it was a smile. A very small, genuine smile.

"Says the one who keeps looking at himself," she teased back.

He rolled his eyes. "Only because I think I missed a spot when I cut your hair, so I try not to look at it."

Oh, her hair. Astra always felt silly for the strange sense of loss that came with having her once-long hair now cut so short. Perhaps it was just because it was one more thing about her that had been lost in the castle. But she refused to let the humor die on her account. "Looks that bad, does it?"

"Well, besides the rather bad job I did, it looks nice." His head jolted up then. "I mean, er, well. It doesn't look bad—I mean, it is very pretty—I mean, I'm not saying you're beautiful—wait, I mean, you are beautiful, but I'm not saying that I'm saying—"

"It's alright, truly," interrupted Astra, not sure what to make of this outburst.

Louko looked wide-eyed and embarrassed, then suddenly asked, "What were we doing again?"

"Trying to dance," Astra answered, now reddening herself. She told herself it was merely the exertion of having been standing and moving for so long.

"Oh. Right."

"Let's try again."

"What are you two doing?" The curious voice belonged to none other than Asher, who had apparently come into the room through the door Louko had left open.

There was an awkward second of quiet, and then Louko began stuttering out indistinguishable explanations. Asher interrupted by raising a hand.

"One sentence at a time, please," he said with an air of exasperated patience.

"Um. You see...I can't...dance." Louko's response was not exactly helpful, and Asher's expression showed as much, waiting with crossed arms for more information. When none came, the physician turned to Astra.

"Astra, why don't you explain." He turned to the second culprit.

The pair of them must have looked like two naughty children caught stealing the maid's pies. Only, Astra couldn't tell if the maid was irritated or amused.

"Louko wanted to learn to dance," Astra mumbled, trying to find a way to make it sound less odd than it looked. "I wanted to get up, and, um, you said I could get up today if he helped me. So, we thought this would be alright."

"We did?" Louko was not being helpful.

Astra gave him a dark look.

"Um. She—we did, I guess."

Asher was somewhere between amused and incredulous. He made a sound in the back of his throat, looking between them. "Well, by the looks of it, you've both been up for too long," he said. "You both ought to rest—and eat. But if you wish to dance further—and by further, I mean later—a little supervision would be beneficial. Who's going to catch you if the other falls?"

Astra did not argue, knowing the physician was right. She ached everywhere, and her legs were now trembling violently. Her side throbbed and burned. Somehow, she had thought she would feel better than this by now. Still, she noticed that Asher looked almost...pleased.

Suddenly, Astra found herself being scooped up by Louko and placed gently on the bed. As odd as the abrupt action was, it was stranger still that it *didn't* feel odd.

Asher seemed to be the most startled, raising both eyebrows. "I suppose that works," he said, more to himself than anyone else. He gave a shake of his head and went on with, "I will be back with some breakfast for you both. Louko, sit and rest. No more, er, carrying people."

"Um...I don't think that will be a...problem," Louko answered.

The physician was not gone long. He reappeared with two bowls of some kind of grain mash. "Eat," he ordered, handing a bowl to each of them.

When they'd eaten enough to satisfy Asher, the physician traded their bowls for cups of warm tea and gave the order: "Drink."

"I'm greatly offended. I have no problem drinking—" Louko broke off from his jest and narrowed his eyes. "Unless you put something in it...."

"I am not obligated to tell you. Now drink."

Astra had given up on trying to argue against Asher's medicines days ago. At least he had taken up mixing it into tea to lessen the strong taste of it all. She sipped the bitter brew down to the dregs then handed the empty cup back to the physician.

Louko stared at his cup for several minutes as if it might bite him. His focus shifted to Astra. After seeing nothing happen to her, he also drank his tea.

"Now sit down, Louko," Asher instructed. "I don't want to have to try and pick you up and get you on that chair."

"What...?" Louko's brow furrowed.

Asher acted as though he was explaining a simple concept to a small child. "With the amount of sleeping draught you just drank, you will be asleep within minutes. I don't feel like having to drag you up off the floor because you fell asleep there."

"Asher you—" Louko's anger melted into confusion and Astra's pulse quickened to realize he was swaying. "No good...physician." He half fell into the chair, and started blinking repeatedly. "I'm going to kill...you when...I wake up...." Apparently, Louko hadn't actually expected Asher to drug him.

True to Asher's words, Louko was asleep in minutes. Astra, though she had to remind herself Louko was *only* sleeping, felt no different. She looked at her friend and then at the physician.

"I don't think it's working on me," she said slowly.

Asher smiled broadly. "Oh, that's because I didn't give you any." He seemed rather pleased with himself. "You have been better behaved as of late, so I decided you didn't need any. But Louko has been rather less cooperative. I hope he will learn from this experience and that you may remember it when you feel like resisting."

Astra might have been more amused by the physician's devious ways if they didn't threaten her so much. "I will keep that in mind," she murmured, carefully laying down and drawing the covers about her. As she fell asleep, she wondered what it was that she had drunk. Astra decided she was going to be more careful about accepting food or drink from physicians.

It was two days before they left for King Dia Tzaro's ball. The fear of what would come next, the knowledge that Tyron had found them, even the simple realization that she would have to face others outside of this room, left Astra too stressed to even sleep at night. She did her best to keep calm for Louko's sake—he was even more apprehensive than she was.

In the meantime, dance practice continued. Astra was able to go a little longer than before, and though she ached with each step, she refused to complain. A maid came in at one point and measured her for a ball gown—Asher was the one who brought up the idea of a veil. It had made Astra realize that, even if others did not recognize her, her scarring alone was enough to make her conspicuous. She couldn't hide it all under shirt sleeves and high collars anymore. The thought made her wish not to be seen at all.

Louko and Astra were sitting in her room when there came a knock on the door. Both startled at the noise.

"Come in," Louko called when he had recovered.

Astra was already anxious. It didn't help when she saw Louko's uncle in the now open doorway, poised and stately as he strode inside.

"I came to see how you both were doing," he announced.

Astra kept quiet, allowing Louko to answer, wishing that she could shrink back against the pillows and become invisible.

"We are well." His eyes darted back to Astra, worry prevalent in the protective gaze.

Aelor Ven, meanwhile, turned to address Astra. "And how are you doing, young lady?"

Astra froze, any words she might have had catching in her throat. It was only when she saw Louko watching her that she was able to break through her own panic and scramble for some sort of response. "Um, better, thank you." Her knuckles were white around the edge of her blanket.

"Good," the lord murmured, adding with abruptness, "I suppose we have not been formally introduced. Since you will be stuck in a carriage with me for the foreseeable future, we might as well try and get to know each other a little."

It had somehow not occurred to Astra that she would have to ride with other people. She managed a nod.

Pulling up a chair, Aelor Ven sat down, stretching his legs out in front of him, and crossing them at the ankles. "Well, I assume you at least know who I am?" He cocked his head slightly—Astra noted how similar it was to the way Louko did it.

She nodded again. "The Lord Aelor Ven," she heard herself say. "Heir to the throne of Nythril and Louko's uncle." Louko had explained that much, at least. She wondered, not for the first time, what piece he could be in Tyron's game.

The man arched an intrigued eyebrow. "Well then," was his comment. "I am afraid I am not quite so well acquainted with you."

What did Aelor Ven want? Astra chanced a look towards Louko, trying to gauge his reaction to all this. It didn't help that he seemed equally uncertain and uncomfortable. So she swallowed hard and forced out the question, "What is it you want to know?"

Aelor Ven's stiff posture gave away his tension, even though his response sounded effortless. "Unfortunately, as much as you can tell me about what happened. Starting with your exile. The more I know, the better I can protect you."

Her exile...Astra's mouth felt dry. She glanced again at Louko, wishing there was some way out from under this scrutiny. But all he gave was a nod of encouragement.

So, mustering what voice she could, she slowly began, "I was exiled for my own safety. There were some who thought me too dangerous to be allowed to walk freely." Her eyes darted towards the spare blanket at the foot of the bed. It had already been replaced at least three times after she'd accidentally destroyed it. Clearing her throat, she tried to continue. "These people wanted me imprisoned or held for experimentation." She fought off the memory of a dark room, of being strapped to a table. "Exile was a way to appease them while allowing me some freedom."

Ven folded his hands in front of his chin, surveying her a while in silence. His narrowed, piercing brown eyes were not unlike Louko's in intensity, but they held a much more jaded personality. It was hard to discern the person beneath. His gaze broke from her and he looked over to the blanket she had just been noting.

"Dangerous, perhaps," he acknowledged. "Funny how they change their perspective to suit them. They called it 'useful' during The War. People never change." He leaned back in his chair. "But will it be safe to bring you to the king? I am not in the mood to sweep him up from the floor, no matter how much I would like him to…" He pursed his lips, a small curl touching the edges. "…disappear."

Astra was not sure if that spoke volumes about the king of Nythril or his heir. She had the uncomfortable feeling that time would tell. "It will be safe," she replied, hoping her acute embarrassment didn't show on her face. "There is a way to restrain my power." A necessary way, since she apparently lacked the self-discipline to do so.

"Yes. So Louko tells me," he sighed. "It will not weaken you too much? I may be no Elf or Bandilarian, but I've heard what red bronze does to those with Gifting."

Remembering what Louko had said about his uncle's dislike of Litashians, Astra was surprised he was so knowledgeable. "I have used it often and am accustomed to its effects."

He did not seem entirely satisfied, but all the same gave a terse, "Very well. But I am not about to watch my physician's work go to waste—nor my great-grandmother's woven blankets."

Now a little lost, Astra turned to Louko.

Louko just waved a hand and shook his head, muttering something about Nythrilian humor.

Aelor Ven went on as if nothing had been said. "Now, as sensitive a subject as it is…there are other matters we must discuss. He is alive, then?"

Astra's breath caught. She tried to answer, couldn't get the words out, and settled for a nod.

"And he is Kaeden?" The man's jaw was taut as he asked.

"Yes." This time Astra forced the answer out from between her teeth.

Aelor Ven took in a deep breath, clearly not pleased with the next question he was about to ask. "What did he want?"

Astra's gaze fell to the blanket that covered her legs. She hadn't noticed that she was grasping fistfuls of it, knuckles white over the bunched-up fabric. "Um…" *Breathe. Just breathe.* "He, um, I don't know. He was…." Her vision swam, and she closed her eyes. "He was experimenting. I thought that-that maybe he was trying to do something with my power. But he always kept me in red bronze." She opened her eyes but saw nothing more than before. "He kept demanding that I 'open it.' I don't know what that means."

Aelor Ven did not immediately reply. When he did, all he gave was an "I see," before going on. "Well, the capital will be very busy, but I doubt anyone will recognize you outside of the palace. Dia Tzaro will know who you are, of course, but I doubt he will want that news spread, any more than we do." The ease with which the man moved on in conversation was dizzying. "I will make sure you and Louko are safe, don't worry. But you will have to do exactly what I say."

Astra looked up in time to see his eyes flicker from her to his nephew.

Both nodded in unison.

It took all of the silence that followed for Astra to work up the nerve to say, "Thank you."

"It is my pleasure." He stood up. "We can discuss it more in the carriage, of course, but for now, just know that Nythril...likes politics. So, we will have to tread lightly." His smile turned humorless.

The warning was a heavy one and effectively closed the conversation. Aelor Ven exchanged a few more comments with Louko, bowed, and went off in search of Asher. Only then did Astra look back to her friend.

"It'll be alright," he reassured quietly. Astra wasn't sure who he was trying to convince—her or himself.

So, for Louko's sake, she nodded. "I know. I trust you." Yes, she trusted him. *Only* him.

CHAPTER VIII

Louko:

"So, have they found you something to wear, or are you really going to the capital in a nightgown?" Louko said with a smirk as he danced with Astra in her little room. She was doing better every day, but he could not help the worry that her condition would worsen after they left today. He didn't let her see that, though. His uncle had shown himself to be true thus far, even if Louko's years of experience set off warning bells in his head. *Don't trust. You'll get both you and Astra killed. What are you thinking?!*

"It seems no one realized I couldn't wear a ball gown for days while traveling," Astra replied, a small measure of her old, dry humor showing through. "I believe your uncle was trying to procure something for me." She switched back to instructing him. "Careful not to drag your toes."

Louko tried to do as she said, tripping in the process. He rolled his eyes at his own clumsiness. "I promise Asher didn't drug me...this time," he muttered, trying to resist the urge to look down at his feet. He kept trying to think of dancing as a sword duel. He couldn't tell if his slow learning was due to stubborn pride, being a slow learner, or just the fact that he really was a bad dancer.

Astra shook her head. "As I recall, the only time he did that was after you tried to stay up for three days straight."

"That's it. You need to sit down. I think you're getting delirious again." Louko gave her a mock glare and stopped dancing.

Astra obliged and sat down, which made Louko decide she must actually be growing tired.

"Me? Delirious?" Astra said, shaking her head. "Clearly you do not remember the few minutes between Asher drugging you and you falling asleep."

Louko gave an awkward cough and looked around. "Do you think it's time to leave, yet? I do believe Asher said everyone was almost ready.... Maybe I should go see if Uncle Ven managed to find you something more fitting to wear?" It still felt odd to call his uncle anything but 'sir.' But then again, he'd had this issue with Entrais during The War. Perhaps he could get used to it. It could be nice, even.

The only reply he got from Astra was a shrug. But then, when Louko turned to leave, he heard her quietly ask, "Have you packed the chess set?"

His hands clenched into tight fists, but he undid them swiftly, hoping Astra did not catch on to his tension. "Yes. Uncle Ven is bringing it," he said without turning around. He knew they had to. He knew they couldn't ignore it, and yet he wanted nothing more than to throw the stupid thing away. Tyron had them, now. They were stuck trying to figure out what it all meant and what he wanted.

"Why do you call him Ven?" Astra's quizzical tone made him turn around.

Louko blinked. "Uh. Because...that's his name?"

Astra's head tipped to one side. "It's not Aelor?"

"I mean. That's his family name. But *his* name is Ven. Oh...*oh* right, you have...oops. Uh. Yeah, Nythrilian names are inverted." His lips tipped up in an amused smile. "You thought his name was Aelor, didn't you?"

"Um...." Astra's cheeks turned pink. "I may have."

The snort that came from Louko was less than dignified.

"I thought you were going to go find me something to wear," she mumbled.

Turning up his nose, Louko made another sniff and stood up. "*Fine, Verzaer.*" He tried not to smirk as he threw out her family name. "I am always at your disposal."

Enjoying her still-reddened cheeks, he ducked out into the corridor and looked both ways for his uncle.

He didn't want to wander very far from Astra—in case she fell or did something—so he simply walked up and down the corridor and peered into some of the rooms to try and find Uncle Ven. This brought no success. Louko had just begun walking back to Astra's room when he heard someone trotting swiftly up the stairs. It was a maid, carrying a bundle wrapped in some sort of parchment or paper.

"Prince Louko?" She spotted him and came over, bowing in the usual Nythrilian fashion.

Louko still despised being bowed to, even if it was simply the standard greeting in Nythril.

"This is the best we could do. It has a dress for the princess and some other clothes for traveling."

Well, wasn't that well-timed? "Oh. Thank you." Louko took the wrapped bundle carefully and brought it back to Astra's room.

"They found something," Louko announced before entering the still open door.

Astra got up from her seat as he entered and took the package. She laid it out on the bed and opened it, sighing at the dress. "At least I can wear breeches while traveling," she murmured.

"I'll let you get dressed." Louko decided not to argue with her. Otherwise, he might find *himself* wearing a dress one day….

He stepped out of the room and closed the door, running his hand through his hair as he waited. As hard as he tried, the uncertainty of what they would find in the capital was impossible to escape. He feared both for Astra's health and her safety. What if the king decided Astra was to become a prisoner? What if he tried to use her for some personal gain? Uncle Ven had tried to reassure them that he would keep things under control, but Louko had caught the look in his eyes; Ven wasn't king yet, and he only had so much power. All they could do was hope that the king would see Astra as an asset and not a threat.

Louko heard Astra call out that she was done, and he re-entered the room. For the first time since the castle, she was back in her usual attire: breeches, a tunic, riding boots, and an overcoat. Not all of it fit very well, making Louko wonder if they had not actually been able to find much in the way of women's clothing. The oversized apparel made Astra look even smaller than she was.

"You look…nice." He tried to break the awkwardness but only made it worse.

Astra blinked at him. She looked down at herself then back up at him. Her brow furrowed.

"Are you two about ready?" Uncle Ven chose that moment to walk in, saving Louko from saying anything strange...er.

There was a simultaneous 'yes,' from Louko and Astra.

"Well. That's...good." Louko's uncle looked almost confused. "Everybody else is, as well. The capital is nearly three days away if we make good time."

"Um, sorry," Astra broke in then. "What is the capital's name, exactly?"

Louko smiled slightly at that topic, but allowed his uncle to answer.

"If you ask me, it's a rather supercilious title. Unfortunately, no one asked me when they named it Kythdexlentu-Orsha."

Astra cocked her head. "What?"

Louko repeated it to her. "Kythdexlentu-Orsha." His mouth felt numb by the time he finished.

"Its translation is some nonsense about conquering Dragons and all that," Ven explained with a distasteful expression.

She still looked wildly confused.

Louko realized suddenly that Astra must be translating it. "Why? What does it sound like to you?"

"Um," It was hard to tell if she looked sheepish or mischievous. "It kept sounding like 'the house of the friends of dragons.'"

"Oh?" Uncle Ven spoke slowly, evidently lost. He gave Louko a strange glance.

Louko smiled. "I love Elves."

Uncle Ven gave a scowl, but just as he opened his mouth to reply, he was interrupted by Asher entering the room.

"Everyone is ready," the physician announced.

"Right." Ven's demeanor changed almost instantly, and he looked at Louko and Astra. "Are you ready?"

Louko glanced at Astra, worry washing over him. He felt a strange sense of protectiveness for her and didn't like the thought of all the knights seeing her so vulnerable. He'd seen how Astra had been anytime his uncle had visited, and he had noticed her discomfort and feelings of exposure. Indeed, Astra had one hand at her wrist—a thing Louko had grown to realize was a subtle sign of her inner nervousness.

So, ever so gently, Louko drew close by her side, taking her hand in his. "I'll be with you. Don't worry," he whispered.

"Thank you," she whispered back.

Louko saw an oddly displeased look from his uncle, but it disappeared as quickly as it had come on.

"We're ready," Louko said, turning to Asher, who seemed to be fighting a smile. Everyone was acting rather...odd.

They headed out the door and down the corridor. When they reached the stairs, Louko let go of her hand and gave her his arm instead so she could lean on him for balance. "Ready?" Louko whispered. She had yet to try anything so challenging as stairs.

Astra faced forward, took a deep breath, then nodded. She looked at him again. "Are you?"

Louko was taken aback by the question, and not really sure what to say, just rolled his eyes. "No. But at least your hair is more noticeable than mine." Wait—what? Louko mentally kicked himself for saying such a thing.

"At least the servants fixed it up some." She wore it a little to the side as if trying to hide the scar that now curved around one eye.

"I suppose that explains why it looks so nice," Louko replied before he could think over what he was saying.

They both fell silent as they got closer to the bottom. Astra tugged slightly at her sleeve with her free hand, then she rested it on Louko's arm for more support. He realized she was trying to hide the scarring from the manacles. So, even though it made balancing harder without the side rail, he laid his hand over her wrist. She looked up at him with gratitude written clearly in her expression.

And then they reached the bottom.

The knights and Keeshiff were waiting there, and Louko felt instantly uncomfortable under their clear stares. He was sure Astra felt even more so, and he wished he could hide her so she didn't feel so exposed.

To make things even more uncomfortable, all the knights bowed as soon as the pair stepped off the very last stair. Louko felt Astra stiffen and grip his arm more tightly. He didn't blame her.

The knights rose as they passed by, and the two made their way to the door.

"Oh, Astra." Louko suddenly remembered something, and hoped it would get her mind off of the unpleasant publicity. "There is someone who has been waiting ages to see you." They walked out the door and into the courtyard, where a carriage waited. Tethered to the back with a couple of very displeased grooms nearby—not *too* nearby—was Dannsair.

Astra's eyes lit up immediately, and she let go of Louko's arm. Dannsair whinnied loudly, pawing at the ground and tugging at her restraint. The mare stilled as soon as Astra laid one hand on her. Astra smiled and whispered something to the animal as she stroked her horse's neck. Dannsair, in turn, nibbled at her owner's sleeve. Considering how much the little "window visits" had improved Astra's mood, Louko hoped that being reunited with Dannsair would do even more.

"Unfortunately, Princess Astra, I am afraid I will need to charge you for every groom or stablehand that your possessed cow has injured, harmed, or otherwise insulted." Uncle Ven's voice came from behind Louko, and it was hard to tell whether or not he was serious.

"I will let you settle that with Dannsair," Astra replied, without even looking at him.

"If you can survive that, Uncle, you'd be the first," Louko said with a small smile. Or would his uncle be the second? Technically, Louko realized he, himself, had been the first.

Then the wind tugged at his coat, and he realized how cold it was. So he called out, "Why don't we get you inside the carriage, Astra?" Last time she had been out in this kind of weather, she had come down with a fever.

Though visibly reluctant, Astra complied, leaving Dannsair and allowing Louko to help her into the waiting carriage.

Uncle Ven climbed in behind them, and to Louko's surprise, he was closely followed by...Keeshiff.

Keeshiff nodded to both of them and sat down across from Louko.

"Are you alright, Astra?" Louko whispered to Astra after they had settled. What would the hours of sitting up do to her?

Astra nodded. As the carriage jolted and began to move, she returned the question. "Are you?"

"Yes," Louko said softly, with a pang of guilt at the fact that she felt the need to ask. He was the last thing she needed to worry about.

Silence fell after that. Keeshiff and Uncle Ven sat next to each other—albeit as far away from each other as physically possible—both looking out the window and saying nothing.

It was hard to tell how much time had passed when everyone sat in such wordless fashion. Louko guessed it had been an hour or two when Astra seemed to tire. Her shoulders drooped first, then she leaned her head back against the rattling carriage wall and closed her eyes.

Worried, Louko made more room for her and said, "Why don't you rest your head on my shoulder? Stretch your legs out on the seat a little more?" It would be the closest thing to lying down and resting she would have for a little bit. Louko only wished he could do better.

Astra looked up at him. "Wouldn't that make you uncomfortable?" she asked, searching his face.

"No, don't worry," Louko encouraged. He would much rather be uncomfortable than have to watch Astra fall ill. She already seemed much paler than this morning.

She studied him a moment more, then gave in. Once her legs were curled up on the seat, Louko realized the bumps on the road could cause her to eventually fall forward. So, ever so gently, he put his arm around Astra's shoulders, hoping that would be enough to keep her steady.

"Thank you," she murmured, already beginning to doze off.

Louko just gave her a slight squeeze in response.

It was then that he noticed Keeshiff was no longer looking out the window. He was instead looking directly at Astra with an expression Louko had never seen before. Uncle Ven looked almost...perturbed, quickly going back to gazing out the window when he caught Louko looking at him.

"Is that better?" Louko asked, trying to ignore the odd reactions of the others in the carriage.

He got a faint 'mmhm' in reply.

"That's good," he said, leaning his head on top of hers. Slowly, his eyes began to flicker, and darkness overcame him.

They were within a day of the capital, now, and Uncle Ven was trying his best to catch them up on etiquette, politics, and the other such nuances that Louko despised. If nothing else, it was clear from his uncle's tone and expression that Louko wasn't the only one to hate them.

"He won't be permitted to dance." Ven had yet to warm up to Louko's brother, and the feeling appeared mutual by Keeshiff's expression.

"Suits me," he mumbled, "I hate dancing."

Ven continued on, "Our events are quite different from those dull ones I *used* to be invited to in Merimeethia." He cocked an eyebrow at Keeshiff. "The elderly usually watch the younger participate in dancing, so there will be a *Karja* board out—that stupid word game is a waste of time and simply to show off one's extensive vocabulary. There will also be a few other meaningless trifles of entertainment to keep those not dancing engaged, but I would, for the most part, avoid them unless you are somehow acquainted with them." This was addressed at Louko. "Though if someone offers to teach you, I suppose there would be no harm in it. They will be patient with you for the lack of knowledge in our culture. That was not your doing."

Louko shifted uncomfortably. "They...will?" He wasn't comfortable with the way Ven kept seeming to address Louko so specifically. Kae—

Tyron had taught Louko a bit of Nythrilian culture and etiquette when he had originally tried to run off. It hadn't been much, but he at least knew enough to know Nythrilians were very particular in their customs. But Louko's focus was suddenly drawn to the memory of Tyron, and a shiver snaked down his back as he tried to breathe and ignore the all-too-recent events.

Uncle Ven's voice was all that dragged him back. "I will be acting as guest of honor as KingsHeir, and as such will be the one commencing the activities of the evening. I will—" his uncle almost visibly gagged— "be the first to dance. Our dances are similar to your quaint little things in Merimeethia and—from what I have seen—Litash, but with a little more elegance." He appeared to catch Louko's distress at this and quickly added, "The opening dance is always slow. You will get the hang of them. But you will be my second, as this is your official introduction into Nythrilian court."

"Official introduction? I—uh—huh?" Louko was so very confused. And panicked. Mostly panicked.

He felt Astra turn to look up at him.

Again, Ven's expression turned perplexed as he slowly said, "Yes. We have been trying to get you here for quite some time. I'm afraid your arrival will be quite the thing…."

Louko just blinked. He was joking, right? He turned to Astra in the hopes that she perhaps would look amused.

Astra's expression gave little away. She addressed Ven as she quietly asked, "That is a good thing, isn't it? If Louko is so public—and so popular—the king will be pressured to treat him well, won't he?"

"Yes. Louko will have no fear in that department. It's his brother and you that are the primary issue." Ven's tone was hard to discern.

It didn't help that Louko was trying to process all this. He didn't like the idea of all the attention being on him, and pressure was already building in his chest as he thought of a thousand eyes staring at him for an entire evening as he tried to keep in the king's good favor and stop his brother and Astra from being taken—or worse.

Ven cleared his throat and moved on. "At some point amid the dancing, the king will make his appearance. All dancing will pause until he and his entourage are seated at the head of the room. The dancing will resume, but we will be expected to go forward and pay our respects."

Louko nodded in understanding, even as he tried to avoid looking at Astra or Keeshiff. He was afraid of what he'd see in their eyes; were they as worried as he was? What if the king sent Astra...sent her to Litash? Or...or...no. Louko would die before he let her be taken by Tyron again.

"When the meal is set, they will bring in tables. The elderly will be seated first—that's you, Astra." Ven nodded towards her.

Louko's uncle had already mentioned that the elderly often wore veils and long, loose clothing, making it Astra's best disguise.

"Then come the guests of honor, meaning me, and Louko with me." Ven's voice dulled and he glanced at Keeshiff. "You will likely be seated at the end somewhere—just keep your head down and try not to talk." Uncle Ven didn't even give time for Keeshiff to answer before changing the subject.

"The king's niece—well, grandniece, technically—is Dia Jahng. She is probably the one you will want to avoid the most—but don't look like you are avoiding her. She isn't happy I'm going to be king...." Ven shuddered. "Spitfire of a rebel, she is. She's tall...dark-haired...well, you'll probably know her if you see her. But she's been on some patrols and Drogan hunting in the West, so we might be relieved of that encounter. All the same, if she catches wind of what her great uncle is doing and how I'm involved, she won't make things any easier. Drogan Hunters, as a whole, are best avoided. Distasteful occupation."

All Louko did in reply was sigh and turn to Astra. "Are you doing alright?" he asked quietly, wishing the carriage didn't jolt so much. Wishing a lot of things, really.

She seemed pale and distracted as she nodded. "You?" she returned the question, meeting his gaze.

Louko couldn't help but remember again how ardently he'd promised her it would be alright—that allowing him to help wouldn't end in disaster. And what had happened? He had failed her and, seeing how frail she still was, he couldn't help but feel responsible. If he had been more—perhaps he *could* have protected her.

He realized he hadn't replied. "Tired." He tried to give a truthful answer, because Astra was too smart for a lie. And she didn't deserve that.

"Since we are arriving at my home in the capital only a day before the ball, I doubt Dia Tzaro will call for you until after the event." Uncle Ven's statement reminded Louko that private conversations were non-existent within the confines of a carriage. "You should both have some time to rest before going out in public."

"Thank you," Louko managed a murmur.

Ven nodded, though his lips were pursed as if he wished to say more. Instead, he returned to his lecture and turned it towards Keeshiff. "Now, you will have to stay near me," he instructed. "The last thing we need is you making a mess: You're an outsider, so everyone there will be looking for you to slip up so that they can...." Louko's uncle seemed to remember his audience and let the sentence drop. Stiffly, he finished with, "If you can manage it, it will be best to just keep your mouth shut."

Keeshiff—who had barely spoken a single word since the start of the trip—only nodded.

"You'll be fine." Louko didn't know what in Eatris possessed him to speak, but he couldn't help it. Not when he was a little aggravated with how his uncle had been treating Keeshiff. Besides Ven, Keeshiff was the only family Louko had left...and he had saved Astra, after all.

This only seemed to make Keeshiff more tense. His lips turned up in a smile that did not match the rest of his expression. "Of course. We all will be." His gaze drifted briefly towards Astra.

Louko could not give a reaction for fear of Astra noticing. But then, of course, she would notice his *lack* of reaction...there was no winning.

Keeshiff cleared his throat suddenly. "So, um, you've been here before, right, Louko?" His words sounded uncharacteristically forced. "You told me about a play or something like that...back when we were, er, younger."

Louko looked confused. "Um. Did I? I really don't remember...." He had been quite young the last time he'd been here. "But I'm sure it was lovely." He was not helping. Poor Keeshiff was trying to—er, what exactly *was* he trying to do?—but here Louko was, being the typical unhelpful one in the family.

"That was in the countryside," Uncle Ven cut in tightly. "A lord's manor—not the king's palace."

"Oh." Keeshiff visibly shut down under the weight of Ven's scrutiny.

Louko again felt bad. "I don't remember very much, but at least it doesn't rain all the time here." He tried to give some shattered semblance of a smile to his brother but felt the attempt came off as inauthentic.

His uncle huffed slightly, but Keeshiff dared the response of, "Yes, one can actually tell that the sky is blue here."

"And I was beginning to wonder if there was any other kind of ground besides mud." Louko was not doing very well, and yet still he tried. For Keeshiff. And it was odd...Keeshiff trying to talk to him. He'd not really tried to for so, so long.

"By the way you two speak—" Astra's voice was so soft, it took a moment to register— "I'm beginning to think that Merimeethia is not meant for permanent habitation."

Without thinking, Louko replied, "I think you are correct."

A GAME OF WITS

CHAPTER IX

Astra:

Astra stared at the giant set of stairs before them, the marble illuminated in the warm light of the street torches and the setting sun. The whole area was a buzz of activity, with innumerable servants scurrying about with orb-like lamps on long poles, helping nobles out of carriages, taking horses from those arriving on horseback—though that was rare— and offering light to those climbing the steps to the palace that was perched so high above the rest of the city. Astra almost wished she'd been able to get a better look at the city when they'd arrived; this all seemed so different from Merimeethia or Litash—or even Alarune.

"Oh, yes, I suppose I forgot to mention this." Aelor Ven straightened his collar and said under his breath, "The elderly are escorted up the stairs on a litter."

"*What?*" Astra hissed.

"Just go along with their instructions," the lord murmured quickly.

She had just enough time to cast a horrified look at an equally horrified Louko before she was rushed by fretting servants, ushered over to an unnecessarily ornate litter, and helped up onto it. She wanted to pull away and scream at them not to touch her. It didn't help that the whole thing seemed to wobble as two servants on each of the four poles hoisted her up and began the precarious journey up the endless set of stairs.

Besides her complete mortification at being *carried*, Astra spent the entirety of the ride clutching the sides of the litter. She could barely keep herself from jumping up when they finally put the thing down. She waited, forcing herself to let the servants take her hand to help her out. *It will only last a second—just one second.*

"There you are, my dear," Aelor Ven was all smiles and cordiality as he, Louko, and Keeshiff came up to meet her, having gotten up the stairs a little quicker than her...entourage. Astra also noted the change in Ven. His shoulders were relaxed, his expression no longer constantly disapproving. It was unnerving. Before, she had wondered how such a seemingly particular person could stand society, but now, the ease with which he changed left her even more uneasy.

"Are you alright?" Louko asked her as he moved forward and offered his arm—something that had previously been deemed acceptable by Ven.

Since Astra had been told to keep speaking to a minimum, she only nodded as she took his arm. As they moved away from the stairway and the servants there, she muttered, "Next time, I'm sticking my veil on your uncle and *he* can go for a ride."

Louko's eyes bulged and he actually looked like he was fighting a smile.

"Quite a threat, I must admit," Aelor Ven commented from ahead of them as he led the way. "I would be amused to see the sight, myself."

Just as amusing was the sight of the lord wearing a highly ornamented cuff around his neatly coiled hair. He was arrayed in full Nythrilian court regalia, draped in layers of blue and white silks that were edged with gold stitching. Patterns in jade green lay at the borders before folding into a wide belt at the waist. He wore a cloak over all of it.

Louko was dressed in similar fashion, though his hair was not long enough to be worn up. Instead of blue, he wore silks of striking red with silver embroidery. It was strange how much the style should suit him when he'd never worn it before, even if he did appear quite uncomfortable in it.

"I'd be glad to help," Keeshiff grumbled from behind them all, barely loud enough for Astra to catch. He, unlike the others, was dressed in formal Merimeethian attire and looked barely different from any other time Astra had seen him. Except, perhaps, for the fact that he was clean-shaven.

They approached the entrance of the palace—its massive jade pillars bathed in golden light—the elevation of the palace allowing the sun to catch it with much more proficiency than the lower city. Soon, they were past the pillars and under the rich red-tiled roofing, chatter echoing off of the stone walls. Only, the closer she got, the more she realized that the walls were not plain stone but intricate murals: mosaics of dragons, scenes of mountains and valleys, mysterious and colorful birds, and much more that Astra was unable to catch. The vibrant chips of colored stone sparkled in the light of the braziers and torches, and Astra marveled at the beauty of it all before being led through the giant, open double doors—wooden but no less colorful than the rest of the palace's exterior.

As soon as they passed through the doors and were out of the cool evening air, more servants appeared. Ven held out both arms, allowing them to take off his cloak. Astra stepped aside while Louko copied his uncle—albeit with much stiffer gestures. Keeshiff, wearing a long overcoat, took his off himself and simply handed it to the waiting attendant.

"Shall we?" Ven motioned with a hand as he led the way once more down the busy hall.

Astra noted the frequent stares they were getting now, the admiring looks towards Louko's uncle, the astounded ones at Louko, and the ones of disgust pointed at Keeshiff. Astra, it seemed, was entirely invisible for once.

They walked through the hallway easily despite the crowd. Astra noted the way people would bow their heads in deference and step out of the way. Perhaps it was not so bad to have Ven leading the way. Even if his brisk pace was leaving Astra short of breath…. She tried to breathe more deeply, just to ease the ache around her ribs.

"Uncle, our legs are not quite as long as yours." Louko sounded equally breathless as he called ahead. Astra noted, however, that seeing as his uncle was quite short, the legs were not likely the issue as much as Astra and Louko's health. She was growing quite tired of being sick.

Ven looked back with a brief apologetic look before slowing down and taking a left down the hall. Soon, they stood before another set of doors, which opened with a wave of laughter and noise from inside. Servants stood at either end, managing the line that had formed at the entrance. Astra could hear constant announcements of the arriving guests from just inside.

But Ven did not wait in line. He stepped right up to the set of doors, and the servant there bowed upon recognition.

"Might I have the names of your companions, Aelor KingsHeir?" The man asked as he straightened.

"You may announce my nephew, Prince Louko of Merimeethia, son of the late Queen Ravyen," Ven replied evenly. "As well as his brother, Prince Keeshiff, and Lady Vyr Zhai."

"Very well." The attendant bowed again, and darted away behind the doors.

Astra could not catch the exact words amid so much sound, but she heard the call through the thick wood—and the silence that followed. Then the doors swung open, and Ven strode through.

It was so bright that Astra was again thankful for her veil—the lanterns, braziers, and torches all cast a glow against the brilliantly colored walls and pillars that was enough to blind anybody. The noise was hardly any better, overwhelming Astra until she felt she couldn't breathe, let alone discern what was going on. It was all she could do to cling to Louko's arm and move forward.

She felt more than heard the doors close behind them. But it wasn't until everyone in the crowd stood up that she realized that they had been bowing. Ven stopped suddenly, and Astra and the two princes stumbled to do the same. He bowed his head, held it there for several seconds, then looked back up. The small motion seemed to release the entire room, and the conversation around them resumed.

"Now what?" Astra heard Louko breathe.

"We wait for the music to begin," Ven replied, equally quiet. "In the meantime, it's only respectful to help our elderly companion over to a seat."

Louko obeyed by slowly helping Astra find a seat in the corner, quietly asking, "Are you alright?" as she at last sat down.

At least pretending to walk like an old lady wasn't difficult. Astra just wished she was half as deaf as she was supposed to act—she'd forgotten how *loud* parties could be. Especially in a hall where the ceiling was not as vaulted as the ballrooms of Litash.

"Can you hear me?" Louko's voice held a prick of concern.

She nodded quickly, realizing she'd never answered. "Yes, sorry," she said softly.

"You going to be alright?"

Another nod. She didn't want to risk speaking when so many people were nearby.

Louko didn't appear convinced, and Astra noticed he seemed just as strained by the noise as she.

"Are you ready?" Ven cut in, addressing Louko.

"No? Can I say no?" Astra perhaps would have been amused by her friend's reply if not for the fact she shared his sentiments.

The way Louko's uncle pursed his lips made his expression hard to read. It was somewhere between concerned, displeased, and yet somehow understanding. "Not easily," was the lord's reply. He turned slightly, shifting so that he was looking towards someone. "See the girl in the pink-and-gold robes? Pick her as your first partner. Her family's good favor may yet be important for us, and she happens to dance quite well— she can help make up for any steps you may miss."

Astra caught Louko's dismayed look before he hid it beneath the sigh of acquiescence. "Alright. Let's get this over with…" he murmured.

Ven glanced towards Keeshiff. "Stay with her. If anyone tries to talk to you, pretend you don't speak Nythrilian."

As the lord walked away, Astra heard Keeshiff mumble, "I don't have to pretend."

With a last reluctant look, Louko followed his uncle away into the crowd.

Astra tried to ignore the way anxiety wrapped around her throat. But it was difficult when there was so much that could go wrong and, as silly as it was, Louko being out of sight only added to those fears.

An unexpected sound nearly startled her out of her skin.

"Woah, you okay?" Keeshiff asked, sitting down next to her. "It's just the musicians."

Realizing he was right, Astra felt her cheeks redden as she nodded. Now she could pick out the distinct timbre of several different flutes, some kind of plucked strings, and a deep-voiced drum. In her defense, the sounds were completely uncoordinated. Yet the crowd responded to it by moving to the edges of the room and leaving the center clear. Just when Astra thought the press of people would be too much, a man in dark green noticed her and tapped his companion on the shoulder. Both stepped out of the way and left her a clear view to the open floor.

As suddenly as it had begun, the random cacophony of instruments ceased, taking all conversation with it. Only a single pair of footsteps dared to break the hush. When she leaned forward, Astra could just barely see Ven step out into view. He halted in the very center of the room, and the music began.

As a pair of flutes struck up a stately tune, the solemn lord held out a hand. A woman in pale blue came forward from the edges of the crowd. She stopped one pace away from him, waiting as he gave a precise bow.

Then she inclined her head in a similar manner, the tassels on her ornate headpiece bobbing as she did so.

Ven took her hand, and the dance began. Though there were several differences—such as the woman placing her hand at the man's elbow instead of his shoulder—Astra was relieved to see that the basic steps were the same as what she had taught Louko. With the restrictions of such extravagant clothing, the dance was kept to a slow pace. It seemed to emphasize the dignity and the ceremony of the moment rather than the grace of motion.

A minute or two later, the music came to a close and so did the dance. Astra watched as Ven and his partner stepped back, bowed, and returned to their places. Then it was Louko's turn.

He looked like he was about to die, honestly. Even paler than he had been of late, he mimicked his uncle's steps and waited in the center of the room until the music began. Then he held out his hand and a young woman in pink and gold joined him from the crowd. Louko gave his bow, she dipped her head, and both stepped into the dance.

Sitting and watching the two glide across the tiled floor, silk robes reflecting the soft light of paper lanterns, Astra couldn't help but recall her clumsy lessons with Louko, and her cheeks began to burn. This young lady was nothing short of lovely, with her embroidered gown, her glossy dark hair done up in intricate braids, and her cosmetics that made her look ethereal. Astra was not prepared for the wave of self-consciousness that swept over her. She couldn't block out the thought of the ugly scars that raked across her arms, the harsh cut of her now ragged hair, the thinness that came from long illness, and the cut that curved in a half circle around her eye like a slave's brand. She had never been so glad to not be seen.

Louko stumbled, wrenching Astra from her thoughts. He picked the dance back up almost immediately and gave that awkwardly apologetic smile. Though she was too far to hear him, Astra was almost certain he was now launching into some run-on dissertation about his own clumsiness. The guess was confirmed when Astra heard a fluttering laugh from Louko's partner.

The exchange seemed to set the whole room at ease, for conversation resumed among the observers. By the time Louko bowed to the lady in pink, several other couples were heading for the floor.

"I knew he would do just fine." Ven's comment startled Astra, and she found the noble suddenly next to her.

Keeshiff got to his feet, as if making room for the lord to sit.

When it seemed Ven was still waiting for a response, Astra said quietly, "And so he did."

An attendant walked by them, bearing a platter of porcelain cups. The lord waved them to a stop and plucked one from the tray. He handed it to Keeshiff, and took two more, sitting down next to Astra.

"Would you like something to drink, my lady?" he asked politely, all charm and manners in the court, it would seem.

"I am alright, thank you," Astra murmured.

"Are you sure? It can get insufferably stuffy at these things," he continued.

Her gaze still lingered on the crowd, trying to pick Louko from its midst. "I really am alright, but thank you."

"If you are certain." Astra heard him set the cup aside.

When she glanced at him, he appeared the very picture of ease and calmness. Yet, as he held the cup to his lips and drank, each movement seemed *too* planned—as if he was nervous and had to think every miniscule action through.

And if Lord Aelor Ven was nervous...what did that mean for them?

Then, out of nowhere, came the question: "What exactly are your intentions regarding my nephew?" It was guardedly, though still respectfully, asked.

Astra looked at him blankly before remembering he could not see her face. What did he mean? Was he questioning her motives? "I am not sure this is the best place to discuss such a political topic," she replied in an undertone.

"Political? My dear, I am not sure you quite understand my question." His gaze was fixed keenly on her, not even wavering for a moment.

She was less intimidated knowing he couldn't properly meet her eyes. Still, Astra found herself wishing to move or at least look away. "What do you mean?"

There was a sigh. "I mean your—how shall I put this—personal intentions?"

"I'm sorry?" Perhaps sitting up so long was making her slow and foggy. The noise of the room certainly wasn't helping.

"Love is not something my nephew is accustomed to." This was clearly extremely uncomfortable for the lord to say out loud. "I am afraid of him being used. I do not mean to imply that you are trying to use him...but I worry for him. And I worry he does not realize where his heart is going."

Veil or no, Astra stared at him in bewilderment. *Love?* Then she realized what he meant, and was thankful again that Ven could not see her face. "I am aware of what his—" Astra veered off from the word 'family' at the last minute when she remembered Keeshiff was standing mere feet away— "his father deprived him of. I have no intention of using that to manipulate him."

Ven raised an eyebrow. "But what are *your* intentions towards him?"

"To help in whatever way I can," Astra said. She did not take offense at his questioning, considering how tremendously she had failed in this regard, she understood the lord's doubt. If it wasn't for her, Louko never would have ended up in the castle, in that dark room, in such…. She swallowed hard and made herself take a deep breath.

Ven appeared only more perplexed by her reply. "My dear, in all honesty, I think you are missing the point." He looked from her to where Louko was dancing. "You've been glaring at every woman who dares approach him. Even *I* would be afraid for my life."

Glaring? As in, *jealous?* What in the world was he talking about? "My apologies, but is my veil still properly in place?" she asked with mild sarcasm before she could bite it back.

Astra heard Keeshiff choke on his drink, clearly listening to the whole exchange.

Ven made a face not far from Louko's own roguish half-smile. Slowly, the lord sipped his drink, one eyebrow raised as he gave Astra a sideways glance.

This irritated her all the more. She wanted to protest and yet was too flustered to really piece together what exactly she was protesting against.

She settled for a less than gracious silence and hoped her veil actually hid it.

It didn't help that the dance ended at that very moment, and Louko returned in an awkward hurry to their group.

"Are you alright?" He looked with worry at the still-coughing Keeshiff.

"Yes—quite." It sounded like some strangled laugh came from the older prince. "How was your dance?" His smugness only grew.

Louko did not answer, only his eyes pleading with Astra. "I much preferred our lessons," he mumbled.

Astra did not want to think of those right now.

"You are doing marvelously, Louko." Aelor Ven seemed to at last get a hold of himself and turn the subject. "You'll have half the room charmed before the night is through."

Louko didn't appear convinced, giving Astra a dismayed look that just screamed 'save me.'

But before Astra could think of any way to comfort him, a young lady hardly older than herself swooped in, her silver-and-purple dress floating as delicately as the rest of her.

"KingsHeir." She inclined her head to Ven—who returned the gesture with a nod—before turning quickly to Louko. "Prince Louko, this next dance is perfect for a beginner—not as complicated as the previous formalities. Pardon my lapse in etiquette, but would you like to try it with me? I would be honored to help you."

"Oh, um." Astra caught Louko's brief glance to his uncle before replying, "That sounds marvelous, thank you. I am really at a loss…." He offered his arm with seeming ease, though Astra easily caught his flinch as the girl took it.

For a brief flash, Astra wished she was not quite so invisible. She remained in her seat as Louko walked away.

"Well, how fortunate that the KingsHeir actually graced us with his presence." A man's voice jolted Astra out of her thoughts, and she turned to find a man and woman approaching them.

Ven did not get up but smiled congenially.

"We have missed you of late, but perhaps I now see the reason for your absence." The man looked to where Louko and the girl were now dancing—the latter, laughing and smiling constantly.

"Lord Eren, do not be so presumptuous," Ven replied. "It was, of course, to avoid your company."

This was met with smiles and chuckles, and Astra guessed that these were friends. "Come now, you can't go complaining about my manners when yours are so poor," Lord Eren replied. "It is a blessing for us all that your nephew took after his mother instead of his uncle." The tone of the jest softened. "Though I suppose all of us now see why you fought so hard to bring him home."

Astra watched Ven very closely. And she saw the way his smile went brittle at the edges, and his hands tightened around his porcelain cup. Yes, Louko was in Nythril and yet in more peril than ever.

"It would be nice to see him have easier days ahead," Ven replied, looking beyond the pair and to the dance floor. Astra still saw the hidden tension in the man's shoulders. "Time will tell."

It felt hard to swallow, and Astra suddenly wished that she had accepted Ven's drink offer. She saw how Keeshiff, too, had his eyes glued to the dance floor.

"So, when is the king to make his entrance?" Lord Eren's tone changed ever so slightly.

Aelor Ven emptied his cup. "Before the end of the hour, I would expect."

"You seem thrilled, Ven," Eren's wife spoke now, looking very amused. "Another fun evening in store for you?"

"As fun as ever," he grumbled under his breath but picked back up in an almost pleasant facade. "But that is duty, is it not?"

It was hard for Astra to tell if Lord Eren's quiet sigh was an agreement or a protest. Either way, the conversation shifted to lighter things: gardens, music, the new decor of the palace tiers. Sometimes another noble would wander by, everyone would exchange bows, and they would chime in on the conversation before moving on. In the background, Astra managed the occasional glimpse of Louko still dancing as the evening wore on. Neither she nor Keeshiff said a word.

At last, Louko again returned to the group, the young lady in violet and silver on his arm—to Louko's apparent chagrin. As soon as they had made it to where Astra was sitting with Ven and the others, Louko managed to politely extract his arm from the lady's with the guise of needing to run his hand through his hair. A lot. Astra wished that, if she had to be invisible, she could at least be blind, too.

"Ah, Louko, I see you have met Miss Eren Qura," Ven said cordially, getting up from his seat. "This is her father, Lord Eren Lusan, and her mother, Lady Eren Si. Perhaps you remember them? You and I visited their manor when you were quite young."

Louko's cheeks reddened, and he blinked very slowly before giving that sheepish smile. "I fear I do not, my apologies."

Lord Eren smiled warmly. "Oh, no apology needed. I did not expect you would, considering how long ago it was." He chuckled when he added, "Though, I do remember you being quite enamored with the theatre players who were residing at my estate then."

Astra saw Ven brighten in apparent recollection. "Oh yes, he chattered about them all the way home."

In the background, Keeshiff shifted slightly.

"Oh, I did? Sorry. I hope that wasn't as annoying as that sounds...." Louko gave a nervous laugh.

Lord Eren's daughter smiled and shook her head. "I don't know that I've ever met someone so apologetic and yet so polite." Even under the white powder the girl wore, Astra could see the tell-tale flush of red.

"He was equally solemn as a child," Eren chimed in. "Though I must say, his Nythrilian has improved immensely."

Running his hand through his hair, Louko gave Astra a fleeting glance before saying, "That really isn't saying much, I'm sure I'm still mixing up the words 'food' and 'couch'...I mean they are very similar in Nythrilian, and my accent must be terrible...all the vowels really clutter up the tongue—not that it's an inelegant language, it's quite beautiful when someone can speak it properly...I am...going to stop talking now." He looked like he wanted someone to impale him.

Astra wished she could step in and speak up.

With a hearty laugh, Ven clapped him on the shoulder lightly. "To be fair, the last time you met Lord Eren, you couldn't speak Nythrilian at all."

"Not quite true." Lord Eren grinned. "As I recall, he gave a perfect farewell. His accent was so exact that Lord and Lady Faizos were *certain* he'd understood all those snide little comments they'd made." The lord chuckled. "I still remember the looks on their faces."

That seemed a very Louko thing to do.

And that was when the deep voice of a gong rang through the room, causing both her and Louko to nearly jump to the height of the painted ceiling far above them.

"King Dia Tzaro of Nythril, High Seat on the Council Ezai," a grand voice boomed, and the crowd pressed towards the sides of the room.

"*Here*," the single word in Litashian snapped her into the language and she turned to see Keeshiff offering her his arm. "*Let me help.*"

Astra hesitated only a second then took his arm. He helped her to her feet.

They bowed in unison with the entire room and remained that way. Struggling to stay in that position, Astra still looked up to try and catch a glimpse of this man who held so much power over them. His entourage was impossible to miss. First came several guards in intricate, elaborate armor, marching at a slow step. Next came several attendants in an equally formal array. And then the king himself. It took Astra a moment to realize that the tall young man was not the ruler but rather an assistant to help the king walk. It hadn't occurred to Astra that the king would be so *old*.

He was brought across the room to an ornate chair that sat on a raised platform and helped to sit down. The king surveyed the hall from his comfortable vantage point even as everyone held the precisely angled bow. It was a moment longer before the king at last waved an idle hand for the music to recommence.

Keeshiff helped Astra straighten and sit back down.

"*Thank you*," she said under her breath, too winded to say more.

"We will have to go up," Ven muttered, sounding again on edge. "But rest a moment first. There are several others who will want to be first to pay their respects to the king." This comment was smug, and he eyed Lord Eren. "Insecure, petty things that they are."

"Why Ven, you couldn't be referring to certain lords, could you?" Eren poked back.

Ven's expression turned less brittle and more conspiratorial. "Whatever do you mean?"

"No, come, dearest, let's go grovel at the senile piece of decor before you and Ven start up a public conversation on insurrection...again." Eren's wife rolled her eyes and tugged him in the direction of the dais. She motioned for her daughter, who gave Louko a fleeting smile before she followed behind.

Louko's breath of relief was all too audible as his shoulders sank.

Astra hoped that so much dancing wasn't too much for him. Neither of them had had very much activity during their recoveries. Though, if she was to be honest, perhaps she had other reasons for being glad that the Eren family left. One of which wore violet and silver....

Louko:

Louko wanted nothing more than to crawl into the nearest hole and curl up and not have to talk to another soul again. Well, perhaps besides Astra. She didn't count. But everyone else...Louko much preferred the dance lessons Astra had given him. There had been no one staring, no one judging. Their lives hadn't depended on Louko making a good impression, and it had just been a moment between friends, not a facade to save their hides.

But now Louko's anxiety was redirected once more to the newest threat: King Dia Tzaro. After a brief moment to let him catch his breath, Louko's uncle had ushered them towards the throne at the far end of the room. Louko had whispered thanks to Keeshiff and taken Astra's arm to help her walk.

The king sat there, head drooping under the weight of a tasseled gold headpiece, with a cape spilling around his shoulders and down to the floor. It glimmered as he moved, and Louko realized it was covered in metallic...feathers?

"Exalted One." Ven made a sweeping gesture that led into an exact, elegant bow as he stepped ahead of Louko and the others. "May the four winds guard your throne." There was a pause, and then Ven added, "May I introduce you to the guests you so anxiously desired to meet."

Dia Tzaro appeared barely interested, lazy eyes rolling from one person to the other until they settled on Astra. He waved an idle hand at her. "And you are the Lady of the Stars, then? Hm." The comment held disappointment.

Astra let go of Louko's arm and stepped forward by herself, veil bobbing as she nodded.

Louko felt his stomach twist and his mouth go dry. The sudden urge to protect her was only drowned by the overwhelming sense of helplessness, and he sat there like some idiot, wishing that just once he could be more than a bystander watching as she fought for her life.

"There are some people who are quite keen to see you, my lady." There was a slow sort of smile on the king's face.

Dia Tzaro filled Louko with revulsion. Age, a quality which lent others an air of gentleness, had only endowed him with the appearance of greed. He slouched on his ornate chair with a lazy sort of confidence. He was not threatened by them in the least.

"What do you mean, Exalted One?" Astra asked. The disgust in her tone was so thinly veiled anyone could have heard it.

The king's smile grew. With one gnarled finger, he traced a crescent shape near his temple, as if highlighting the scar Astra hid beneath her veil. "Oh, I believe you know what I mean."

Louko couldn't breathe. For one paralyzing moment, he couldn't even think. All he could remember was that dark room, and Astra fighting for her life as they waited for help that wouldn't come. The fear of Astra going back to that was more terrifying than Louko could even put to thought, and he struggled to remain steady as he stood there, silent amidst Astra's battle of words with the king.

"But frankly, as much as I would gain from such a handover, we have better uses for you, isn't that right, Ven, KingsHeir?" The king's words were like poison on the lips of a viper.

Ven did not appear pleased. "Your Majesty?"

"The little winged problem." Dia Tzaro gestured loosely with one hand. "But I suppose this is not the place for business. Bring them to me in the morning, and we can discuss this in detail. In the meantime...." He smiled again, this time revealing many gold-capped teeth. "Enjoy the party." The vulture's glazing eyes turned on Louko next, the smile slimy and no less repulsive than that of a corpse. "Now, Prince Louko, my apologies for that little bit of business. Come, come forward, I want a good look at you!"

Louko would much rather have run into the nearest sword, and yet he had no choice but to replace Astra in the forefront. He saw her look his way as she stepped back.

Louko gave a bow similar to Ven's. "Exalted One. Your hospitality is more than generous." The words tasted like the bile rising in the back of his throat.

"Nythril has long awaited your return." Dia Tzaro gave another horrible smile. "We were all devastated when we heard of your mother's death— those Merimeethian snakes did not deserve her." Louko saw the king's eyes narrow towards Keeshiff. Then he held out both hands. "But Nythril shall be a new start for you, yes? You are no longer bound by your previous circumstances." He tilted his wrinkled head towards Astra and Keeshiff.

Clearing his throat and trying to remain upright, Louko gave a tense smile. "Of course, Your Majesty. Thank you."

Dia Tzaro's attention shifted towards whoever was behind them. "Yes, yes." He gave a dismissive wave. "You are welcome. Now go enjoy yourself while the night is young."

Ven placed a hand on Louko's shoulder, causing the prince to swallow a flinch in surprise. "And so he shall, Exalted One. Thank you."

With that and a couple of strangled bows, they turned and retreated, Louko giving Astra his arm and helping her back down to the seating area of the ballroom.

He barely had the breath to sigh as he muttered, "Did I ever tell you I hate politics?"

CHAPTER X

<u>Louko:</u>

This was beyond bad. Ven had been almost silent for the rest of the night, and now, come morning, he looked like he hadn't slept. And if his uncle hadn't slept, then this had to be bad. But nonetheless, it was fruitless to try and leave without appeasing the Nythrilian king. To do so would basically alienate Astra and Keeshiff from almost every country on this side of the Macridean Sea. If Nythril cast them out, then they would have nowhere to go, and Tyron would easily be able to get ahold of them.

And so here Louko and Astra were, standing outside of the throne room. Without his uncle. Where was he? Why had he left? Louko's throat stuck together as he thought of a million possible answers to those questions. He was all too skeptical of people—especially family—and while his uncle had seemed trustworthy, he was also heir to the throne of Nythril. Why had this king picked Ven, exactly?

"You may enter, now," a servant announced, having just come from the room. "He awaits."

Louko gave a nod in acknowledgement, and with Astra clinging to his arm, he walked through the open doors and into the ornate throne room.

It was so much different than any other architecture he had ever seen, lacking the towering ceiling of the grand halls of Merimeethia or Litash. And yet, it was no less a formidable and jaw-dropping sight. Red beams crisscrossed overhead, and golden, rune-like chimes hung along them in intervals; their low, doleful tones created a constant murmur that filled the hall. The floor had the texture of wood and yet the firmness of stone, and their footsteps were almost soundless upon it. The throne, at the other side of the room, was a complex fusion of red-green stone and gold. It depicted a mountain as the backrest with golden smoke petrified above. The sides of the chair each held a different sculpture formed of gold: on one side, a man, soldier-like and determined, a halberd in hand and ready for use; the other side was a dragon, wings spread over it and holding the red velvet seat.

In fact, the throne alone was such an awe-inspiring sight that the decaying form of Dia Tzaro somewhat diminished it. Louko couldn't help but think of the command Ven would have on such a seat.

"Well, well, good to see you didn't try and run off in the night." Dia Tzaro gave a half-gold grin at the sight of Astra, but as his narrowed eyes settled on Louko, he frowned. "There must have been some error, my dear Prince Louko. You are not needed. You need not be bound to this Litashian any longer." He waved his hand dismissively.

Louko could feel Astra's hand stiffen on his arm.

"I will remain with my friend, Exalted One. I go where she goes." It took all of his composure not to scream the words, and Louko was surprised with just how calmly he was able to speak them.

He felt Astra look at him.

"Hm," Dia Tzaro mused, displeasure on his face as he seemed to think this through. Finally, he shrugged. "I suppose time will tell just how firm your resolve is...or how thick your skull."

Jaw so tight it threatened to break, Louko did not reply. He kept his focus on his breathing, and on keeping his expression from showing the king just how much he loathed him.

Dia Tzaro jabbed a bony finger towards Astra. "You, Lady—it isn't Princess anymore, is it? Or are you still allowed the title?—are known for a set of skills. And I have some criminals that need...tracking down."

The way he showed knowledge of Astra's exile was only overshadowed by the request that followed. Criminals? Really? *That* was what the king wanted? Louko wasn't sure whether or not to be relieved. Surely there was something more to it than this.

This time, it was Astra who asked, "Criminals, Sire?"

"Yes, escaped from the palace dungeon. They are dangerous murderers and are very...Gifted." He raised a withered eyebrow.

This did not sound good. Astra was not recovered enough for this! She could get herself killed....

"And you want me to track them down and bring them back here?" Astra's voice was measured and even, though it had never lost its hoarse edge.

"Correct. That is, if you don't want that rascal of a Prince Keeshiff and his rebels shipped back to Merimeethia."

Louko's heart froze.

"What?" The word was taut coming out of Astra's mouth.

Dia Tzaro's lips twitched in ill-hidden amusement. "Did you think I didn't know about those knights that dragged themselves over the border?" His chuckling sounded more like a cackle. "Don't worry—they are already well housed here with me. They'll be quite safe until your return."

How had he gotten them? They'd been in Ven's care...Louko's free fist clenched until it hurt.

"But how can we be expected to detain and bring back several 'dangerous Gifted' criminals?" Louko felt Astra's fear as she spoke. "We have nothing: no supplies, no information, no support—not even any weaponry."

Astra's bow and Louko's sword had been among the things that had not made it out of the castle.

"Oh, don't worry. Weaponry will be provided." The king waved his hand dismissively.

This was insane.

"And if we fail? If we are overpowered?"

"Well, Merimeethia will give me a pretty penny for my efforts.... Though with your reputation, I doubt that will be the case. All the same, I'm prepared to give you three weeks to complete the task. I have their last known whereabouts and any other information you may need."

Louko wanted to punch the stupid grin off of the king's face. This was going to get Astra killed. What had he gotten them into? He met her gaze only briefly but knew that she shared his thoughts: What choice did they have?

Finally, he heard Astra draw a shaky breath to ask, "What assurance do we have that you will honor your promises?"

"My word will have to be enough. I don't want my last days to be known as a liar. Besides, Ven would kill me." A smile grew on his face. "Or try to, anyway."

Ven. "And is he the one who suggested this?" Louko almost didn't want to know.

162

Dia Tzaro laughed, a grotesque mimicry of humor. "He's not king yet. No matter what he tells you, he is not privy to everything—nor can he control it all."

Louko wasn't sure whether he was relieved or felt further betrayed. Not knowing what was going on wouldn't have stopped Uncle Ven from handing over the knights. He hated them well enough…. Oh, what a mess.

"I request to see the knights personally, that I might verify your claims." Astra's tone was strained. "And if they are true, then we have no choice but to accept your offer. I only ask that you consider sending more men with us, that we might be sure of success."

"Please. You would whisk them away the moment you saw them. No. You will leave today and return with what I need." The king's face was more deadly as he said this, somehow creasing the wrinkles into a somewhat menacing expression. But he didn't need to look menacing: The words were what counted. Then he sat back, and his tone eased. "But seeing as there are two criminals, I will let you bring along one more companion so that you can outnumber them. He is already waiting with your horses and supplies. My attendant will take you to him and give you the written information regarding the fugitives."

Louko forced his breath to remain steady, and he replied with, "Thank you, Your Majesty."

"Now go. Three weeks." He waved his hand dismissively, and the sound of doors opening behind them gave the cue to leave.

As soon as the doors were safely closed behind them, Louko grabbed Astra's hand. He wasn't sure if he was trying to calm her or himself. "It's going to be alright…it will be fine," he murmured almost feverishly. Stupid,

stupid king. *Idiot of a prince.* How had they let this happen? And where was that uncle of his when they actually needed him?!

Astra squeezed his hand back but did not speak.

A servant in a blue-and-jade uniform stepped up from nearby, a scroll in one hand. He bowed from the waist and motioned for them to follow.

They were led around and down until at last they were in the courtyard; two of the three horses were already saddled up and ready with supplies. A third was being tacked up by a set of grooms.

"You're both alright!" The words of relief came from none other than Keeshiff. He had been standing pale-faced by the horses but, upon seeing Louko and Astra, he ran forward. He stopped short in front of Louko in the most awkward of fashions. "Ven was all in a hurry and left soon after you did. Next thing I knew, two palace soldiers dragged me out here…. What happened?" Keeshiff's eyes shifted around suspiciously.

Again, Louko found his free hand tightly wound in a fist. He hated kings. He hated politics. And he was starting to think he really just didn't like people in general.

Apparently, his silence was enough to spur Astra into answering Keeshiff's question. "Dia Tzaro found your men and is holding them somewhere. If we want to get them back, we must capture and bring back two criminals that escaped from here."

His brother looked dumbfounded, staring at Louko and Astra. "W-what? The knights?"

There was horror in his eyes, and Louko understood why. The group of men had been Keeshiff's *real* family. The ones he had always felt comfortable around. The thing Louko was never able to be.

"We'll get them back." He tried to sound reassuring, but he wasn't exactly a naturally positive person to begin with. Things were looking worse by the moment.

"They-they all have *families*. If anything happens to them—"

"It won't." Astra surprised Louko by stopping the devolving reaction. Even more so when she stepped forward and put a hand on Keeshiff's arm. "We are going to do this, and we are going to get all of them home. And that starts with keeping our heads and getting to work."

The servant who had led them out cleared his throat and interrupted in Nythrilian. "This is from the king," he said. "It's all the information you need."

Louko went to take it, but the servant did not let go.

The man looked side to side, then, in a low voice, said, "They are not what everyone says they are. Be careful who you trust."

The servant released the scroll, bowed quickly, and left.

Louko's brow furrowed. "Fun," he grumbled under his breath as he opened the scroll. This was going to be great.

Just. Great.

Astra:

The two moons shone in the evening sky, empty and alone. Or maybe it was just Astra.

"If we are able to keep this pace, we could reach Tehng in three days' time," Keeshiff said in a monotone.

Tehng. The last village where the criminals had been spotted, southeast of Kythdexlentu-Orsha. The fugitives were likely heading for the southwestern border of Litash. Louko had given Keeshiff the map and information in what was likely an attempt to get his mind off the fate of his men.

"Hopefully they'll still be nearby," Louko said. "The mountains are too high and too dense to cross easily here. They'll probably have to cut further south before crossing."

Astra hoped so. But she couldn't help but think of the servant's sincere expression when he had warned them that these 'criminals' were not as they were made out to be. She almost hoped he was wrong. After all, if these people were innocent, how could they turn them in?

"The description, at least, is helpful. Not many girls have silver hair...." Keeshiff commented in some strange combination of doubt and optimism.

Astra was more concerned over the girl's age than hair color. All the scroll revealed was that she was young. But Astra kept this anxiety to herself. She refused to add to the air of worry, especially when she knew herself to be the weakest of the party. She had already resolved never to ask to stop early, no matter how much her whole body ached. They did not have the time to cater to her comfort. And Elves were said to heal quickly—surely, she would be alright in another week or two.

Louko, of course, seemed ever observant. He would never say anything about her condition but was always the one to suggest stopping for the day, always the one to call for breaks.

And today was no exception. "It's getting rather dark. We don't know this territory well enough to keep going without daylight." Louko peered around their barren surroundings as if to prove his point.

And somehow, as usual, Keeshiff agreed. "You're right. Let's stop at the foot of that rise up ahead. It might break some of the wind for us."

Astra said nothing.

Making camp was as quick as it had been the last two nights, what with none of them having a tent. All it took was rolling out the heavy bedrolls and collecting brush to build a fire—chores which Astra was not allowed to do. She settled for untacking Dannsair.

"So much for Aelor Ven being on your side," Keeshiff growled the man's name. "He only seems to care about how Louko can advance his popularity."

Astra took out a thickly bristled horse brush. "I don't know," she murmured. "It seemed like it was more than that." She thought of the carriage ride, and those expressions of concern Aelor Ven always wore. Or how he had made sure Louko had enough time to rest before the party. And then the conversation he'd had with Lord Eren. Why bother if he had only been using him?

Either way, despite Astra's initial hope that perhaps Ven would send help once they were out of the king's sight, they were on their own. She noted how Louko did not say a word, only caring to the small fire he was building. Yet Astra did not miss the way he snapped a twig more like it was someone's neck than a piece of kindling.

"Well, if it was, I feel like we wouldn't be here right now, and you would be healing and resting instead of gallivanting across the countryside acting as bounty hunters." Keeshiff unrolled a bedroll, rage clear in each jerking motion.

Steadying herself against Dannsair, Astra began to brush her down. "The king seemed to make jabs at Aelor Ven's ignorance." She tried to recall Dia Tzaro's exact words. "He said something like, 'He's not king yet.'"

"I don't know that it matters," Louko spoke up at last, so quiet his voice almost blended with the newly crackling flames. "Whether he's powerless or power hungry, we're on our own nonetheless." The way he said that....

Astra finished her work in silence, returning the brush to her packs. Then she noticed again that the portable chess case was attached to Dannsair's harness. It had somehow been among their belongings. The past two days, Astra had been too exhausted and too afraid to touch it, but she couldn't avoid it forever. She unclipped it and brought it over to the campfire.

She sat down, her aching body protesting the motion. It seemed ages since she had ridden a horse, and even longer since she could do so without pain. She tried to ignore the repercussions as she opened the chess case and began to arrange pieces. Then she pulled out the note that had come with the case...only to find that there were now two. Bewildered, she opened the folded piece of parchment.

Black Bishop No. 1 forward/right three

Lord Aelor Ven takes in the refugees—White Bishop No. 1 forward/right four

King Dia Tzaro sends for Princess Astra—Black Castle No. 2 forward six

Lord Aelor Ven's party arrives in Nythril—White Queen forward one

King Dia Tzaro captures the knights of Merimeethia—Black Castle No. 2 left two

Prince Louko, Prince Keeshiff, and Princess Astra accept King Dia Tzaro's deal—White Pawn No. 6 forward two

White Pawn No. 3 forward one

Black Pawn No. 5 forward one

The parchment trembled in Astra's hands. He knew. Tyron knew. This whole time. He had known every move they would make, enough to write it on paper and put it among their things far in advance.

"Astra? What's the matter?" Louko's voice came from right behind her, making her jump.

She couldn't even reply. She held out the fluttering note.

"Is that…." He snatched the note, clearly in the same panic she was descending into. She listened to his shortening breaths as he tried in vain to read the encrypted note, and no words had to pass between them to acknowledge the quiet horror that he already held.

How had he known? He must have been the one who had betrayed their position to Dia Tzaro. He somehow had orchestrated this whole thing. How?

"What's wrong?" Keeshiff dropped his armful of brush nearby the campfire.

"T-Tyron," Louko sputtered out the name. "He somehow got another note into our things."

Keeshiff gaped. "What do you mean, another?"

"He knew." Louko sounded as empty as Astra felt. "This whole time. He knew."

Astra felt like she couldn't breathe. He knew where they were. Where all of them were. The urge to leap to her feet and tell them to leave, to get away from her, was sudden and strong.

And then she felt his hand. Somehow, in all of the panic, Louko had come and sat by her, his clammy, sweating hand finding hers in an attempt to reassure her. He didn't say a word, only sat there, ever stubborn and refusing to leave her.

"I-If he...if he catches us," Astra could barely say. "He...he...." She gasped for air.

"Won't." Louko's voice was suddenly firm, matching the fervor with which he squeezed her hand. "He won't," he repeated.

Astra gripped his hand like a lifeline. She wanted to believe him but didn't know if she was capable of it. *Get a grip—what will this help?* If only to make him feel better, Astra forced herself to nod and give in to Louko's assurances. Yet the terror of what would happen to him if they were caught could not be stamped out—only swallowed for appearance's sake.

"You're right. I am sorry," she managed to say. Her gaze dropped to the note in his other hand.

"Don't be sorry." His voice was gentle. "You have nothing to be sorry for."

Astra did not dare reply. After a few moments more, she held out her hand and he gave her the note. She opened it, read it again, and turned back to the chess board.

"So, it is a game. And we need to play," Louko said. Astra could feel his gaze settle on the board.

Her reply came slowly. "It doesn't have to be 'we.' The game was sent to me. Even Dia Tzaro offered you a way out." She flinched at the sudden sound of Keeshiff throwing sticks on the fire.

"We're friends, aren't we?" Louko's exhaustion seemed temporarily diminished by determination.

Astra swallowed hard. Weren't friends supposed to be equals? Why, then, was Louko always having to bear her burdens? Astra was saved from replying by Keeshiff's interruption.

"Neither of you are working on that until you have taken care of yourselves and actually eaten," he said. "How can you deal with things like Tyron if you're too weak to even stay on your feet?"

Both Astra and Louko just stared at him, taken aback by the sudden comment.

The scrutiny appeared to make the elder prince uncomfortable, but he stayed outwardly stern. "Don't make me take it away. Come on." He held up the rations bag.

Astra did not want to eat. She was tired and sore, and her stomach was tied in knots over the thought of Tyron. But she saw the way Louko glanced at her and knew that there was no way to refuse without making it harder for him.

So she folded the note and stowed it safely away with the other. "Alright."

"Good." Keeshiff gave a nod, and brought over their rations of hard tack and cheese. "I'm taking watch tonight," he added firmly.

Astra took her rations, already feeling ill at the thought of eating. "I can take second watch," she offered.

Keeshiff scoffed. "After seeing the habit you both have of 'forgetting' to wake me, I think I'm entitled to as many watches as I want."

Astra saw Louko raise an eyebrow. "A valiant effort."

"No. It isn't an effort. I'm telling you. You both are getting some rest. I'm tired of looking at your...um...tired faces." Keeshiff's stern mood was lessened by the odd choice of words, but he went on more severely. "If we get attacked by bandits or something, then neither of you will be very much help in your current state. And you are very well aware that my sword fighting abilities are not as accomplished as yours."

Now both Louko and Astra looked up. "Did you just...say I'm better than you?" Louko asked.

"N-no. That's not what I meant." Keeshiff recovered quickly. "I was talking about Astra."

"Good," was all Louko said, and Astra saw his gaze return to his half-finished dinner.

"But my point stands. Both of you are getting sleep," Keeshiff insisted.

"He's right. You need rest." Louko turned to Astra.

"In a bit," Astra replied as she refocused on the boards.

Keeshiff snorted, "I've heard that one before. If you don't, Princess Astra, I may throw those boards in the fire."

Astra froze, having no idea what to make of such a comment.

"He's not kidding." Louko looked at her. "I beat him in something once, and he told me if I ever beat him again, he'd lock me in his closet. Idiot that I was, you know, I did it again. So he locked me in the closet for four straight hours."

Astra stared at him, horrified. Out of the corner of her eye, she saw Keeshiff doing the same.

"You…still remember that?" Keeshiff asked.

Louko's expression changed to something mischievous. "I mean, it was a blast, really. He shoved me in there and told me to stay put until he came back. And to not make a fuss."

Keeshiff's face was crimson.

"Thirty minutes in, I realized he'd probably forgotten about me. He'd also forgotten to lock the door." Louko was full on grinning, now. "I mean, I wasn't going to disobey him. But I was hungry…. First time I'd had a picnic in the closet, but it was quite fun. Graece didn't ask twice when I said I was having a picnic for lunch. Got a lantern, some tin soldiers…I made sure it was all cleaned up before he came back, of course."

Astra looked back at Keeshiff, who looked like he was about to burst. "What?"

Louko's smile wavered. "Um…."

"You could have told me!" Keeshiff blurted out. "Do you know how many years I've felt bad for that whole thing? I was supposed to meet Father for a lesson and completely forgot—and you looked so lonely wandering around aimlessly so I let you in my room even though you weren't supposed to ever be there, and when Father came to get me, I panicked and put you in there thinking I'd be back in half an hour. But then Father wanted to go all the way out to the sparring fields instead of the gardens and some knights got involved and it was almost the whole afternoon and…." Keeshiff came to a sputtering stop, apparently realizing everything he was saying. His hand went to the back of his neck. "Wow. I sound like you."

Astra, still trying to absorb the onslaught of information, couldn't help but agree with the last statement.

Louko blinked and just stared at his brother for a while. "Oh. Uh. My bad?"

Still rubbing the back of his neck, Keeshiff sat down by the fire with the rest of them. "I sort of figured that it was part of why you stopped coming around," he admitted, still visibly and painfully embarrassed.

If possible, Louko looked even more confused, and now perhaps a little uncomfortable as he ran his hand through his peppered hair. "Right. No, uh, that wasn't it at all. Sorry."

The two brothers sat in silent impasse, neither looking the other in the eye.

So Astra asked for them. "What started it, then?"

Louko laughed nervously. "Well, uh, you know. Things...I got busy...and just bored of following him around." It had been a long time since Astra had heard Louko lie through his teeth, but she recognized it instantly.

"Why don't you want to say it?" she asked.

Louko still had one hand raking through his messy hair, the free one tapping in his lap. Astra almost thought he wasn't going to reply, but then: "It was just some of the knights. They worried I was just trying to use you and told me to stop getting you in trouble. I guess Father kept noticing me around." He shrugged. "Father had been keeping you busy anyway, and I figured I was getting on your nerves or hurting your situation, so I just thought it was best to leave it."

"The knights?" Keeshiff's jaw hung slack but only for a moment. Astra saw his hands turn to fists. "Why, those absolute...." His rant turned to

174

unintelligible growling. "We are going to find Dia Tzaro's runaways, go back and save my men, and then I'm going to bash some heads together."

Louko was staring rather aghast at his brother, but Astra found she was on Keeshiff's side.

"Uh. I'm...sorry...." Louko's brow was so furrowed it threatened permanent wrinkles.

"No—don't apologize." Keeshiff was on his feet now. "Just, just—" he made a shooing motion. "Just get some sleep, both of you. You've been up too long already."

Louko's cheeks flushed ever so slightly. "Alright."

Astra said nothing, only silently beginning to put the pieces back in the wooden case. Perhaps it was best not to aggravate either brother. Surely the game could wait 'til morning....

"We're almost there," I say.

Little Louko trundles behind me, trying to keep up. "Will I get in trouble again?" he pants.

Sorrow tugs at me. He keeps asking that. "No, Louko, your father will never even know," I say again.

I look down at him as he catches up to me. Seeing he is tiring, I take his hand.

I am glad when he finally asks something else. "What are cities like?" Louko asks, looking up at me with those big, brown eyes.

"Big," I say with a smile. "Busy. There are people and animals and houses everywhere."

Louko's mind is churning visibly, trying to comprehend such a thing. He has never been outside the castle walls.

"We're here," I announce, pulling the last bit of brush aside and revealing the bustling city of Melye.

Louko's eyes widen in awe and wonder as he stares out at the lively streets. His mouth, having dropped in surprise, now snaps shut. He looks up at me. "We-we get to go in?" His question is full of excitement.

I nod, smiling again. The child's enthusiasm is contagious, even for me.

This time, Louko is leading, tugging on my hand as he pulls me forward. "I didn't think that there were so many people in the whole world!" he exclaims.

The statement is both sweet and sad. I say nothing.

"Hurry, Tuloi," Louko calls, using the Merimeethian title he gave me. It means "Protector."

I quicken my pace, letting the little boy lead me into the crowd.

Louko's curiosity wars with his excitement. We look at a stall, only to be torn away to go look at another one. He wants to pet one of the resting horses but gets distracted by a stray dog that is running by. But I do not try and stop him. This is his day.

By the time it is growing dark, Louko is exhausted, little feet dragging as he tries to pull me on. "Just a little longer," he begs.

Oh, how hard it is to refuse his sad eyes! "We'll come back," I promise.

Louko perks up then and allows me to turn us back towards the castle. "Really? Can it be soon?"

"Yes," I laugh. "Soon."

I scoop him up and carry him back home. I am content to hear him chatter of all the things he saw. I am glad that his mind has been taken from the abuse of his father and captured by the wonder of the wide world.

A GAME OF WITS

CHAPTER XI

Louko:

Louko was trying not to be paranoid over how much Astra was riding. She shouldn't be doing this…. In fact, why in Eatris was she still so sick? In his time with Astra and Entrais, Louko had never seen either of them sick *this* long. Was it the stress?

Stupid king.

Stupid uncle.

Honestly, Louko wasn't sure who he was more angry at—but the family betrayal was getting old—really old.

"So…Tyron gave you the chess set, then?" Keeshiff's question was not exactly a pleasant break from the silence as they rode, but Louko couldn't fault him for asking.

Astra gave a tight-lipped nod.

There was a brief silence, and Louko hoped Keeshiff wouldn't ask the question he knew he would.

"Why?"

His jaw set and he closed his eyes—though only briefly, so as not to crash his ambling horse—wishing Astra did not have to answer. Wishing he didn't.

"I don't know," came the hollow response. "I don't know what he wants, nor what he'll gain from sending us the game. I'm sure there is something. Until then, we have little choice but to try and play it to figure everything out."

Another pause, then, "Is there any way I can help?"

Louko thought again of the conversation by the fire, and the look of horror and guilt in his brother's eyes. He had not expected Keeshiff to react so...strongly.

"None besides what you are already doing," Astra said quietly. The taut set of her shoulders gave away her hesitation when she spoke again: "But I am sorry that this game has already cost you; I will do whatever I can to help free your men."

"You have done more than enough already, Astra. This is not your fault," Keeshiff replied firmly.

Louko sighed, wishing Astra would believe that, even as he knew she wouldn't. The way Keeshiff's shoulders slumped from up front told Louko he wasn't the only one who knew.

"I just...." He could see Astra's grip tighten on Dannsair's reins. "I just cannot understand how he is so far ahead of us. He would have had to know where we were going several weeks ago in order to get a note across the border and to someone who could stow it in our things. *We* didn't even know what we would do yet."

"Well," Louko said, "Honestly, it wasn't hard to deduce."

"Except it wasn't deduction, was it?" Astra shook her head. "It was *control*. He knew to hurt me just enough so that we would be at your uncle's for weeks while I recovered. And then he knew enough of Dia Tzaro to offer him information in the guise of a deal—a deal Dia Tzaro would ignore in favor of his own plans. And all of this in perfect timing for the celebration of Dia Tzaro's reign, when Ven would be called to the capital and away from his estate and the knights there."

Exactly. Tyron knew Astra had few options in places to hide, rest, and recuperate. Louko was a fool for thinking they would be safe in Nythril. Clearly, since all of Tyron's last hints had come to pass, these notes were real, and not some attempt to mislead them. But why? Why would Tyron risk telling them things ahead of time? Was it just for the pleasure of control?

"The question is, how to use his own game to control him, in turn," Louko murmured half to himself.

"How can we do that when we have no resources?" Keeshiff voiced the question in all of their minds. "And even if we knew half of this stuff, it doesn't mean we have the means to actually change any of it."

Louko's expression hardened. "Well, we have pieces on the board. There's a reason Tyron didn't just give us a list of what they were; he is trying to keep us from knowing our resources. We just have to...find out what they are." Right?

Astra closed her eyes and recited the two lists that Tyron had sent them. Then she opened her eyes and continued, "That gives us some of them. Mariah, we already know. Since the white queen moved in correspondence to me leaving Litash, that must be me. And the second white knight, which moved with Keeshiff escaping to Nythril, must be either him or his men."

Louko wondered at all the moves that weren't being listed. Was it up to them to figure those out? "And the first white bishop shifted when we escaped to Nythril. That must be Uncle." He wondered again at Ven's intentions, and the pain of again being left to figure this out on their own was raw and too fresh.

"Which was then blocked by the black castle...Dia Tzaro?" Astra didn't seem to be asking anyone in particular.

Louko thought of where that left them on the list Astra had recited, imagining where that placed each piece on the TetraChess board. "Right. The list put the second black castle forward six and left two, meaning it blocks both the white castle and pins the white knight." The latter seemed pretty obviously the knights.

"...I'm pretty sure that I'm lost," Keeshiff muttered. "I don't know how you two do it any more than Tyron does, but you seem to have a good grasp on it already."

Astra frowned. "Except that we're missing an entire side of it. Mariah's name was carved on two pieces—the second black bishop and the eighth white pawn. Meaning each person has, or might have, a piece on each side of the board according to their usefulness."

"Yes...so what's Tyron's white piece?" Louko bit his lip. And what was his own piece?

With a terse shrug, Astra replied, "I do not know. I suppose there's nothing to prove he would even have one."

Louko frowned, saying no more for now. It made sense that even Tyron would have a white piece—everyone's actions in turn affected others for good or bad. He'd never thought of it, but now it made sense the way the pieces danced with each other even on a TetraChess board. Partners. But how to find each one? And what to do once they did know?

"I'm not *that* stupid, Louko. I'm coming in there with you both."
Keeshiff's face was red as he argued.

Louko sighed. "One of us has to stay with the horses and supplies.
We don't need to get robbed. And if Astra...." he trailed off. If she were to
have a flashback or a moment of panic or...something...he knew he would
likely be the only one Astra would recognize. He didn't like doing this to
his brother, but it had to be done.

Keeshiff's fire dampened, and his eyes fell a little. "Alright. But how
will I know you haven't gotten abducted or killed?"

Raising an eyebrow, Louko replied, "Um. Well. We'll come back, for
starters."

Keeshiff huffed impatiently. "No, I mean how long should I expect you
to be?"

"Oh. I'm hoping no more than about an hour," Louko replied with a
shrug. Hopefully. He didn't like this at all.

It was clear that Keeshiff was not comfortable with this. "If you aren't
back by then...." His voice went thick, and he clenched his jaw. "Just, be
back by then. Or this time I will follow you all the way back to Melye."

Louko grew very quiet and gave only a nod, turning around and going
to find Astra. She had been so stubborn since leaving, and he knew why.
She was afraid...of so many things.

He found her still grooming Dannsair. She was much slower at such
things nowadays.

"Do we have anything else we need to bring?" he asked her, giving
Dannsair a gentle pat on the neck in thanks for the way the mare
comforted Astra. Sometimes, he worried the horse was better than him.

Astra stowed the brush back in her pack. "No." She shook her head. "We have no need for disguises, since Dia Tzaro is the one who has sent us."

"Alright. Are you ready, then?" The question sounded so weighty. When *had* they been ready? When had they even had a chance to breathe? Louko longed for Astra to be able to properly recover and be rid of the burden Tyron was set upon giving her. Yet, no matter how hard he tried, Louko appeared incapable of helping her. He was only adding to the burden, just like he had been in the castle.

Useless.

Astra just nodded. Picking up Dannsair's reins, she walked with Louko back to where Keeshiff was tying the other mounts.

"Here." She held out the reins.

The eldest prince and the painted mare both looked displeased. When Keeshiff reached for the reins, the mare bared her teeth and snapped them together inches from his fingers.

"Back off!" Keeshiff looked almost more ferocious than Dannsair.

Louko held in a small smile.

"*Be nice,*" Astra said in Litashian and nudged Dannsair's leg with her elbow. "*It's only for an hour.*"

Dannsair shook thoroughly as if trying to get rid of a fly, then she rested her large head on Astra's shoulder.

"*I'll be fine,*" Astra said, pushing her off.

The mare snorted, looking back at Keeshiff with flattened ears.

Astra switched back to Merimeethian. "I'll leave the reins around her neck. If she tries to wander off, just scold her."

"What if she doesn't listen?" Keeshiff's voice was doubtful as he glared at the mare.

Astra gave the mare a stern look. "Oh, she will. Won't you, Dannsair?"

The black-and-white mare snorted again, but she walked over to stand near Keeshiff and the other horses. Louko was certain she was pouting, especially once Dannsair flicked Keeshiff directly in the face with her tail.

Louko couldn't help but comment to Astra, "What a fitting pair," and finally let a smile briefly slip onto his face.

"Let's just hope they haven't killed each other by the time we get back," Astra returned dryly.

With that lovely thought, Louko and Astra left the unlucky pair to their misery, slowly trekking off into the peace and quiet of the sparse woods. When they reached the road, Louko noticed Astra putting her hood up and realized that she had been wearing it up more often than she used to. He'd assumed it had been from the cold, but his gut formed a knot as he suddenly wondered if it was more to hide the scar on her temple.

He fought to keep anger from rising in his throat, instead walking in silence with her into the village of Tehng.

Louko had never seen a settlement that looked like it had grown right up out of the ground like this. It was only as they passed the first home that he could make out what caused the effect: The houses had been partially dug out of the ground, and the removed soil used in slabs to form the walls. He could tell which houses were older simply by how much grass had grown over them. From what he could tell, the only woods used in the whole structure were the beams of the roof and the frames of the door. It made sense out here on the plateau, with so little forest nearby.

As they walked, there were at least a few familiar Nythrilian trademarks—some ceramic roof tiles, woven thatch window shutters, a few houses with plaster walls. Smoke drifted up from hidden courtyards and filled the village with savory scents of meat and cooking grains, signaling the preparation of the evening meal. Louko hoped they wouldn't be too late to reach the market square.

The 'square' was really just a patch of well-trodden dirt at the center of the village. A few carts were parked at its edges—some with oxen still harnessed—and laden with varying produce. One woman had a handcart stocked with yarns and a few bolts of thickly woven cloth. Louko noted three elderly women sitting in chairs beneath the eaves of a nearby house, pointing out things and chattering in turn. They were just the people he'd been looking for—the town gossips.

Skirting a group of children playing a boisterous game of kickball, Louko and Astra entered the square and stopped at the first cart. They'd already agreed that buying a few supplies and thus providing revenue would increase their chances of congenial treatment.

"How much for these?" Louko held up a piece of fruit from a vendor's wagon.

The aproned lady squinted at the produce and began to reply, only to stop mid-sentence. She leaned forward, and Louko, thinking it was to inspect the fruit, held it out. Then the woman reached a hand towards Astra's face. Astra jumped backwards and away from her touch. Her hood fell back, revealing wild eyes.

"Oh, it is you," the woman said, withdrawing her hand. "I just needed to make sure it was you." She tapped her temple in reference to Astra's scar. "He was quite insistent that I make sure I gave this to the right person."

Louko watched as she pulled a folded piece of parchment from her apron. *Tyron.* This was maddening. *How?!* But he had the sense not to show the panic that swelled—the panic Astra was no doubt feeling.

When Astra didn't reply, Louko took the letter and spoke for her, "Thank you." Hopefully that sounded sincere...and not how he felt.

The lady just nodded, wiping her hands on her apron and adding, "And the fruit is a copper apiece."

Louko quickly fished out the money and handed it to her as he asked, "Do you get many outsiders here? I'm not sure which of our cousins were the ones who dropped this off? It's so hard to keep them straight sometimes." He gave a laugh and rolled his eyes.

"Oh." The vendor thought a moment. "He was rather tall. Black hair. Yes, I remember now—he had the strangest eyes I've ever seen. Such a vivid green."

No. No, no. "Oh. That one. Wonderful," he grumbled, the woman chuckling as she fortunately misinterpreted. "I was hoping it was my younger cousin. She's rather peculiar looking. Contracted *drora fever* when she was five and went prematurely grey." Louko may have been pressing his luck a bit, but it was worth a try.

The vendor, now looking somewhere between suspicious and bewildered, shrugged it off and merely handed him the rest of his purchase.

As soon as they turned away from the old lady and her cart, he heard Astra speak in Litashian under her breath. "She knew who you were talking about." She pulled up her hood again. "They must have come here."

Louko nodded subtly. "Someone has to know. Better keep with the cousin story, though. Gossip is definitely prevalent around here."

They tried every single vendor, a few passersby, and even the town gossips: No one would acknowledge anything. Not out loud, anyway. Louko saw enough sideways glances and nervous shifting to tell him that they knew. Why were they so willing to protect these people? Whatever the reason, it didn't bode well for them rescuing the knights.

"Well, I think we've gotten what we can out of here," Louko muttered, hoping that perhaps this meant that at least those they were searching for were still not far from the village.

Astra, still visibly pale since the woman had given them the note, nodded. "Agreed."

They were nearly clear of the village limits when he heard someone call, "Hey—you!"

Both Louko and Astra spun around, daggers at the ready. Louko hid his when he realized it was only a boy, perhaps a few years younger than Astra.

The boy jogged to catch up to them. Still puffing, he asked, "You were the one asking about the girl with white hair, right?"

Keeping Astra behind him, Louko nodded.

"And you said she was your cousin?" This question was more guarded. "You're here to help?"

Guilt deepened as he nodded. "Is she alright? Is she safe?"

The boy relaxed all at once. "Yes, she's safe. Her and her friend are just west of here. They made their camp in the old ravine," he explained.

"But you might want to hurry. There's been a few other strangers asking around—some of them soldiers."

Louko pursed his lips, conflicted. "Thank you. Hopefully we can help her." He was pretty sure this was branding him a horrible person, but the glance he and Astra shared proved she was thinking the same thing: They needed more answers before they decided what to do with these "criminals." Why were locals helping them?

The boy smiled, nodded, and said, "I hope so, too," then ran off back towards the village square.

Now thoroughly shaken, Louko and Astra turned back to the road. The hood obscured her face, but Louko didn't need to see her to know how terrified she must be. Then he saw her head snap up.

"Riders," she breathed. "A lot of them."

Louko took her by the arm and helped her move out of the way just as a large group of riders came barreling around the corner, a jail-like wagon in the middle of the caravan of Nythrilian soldiers. At the head was a woman, hair up in a bun held together in a shining metal ring not far off from what Ven had worn to the palace ball. Her jaw was tight, her eyes hard, and she only glanced briefly at Louko and Astra as they passed by in a flurry.

As soon as the company had passed, Louko and Astra stepped back onto the road. Louko was eager to get moving, but Astra stood staring after them. When she finally turned around, he heard her murmur, "We'd better hurry."

After they were safely out of the possibility of earshot, Louko gave a long sigh. "I don't like how this is going."

He saw Astra's hand go to her wrist in that old habit. Only there was no more red bronze cuff there. Did he imagine the sparks of blue that raced over her fingers?

"Are you alright?" Louko asked.

Her hands became fists, and the sparks vanished. "Yes. Sorry." Astra's voice was tenuous. "May I see the note?"

How he wished to withhold it. But that would have been wrong and just as he wished her not to hide things from him, he could not do so to her. So he handed it to her, gut wrenched in too many directions.

Astra unfolded the parchment as they walked, considered a moment, then folded and pocketed it. "He knows," was all she said.

"May I see?" he asked, extending his hand. He should have read it first—not that he could really decipher the mix of languages. *Idiot.*

It was impossible to miss Astra's hesitation. She pulled it from her pocket, only to falter again. Her hands were shaking when she glanced up at him and tried to speak. Only, nothing came out. She stopped in the middle of the road.

Slowly, Louko reached forward with both hands, one for the paper and one to clasp her hand. "Astra." He turned and faced her head on, even as she didn't meet his gaze. "What is it?"

He knew what it was...he knew how much was on her shoulders. But she had said nothing—had hidden it beneath the guise of composure as she always did. Only, with how sick she was, she couldn't quite hide it with the same ability she once had. Or perhaps Louko just knew her so much better, now.

She opened her mouth, then closed it with lips pressed together. He heard her let out a shuddering breath. "This isn't right. You shouldn't have to do this—you've suffered enough. I-I told you once that I would help you, and now...." She shook her head rapidly. "...now look at us."

Louko did not let go of her hands. "It's not right, but that's because of Tyron, not you. And you have helped. You're the only one still here with me. You gave me a friend and a *reason* not to give up in that stupid cell. You're the only reason I'm here, Astra."

"I was the only reason you were in there in the first place!" She seemed to realize how loudly she'd said it, swallowing hard and looking back down. "I was the one who fell for a trick and was captured, remember?"

"I don't think you understand, Astra. I don't know where I would be if you hadn't shown up in Melye." Every word was said with a deliberate slowness, as he wanted her to see just how much she meant to him. Just how she'd saved him. Every word of it was true, and he needed her to know that.

Astra met his gaze, fear momentarily subdued. "What do you mean?"

"I would have ended up dead or worse. Astra, if Tyron had asked me to help a year ago...." He winced, and now it was his turn to turn away, eyes riveted on the empty space to his left. He looked back. "...I would have said yes."

The only sound was that of the wind tugging across the brush-strewn landscape. Then Astra gripped his hand a little tighter.

"You would have come right in the end," she said with quiet assurance.

"Maybe you're right." He held the same conviction. "But I wouldn't ever have been able to forgive myself. Ever." Even now, it caused Louko to shudder; if he had been helping Tyron...only to find Astra caught, or

Keeshiff killed…. It still scared him how close he'd been to saying 'yes' to Tyron. And perhaps deep down, he still felt guilty for the fact. He just wanted Astra to see all she had done—just like everyone else saw. All the people she'd saved and the lives she'd changed. Keeshiff and the others would never have made it to Nythril without her. And no, Louko would not be here if she hadn't cared.

Astra was unnaturally still. "Do you really think it was all worth it?"

"Yes." And anything that wasn't was Tyron's fault, not hers. Louko's jaw tightened in determination. "You're the only person who's never left me"

He felt her waver, looking away and then back down. She took her free hand and placed it on top of his. "I trust you," she said softly. "If you believe it, I trust you."

Before Louko could say anything else, a shout rang out. "Get back here, you stupid horse!"

There was the sound of hoofbeats from down the road, and Louko turned around to see Dannsair trotting down the road calmly. She was followed by a rather aggravated Keeshiff, who, at present, was all but dragging the other two reluctant horses behind him.

"Dannsair, *what* are you doing?" Astra called out.

"We told you both to stay put," Louko added somewhat irritably, running his hand through his hair.

Dannsair ignored everyone, trotting right up to Astra. The girl said something in Litashian, taking the mare's reins and swatting her on the side with them.

"Next time, I'm going to just eat her for dinner if she misbehaves." Keeshiff caught up to them, giving an evil glare at the horse. Then he looked between Louko and Astra. "Did you find out anything?"

"They are nearby." Louko barely got the reply out without laughing, still registering his brother's comment.

Keeshiff glanced towards the sky as if gauging the time. "Then do we find them now, or wait for nightfall?"

Louko turned to Astra. "Perhaps nightfall?" he suggested. They needed to catch their breath and be ready. And night was always the best. "Unless you think the villagers would warn them of our coming?" he added.

Astra, still holding her mare, paused to think. "I do not think they would. Those who distrust us would not risk going to them while we are still so close."

"Then nightfall." Louko nodded, taking a deep breath. They had until nightfall to figure out what to do. Oh, how he hoped these were indeed criminals. And how his doubt grew.

"What is the matter?" Keeshiff seemed to address them both.

Louko ran his hand through his hair and muttered, "I don't know about this."

Keeshiff still appeared confused.

"These people do not sound like criminals," Astra explained, as they started to move off the road and into the shelter of the woods. "They are outsiders, yet the villagers were protecting them." Louko noticed she was still holding the note from Tyron.

"Oh, no. They're going to be like us, aren't they?" Keeshiff sounded as exasperated as Louko felt.

"We will see," the younger prince muttered. They would figure it out, right? They always did.

CHAPTER XII

<u>Astra:</u>

It was decided that they would find the gorge the village boy had described, then backtrack a good half mile before settling down to wait till nightfall. No sooner had they picked a well-hidden spot than Astra was pulling out the chessboard and the newest note from Tyron.

"Is that a good idea? Rest might be better?" Louko asked, appearing hesitant as he sat down. "Even Keeshiff is resting."

Astra had no desire for sleep; not when all she ever dreamt of was Tyron and being in his head. "I'm alright," she said as she set out the pieces. "I need to add this new one to the game."

"Alright." He didn't move. "Do you want company?"

Astra went very still. She wanted to say no, but now she thought of their conversation on the road. Louko wasn't going to leave her; to exclude him would only force him to watch while tying his hands. "Sure."

And so he stayed. Astra could feel him keenly watching each move she made as she set up the board and took careful notes of every piece and their function in this sickening game. This last note had held no explanations, only predictions:

Black Knight No. 2 forward three, left two
White Bishop No. 1 takes Black Castle No. 2
Black Pawn No. 2 takes White Pawn No. 7

A GAME OF WITS

White Pawn No. 8 forward two

What did they all mean? Who did these pieces represent, and could those representations change? And what about all the moves and pieces that Tyron didn't dictate? Surely those were of importance, too. Perhaps if they could decipher those, they could actually get ahead of all Tyron's predictions. This hope, as futile as it felt, brought up another question: What did Tyron have to gain from this? Was it just the enjoyment of taunting her? Was it a means of manipulating her? It seemed as though he did that easily enough without a board game to help.

As her mind wore its way through the same unanswerable questions, her thoughts began to drift to their current mission: the knights. And now, the so-called criminals they were meant to capture as soon as dark fell. "How do you think we should go about detaining them? The fugitives, I mean." She began to play through the indicated moves on the chessboards.

"Hopefully by reasoning with them to help us." Louko sounded uncertain. Then he added, "So how can I help?" She didn't immediately register that he was talking about the game.

Astra hesitated. She knew they'd gone over this. She knew what he'd said, and now she repeated it to herself over and over: *It was worth it. You were worth it.* But she couldn't help but offer him one last chance to escape: "Are you certain about this?"

"Yes." The reply was firm, even as his face showed the severity of his resolve.

"Alright." She had to trust him. She had no other choice.

With that, he came over and sat beside her instead of across, patiently watching her play through the newest moves. His jaw set as she finished, and he asked, "Have we seen the second black knight yet?"

Astra shook her head. "Not directly, no."

"Hm." Louko glanced at the board and pointed out the arrangement of the black knight and the white knight nearby. "Well, whoever it is, they and the black castle are blocking off the knights. The black castle was Dia Tzaro, right? Maybe the knight is one of his underlings."

"But doesn't it also say that the first white bishop takes the second black castle?" Astra pointed to Tyron's second note before remembering that Louko couldn't really read it. "This one says that the first white bishop moved when your uncle took us in."

Louko's brow furrowed.

"What would that mean, then, if his piece took Dia Tzaro's?" Astra asked.

Louko did not reply right away. His gaze flicked back and forth between the two pieces. "I'm not sure," he finally admitted. "And I'm not sure whether it's a good thing or a bad thing."

Astra didn't know what to say. She wanted to reassure him, but what assurance could she offer? She knew even less of his uncle's intentions than he did. She decided to use the rules of the game instead: "Well, if it is a white piece, then theoretically it is in our favor."

"Theoretically," Louko murmured. Then he sighed. "We need to get ahead of Tyron...somehow."

"But we don't know what he wants." Astra couldn't help her frustration. "How are we supposed to beat him if we don't even know the prize?"

"Well, if he wants to win the game…." Louko frowned at the board. "That means taking out the king—whatever that means…. Although, in TetraChess, that usually requires killing the queen first…." He trailed off a moment. "So yes, I suppose this is more complicated…." Another pause.

Both were distracted by Keeshiff who sat up abruptly. "But what does he *want?* I mean, we know he's not right in the head and all...but this all has to be for something, right? Does he want Litash back? But wouldn't he be going after Entrais and not you, if that were the case?"

Astra turned to Louko, but neither of them had any answer.

"Well, um," Keeshiff's voice dropped and he rubbed the back of his neck. "Did he, you know, say anything? While you were in there?"

He spoke so quietly, and yet the question hit Astra square in the chest, robbing her of breath.

Louko took the answer up in her stead. "I guess it's hard to remember…." Astra saw him shudder. "But now that you mention it...he kept asking about 'her.' Where 'she' was. He kept saying that we couldn't keep him from 'them,' and vague things like that. Everything was so vague and scattered and...well, I gave up trying to figure out what he wanted. It didn't seem like we could give it to him either way."

The silence seemed to roar in Astra's ears. She couldn't tell if no one else dared to make eye contact either, or if they, too, couldn't tear their eyes from the chess boards.

"He kept goading me to try and escape." She barely registered the voice as her own. "He told me I could get out if I really tried."

She felt both princes look up.

"Maybe I am just misremembering." She forced herself to exhale. "I have so many dreams of him."

"Dreams?" Louko looked troubled.

An odd sense of shame swept over her, and Astra turned back to the board. "I...." She didn't even want to say it. "I keep having dreams that I am him. They're all disjointed, but they're so..." She gave a shrug. "...vivid. Specific. Out of place. Things like...like reading to a group of children. Or walking through the forest. Or taking you into Melye for the first time. They aren't always awful like...." She stopped speaking when she looked up and saw Louko's horrified expression.

"Taking me to Melye for the first time? Tell me that one. In detail." His eyes were wide.

Too frightened by his reaction to even ask why, Astra relayed the dream as best as she could remember.

Louko was very pale by the time she finished, and his voice was hoarse as he said, "Astra...that...that's not a dream...that-that happened."

Astra felt cold. "What do you mean?"

"That *happened*, Astra," he repeated. "As in, that is one of my earliest memories of him. I don't understand how...but that isn't some dream. That's too clear to be a coincidence...."

She began to shake her head. "No...no, that isn't possible." She didn't remember standing up, but somehow, she was on her feet. "Are you saying I am *actually* seeing inside his head?"

He grabbed her hand, a desperate attempt to calm her down. "Astra, I don't—"

"Woah, let's just take a deep breath." Keeshiff tried to step in.

Astra barely heard him. "What if he is seeing mine? What if that's how he is finding us?"

"You've only seen old memories, though, right?" Louko didn't sound very confident.

"I-I don't know. Some of them are dark a-and disorganized." She was going to be ill.

"Wait! if you can see his memories, maybe you can see what he wants—or even what he's planning." Keeshiff seemed...excited.

It interrupted Astra's rising panic. "I-I don't know. Everything is all mixed up—I can't control it. It's like...." The realization came all at once. "Like when I was taken over by the Miadoris."

Louko's brow furrowed. "Didn't you go crazy last time...?"

Astra winced and nodded. "Yes. It nearly killed me."

"So, how exactly is it happening again, and how are you not going to die?" Louko's voice cracked, revealing the fullness of his anxiety.

"I don't know. Maybe that's what he was trying to do with his experiments," Astra said again, wishing she had some sort of answer for him. Then a new fear struck. "It's not possible that he has obtained the Miadoris." ...was it? Had he already reached Ent? Surely such drastic news would have been the talk of the party when they were at Dia Tzaro's ball.

"Can you write to your brother? Have you written to him since we got out?" The fact that Louko hadn't immediately dispelled the idea was frightening.

"N-no, your uncle warned against it lest someone intercept it." The last letter she had sent had been before her capture—nearly two months ago by now. She had mentioned then that they were heading for Aelor

Ven's estate. What if the reason he had not sent anyone or done anything was because….

Louko ran his hand through his hair. "Well. We haven't heard any news—surely it would have been all over the capital while we were there."

The assurance was not enough to quell Astra's trembling. "Then how would Tyron be linked to the Miadoris?"

Louko was silent.

"Did the link to Tyron happen in...there?" Keeshiff offered.

Astra wanted to curl up and hide. "I don't know. But I was in red bronze for the whole duration."

"Then maybe…." Louko started in. "Wait...maybe your link to him is older. You haven't been without your red bronze cuff until after we got away—you've worn it ever since The War. What if...you've always been connected?"

Astra couldn't suppress a shiver. "Maybe. I don't know." Her shoulders rose and fell in a helpless shrug. "But if that is true, then maybe I can put a stop to it by putting the bronze back on." She knew that they had brought two of her old cuffs along.

"Astra...that's not a good idea." The worry in Louko's tone penetrated even further than the look he gave.

"I agree...you really haven't been looking well. Asher didn't even like the thought of you traveling when we were just going to that stupid dance," Keeshiff added.

Astra tried to argue, but Louko cut back in. "You'll need your full strength for tonight, anyway. Dia Tzaro said the people we're going after are Gifted—innocent or not, they can still be dangerous."

This was enough to make Astra bite her tongue and try to swallow her fears. He was right. She couldn't risk making herself even more of a weak point for them. But the thought that she was *really* seeing Tyron's thoughts...and that he was seeing hers....

Louko just took her hand, squeezing it softly and not saying a word. He didn't have to.

"Maybe we should put this away for now," Keeshiff suggested, looking back down at the boards. "We might be better off planning for tonight."

"I agree," Louko said, stooping to help his brother pack it up.

Astra did not say either way, but she knelt to do the same.

Astra held up a hand, and the sound of muted footsteps to her far left went still. Through the dark of the evening, she could just make out Louko looking her way.

Over the distant hum of churning water, she could hear two voices, one male, one female: an argument.

Tactically, that was perfect. A distracted target meant an easy target. Yet, somehow, it only added to Astra's uneasiness as she signaled to move forward again. At least the sound would help cover Keeshiff's approach. She had been worried about him slipping on the loose shale and so giving himself away before she'd had a chance to step out and draw their attention from a safer distance.

The closer they drew to the hidden camp, the higher the disagreement escalated.

"Just let me fly you! You will never make it to Litash on that leg," a young, female voice argued in Litashian.

The voice that replied was definitely older and definitely male. "And you wouldn't make it halfway over the forest without getting eaten—just let me rest a day or so longer, and then we can walk through and—"

"—A day or so longer and we'll be caught!"

"Would you please let the matter go?" The man's exasperation made it clear that this was not the first time they'd had this debate. "This is no time for arguing. Someone might hear us."

Astra took that as her cue. She drew her borrowed sword and came out from behind the cover of the underbrush. "He's right. Lay down your weapons and keep your hands in sight."

The two looked startled, spinning around and—of course—reaching for weapons.

"Behind us!" It was the silver-haired girl who cried the warning as Keeshiff and Louko stepped out from their closer vantage points.

The targets, now realizing the trap they were in, stood back-to-back. Astra saw the way they looked around in a panicked search for a way out. She knew the steep-walled gorge offered no natural escape, but readied her Gifting in case they had other methods.

"Stay back!" yelled the girl, lashing out with her blade in threat.

"We just want to talk," Astra assured.

The girl narrowed her eyes. "Oh, *sure*." Her sword drifted towards Louko, and her stance turned from defensive to hostile.

Astra did not think, she acted. She didn't even realize it until the girl screamed and dropped her weapon. The sword lay on the damp pebble bed, sizzling and glowing red. There was another clatter as she dropped to her knees, gasping.

"Get away from her!" The man raised his sword and stepped between Astra and the girl, limping painfully as he did so. "Mitheau, are you alright?" He called over his shoulder.

The silver-haired girl was visibly breathing hard. "Yes, I...just...." She couldn't seem to get the answer out.

Astra was baffled. All she'd done was heated the blade. Why was the girl so affected? Whatever the reason, Astra had to take this advantage. "If you would put away your swords, we would like to have a decent conversation."

"Who sent you?" The man's blade did not drop so much as an inch, even though he wasn't putting any weight on one foot.

He was wounded. That's why the two hadn't moved. "King Dia Tzaro. But we do not trust him," Astra answered plainly. "We decided to see what you were for ourselves."

"And you are not helping your own case." Louko walked over and picked up the cooled sword that the girl had dropped. Then he stepped back so that they still formed a loose circle around the two outlaws.

The girl—Mitheau, the man had called her—only watched.

"Now, please, your sword." Astra gestured for the man to toss his to Keeshiff.

Surprisingly, the man obliged, laying his blade down carefully and sliding it over the rock bed towards Keeshiff.

Astra's attention went back to Mitheau, who was still on her knees behind her friend. "Are you alright? Are you wounded?"

The silver-haired girl looked up warily. "I am unharmed," was all she said.

"Then let's all have a seat," Astra said, gesturing to the neglected little fire where the fugitives had dragged large stones for seats.

Both obliged, the man then making startling eye contact as he seemed to size Astra up.

It made Astra glad that she'd put her hood up. She tilted her head in acknowledgement and said, "My name is Astra. How may I address you?"

He limped his way to the stones and eased himself down onto one of them. In the firelight, Astra could see all the bandaging wrapped around the man's calf.

"Grenedil," he answered then paused. "Please, don't turn her in."

Astra glanced towards the silver-haired girl, who was still eyeing Keeshiff and Louko from their positions beyond the fire. Astra let out a sharp breath. The way Grenedil had spoken reminded her of her brother. She pushed away memories of when he had stood between her and their enemies, making similar pleas. "Why don't you start with explaining why the king of Nythril wants you both so badly."

Grenedil's fingers drummed against his uninjured leg, the only sign of tension as he calmly cleared his throat. "Well," he started, "They are after us because I didn't approve of children being locked up in dungeons. When I broke Mitheau—" He pointed to the silver-haired girl— "out of the king's palace, they came after us."

The story was eerily similar to Astra's current situation. Perhaps too similar. "Why did Dia Tzaro want her detained in the first place?"

"Um, well...."

"I'm one of the Myrandi." The girl's voice was calm enough but the set of her shoulders gave away her tension.

Astra glanced to Louko, who looked just as puzzled as she did.

"You may better know the Myrandi as Drogans," Grenedil added.

Now, Louko made a small sound of surprise. Astra could only second him. A Drogan? So that's what Dia Tzaro had meant when he said 'Gifted.'

After muttering something about 'mispronouncing Dragons,' Mitheau said, "What does it matter? There are few of us left." The words held a weight that did not befit the girl's age. "And those of us who remain are being hunted down for a prize. King Dia Tzaro has always paid well for us."

And here Astra thought Dia Tzaro could not be any more revolting than he already was. Anyone who put a price on another person's soul was not worth the air they breathed. She quieted her anger, knowing she needed a cool head in order to judge this wisely. It would not do to buy their story so easily. She steadied herself before asking, "Why do they hunt you?"

"There was a leader among us by the name of Ovok," Mitheau explained.

Astra heard Louko shift at the name.

"Over fifteen years ago, he rallied our kind and led them to war," Mitheau went on. "None who went with him returned. With so few left behind, there was no way to defend our homes from jealous neighboring countries. We faced either eviction or extinction, so it was decided we should scatter. Only…." The girl let out a long breath. "It seemed that hiding just made us more sought after."

Rarely had Astra ever understood a statement more. She kept herself from sympathy and looked to Louko. He would be more informed on these things and would be better able to tell if Mitheau was lying.

His shoulders drooped ever so slightly as he gave a nod to corroborate the Drogan's story.

Astra suppressed the urge to sigh. She thought of the knights, and how much harder this was going to make rescuing them. Nonetheless, she asked, "How did you come by that?" as she tilted her head towards Grenedil's bandaged calf. Even in the dim lighting, she could see the dark stains that bled through the fabric.

Grenedil's guarded expression intensified, but he replied nonetheless. "When we drove out that idiotic band of ruffians draining the town of life," he muttered.

Ah. So that would be why the villagers had been so tight-lipped. "How bad is it?"

"I've had worse." His shrug was unconvincing.

The problem was that he couldn't walk—not even well enough to defend himself when they'd caught them by surprise. Astra didn't dare look at Louko. "Where do you plan to go?"

"We were trying to make it to Litash." Grenedil's admission was accompanied by a near sigh. "They have plenty of races that won't bat an eye at you having two forms, and there are other Myrandi that stayed on Eatris and have fled there."

The last sentence surprised Astra. She had not known that any Drogans resided in Litash. Then again, she'd not been allowed out much. She thought for a long moment before getting to her feet and brushing herself off.

"Pardon me for a moment while I confer with my friends."

In response, Grenedil nodded.

Astra walked around where the two fugitives sat and joined Keeshiff and Louko. In Merimeethian, she said, "*We cannot leave them here.*"

Louko sighed, "*Not with that leg and the soldiers we just saw.*"

"*But what can we do?*" Keeshiff asked, jaw taut.

Astra let out a long breath as her attention wandered back towards the trio. "*Maybe I can heal it. This will be easier if we can get him moving.*"

"*No.*" Louko's reply was firm. "*It could kill you.*"

Astra opened her mouth to argue, then stopped when she turned and saw the look on her friend's face. She swallowed and looked away. "*What if...*" The threads of an idea began to weave into a sort of plan. "*...what if we accompanied them for some of the way? Then we could put him on one of the horses.*" She recalled their map and where they were in regards to the capital. "*If we travel straight north of here, it will bring them closer to the northern mountain passes and us still nearer to the capital. That would bring them past where the king's hunters are searching, and then we could approach Kythdexlentu-Orsha from a direction Dia Tzaro would not expect.*"

"*But what about...what about our problem? Astra, I know you want to help, but we are in just as much danger. And not just us.*" Keeshiff rubbed the pommel of his sword with a ferocity that equaled Louko's stillness.

Astra looked back towards the fugitives, warily talking in low voices and glancing back at them. "*But we cannot condemn them to the same fate we are trying to escape,*" she replied. "*There has to be something we can do.*"

The following silence passed from Astra to Louko to Keeshiff.

"*I guess there is no other option.*" Keeshiff threw his hands up in exasperation.

Astra bit her lip, looking to Louko.

Louko did not speak for a long while, face drawn tightly and eyes glued on the fugitives—especially Mitheau. The constant shifting of the firelight only added to the conflict in his expression.

"*I'm not going to be a pawn in anyone's game.*" Louko's gaze shifted to meet Astra's, and he reiterated, "*Anyone's. We'll make a plan on how to get the knights out on the way. I'm sure we'll come up with something.*"

Astra hoped so. She hoped she was right to do this. "*Then it is agreed?*"

Louko dipped his head.

Jaw set, Keeshiff gave a terse nod.

Astra returned to her spot across from Grenedil, and sat down. "My companions and I are willing to take you closer to the border. You would be able to ride one of our mounts while you recover," she said in Litashian, remembering that they spoke the trade language. "We have matters of our own to attend to and must ride north; where our path turns from the border, we would part ways. But it will at least get you away from this village and the company of soldiers that rode into it earlier today."

"Wait...you...you're *helping* us?" Mitheau stood up abruptly, astonishment clear in every inch of her body.

"If you will accept it, yes," Astra replied.

Grenedil's eyes narrowed. "Why?"

Astra was struck by the sudden, strangely vivid memory of Keeshiff carrying her through the rain, helping her onto a horse and away from Tyron. "I have been in your place. We are simply doing for you what was done for us."

209

Neither of the fugitives gave an immediate answer, sizing up Astra and her companions in a mixture of shock and disbelief. At last, Grenedil breathed an unsteady, "Thank you. Then we are at your mercy."

"Thank him," Astra said, inclining her head towards Keeshiff. "It costs him the most." She stood up, taking a moment to steady herself. "We will go retrieve our mounts. Please pack your things—we must be off as soon as possible."

Grenedil inclined his head towards Keeshiff, "Thank you."

Keeshiff, lips pressed into a thin line, waved the thanks away. "Let's just get going," he said in heavily accented Litashian as he turned away.

CHAPTER XIII

Louko:

Louko didn't like this at all, and yet as far as he could tell, their story rang true. And that only made their situation worse. What were they supposed to do in the face of this? They *had* to help, and yet they barely knew these strangers. How did they know they weren't lying…?

Oh, but they knew. The fact they had been shielded by the villagers proved their claim about driving out thieves. And the girl looked so young...these were definitely no villains. No more than the rest of them.

They had traveled all through the night and most of the day, leaving everyone exhausted by late afternoon. Especially Astra. She looked so worn and so anxious. Yet he dared not say a word in the presence of their temporary companions.

So he kept quiet, instead helping with what he could—the fire, the unpacking of necessary supplies...the extra set of eyes on their mysterious new companions. Louko still didn't know what to think of them. A Drogan? The race, by a rule, was feared and shrouded in myths and half-truths. But then again, so was Astra.

As soon as the bedrolls had been laid, Louko saw Astra half-collapse onto hers. Then she sat back up as if remembering something. She hauled herself to her feet, went over to her things, and brought the chess set back to her sleeping mat.

"I don't know about you, but my feet are killing me," Keeshiff groaned as he sat down on his own bedroll, stretching.

The other fugitives were all doing the same.

Louko rolled his eyes. "Out of shape, hm? Maybe walking will do you good."

That's when he noticed Astra had paused in setting up the chess boards. Her brow was furrowed in bewilderment.

Louko realized suddenly that it was the turn of phrase that had gotten her confused. Ha. Elves and their language slips. His smile slowly grew. "What, Astra, tongue-tied?"

He saw Keeshiff turn and look at her.

"I think I am more tired than I thought…." Astra said slowly.

"I...I don't get it…." Keeshiff's confusion was open now, only furthering Louko's smirk.

"Astra has that little problem of not being able to *read between the lines*."

"I can if I know the lines," Astra shot back half-heartedly. She looked almost embarrassed when she added, "But I'll admit, I'm not really sure what one's feet have to do with murdering people."

Louko snorted. "I mean, honestly, you did kick me once and that was *pretty* deadly."

Astra's cheeks colored fiercely.

"I do believe that I've missed the joke." It was Grenedil who spoke, apparently observing everything from where Keeshiff and Mitheau had helped him sit.

Keeshiff chuckled. "I think I have, too, but apparently it's making Louko laugh, so I'm completely satisfied."

Giving a cough in an effort to control himself, Louko let them in on the jest despite Astra's feigned glares. "Elves have this nasty problem with turns of phrase. Things like 'oh my foot fell asleep' or, well, 'tongue-tied.'"

"My tongue is not tied," Astra grumbled.

"Wait, Elves?" Mitheau drew closer in visible interest. She cocked her head. "But aren't Elves, well, you know..." She seemed embarrassed. "...tall?"

Louko couldn't help but smirk at this, allowing Astra to answer.

A little reluctantly, she explained. "I'm only half Elvish, which seems to have let me inherit the downsides of both races. I have my father's height."

"Wait." Grenedil's tone did not match the humor that had been going back and forth, and Louko looked over, confused to find that the man's eyes were wide as he said, "You're...you're the Verzaer girl?!"

Astra went rigid, looking at Louko in alarm before asking in a low voice, "Where did you learn that name?"

"So you *are*...your brother is the king of—what are you doing out here?" Grenedil seemed in such a suddenly frantic state that even Louko was concerned, and he took a slightly protective step closer to Astra.

"What's it to you?" Keeshiff interjected, also drawing closer.

"Have you any idea how long I've been *looking* for you? I was on my way to Litash when Mitheau got caught—" He laughed. "And you just show up here all by yourself. I never—"

"—I'm *sorry*?" Louko was not in the mood for riddles, and after the last fifty thousand people that had wanted Astra for something or other, he wasn't exactly liking this.

He heard Astra stand up from behind him. "Explain yourself," she demanded.

"Right...sorry. I suppose that was a bad lead in. You see...oh, how to explain this...you, uh. Hm, no...."

"Would you spit it out?" Louko was surprised at his own vehemence.

Grenedil stopped his ramblings and stared at Louko for a good half a minute, and Louko realized all at once that the man's eyes looked much older than the rest of him. But there was also desperation in there, and desperation was something Louko both knew in himself and feared in others.

"Maybe we should all just calm down a moment." It was Mitheau who stepped forward, both hands raised in a placating gesture. "Please, we mean you no harm."

Louko heard Astra sit back down. "Explain yourself," she said again, each word with deadly evenness.

"Mitheau is right, I have no intention to harm you or any such thing. But what I'm about to tell you is not really as easy as a quick explanation. Though if I hazard a guess, you have issues controlling your Gift, don't you? Things you do that can't be explained through the rules of Gifting."

"If you are trying to impress me with some uncanny knowledge, I have to say that you're failing miserably—everyone knows that I've come into contact with the Miadoris and have been unstable ever since," Astra answered, with a coldness that surprised even Louko. "Try again."

Grenedil made a sort of startled noise, "Well, yes, I suppose that would cause issues in and of itself, but no. I'm talking about breaking the *rules* of Gifting. But anyway—" He waved his hand then stopped. "You know what, I give up. You're supposed to be the next Guardian of the

Doorway, but I can't find the original one because he got attacked by Ovok when he and his group laid siege to The Maze's doorway and left for Baeno, and I've been stuck here trying to find him or you because I can't get through into The Maze, and who knows *what* Ovok's been doing running loose in Baeno, or why he's there, or when he's coming back...and apparently my idiot brother leaked that you were the next Guard to Ovok's son-in-law, Tyron, and I was trying to find you before anything came of that...and.... This is such a mess."

Louko blinked, shifting on his feet as he tried to process the tangled mess of information. Maze what now? Ovok...wait, that Drogan? Tyron was his *son-in-law*?

"Was any of that supposed to make sense?" Keeshiff didn't seem to be asking anyone in particular, sitting down on the ground not far from Astra.

"Look, there's a lot more going on here than your small little world, and there's been no one but me trying to hold it together for the last ten years because of the mess Ovok made, and I was never meant to *communicate!* I don't know how to explain any of this to any of you." Grenedil's exasperation mirrored Louko's own boiling confusion.

"So, wait. Let's get this much straight; Tyron wants Astra because she's some Guard or something?" He turned to Astra. Was *this* what The Game was about?

Grenedil's brow furrowed. "Oh, great, Tyron's already come after you?"

Astra, face pale, pushed back her hood and traced the dark scar that curved from brow to cheekbone.

Louko winced.

"I'm sorry." Grenedil's words rang sincere. "I was too late, again."

Now, that was something Louko could sympathize with, but all the same, he kept his guard up and refused to sit.

"What *exactly* is he after?" Astra asked.

Mitheau took a deep breath, looking to her companion as she said, "Well, seeing as we have nothing to do for the rest of the evening, perhaps it's best if you start at the very beginning? I feel like you will make a little more sense if you start there. Just don't go full long-winded Myrandi odyssey on them? Otherwise, we'll all be dead before you finish."

Grenedil grumbled something along the lines of, "Which one of us is actually Myrandi," before nodding his assent and adding, "Let's just get settled and have some supper first."

Louko wasn't sure what to think of this, but Mitheau was right: They weren't going anywhere tonight, and if nothing else, it would get Astra to sit down and rest. Hopefully, it would also give them answers.

All those who had been on guard and on their feet now found a spot to sit. Keeshiff passed out the evening rations, which everyone pretended to eat while waiting for Grenedil.

"So, I suppose the simplest way to start is for you to look up," Grenedil began.

...Look up?

"See the two moons?" Grenedil went on. "The one with rings there is a world called Baeno. The smaller one, the one with all the white patches of clouds, is a world called Kryso."

Those were *worlds*? As in, lands full of peoples and cities and animals?

"Wait. Kryso? I've heard of that name—but...I thought it was just an ancient civilization or something lost from the Destruction of the West?" Louko piped in. "And Baeno...that's just a country out east, isn't it? I'd thought so anyway, with how incomplete the maps of Eatris are and all." In all honesty, he thought perhaps Kryso had been west—past the Wildlands where few dared go.

"No, not a country. A whole planet," Mitheau said with a shake of her head.

Grenedil took a deep breath and charged on, "Up until about two thousand years ago, these worlds interacted through the open Doorways. The three worlds are Eatris—obviously—Baeno, and Kryso. The Creator of the worlds gave each world a source, and he has always provided Guardians of the worlds, to keep them in relative order. The Myrandi—or the Drogans—were the most recent Guardians." He turned and looked to Mitheau, and Louko noted the pained expression the girl bore. "But they neglected their purpose and closed off the Doorways to the other worlds and, over time, the worlds faded into legend. Only three Drogans kept to the daunting task of keeping the worlds safe: Kassander, Xyridcylduin, and Ovok." The last name was said in a dark tone. "Ovok's wife killed Kassander, and then Ovok targeted Xyr—er, Cyl, as his friends called him. If Ovok has gotten off world, then he went through Cyl. But if the Doors to the worlds are still closed, then Cyl must be the one keeping them that way. I haven't managed to track down either one yet."

Louko perhaps would have been fascinated by this tale under any other circumstances; the falsified history he'd read had omitted any mentions of portals or such nonsense. Though...Grenedil had referred to the 'Doorway,' and now that he thought about it, Louko realized he'd seen mentions of doorways in various ancient history books. He'd just always chalked it up to a mistranslation or some antiquated term. He also recalled the vague account of Ovok disappearing well over a decade ago—but Nythril had made it sound like they had eradicated the Drogans; not that they'd *left*. Had Nythril known about the portals? Did his *uncle* know?

"Wait, I thought Nythril had killed all the Drogans?" Keeshiff broke in unexpectedly. "Now you're telling us they went to another *world*?"

"Yes. Dia Tzaro likes to...exaggerate the truth—especially when it gives them more glory. I don't know fully what Ovok wants, but his last irrational siege on the Doorway in Nythril was seemingly prompted by the death of one of his daughters, Rhioa. But I worry he is also trying to locate his replacement...." Now Grenedil was looking knowingly at Astra. "The Creator has decided three new Guards are to be raised up. Ovok has chosen his path, and with Kassander dead and Cyl presumably trying to hold up the Doorways on his own, it is time for new Guardians for the TetraWorlds."

"Woah, wait. The *Creator*? Sure. And how exactly do you know all this when you can't even get a *child* out of the country without getting found?" Keeshiff challenged.

Grenedil's sigh was an exasperated one. "Look, there is a lot more out there than your mind could possibly comprehend, and usually I'd have a lot more tools to work with, but I'm trying to run with what I have, and that's not much. But if you must know, The Creator has given many prophecies through the Living Stone—Baeno's equivalent of your Miadoris. I happen to know Alenor, the lady who is its keeper."

Mitheau interrupted, "And this prophecy stated a daughter of Elves and Humans would be one of the new Guards. Seeing as there hasn't been a Half-Elf since Astinian Fox over a millennia ago, and your only sibling is male, it was safe to assume it was referring to you."

Everyone looked to Astra now. In the dimming light, she looked more frail than ever. "How am I to guard a whole world when I cannot so much as protect my friends?" she finally asked. Then she shook her head and went on before Grenedil could speak. "So, what does all of this mean? Are you saying that Tyron is working under someone else's direction? And why come after me? 'Guard' or no, I know nothing of these other worlds that would be useful to anyone."

"There is no way for Ovok to communicate while he's off-world," Grenedil said with a shake of his head. "That's how I knew Cyl was still alive—he's the only thing preventing Ovok from returning. The Doors are almost all sealed except for a few back doors, and it seems Cyl is the one keeping them closed against Ovok's constant banging." He sighed. "As for Tyron's motivations...I don't know. All I know is that he wants to get off-world, and so he's coming after you to try and make you open a Door."

Louko saw Astra's hand go to her wrist. She looked at him with widened eyes. "That's what he was trying to do," she whispered.

She didn't have to specify; Louko knew she was talking about the castle.

"Is that even possible?" Astra asked abruptly, attention back on Grenedil.

"For you to open one? Yes...but you'd need Cyl to teach you."

Louko's brow furrowed.

Astra's frustration was evident. "So there is no way for me to even do what Tyron wants, and no way to convince him of such." Her voice turned bitter. "How marvelous."

Louko sat down and took her hand as discreetly as possible, the only form of comfort he could think to offer her. Of course it would end up like this; they'd finally figured out what Tyron wanted...only for it to be impossible.

Grenedil looked apologetic. "I'm afraid not. But we wouldn't want to give it to him, regardless. The three worlds are all in very...precarious situations at the moment. But that is a matter for me to worry about. For now, since I have *finally* found you...we need to get you off world and away from Tyron. As soon as Mitheau is safe."

"Off-*world*?" Astra echoed. Louko saw her shake her head and try to orient herself. "I don't think you quite understand—Tyron will do *anything* to get what he wants. He will go through every single member of my family and every last one of my friends if that's what it takes. If I disappear, I condemn them to death." She let out a sharp breath. "Who are you, anyway? How do you know all this? And if you are not one of these 'Guards,' how can you offer to get me off-world?"

Grenedil sighed in exasperation. "I am nobody. That is the problem...I was *supposed* to be assigned the role of The Merchant, but my *charming* brother stole it from me, and honestly that's half the reason the worlds are such a mess right now...."

Louko decided to jump in, then. "The Merchant?" He noticed the sour expression on both Grenedil and Mitheau's faces.

"Yes. A dumb name, really. But we are meant to work with the Guardians. I—well, The Merchant collects dangerous and rare items and keeps them out of the hands of those that would use them for ill. We have our own backdoors into The Maze—er, that's what the space in between the worlds and doors is called—but with all this chaos going on, and the fact that I am not *actually* The Merchant, my ability to help has been...limited."

"What of your brother, then?" Astra raised the question. "Is there no way to get your position back from him?"

"Not unless he offered it willingly. Which he was not inclined to do. Havirax is a jealous half-wit." Grenedil's jaw clenched. Apparently, tough family dynamics were a bit of a common thing. Great.

The circle fell quiet, everyone apparently trying to process this.

"So basically...." Keeshiff was rubbing the back of his neck. "This is all worse than we thought, and there's still nothing we can do about it. Did I miss anything?"

Yeah...that was about how Louko was feeling right now.

Grenedil ran his hands over his face. "I...I guess. I'm trying—I am. I'll come back with you after Mitheau is safe, and then we can all figure it out. If I could just get to one of the rifts, I could at *least* try and get through again to see what in the worlds is going on in Baeno."

"I suppose that brings up the other catch," Astra sighed. "We were sent by Dia Tzaro to capture you two, but we didn't do so willingly: He has several of our friends and will send them to Tyron if we don't return in two weeks' time. We cannot go to Litash."

The reminder knotted Louko's already tight stomach to the point of bursting.

Grenedil looked pensive. "I can help with that, too."

"So can I," Mitheau added with determination. Grenedil tried to interrupt her, but she plowed ahead. "I never said that I wanted to go to Litash, and I'm certainly not going without you."

"You *can't* stay here, Mitheau."

Louko felt uncomfortable, looking to Astra. It would...be rather nice to have a Drogan's help. But she was only a child, and the last thing Astra needed was another weight on her shoulders.

Mitheau opened her mouth with clear intent to argue.

"Look, it's late, we're all exhausted," Keeshiff spoke up from the side. "How about you two argue about it tomorrow when we have to ride all day just to keep from getting caught? I don't know about all you 'Guards' and 'Merchants,' but some of us are Human and still need sleep."

There was very little chance Louko would be able to sleep, and he knew Astra would be the same after all of this. Still, they had to try. Astra couldn't afford to keep running like this. "Yes. I suppose so," he replied with a sigh.

"Then I'll take first watch, and you all get some shut eye," Keeshiff said simply. "We have a long day tomorrow, followed by even more long days."

He was right, they did. Louko only hoped these long days wouldn't last forever.

So...Louko hadn't thought Mitheau would *actually* spend the entire day's journey arguing with Grenedil about going to Litash. But that was indeed what was currently going on. It had gotten to the point where Louko was concerned about them being heard, and he finally broke in with, "Can we please keep our voices down? We weren't the only ones looking for you, if you recall." He tried his best to be patient, but a poor night's sleep paired with the stress of all this new information was not exactly a good combination.

"Yes, *our* apologies," Grenedil murmured.

Mitheau huffed. "Stop treating me like a child."

From behind them, Louko heard Keeshiff grumble, "Stop acting like one."

"Excuse me, but need I point out that I am the oldest one here?" Mitheau looked over her shoulder with narrowed eyes.

"Uh, I'm...sorry?" Louko turned in his saddle so that he could look back at the girl. "You're...what?"

Her annoyance wavered for the first time all day. Adjusting her silver braid and tilting her head, she said, "I'm the eldest here, unless one of you happens to be older than sixty-three."

"You're kidding," Louko choked. Next, someone would be telling him unicorns existed after all.

Now Mitheau seemed to be enjoying his surprise. "Not at all. Myrandi are not considered to reach adulthood until we're a hundred years old— sometimes even later, depending on when we first molt."

He stared at her. "Oh...um...good to...know?" He turned to Grenedil. "I take it, however, her level of maturity is still quite that of a child, given the...arguing?"

Grenedil smirked and gave Mitheau a sideways glance before replying, "Indeed, she's quite the feisty little sprite."

"Little?" Mitheau puffed, stride lengthening. "I can be five times your size if I feel like it."

"Please don't," Louko interjected now, half joking...but only half. "I think my mind is blown enough for one day, and you're loud enough as it is."

"Well, having you on our side might be good for my men after all," Keeshiff mumbled as he walked.

"How do you two know each other, anyway? I mean...that makes her older than you are, right?" Louko's curiosity got the better of him.

Grenedil laughed. "Oh yes, older by numbers, for sure. But definitely not by maturity standards—ouch!" He cut himself off as Mitheau pinched him. "My brother and I were orphans taken in by the Drogans. Highly unusual, but our parents had been kind to them. Mitheau and I grew up together. Well. I grew. She sort of...stayed the same." He grunted as Mitheau elbowed him.

"You really should keep it down...." Keeshiff murmured.

The mood now sufficiently killed, everyone quieted into an unpleasant silence. Louko's nerves were just...so frayed. Nothing was going right, and it just felt like the further down the hole they fell, the less likely it was that they'd be able to climb back out again. The little voice in the back of his head just kept whispering worst-case scenarios until they echoed like the toll of a bell. What if they really couldn't get the knights out? What if they were sent back to Merimeethia? Executed or worse?

Such were Louko's less than optimistic thoughts as they traveled until dusk, Astra suffering in silence while Louko wished he could offer help. When at last they did stop, everyone was clearly exhausted and had caught on once more to the sense of urgency, quietly setting up a small camp and divvying up rations in silence.

Astra, however, seemed more interested in the chess boards. She set up the three boards despite the fading evening light.

Louko sighed and walked over. "I suppose this does change things...though I don't know how much it really helps to know what he wants." All those sleepless nights wondering, and it only added to the distress. Louko had somehow hoped knowing would help, not add another problem to the list. And yet, now the game seemed to make even less sense than before. He must have figured out Astra couldn't open the portal in his...experiments. But why The Game? Did he hope to somehow drive her to it some other way?

"Perhaps," Astra murmured, not taking her eyes from the boards as she played through all the moves they already knew. "But we still don't know what it looks like in the game, meaning we can't figure out how he plans to get there." She sat back and finally looked up. "And what happens when I can't give him what he wants?"

Louko registered the urge to move—to run his hand through his hair, or clench his teeth, or fidget...or…. He had to stay focused. He had to keep calm, so that Astra didn't have to feel alone.

"Then we'll deal with it." Louko wished that sounded a lot more convincing that it had come out. "But...still, we don't know *why* he wants off-world."

Astra put one hand to her temple and studied the marble pieces again. "What did he want when he left Merimeethia all those years ago? Was he after something in Alarune? Or was he looking for me, even then?"

"I...I'm not sure." Louko scowled in thought. How ironic it was that Louko had known Tyron for so long, and yet very little of his information on the man had ever been of use. Sometimes Louko wondered if Tyron had ever really cared about him at all, or if the man had always just been using him. The thought stung, but he pushed it out of his mind. It wasn't important.

Astra's brow furrowed. "Wait...didn't you say something once about my father traveling with him? How does that all fit in?"

"I don't know. He just used to come by. But wasn't your father caught by Tyron in The War? I suppose it could have been to keep an eye on him. Though I always thought it was because your mother was kept in Merimeethia."

It was a moment before Astra said, "Perhaps we can find a way to write to him once the knights are safe." Her expression seemed pained. "Him and my brother."

"Yeah, I'm sure you can." Louko was disgusted with himself for the way he'd forgotten Entrais and Astra's family. Everything had gone south so quickly, they had hardly come up at all. But come to think of it, Astra hadn't written Entrais since before the castle. And yet, nothing had apparently been done—no rescue party, no uproar in Litash. Why did that make him feel so angry? "But why don't you get some sleep, for now?"

He saw the way she swallowed before answering, "I suppose I am not getting anywhere. I might as well."

He didn't say another word, wishing he could offer comfort, but knowing anything was just empty promises, at this point. They were all alone in a foreign country, with no help, and time running low for their friends. Yes...perhaps sleep would help. Perhaps the morning would bring with it some refreshed hope. Louko could use some, about now.

A GAME OF WITS

Astra:

"Not so fast!" I call to the gold-and-white dragon flying ahead of me.

I am rewarded with only a rumbling, contagious laugh. "Or maybe you should just hurry up!" She arcs her wings and leans into the wind, a beautiful spiral of feathered gold in the cloudless blue sky.

How does she always take my breath away?

"To be fair, I haven't had as much practice as you have," I call ahead in Dragonspeak.

Only recently have I developed my wings, yet that has been enough time for me to find myself addicted to the rush of flying. To fly is freedom itself. I now understand why Rhioa always longs for the skies—I just can't figure out how she can stand her Human form so long.

Suddenly, I feel my strength waver. It's as if my wings are threatening to give out. Rhioa seems to feel it, too. I see her tail bobble in an effort to balance herself as we both lose altitude.

"Tyron?" she calls my name in question.

I start to reply, then get distracted by movement from the corner of my eye. It takes me a second to register that the movement has a blazing blue hue.

"Get down!" I shout in terror. "Rhioa, land!"

The gold-and-white dragon folds her wings and dives, but it is too late. The Essence slams into her from the side. For a moment, she is obscured by blue light. Then she reappears in Human form. Unconscious. Falling.

"RHIOA!" Her name is torn from my lungs in a scream.

I dive after her, pulling my wings in as close as I can to speed my dizzying descent. The green blur of the field below is broken only by the golden color of Rhioa's hair. I reach her only a few hundred feet from the ground and catch her as gently as I can in my talons. It feels like a wave of icy water hits me, and I am forced back into Human form before I can land. We both fall the few remaining yards into the field below.

I land hard but take no heed. The pain in my mind far overcomes the bruising of my body. I stagger to my feet and rush to my wife's side. My heart drops to see that her eyes are still closed, and I put a hand to her wrist to feel for a pulse.

At first, nothing.

Then, faintly, but very surely there, I feel her heartbeat.

My relief is dizzying but far from complete. I know I must get her back to the palace instantly.

"Hold on, Rhioa," I whisper as I shift back into dragon form and gather her up again. "Don't you dare leave me. Don't you dare give up."

I fly faster than I ever have before.

Astra woke with a scream stuck in her throat. Instinctively, she wrenched away from the figure in front of her.

"Astra, Astra it's me, Louko," the voice called as the figure backed away.

The words made little sense to her. But the voice—the voice stopped her. Still halfway between sitting and lying down, she gasped, "L-Louko?"

"Yeah. Yeah, it's me. Louko. That's right. Just try and breathe. You're safe." His words were said in between breaths, as if he had just run a very long way.

The horror of the scene she had just lived was moved aside only by anxiety for him. "What is it? What happened? Are you alright?" Astra tried to focus, willing her senses to right themselves. Where was she?

"What? Yes, are *you*? You screamed." Louko's eyes were wide.

It seemed too much information at once. She had screamed? She was suddenly aware of the wet leaves under her palms, and her blanket half wrapped around her. When she looked back to Louko, she could truly see him—worry was written all over his face.

Astra's throat felt thick. She opened her mouth to reassure him, but somehow heard herself say, "I saw her die. I saw Rhioa die."

The abruptness with which he got up from where he had been kneeling next to her was only outmatched by the way he feverishly murmured, "Water. You need water. Let me get you some," and with that disappeared.

Astra withdrew, bringing up her knees and wrapping her arms around them. She wished she hadn't said it. She wished it wasn't true. If her stomach wasn't so empty, she would have thrown up.

Louko returned as quickly as he had vanished, a canteen in hand as he knelt by her again, gently taking one of her hands and prying it away so that he could place the canteen in it. But Astra could not bring herself to drink. She wanted to recoil, to hide, to let the very ground swallow her up.

"It's okay. It's alright," Louko coaxed. He let go of the hand with the canteen and then very slowly took hold of the other one, leading it away from where it was gripping her legs. "It's alright," he said again.

It seemed a long time before Astra could say anything in reply. She sat there, gripping his hand and struggling to tame her ragged breathing. She kept hearing Tyron's voice as he screamed his wife's name, seeing that golden blur as she fell, feeling that shock as he reached her....

"It was the Miadoris," she realized, barely audible in her discovery. "Rhioa was hit by the Miadoris and she fell."

Louko acted as if he hadn't heard her. "Your voice sounds hoarse...drink a little?"

Astra was trembling. "No, no, did you hear what I said? I *saw* her."

"Yes," Louko whispered, "I heard you."

Astra released his hand. All the panic of her waking vanished, leaving exhaustion in its wake. She rested her head on her knees, squeezing her eyes shut and longing to shut out the world, too.

Louko didn't say a word, but Astra knew he hadn't left. She could feel his presence next to her.

"Is she alright?"

Astra jumped at the unfamiliar voice before recognizing it as Grenedil's. She recalled all at once their new companions and tried to collect herself. *Idiot.* She made herself sit up, despite the tight ache that protested in her left side.

"Yes, sorry, I'm alright." She hoped she didn't sound as raspy as she thought. Then she remembered Louko saying that she had screamed.... "I did not mean to disturb anyone's rest."

She must have woken them. Already, Grenedil and Mitheau stood near the low fire, and she could see Keeshiff sitting up just beyond.

"I don't think any of us were really sleeping," Mitheau replied for everyone.

This only made Astra more self-conscious, as it meant they had all witnessed her reaction. She felt sick. But she tried to get to her feet anyway.

"My apologies," was all she could find to say.

Louko was the one who replied, "Nothing to be sorry for. Now...please, I think you are still feverish." He gave her a worried look.

Astra didn't feel warm. No, she was still shivering. She shook her head and said, "I'm alright. I think I just want to sit by the fire a bit." They'd had to keep the blaze low to avoid detection, but anything would be better than her current state.

Louko didn't say a word, but neither did he take the canteen from her, only held out a hand to help her up.

"Are you sure you're alright, Astra?" Keeshiff called from his spot, clearly hesitant.

The public scrutiny made her wish she was invisible. But no such luck. She had to let Louko help her up in full view of the awkward little crowd.

"Yes, I am sure, thank you." Astra might have tacked on another apology if she had the breath for it.

No one said anything as Louko helped her over to the little fire that they'd dared to build now that they were in the cover of the forest.

Astra couldn't get Tyron's scream out of her head. "Do you still have my cuff?" she whispered.

"What?" Louko looked incredulous and something more akin to angry, fists clenched. "You can't be serious?"

Flinching away, Astra wished she could take the question back. But the weight of the memories was enough to make her say, "It might help stop them."

"But...it made you so sick—you're *still* sick. I don't think it's a good idea."

"What...happened?" Grenedil asked from across the fire.

Astra did not know if she could have answered, even if she wanted to. She kept her eyes fixed rigidly on the low tongues of flame, kept in by the fence of small stones as they lapped up the tinder. "Long story," she murmured.

"Are you seeing things...from the future? Did someone die?" Grenedil persisted as he sat across the fire from her, his chin resting against his hands.

She wanted to get up and walk away. She might have, if it wasn't so possible that they were being followed. "No, no, they're just..." Her voice withered away, and she had to choke out the last word. "...memories."

His brow furrowed.

"I don't think now is the best time to whet the appetite of your curiosity," Louko growled.

Astra put her hands to her head. Everything seemed so loud. Or maybe it was still Tyron's scream ringing in her ears.

Grenedil's tone went taut as he replied, "I would not prod for mere amusement. Depending on what ails her, I could search for something to help—after Mitheau is safe."

The thought was enough to make Astra look up. "Is there something that could do that?" she croaked. Then she faltered, glancing at Louko. Should she say all this aloud? Did it matter? Grenedil knew so much about them already.... "I...I keep seeing other people's memories."

"Well, depending on why, I'm sure there's something that can help you. That's what The Merchant was *supposed* to do, so I just have to track down my idiot brother who *is* The Merchant." Astra heard him mutter an 'unfortunately.'

Astra's hope dimmed. That did not sound particularly confident.

"Oh, I *will* find him. Don't worry," Grenedil added in a rush, as if sensing her dismay. "But I cannot help what you do not tell me. I know we just met...I know this is all...odd...but surely telling me can do no further harm than what is already going on?"

For a brief moment, Astra closed her eyes and made herself recall the dream. The feeling of wind under her wings, the unsteady moment, the flash of blue, then the golden figure tumbling towards the ground...and when she reached it, when she'd reached out her talons to catch Rhioa, there was a shock that had ripped through her entire body.

"It has to be the Miadoris." Astra opened her eyes. "I've touched it before. I've carried it—it gave me many people's memories. But now I only see Tyron's." She swallowed. "I think it has affected him, too."

Grenedil's brow furrowed, "I see...I'm sure there's something. Perhaps just something with Ithynian Gasper.... We'll want to stay away from anything that includes red bronze, though."

She forced her shoulders up in a stiff shrug. "I have worn it often to contain my Gifting."

"Red bronze is not a healthy permanent solution. No long-term inhibitor will have that. I would be careful using any of them."

Astra knew that red bronze was not always enough to keep her Gift in check, but it was still the only thing that offered any such shred of security. She already had too much terror swirling in her chest for this last comfort to be taken away. "I see few alternatives."

Grenedil gave a long stare but said nothing more.

"What are the long-term effects?" Louko—*of course*—asked.

Shifting uncomfortably, Grenedil replied, "It varies depending on the Gift. Eatrisian Gifting is a manifestation of the Miadoris, and, therefore, a manifestation of one's very life source. It technically cannot kill people in its raw form—as it will never attack itself. That's why Drogans have an adverse reaction to it; they aren't from Eatris and so the Miadoris sees them as foreign. But the greater the Gifting, the greater the person's reliance on the Miadoris for life." Grenedil glanced towards Astra and back to Louko. "So, to suppress a more Gifted person is to cut them off from a greater percentage of their life source. Long story short, they'll be far weaker."

Astra resisted the urge to put her hands back over her ears.

"Why would you want to wear something like that?" Mitheau's question was as incredulous as it was sincere.

It took effort to get the words out from between her teeth. "My Gifting is not always within my own control."

"But didn't anyone teach you?" The question was said with an air of obliviousness that Astra could not understand.

But Astra had given enough explanations for one night. She just shook her head.

"Why...?"

Astra felt Louko put his hand on her shoulder.

That sensation of falling, of choking on fear—it made it hard to breathe. She couldn't sort out what feelings were hers and which were Tyron's. Why couldn't they all be quiet? Why did they have to ask so many questions? Did they *really* want to hear of how she was driven from her home when she was just a child? Astra didn't care even if they did: She did not want to speak of it.

"There was no one who could," was her thin reply.

An awkward silence ensued.

"I think...I think I will take the burden of changing the conversation, because this is...." Keeshiff trailed off and waved his arms at, well, everybody. "I feel like it would be more beneficial not to grate on each other's nerves."

Astra did not argue. She wrapped a hand around one wrist and kept her mouth shut.

Astra did not sleep for the rest of the night, too afraid of what she might see. She lay under her blanket and hoped that dawn would be enough to dispel the dark of her dream. She could hold on that long.

When light came, it came cold, clear, and heavy with exhaustion. Astra did not want to get up. None of the others seemed any better off as they set to hiding the evidence of their little camp. In the half hour it took, no one said a single word.

It wasn't until after some breakfast, and after they'd traveled long enough to warm up, that Keeshiff cleared his throat and asked, "So what are we going to do once we get back to the capital?'"

"Well, we have to locate where the knights are being held, first of all," Louko replied. "The question is how to get in the city and not be seen...."

He was right. They all had pretty defined features: Keeshiff was too clearly Merimeethian, Mitheau's hair was extremely unnatural for a child, Louko was, well, Louko, and Astra....

"I could probably get inside," Grenedil offered.

"Maybe we could contact Aelor Ven." Astra looked to Louko, unsure. "Even if he cannot help us outright, he may be able to tell us where the knights are being held or provide a map of the palace."

"*If* he helps us," Keeshiff murmured. "I mean, the man's first in line for the throne. Why, exactly, is that so? He has to get along well with Dia Tzaro, somehow." The shot was almost accusing.

Astra would be lying if she said the thought had not crossed her mind. But seeing the lord's perpetual concern for Louko had convinced her that, whoever's side he was on, Aelor Ven would never purposefully harm his nephew. The question was just whether that same guarantee extended to the rest of them.

"Yeah. I wouldn't rely on him." Louko's voice rang bitter.

"Wait. You have an in with the KingsHeir?" Grenedil broke in, mouth agape.

"I don't know. He seems just in this for himself," Louko replied. "I don't know if it would be good to let him know we have returned. For all I know, he'd turn Astra over. It's not like he likes Litashians to begin with."

The blunt evaluation did not sit well with what Astra recalled of Louko's uncle. But before she could voice as much, Keeshiff turned the conversation back.

"Do you think they would have sent any of the knights already?" he asked, anxiety evidenced by his shortened step and terse voice.

"We still have time left before Dia Tzaro claimed he would." Louko's show of confidence seemed thinner than spring ice. "We'll be able to get back to the city with time to spare."

"He wouldn't gain anything by sending his bargaining pieces away early," Astra added, trying to remain encouraging.

Keeshiff only grunted acknowledgement, but he did seem a little less downcast.

"Well, as far as getting them out goes," Grenedil mused aloud, "My guess is that they'll be kept in the Orshian Tower. How many men are there?"

"Eight—wait, no, nine. Rhumir's there, too, isn't he...." Keeshiff sighed and rubbed the back of his neck. "Yeah. Nine."

Astra tried to remember the layout of Kythdexlentu-Orsha. It was going to be hard to try and get nine people, as well as themselves, out.

"Then the Orshian Tower is our best bet. It's their most secure cell, usually used for political prisoners." Grenedil snorted. "And right on the palace grounds for political convenience."

Oh, right. Grenedil had been the one to get Mitheau out. He knew more of this than most would.

Speaking of, Mitheau looked rather nervous and was keeping her head down as she walked. Astra did not have to ask why; she understood.

"So, how did you break into it last time?" Louko asked.

Grenedil's mouth twisted into something more like a grimace than a smile. "I didn't. Being above ground is an advantage to the Myrandi, so they kept Mitheau elsewhere. If I remember correctly from the prints, the only way through the Orshian Tower is by going up several stories of stairs and trap doors—we'd never make it in that way."

Astra noticed how Mitheau shuddered.

"What about the roof?" Louko seemed to be thinking aloud. "I mean, if it's just meant to keep people from getting down, they'd have no reason to fortify the roof."

Now, everyone looked to Mitheau. The girl responded by lifting her chin. "A few shingles would be nothing to the talons of a Myrandi."

Astra saw Grenedil's jaw go taut. But he did not argue.

"That's a start." Keeshiff sounded nearly hopeful. "Now, all we need is a way to get everyone out of the city."

And out of Nythril…. Astra wondered where they could even go. She decided to keep the question to herself for the time being. Best to take this one step at a time. Or, perhaps, one round of The Game at a time.

The rest of the day wore away in the same weary fashion, each traveler consumed by their own worried thoughts as they trudged on. At least now they had some semblance of a plan. Astra only feared that Tyron somehow knew this, too. Would they break into the Orshian Tower and find nothing but another parchment note?

And then there were the memories. The many shades of sunset that filtered through the trees usually lifted Astra's heart, but now the golden color made her chest grow tight. She had never been so thankful for the call to stop, for it gave her something to do—something to focus on besides the terror that wasn't even hers. Could Tyron see hers? Did he feel her fear? Or did he simply take the chance to learn more about their plans?

A small fire was built, food distributed, and watches assigned. Astra was not allowed to take one, so Grenedil volunteered. Since she could not seem to focus anyway, she did not protest. She curled up on her bedroll and tried to find a way to rest that wouldn't make her left side ache so badly. Then she lay there and listened as her companions all drifted off to sleep, their deepened breathing audible even above the low murmur of the wind.

As exhausted as she was, Astra could not join them. Not when she saw that horrible memory every time she closed her eyes. What if she got another one? Or what if it showed more to Tyron? Not even her leaden limbs were enough to quiet her scattered mind, and the night hours slid by without reprieve. Surely it was nearly dawn.

And then she heard it. Astra sat up. The sound was nearly imperceptible—even for her. By the time she realized what was about to happen, the only thing she could do was shout, "Ambush!" before the nets came down.

It was as if Astra had been hit by a sack of rocks. She was pinned to the ground, gasping for breath, when the war cries split the air. They were followed by the screams of horses—of Dannsair. Adrenaline spiked, and she fought against the metal chain link that held her down. It was so cold, so very heavy.

Then she heard Louko shouting her name and her mind returned to Tyron, screaming as his wife fell. Something shifted.

With a flash of blue, the metal net fell to pieces around them. Astra staggered to her feet with a strength she hadn't felt in months. She had no sword, yet spared that no thought as she stood between her friends and the ring of warriors that had ensnared them.

"Stay back," she hissed, hands out in warning. Blue rose up like a wall around the camp.

"Are you so sure you want us to?" It was warped by the barrier, but the voice was unmistakably female.

Astra's gaze snapped sideways to where a woman in dark armor stood, her sword leveled to Keeshiff's throat.

Astra did not release the shield. There had to be a way out. *Something!* If she could just get Keeshiff inside the barrier, she could try to transport everyone out of here.

A cry of pain shattered her focus.

"Mitheau!" Grenedil lunged to her aid. "Wait, Astra, you're hurting her!"

Astra looked over her shoulder to see Mitheau, free of the net and yet on her hands and knees. Her face was twisted in a horrible grimace.

"Drop the shield and everyone may actually survive this," the woman in armor said. A thin line of dark red appeared on her blade.

"Stop!" Now it was Louko yelling.

Astra felt soldiers battering away at the shield.

It was all too much. She had to act now, or there would be no more chances. So she dove deep into the sea of blue, reaching for power that she'd never dared to acknowledge. She tried to pull it up and send the waves towards Keeshiff and all those within the wall. In response, the rush of energy swelled. But Astra could not make it back to the surface.

The wave collapsed and she felt herself sucked back in as everything went blue. A sound like a ringing in her ears grew till it was deafening. Then silence. And the world went black.

A GAME OF WITS

CHAPTER XIV

Louko:

"Stop!" Louko yelled as he, again, stood helpless. When Astra collapsed right in front of them, he couldn't help but scream her name. She could be dead—what if she was dead?!

The barrier that had been protecting them dissolved, and with it the woman holding Keeshiff released him with a shove, sending Louko's brother flying to the ground.

"Leave him alone!" Louko growled.

The woman turned on him, her steely almond eyes tearing into him. "My great uncle will be *very* interested to know why you were fraternizing with the criminals instead of bringing them in."

Oh, no. The king's niece: Dia Jahng.

The woman made a motion to Louko's sword, and he dropped it. He tried to go to Astra, but was intercepted and restrained by some of the soldiers.

"You harm a hair on their heads, and I swear I'll kill you myself." Every word was said with a poison that held no danger. For they were caught, and the fear in Keeshiff's eyes as he was pulled from the ground by Jahng's soldiers only proved the gravity of their defeat.

"Oh, yes. Prince Louko, the lost prince everyone so loves to pine after." The woman sheathed her sword as the others who were still conscious were restrained and put in cuffs. "You'll be *happy* to know that

243

I can't legally arrest you, thanks to your uncle. But I am taking you back to the capital where you'll be...less trouble." She walked over to Astra's limp form as she spoke.

Louko pulled at the steeled grip of his captors, trying in vain to put himself between Jahng and his friend.

Kneeling down, the woman felt for Astra's pulse and then snapped her fingers at a few more men, commenting, "*This* is Litash's hero? This is the General of Dragons?" And then she turned to Mitheau, who was still gasping for air as she was being dragged away. "I kill Dragons." Jahng's voice was cold.

With that they were led away. It was clear Jahng had indeed been prepared, for Mitheau was thrown into a metal, box-like cart, barely large enough for a single person. Keeshiff was locked in manacles and chained to the back of the cart. When Grenedil's wounded leg was discovered, he was bound at the wrists and made to ride behind one of the mounted soldiers.

Astra, still unconscious, was chained and put on the back of a horse. Louko saw the red bronze. How did they even have it here in Nythril? His heart plummeted at the thought: Had Tyron given the king some?

"Woah! Get back!" A soldier's shout was followed by the thudding of hooves and a horse's squeal.

It was Dannsair, kicking down two of the men and twisting around to bite another.

"Oh, shoot it already before it kills someone!" Jahng shouted.

"No!" Louko yanked against the man holding him. "I can calm her down—just let me go!"

Jahng looked at him with such contempt that he thought she would refuse him. But then she waved a hand. "Let him try. If the horse kills him, it's one less problem for us to worry about."

Louko's captor let go of him reluctantly, and the prince all but ran up to the horse, putting his hands out and whispering desperately, "Dannsair, please, I know—but if you don't calm down they're going to kill you and then you can't help Astra. Please. We'll figure something out—"

The horse pounded the ground with both front feet, snorting and eyeing the Nythrilian soldiers warily. Louko dared to reach forward and grab her halter, relieved when he was not bitten in response. Cautiously, he pulled in closer.

"If you're dead then we won't be able to help Astra. I—please don't do this to her."

The mare's ears flicked forward and back before pinning flat against her neck. But then she relaxed them, lowering her head in submission.

"Well then. You're leading that animal all the way back to the capital, and if she causes any trouble, I'll put an arrow in her myself. Understood?" came Jahng's contemptuous order as she mounted her steed.

Clutching Dannsair's halter rope, Louko nodded mutely.

"But no riding her. I don't feel like tracking our little lost prince down again. Besides, a little walking might do you good. It's about time people stopped waiting on you hand and foot."

If he was not so dazed and panicked over Astra and the others, he would have been thoroughly confused by the remark. But he couldn't stop the rising fear.

Dawn came, even as reality became a nightmare. The others were pulled into motion and forced to follow the cart, and Louko was only made to walk with Dannsair, close to some other dismounted soldiers and yet clearly given a wide berth so that they were out of kicking range. Panic coursed through every muscle in Louko's weary body. Again, he was untouched. Just like the castle. And again, he was watching: helpless.

It had been a day and a half, and Astra had not woken until that morning. Of course, then she had promptly been tied to the cart with Keeshiff, and Louko was barely able to restrain Dannsair, watching in agony as Astra stumbled to keep up with the cart. It was subtle, but he knew. She was fading. The red bronze was too much—just like he feared.

And Dia Jahng hardly said a word besides the occasional order to her men. There were about fifteen of them, all in full armor and each with a mount. Louko realized now that they were the same group he and Astra had seen at the village of Tehng.

"You can't expect them to walk all the way back to the capital." Louko was barely civil as he walked beside the woman, one hand stroking Dannsair in an attempt to keep her calm. The glares she was giving Dia Jahng were enough to kill, and the last thing Louko needed was for the mare to kick the woman's horse and end up getting shot as punishment. If everything else didn't kill Astra, Dannsair's death definitely would.

"Why? Are you tired already?" Dia Jahng did not even look at him as she spoke.

Louko's reply was vehement as he watched Astra stumble. "Says the person on her high horse."

There was a sound, and Louko turned to find Dia Jahng dismounting, taking the reins of her horse and leading it on. She was now walking beside him. At least she seemed smart enough to keep on the opposite side of Dannsair.

"Astra? Astra, are you okay?" Keeshiff's soft questions instantly sent Louko's attention back to his friend.

Especially when she did not reply.

Astra's shoulders were drooped as if the weight of the manacles was too much for her to carry. Sweat glistened on her forehead even while she shivered in the breeze. And she kept stumbling. Stumbling, then recovering, then stumbling again. Then she fell to her knees and was pulled forward onto her hands.

Dannsair gave a sharp squeal.

Louko made a bolt for his friend, but a soldier promptly cut him by wheeling his horse in front of him, prompting Dannsair to stomp the earth and snort in a clear threat.

"You're going to drive her to her *death*!" Louko shouted as he watched Keeshiff helping her up, the cart having stopped.

"She is fine. We'll stop soon." Jahng's reply was cold, and then she yelled up at the cart, "Be mindful of your speed, Ghazo!"

The cart lurched forward again and the procession resumed. Louko could not catch what was being said, but he saw Keeshiff speaking and Astra nodding. But he also saw the way Astra gripped her chains and used them to help keep herself upright.

"She is going to get *killed*. Please, give her a horse," Louko begged above Dannsair's whinnies.

"Why?" Jahng's question was unforgiving.

Louko looked aghast. "She is *hurt*, don't you see that?"

Jahng glanced again at the prisoners walking behind the cart. "So you say. But I do not see any wounds."

"Right, she's just *falling* and gasping for air. Are you mad?"

The woman's jaw clenched, and for a moment, Louko thought she would not reply. And then she shouted, "The little prince wants us to stop. Poor thing. Let's make camp."

At the next level spot, the group pulled to the side of the road. Astra collapsed the moment the cart stopped.

"Stay here. I'll check on her, but you need to be good or you'll get us all in trouble, understand?" Louko whispered to Dannsair as he secured her to a tree. The horse snorted, but bowed her head in understanding, and without wasting another second Louko turned and ran for his friend. No one stopped him this time.

"Astra, are you alright, do you need water?" He practically fell to his knees beside her, Keeshiff sitting down hurriedly on the other side. They were not released from the cart.

Astra's breathing was rapid and shallow. She gave no answer besides a nod.

"No," Keeshiff was the one who spoke. "You're not."

Louko's hands were shaking as he reached one up to feel her forehead just as a soldier came by and handed Keeshiff a canteen. Astra felt dangerously warm. Keeshiff handed Louko the canteen and he took it, putting Astra's bound hands around it and helping her drink.

"You're going to be fine," Louko mumbled. "We'll figure it out. You're going to be alright."

"What's wrong with her?" Jahng's question carried across the space.

248

"Oh. She was just held prisoner and experimented on for a couple weeks. That's all," Louko spat vehemently. "But glad you care. Thanks for asking."

Jahng registered no reaction. "Zhahn, give her a look over and report back. Prince Louko, step away. I don't need you plotting their escape, thank you."

Louko grabbed Astra's hand, frantic at the thought of leaving her. No, no, no.

Astra, too, began to shake her head. "No." Her protest was hoarse as the soldier—Zhahn—knelt beside her. "Don't touch me."

Louko felt a hand on his shoulder and heard a deep voice. "Prince Louko, please come away."

"No, please. I won't say a word—"

"—I gave you what you wanted. Don't keep asking for things, it only proves you're a brat, little prince," Jahng called again. "Now come sit by the fire and let Zhahn look at her."

Keeshiff put a cuffed hand over Louko's. "I'll take care of her." His reassurance was earnest, though it did little to quell Louko's panic.

Astra said nothing more. Louko felt her push the canteen back into his hands.

"No, no, keep it." He gave it back, watching as the soldiers chained Grenedil next to Keeshiff. "Everyone needs some." And it had been given to Keeshiff, anyway.

He left the canteen, but that was all he had time for before he was pulled away, to the fire their captors had created. There he was sat down, forced to be in their company for the evening. He wasn't even a prisoner.

WHY. All he wanted to do was scream, but instead he could only glare daggers at Jahng.

"Here." One of the soldiers handed him a bowl and gestured to the large pot over the fire. "For when that's done."

"Are they going to be fed?" He didn't bother with civility as he took the bowl.

"We aren't monsters, little prince," Jahng answered.

Louko just scoffed. "Could have fooled me."

But another one of the men was already handing out hardtack to those in chains.

"What about Mitheau?" Grenedil asked as he took his. "Can't you let her out of the cage to sleep?"

"So she can turn Dragon and murder us all?" Jahng spat. "I'm not naive."

"You have her chained by the neck, the feet, the hands; she's lucky if she can lift her head." Grenedil sounded as on edge as Louko.

There was silence, and Louko noticed how everyone was watching the woman, waiting for her command.

"Very well." She turned with a glower to the soldier who had been driving the cart. "Don't give her so much as an inch."

The man nodded, looking nervous, and went to do his superior's bidding.

The barred door was unlocked and Mitheau was helped out. She looked pale and frightened, all of her movements clumsy and slow. She allowed the soldiers to assist her even as she tensed at their touch. They sat her down right next to the cart, chained her to it, and gave her some hard tack.

The soldier they'd called Zhahn got up from his post by Astra and Keeshiff, returning to the fire. Addressing Jahng, he frowned slightly. "She wouldn't let me near her. The other prince told me that she's been fevered for at least three days. She looks pretty frail. I gave the prince something to help her sleep so that he could get her to take it." He paused, uncertain again. "She has some interesting scars on her wrists. Seemed pretty recent."

Louko noted how Keeshiff had known Astra had been so sick and tensed at the remark on the scarring.

"Thank you," was all Jahng said, eyes set on Louko before narrowing.

Louko broke contact and looked over to those by the cart, the sun having gone down so quickly that he could barely make out the shadows of his brother and friend, let alone the others.

"Soup's ready," a soldier announced, and with that held up a ladle to beckon everyone bring their bowls.

Louko did not budge. How could he? How could he even think of it? It made him sick thinking how he was just sitting there, technically free and given proper food while the others were chained and forced to walk and be confined.

"Someone serve the prince," Jahng said in monotone. "He's not used to having to get his own."

The man who'd announced the food laughed and brought over a ladle's worth of soup. "Don't worry," he said in an apparent attempt at humor. "We have to bring her some, too."

Louko gave no reaction.

And nor did he have to, for suddenly a wooden bowl came flying out of nowhere and hit the man on the shoulder.

251

"See?" He defended himself with the now empty ladle. "If we don't, she attacks us."

Wildly lost, Louko looked towards Jahng. Her expression was twisted up in what first seemed temper, only to give way to the smile she was fighting.

"Maybe I wouldn't do so if you weren't so slow about it."

"*Sorry*, Your Highness." A bow followed the sarcastic remark. "I'll try and do better."

The banter continued, similar to that of Keeshiff and his men, but only sickening to Louko. At last, unable to stand it any longer, Louko broke in with, "I mean, my friends are all over there chained to a cart and, you know, dying, but good to know you're all having a good time."

The camp went quiet. Everyone was staring at him.

Until someone started chuckling.

It was Grenedil, dry and humorless. At least everyone was now staring at him instead....

"Oh, is this the awkward moment where I'm supposed to stop laughing?" the man called over when he noticed their attention. "I'm too busy wondering what sort of reply you're going to come up with to rationalize all of this."

Louko scoffed, knowing they would not give such an answer.

"Dia Jahng is answerable to no one but the king himself," Zhahn said firmly. "She does not have to explain herself to wanted criminals."

"Glad to know she hides behind her men, instead." Louko hoped his words cut.

He saw the way the soldiers looked to Jahng. Louko also saw the slight shake of her head. No one said anything more after that.

Louko didn't sleep. He stayed up, alert throughout the night as he wondered in dread what could be happening to Astra. What would happen to Keeshiff...and what would happen to all of his men? Jahng took watch for most of the night, and that only made him more on edge, fearing what she could or would do if no one watched to make sure. Paranoia was an understatement, and when the dawn finally came, he was only worse. For they quickly packed up, preparing to leave as if nothing was wrong. Louko didn't see how they could keep going on like this—not when Astra and Mitheau were both so obviously ill. He knew if they did, that Astra wouldn't last the journey, and that only brought back the strong apprehension that had been his ever-present companion during the castle.

The sound of scraping metal made Louko look back towards the cart. The soldiers, with limited success, were trying to get Mitheau back in the cart.

"Wait, no," she pleaded. "I can walk. I won't escape. Just don't put me back in there."

"Sure," one of the men scoffed. "So you can kill us all."

"Please. *Please*." Even Louko was startled by the amount of struggle Mitheau put up as she began thrashing like a cornered animal.

Louko was about to shout something when suddenly, someone else did.

"Leave her be," Grenedil growled. "You all wonder why the Myrandi lash out, and then turn around and treat them like *animals*. You're the reason we're in this mess in the first place. She's just a *child!*"

Louko hardly registered the pain that emanated from his hands as he clenched Dannsair's halter lead, only taking his eyes off Jahng to check on Astra. She had not said a word. And if Astra was not saying a word in this...she had to be very sick.

Jahng stood in rigid silence, narrowed eyes surveying the scene before her. Then she turned to Mitheau. "You understand that your kind has killed many of my own family, and I will have no trouble killing you should you try *anything*."

Mitheau was nearly trembling. "I won't, I won't, I swear. Please just don't put me back in there."

"Very well." She turned to her men. "Take off the foot shackles. Leave the neck collar—if she tries anything, that will stop her." Jahng turned to face Louko but didn't say a word...only stared.

"And are you going to give my friend a *horse*?" Louko snapped at almost the same time Dannsair pawed the ground.

Dia Jahng's expression was like stone. "If she is that ill, she can ride with one of my men."

Relief did not even have time to register. As soon as the soldiers tried to unchain Astra from the others, she began to resist.

"Don't touch me—*don't touch me!*" He heard her hoarse cry.

Keeshiff tried to calm her but to no avail.

"Fine." Jahng flicked her hand in irritation. "Clearly, she's well enough to fight against us trying to *help* her, so she's fine to walk." She glared at Louko. "I don't take orders from you, *Prince* Louko, so stop testing my patience. Now, we need to get going." And with that, she gave the signal to her men.

All Louko felt was a numbness...panicked numbness as he helplessly continued to watch everything happen around him.

Astra:

Just make it around the next bend. Each leg felt leaden as she stumbled forward, using the chains that bound her to try and steady herself. They reached the bend in the road. *Now just make it to the next one.*

Astra tripped over a rut, sending her to her already bruised knees. Her head swam with swirling flashes of color.

"I've got you, I've got you," she heard Keeshiff say.

She was vaguely aware of him helping her back up.

"You really should ride with someone, Astra," he murmured as he carefully gave her his arm for support, even though he could hardly stay steady himself with his own exhaustion.

The thought of any of these strangers touching her made her sick. But she did not dwell on it long. She couldn't. The mind-numbing miles of road wore away any possible thought. All she could feel was pain, fear, and putting one foot after the other.

They took a break at midday. Astra was too exhausted to eat much more than a few bites of the dry bread and cheese they passed out. Even without the blanket they had given her last night, she fell asleep and did not wake until Keeshiff roused her. She could not get back up without his help.

Somehow, resting made the road that much harder. Every time Astra fell, it took her longer to fight her way back to her feet. Her mouth was dry, her hands cold, the chains biting into her skin. Finally, she took too long in getting back up, and the momentum of the cart pulled her to the ground.

Somewhere, Astra vaguely registered Dannsair's high-pitched whinny.

"Stop the cart!" It was Louko, whose voice blended with Jahng's as she shouted the same thing.

The order was promptly obeyed, and soon Keeshiff was again helping Astra to her feet.

"You are going to *kill* her, Jahng!" Louko sounded almost frightening in the way he shouted.

"She is going to kill herself," Jahng snapped back. "I offered to let her ride, and she was the one who refused. I'm not exactly sure what your country's conception of prisoners is, but I actually treat mine better than most—even though I had two more of you than was expected. The food and blankets you all have enjoyed have been at the cost of me and some of my men going without. The breaks we give you are more frequent than we ourselves take, and the delay puts us even lower on rations." Her motions were brisk as she gave a mocking sort of bow. "But I suppose I can't expect a *prince* to understand that. How could I ask someone who's never worked a day in his life to be patient with those who are actually held accountable for their actions?" She thrust a finger in Astra's direction. "But if that princess could realize that her stubbornness is only hurting herself and others, maybe she would let us help her and we could all get back to the capital."

Guilt was one of the few things Astra could register over her panic.

"You have *no* idea what she has been through—leave her alone! You seem to be the one hiding behind your men."

Louko's harsh words and even harsher tone only frightened Astra more. He was going to get himself in trouble. "Louko—"

"Hiding from what, exactly?" Jahng seemed nothing but annoyed. "You? Your broken friends? None of you are as intimidating as you seem to think."

Louko glared at her. "Oh?" That one word, calmer than the rest, somehow scared her more than the others. "You think you're *so* much better?"

Jahng rolled her eyes. "I think I've had enough of your tantrums. Get back in line." She motioned for her men to start moving again. "Bear in mind that, while I can't have you arrested, I will gladly have you *gagged*."

In a confusing move, Louko let go of Dannsair's lead rope and took off his jacket in a seeming fit of rage, throwing it down in front of Jahng.

"Oh...Louko, you idiot. Of *course*, you went there...." Astra heard Keeshiff groan from beside her.

Astra looked to him in bewilderment, not understanding the gesture, but not having the breath to ask.

"What in Eatris are you doing, *little prince*?" Jahng's voice held disgust. "Pick that up before you get yourself hurt."

"No." Louko sounded more certain than Astra had heard him in months. Or perhaps ever. "I was under the impression one couldn't take it back until *after* the duel, anyway. And if I win, I claim my prize as riding this horse with Astra." He pointed back at Dannsair. "What is *your* claim, *Dia* Jahng?"

Wait—it was a duel?! What was he *thinking*?!

"It's too late," Keeshiff said under his breath, holding her back as if in expectation. "He can't back out now."

"Fine, I accept your claim," Jahng spat. "If I win, my claim is that you ride in the cart and keep your mouth *shut*."

"Sounds exciting." The grin on Louko's face held no amusement. "Now, is someone going to give me a sword, or am I supposed to just tackle you?"

There was a ripple of nervous chuckles from Jahng's men, but someone slowly came forward and provided the prince with a weapon. What was he *doing?* Louko hadn't sparred with anyone since before the castle!

She watched desperately as her friend whispered something quietly to Dannsair, and the horse's ears pinned back as she took a few steps backwards. Something stuck in Astra's throat as for a moment she found Dannsair staring at her, distress showing in every muscle of the mare's body.

Then her attention was turned back to her friend as he pointed his sword in Astra and Keeshiff's direction. "My brother will act as post for your side, and you may choose a man to act as post for mine."

"Very well. If he tries anything during the match, I will have him executed," Jahng warned as she flicked a finger to order Keeshiff unchained. "And I'm a woman of my word."

"*Oh yes, the precocious honor of the Nythrilians. Or should I say hypocritical?*" Louko gave an idle swing of his blade, and Astra realized Louko had now switched to Merimeethian. The fact was especially clear by the look of confusion on the other soldiers' faces.

But Jahng seemed to understand. Her face was red as she replied, "*Better than the puffed fancy of a Merimeethian.*" She spoke the language with the familiarity of a scholar, not as a native.

Unease was added to Astra's anxiety as the soldiers unlocked Keeshiff and brought him away from the line. Without his help in standing, she was forced to sit in the road. Still chained to the cart. Still helpless as her friend fought for her sake.

A man was posted behind Louko, and Astra watched as Keeshiff was given the same position near Jahng, the latter of which was already matching Louko's movements with the blade.

"*Call to begin when you're done, well, showing off.*" Jahng's tone was crisp and stiff even as the rest of her showed ease and preparation.

Louko cocked his head, the unnatural shift in character almost akin to madness. "*Well, I don't see a reason to wait. Let's get started.*"

And then, just like that, the dance began. Sword met sword in a frightening flurry as they locked, eyes ablaze and jaws set. Astra couldn't breathe, but if she'd had the strength she might have screamed.

"*You know what your problem is?*" She could just hear her friend's voice above the clamor of footwork and blade. "*You're so caught up in your own selfish thoughts of revenge that you don't see what's right in front of you.*" He swept his sword at Jahng's feet and the blade was caught in an expert move by her own, Louko jumping back a moment in retaliation and waiting for her move. "*I know who your parents were. Drogan Hunters. They're one of the reasons everyone thinks the beings are extinct. And honestly, if your treatment of them is any indication, I'm not surprised your parents were killed by them.*"

Jahng did not leave him waiting long, using her momentum to bring her blade around at an angle and down towards his shoulders. "*Selfish? You know nothing of me, nor of my family.*" There was a metallic ringing as Louko parried. "*At least I'm not famous for murdering mine.*"

Louko just smiled. "*I hope that makes you feel better.*" He made a side-swipe that was quickly parried away. But Astra had seen Louko fight enough to know that he was simply testing the waters. "*I mean, look at you, all high and mighty. You managed to capture a sick girl after she'd just been to death's door and back. Oh, and let's not forget the child you locked in a practical windowless cage for two days. You're right, she won't have nightmares about that. Silly me.*" His approach changed, and suddenly Louko held no hesitance, each move a flurry of calculated expertise that seemed cold compared to the heat of his rage. Astra had never seen him like this.

Jahng, too, appeared caught off guard, frustration edging into every blow she parried and every one she dealt on Louko.

"*And for someone who hates Merimeethians so much, your great uncle works with them a lot.*" Louko jumped out of the way of one of her aggravated thrusts. "*But what do I know? I'm just a murderer.*" He rolled his eyes.

"*My great uncle is many things,*" Jahng sidestepped and stabbed forward again. "*But you're a fool if you think he has any love for Merimeethia.*"

"*No, you're right. But he's a spiteful little thing, just like you. And he does enjoy others' discomfort. Must be a family trait.*" He spun around behind her and nearly got past her guard, only to be blocked again. But Louko didn't appear fazed. In fact, he didn't appear to be working at all—

he now appeared reckless, completely careless of the outcome of the match. *"But why put this all on you now."* He shook his head and changed his tone to that of a mother addressing a child. *"You look tired, stressed, fatigued."* Again, his sword swiftly found its way around her guard, nicking a button from one of her sleeve cuffs. *"Bad food? Hard bed? I know how you feel—"* He ducked as she swung at him, and Astra saw the anger that had permeated every inch of the woman.

"Oh, wait." He swung at her legs and she jumped back, losing her balance. *"I don't, because I'm a prince. And frankly I don't care how you feel, seeing as you've shown little sympathy for any of my friends."* Her sword went flying in the air, and Louko caught it by the hilt and held both his own borrowed weapon and his opponent's to her neck. *"Yield,"* he growled.

Still on her knees, shoulders heaving as she panted for breath, Jahng did not immediately reply. Every soldier in the group stood strained and listened. Astra listened with them.

Finally, Jahng said in Nythrilian, "I yield."

Louko did not release. Astra began to fear that he did not intend to.

But then, still rigid, Louko dropped his stance and offered Jahng her blade back, hilt first. The woman was slow to wrap her fingers around it, and even more hesitant to take the hand Louko offered her afterwards. But she did so without a word. She brushed herself off as they both stood there, observed by all around.

Then Jahng walked over to Louko's coat, picked it up, shook it, and returned it to him as she kneeled and bowed her head. Somehow, Astra knew that it was all part of the dueling code. She couldn't see Jahng doing this otherwise.

"My claim?" Louko asked curtly as he acknowledged Jahng by taking his coat back.

Jahng got to her feet, lips pressed in a hard line. But she motioned to Zhahn, who had dared to take up guard near Dannsair.

The man eyed the mare before stepping out of her way. In return, Dannsair snorted at him and trotted past to reach Louko.

"Begging your pardon—" Zhahn broke in. "I know the rules of the duel as well as anyone, but it might be better for the girl to be allowed to ride on the front of the cart rather than on horseback. This, of course, would be the winner's decision." He dipped his head towards Louko.

Astra found her friend looking at her. The anger in his eyes seemed to melt away to an anguished worry as their gaze met. "Would that be alright?" It took her a moment to realize he was talking to her.

Everyone's attention shifted towards her, and Astra wished herself invisible. She felt somehow ashamed as she nodded in reply.

"Then I will concede on that point." Louko's austere and collected posture devolved as he ran his hand through his peppered hair.

Jahng gestured towards Astra. Two soldiers began to unchain her from the line while leaving the red bronze manacles on. This time, she was too exhausted to even pull away from their touch.

"Then your claim is satisfied?" Jahng's question held an empty formality.

"Yes." Louko sounded equally void.

The soldiers helped Astra to her feet, the combined movement and pain leaving her senses reeling for several seconds. When they recovered, she heard Jahng say, "By your claim, you may walk beside her. But if you talk to any of the other prisoners, you may yet find yourself inside the cart."

"How thrilling," Astra heard her friend say as he recovered Dannsair's lead rope and walked over to join her.

Jahng regathered herself and her commanding air. "Now, let's not waste any more time with petty squabbles!" she called, urging everyone back into movement.

Getting into the cart was arduous. Astra clung to the side of the box seat just to keep herself from falling. Yet it was still better than walking, having to keep herself upright and moving. That vague sense of guilt still swirled, a soft voice telling her that she was selfish for riding while others walked, that Louko had to risk his life because of her stupidity, that they had all been captured because she was too weak. But none of these accusations settled long. Each bump in the road drove all thought from her mind and sent her back to simply clinging to the rail.

Louko was quiet as he walked beside the cart, eyes darting constantly from her to those around them as one hand absently stroked Dannsair. Astra felt some sort of comfort being able to keep her horse within her line of sight and even more so to see the small measure of reassurance it gave Louko. But he needed far more than a small measure.

"Are you alright?" Astra asked, hoping she did so audibly.

"Yes." His reply was short and strained.

He didn't look alright. He looked pale, jaw clenched and hands unsteady.

"I'm sorry," Astra whispered, once again conscious of her part in all this.

"No, Astra, there is nothing you have to apologize for," he said gently, looking only briefly at her before again turning to face the road and watch their captors.

That wasn't true. But Astra only had so much breath to argue. She saved it to say, "Thank you."

Louko looked up, then looked away.

Neither said anything more.

CHAPTER XV

Louko:

Louko could hardly reconcile what he had done. If Astra was not on the cart, he definitely wouldn't have been able to. What in Eatris had possessed him to be so...ruthless? Of course, he knew, but some of the things he had said...that went beyond just winning the match. He had been so angry and so worried for Astra. And then, when he'd been handed a sword to use, it had only made it worse. It reminded him that the sword Entrais and Astra had given him was still with Tyron, and that Tyron was responsible for all of this. He'd done this to Louko's only friend, and that fury had only fueled the fire against Jahng. But now, everything he had said seemed so over the top and almost cruel.

Night came, and with it a bitter cold, and even the fire didn't seem to add much heat. Jahng's men kept piling more wood on in an attempt to make it warmer but with little success as the wind blew cold over them.

Louko, however, didn't care, thinking only of the others chained to the cart for the night. The blankets they had could hardly be enough for this weather, and even as he himself shivered, he couldn't help but watch them huddle. This weather couldn't be good for Astra's fever.

"Zhahn, Xien, bring the prisoners by the fire. They won't be much used to us as icicles." Jahng's command seemed to read Louko's mind.

Lovely. What a great joke. But he said nothing, only thankful.

Two of the soldiers drove metal stakes into the ground while a few others unlocked the chain of prisoners from the cart. Still in a line, all of them were brought over, and their chain attached to a stake at either end.

"Thank you," Louko whispered in Jahng's direction.

Jahng grunted and turned away. "Someone get some stew going. I think we all need something warm."

Louko hoped Astra would eat something and yet feared she would not. She was already huddled up on the ground with eyes half-closed. He wondered if she was going to die.

Bowls were distributed just like the nights before, but this time with the order: "When you are done with it, fill it and pass it to one of the prisoners."

Intently, Louko watched, making sure his friends did indeed get proper food and actually eat. He especially watched over Astra.

"So, Prince Keeshiff." Jahng took her seat by the fire, addressing Keeshiff openly in the trade language. "What is this your brother says of my great uncle working with Merimeethia?" Her tone was calm and even.

"He has my men held captive, and upon our return he is going to send them to Kaeden." Louko couldn't help but note the defeat in his brother's voice. He felt a wash of helpless guilt as he thought of the inevitability and horror of it. Keeshiff's family was about to be sent to Tyron. *Tyron.* And they'd already seen what he was capable of.

Jahng frowned. "I mean no offense, but your steward seems more reasonable over foreign affairs than your former king. Would he really punish eight palace knights for following their prince?"

"He is not what he seems. He's the one that killed our father," Keeshiff replied, just as even.

The circle went quiet.

"Can you prove this?" asked Jahng.

"No. It's our word against his. And I would have been next, so Louko...got me out before he could kill me, too. But in doing so made us both look guilty." Keeshiff sounded as disheartened as Louko felt. They never could prove it to anyone...and no one would believe them about Tyron—especially anyone in Nythril, who barely knew of him.

Jahng seemed to think on this, silently accepting a bowl of soup from one of her men. She moved on with, "How do you know that he is working with the king, exactly?"

Louko pointed in the direction of Mitheau and Grenedil. "Your great uncle informed us of his correspondence when he gave us the ultimatum of capturing them or having the knights sent back."

"Hmm." Jahng looked over the row of prisoners before raising one brow and turning to Louko. "So why doesn't that *lovely* uncle of yours do something about this?"

"I don't know what he is doing, and I don't know if he *is* doing anything." Louko's response was dark. His uncle had seemed of little use thus far. Perhaps he didn't care.

Jahng said nothing more, turning her attention to her dinner. Her expression was unreadable. She finished her soup, wiped out the bowl, then refilled it. She carried it to Mitheau and returned to her seat.

Quietly, she asked Louko, "Is there anything more we can do for your friend that she will allow us to do?"

Louko turned and looked to Astra, whose ragged breathing could be heard as she slept. "You could take off the stupid red bronze."

"I can't do that." Jahng's eyes seemed to flicker with doubt.

"Then I don't know," he snapped, even though he had guessed Jahng wouldn't do it.

She did not react to his brusque tone. "It is severe?"

"I don't know what's wrong," he admitted through clenched teeth, knowing there was no point in hiding it from Jahng. If Astra was going to die, anyway, Jahng might as well know what she was bringing about. "I thought she'd been getting better. But then..." ...then she'd gotten the fever, and they'd gotten caught. Then this mess had happened.

"Better?" Jahng echoed in question.

The one word was like the call of a half-forgotten nightmare that begged to be let back in, and he shook his head to try to chase it away. But it wouldn't go away; he found a shudder running down his back.

The lack of an answer seemed to be enough for Jahng. "Well, if you think of anything more that we can do, let someone know."

"Yeah. Thanks," he replied listlessly. She couldn't die. She just couldn't.

Jahng gave a half shrug. "She's no use to anyone dead."

His whole body stiffened. "Yeah. Of course."

The remainder of the journey was swift and uneventful; Astra stayed alive but was not exactly improving. Jahng had even had Zhahn give her more medicine, had wrapped her in a blanket, and had been feeding her as much as she would eat...but nothing. All Louko could do was try and make conversation to keep her awake, wishing he could somehow do something.

And then, at long, dreadful last, they arrived in the city, taking a small back entrance. Louko guessed with disgust that it was so no one saw them. Somehow, the sight of Keeshiff and the others being led in chains through the street might cause some interesting theories on the part of the city gossips.

Now in the palace courtyard, they were greeted by more guards, and several came up to take Dannsair. The mare instantly began her screaming, and Louko was barely able to calm her down.

"Please, please, for Astra. I'll figure this out, I will but you *have* to be good," Louko begged the horse, staring hard at her until she stopped bucking enough to be handled by the guards.

Louko felt frozen, cold all over as he watched Dannsair being dragged away, ears pinned flat against her neck.

Then someone spoke.

"Dia Jahng, we did not expect *this*." A man clad in the robes of an advisor said as he met the woman.

"Ren Dhag," she greeted the man with a bow of her head.

In the meantime, Louko was allowed to help Astra off the cart. She was so frail—he wished he could just carry her.

"And why is the Merimeethian prince in chains?" Louko heard Ren Dhag ask, referencing Keeshiff.

"His group was found assisting the fugitives." Jahng's explanation was prim.

The way in which the man turned on Astra and Louko showed only disgust. Not a good sign.

"Then they are not the ones who caught them?" Dhag asked.

Jahng gave a brittle smile. "No. *I* did. And the king will be informed of such."

Ren Dhag returned the empty smile, adding narrowed eyes as a finishing touch. "Of course, he will, Jahng. But I think the king will want an immediate audience with them. I will inform him myself and take the three miscreants off your hands."

Louko's mouth was dry, and he couldn't tell if it was Astra that shuddered or himself. He gave her a brief look and could tell nothing besides the extent of her paleness and the glazed look in her eyes.

"My men are more than capable of handling the others. I have no desire to let you walk away with my prize again." Jahng turned back towards her soldiers. "Zhahn, see them to the Orshian Tower. Take the Drogan below."

"Unlock the Merimeethian prince," Dhag ordered the palace guards. "And accompany me as I bring these three to the king." His gaze settled on Louko. "I think it is time we talk about ridding Prince Louko of this bad company."

The grip Astra had on Louko tightened, and he didn't mind the pressure, for he was returning it subtly. *No, no, no, no, no, no.* He wasn't going to leave them—shouldn't he be imprisoned with the lot of them? The thought of Astra being shipped off somewhere—Litash or, even worse, to Merimeethia—without him was an unbearable thought. And if Keeshiff was brought back to Tyron....

He couldn't really get much farther in that thought, however, as Keeshiff was practically dragged from the cart by the guards, and the three of them were pushed towards the palace doors.

"Are you alright?" Louko asked his brother, having seen the clear exhaustion on his face for days, and yet been unallowed to ask.

"Chipper," Keeshiff whispered back.

Dia Jahng came up alongside them, ordering one of the guards, "Take the rear. If anyone tries to run, use whatever force is needed." As soon as the man had gone, she switched to Merimeethian and said under her breath, "*Just play it safe.*"

Louko whipped his head to face her and just glared at her. Right. Play it safe. She was one to talk. But he didn't say anything, only stared a moment longer before again turning back to his friend and brother.

How were they ever going to get out of this one?

It was slow going to get to the throne room, what with Astra's barely functional legs and all, but the soldiers did nothing to help, and Louko knew she would refuse to be carried. And so they went, Keeshiff holding her up on one side and Louko doing the same on the other until they stood before Dia Tzaro.

"Exalted One." Jahng gave that precise bow, holding it for several seconds before straightening. "I have returned with the fugitives you so desired. I have also returned with these three, who were abetting the criminals' escape."

Dia Tzaro gave a crackling, ancient laugh, "Thank you, my dear. For once, you've actually managed to follow your orders." There was a smile. "Leave us, and rest; you look tired. Dhag, make sure she and her men are properly rewarded with refreshments and anything they need."

Jahng bowed again and spun on her heel. Only as she passed them did Louko see the uneasy expression she wore.

Oh yes, of course, feel guilty *now* and leave them to the consequences.

"Well?" Dia Tzaro asked, the question ringing around the room. "What is the explanation for this? I gave you an opportunity, a simple, easy opportunity to be welcomed here, Princess Astra, and this is what you've done with it? I expected as much out of Omath's spawn, but really, you and our lost prince I would have expected better of."

Louko's jaw clenched at every word. He wasn't a pet, and Astra wasn't some *thing* to be used. But apparently this old, decaying puppet of a man couldn't see past his own wrinkles.

With Astra leaning on him so heavily, Louko didn't think that she had heard the old king—much less that she would reply. But then came the soft, steady voice, "Expected better? What path was better than the one I chose? Your so-called 'fugitives' are the mere victims of politics—a position I quite understand." There was a slight pause between each sentence as she caught her breath. "So I made the choice to aid them. Prince Louko and Prince Keeshiff merely did as I instructed."

Louko was about to protest when Astra's grip dug into his arm, her wide eyes saying what she did not: *Trust me.*

And that was all he got before Dia Tzaro waved his hand. "Then I think Dhag is correct. You and Prince Keeshiff will be placed in the Orshian Tower, and we will begin official negotiations to ship them back to Merimeethia. Steward Kaeden seems *very* interested in you, Princess Astra."

"No! Leave her alone!" Louko practically screamed it at the thought of Astra back with Tyron. He could feel her shaking. No. No, she couldn't go back there. No!

"And on that subject...." It was Dhag. "Exalted One, I believe Prince Louko has been corrupted by Litashian and Merimeethian ways. I suggest replacing him *alone* in his uncle's custody, to be properly taken care of away from manipulative hands."

Thought and reasoning was gone, as Louko barely registered anything that was being said. He just found himself holding Astra even tighter as he helped her stay upright. He couldn't leave her. He couldn't.

"A worthy suggestion," Dia Tzaro mused, one hand going to his chin as he surveyed Louko carefully. Then he nodded. "Yes, I agree, take him to the KingsHeir." He clapped his hands, and the guards came forward.

Astra was clinging to him, eyes wide.

"Please, no, Your Majesty, please—" Louko gripped Astra's hand almost deliriously.

"Dhag, take him away. The prince seems unwell."

Louko was torn from his brother and Astra, and fought with every fiber left in him to get back, not caring what was going on and what it could mean. Astra couldn't go back there, she couldn't die—and she couldn't be alone.

"Louko, Louko, stay calm." Astra's voice was hoarse. Keeshiff was trying to keep her from falling. "You won't be helpless there."

And with that, he was practically carried away.

Agony was an understatement as the closing of the door separated him from the last familiar thing in this forsaken place, and the knowledge that it could be the last time he ever saw his brother and best friend was too much. Louko only barely noticed he was shaking, too distracted by the ringing in his ears and the sudden dizziness. He only barely registered collapsing in the hall.

"Sir? Sir?" One of the soldiers was tugging at him. "Someone fetch a physician!"

Louko bolted upright to find himself in a large room, full length windows letting bright daylight in through the shining panes with unwelcome joviality.

Astra. Keeshiff.

The prince practically fell out of the bed, not sure what he was going to do or where he was, but knowing he had to do something. He could hardly breathe.

"Louko, sit down before you kill yourself, please." There was a firm hand on his shoulder, and then he came face-to-face with none other than his uncle. Aelor Ven. The one who had disappeared when he had promised to help them. When he had promised their safety.

"You're safe. We're in my city estate now, and we can—"

Where had he been?! Without thinking, Louko punched him square in the face.

His uncle blinked at him, swallowing a pained expression. Then his features set, and he raised one eyebrow. "I think you might have just broken your knuckles." As he turned away, Louko heard him murmur, "And possibly my face." He called towards the door, "Lena, fetch my physician!"

Louko was practically possessed at this point, ignoring the pulsing in his knuckles as he again swung at Ven's face. "You lied!" he shouted.

Ven grabbed him by the wrists with what seemed to be a sigh. "And you're yelling in my face," he said irritably. "When you can sit down and ask questions nicely, then we can talk."

Louko writhed a good thirty seconds more before concluding his uncle was much stronger than he was at the moment. He forced himself to obey and sit down, taking three shaky breaths.

Just as his uncle finally let go of Louko's wrists, the door opened, and Louko jumped back to his feet.

"You called, sir?" A lady in a long, full apron entered and bowed to Ven.

"Yes." He nodded, one hand now on his jaw. "My nephew is awake and in need of your attention."

The lady bowed again and drew closer to the bed. Her brow furrowed even before she reached him. "Oh my, what have you done to your hand?"

Louko looked down to find his knuckles had already begun swelling and turning purple.

"I think a better question is what he did to my face," Ven grumbled. "And here I thought your stupid horse was bad...."

The lady didn't say anything to that, turning aside and opening one of the cabinets that lined the left wall. She pulled out a bowl and glass and filled both with water from a nearby pitcher. She brought both to the bedside.

Setting the bowl on the stand, she said, "Soak your hand in this. And then drink this." She offered him the glass.

What? No! They were treating *him*?! Did they have any idea how sick Astra was? And *she* was in a prison cell!

"Louko, unless you plan to punch my physician as well, I would recommend doing as she asks." Ven stood with his arms crossed, but at a notably safe distance.

Jaw clenched until it hurt, Louko put his hand in the cold water and took the glass. But he did not drink. He just wondered if Astra was being given any water and, if she was, whether or not she was even able to drink it without help.

The physician put a hand to his forehead, making Louko flinch. He went tense just to stay still as she continued her examination. After checking his pulse and asking a few questions that received monosyllabic answers, she turned to his hand. She left it in the water as she felt each joint with careful, methodical motions. Her gentleness did not stop the needles of pain that spiraled up his arm.

Finally, she let go and turned to Ven. "Besides having two broken knuckles and the others being quite bruised, he is alright," she reported, wiping her hands on her apron. "He simply needs good food, plenty of water, and a lot of rest."

"Not unless you want to lock me up." Louko withdrew his hand like a wounded animal and frankly sounded like one, too. "She's going to *die* and you're all just sitting here!"

Ven addressed the physician as if he hadn't even heard him. "Will he need a cast?"

"No." She gave a shake of her head. "A splint and keeping it still will be plenty. It is only a slight fracture."

"I'm *fine*," Louko insisted vehemently. "Just give me something to wrap it with. Is anyone even listening?!" He waved both hands, ignoring the shooting pain that it brought. "Do you even care?"

The physician moved to stop him, but Ven waved her off. "Go fetch what is needed," he told her.

She bowed and exited.

"Sit," Ven ordered, already pulling up a chair for himself.

Louko did so, listless and despising himself. Here he was, again, sitting all nice and safe while everyone else prepared for the most horrible of fates.

"I already have that man-eating horse, and I know where your brother and Astra are," Ven said with a terse sort of patience. "And I am already working on getting them out. The best thing you can do to help them is to lay low and not draw any more of the king's attention."

Louko shook his head violently. No. No, no. He couldn't just sit here, not anymore. "I can't...I can't." His voice came out choked.

The last traces of annoyance disappeared, and Ven looked troubled. "Louko, this is the best way you can help them."

He just kept shaking his head, again struggling to breathe. "She's going to die, and she's going to die alone or worse...with *him*. I can't. I can't let her go back—I can't—"

"—I know," his uncle cut in, stopping him in the midst of his stammering. "I can't, either. I remember how all of you were when you first escaped, and I refuse to let that happen again."

For a moment, Louko just stared at his uncle, registering what had just been said. "You...you can't?" the words stuttered out of him.

Ven's brow furrowed. "Of course not. Never."

"But...but why did you leave us? You promised you wouldn't—how can we even get them out?" It all seemed so impossible.

"I left to address a message from my chamberlain, which told me of the seizing of nine men from my private manor," his uncle said, sounding angry at the memory. "And by the time I had gotten into the throne room to ask Dia Tzaro what this was all about, he had already sent the three of you off."

Louko had only really begun to wrap his mind around all this and decide whether he could believe it when a servant entered the room.

"My Lord, Dia Jahng requests a hearing."

"Oh great," Ven sighed. "*Just* what I need."

CHAPTER XVI

Keeshiff:

"Keeshiff!" Farian was the first to run towards the prince, stopping short when he realized how Keeshiff was the only thing keeping Astra standing.

"Help, please," he managed through his effort as he struggled to keep her up. She was exhausted; that much was clear.

"What happened?" It was Asher who kept his cool and came to Keeshiff's aid. "Where's Louko?"

"We got caught by Dia Tzaro's niece," Keeshiff replied tautly as they helped Astra over to one of the few cots they had apparently been given. "They've turned Louko over to his uncle's care." Was Louko being with Ven really a good thing, though? Keeshiff wasn't so sure. "Where's Grenedil?" He suddenly realized he should be here, too.

Keeshiff spotted him standing awkwardly in the corner, looking as if he had just gotten up.

"I told them what I knew," Grenedil offered. "But judging from the questions that followed, I didn't have the full story."

"Neither do I, really," Keeshiff said, distressed.

But he quickly turned back to Astra and knelt beside her. "How bad is it, dare I ask?" He would explain as well as he could to everyone, but not until he got proper stock of just how bad this situation was. And that started with Astra. She was all Louko had, and Keeshiff couldn't even fathom how his brother would go on without her.

Face ashen, all Astra did was shake her head.

"So help me Astra, if you die, I'm going to kill you." Keeshiff didn't even have time to be surprised at the words that were coming out of his own mouth. "Louko needs you and, well, frankly you're annoying enough to be a proper little sister, so you can't walk out now. You hear me? You just can't."

He wasn't the only one startled by this little speech. Astra seemed unable to reply. Then her brow furrowed and she looked away, as if to try and hide the emotions playing out in her expression. But her voice was thick when she admitted, "I do not know what is wrong with me. I've never receded so far after recovering. It's...it's...." She swallowed. "It is bad."

He turned to Asher. "We *have* to be able to get medicine. They need her alive, after all." His blood ran cold as he remembered why. But he had to believe Louko would get them out. If anyone could, it would be his brother.

Asher started to speak, only to stop at the sudden sound of keys jangling at the door. Everyone in the room turned in time to see Dia Jahng enter.

Keeshiff moved so that he was in front of Astra. "What do you want?" he growled. Surely they wouldn't take them so soon.

"I have petitioned the king and he has heard me. She is to come with me to receive proper medical care. Your physician is to come along to provide aid, as well as one assistant." She stared at Keeshiff, who had beheld her carefully as he noted the Merimeethian in which she spoke.

"One assistant," she repeated with meaning. "So if one of the others plays the part of prince, *you* hardly look the part at the moment...."

The prince did not move. He did, however, notice that he was not the only one who stood between Astra and Jahng. Several of his knights had done the same.

Keeshiff didn't trust this woman—but did he have a choice? Yes, she could be trying to separate them and make escape harder for them, but, honestly, their chances were next to none as it was. And they really didn't have the grounds to refuse when it would mean Astra's death.

"Asher is our physician," he finally said, nodding towards Asher. Then he looked around. "Who wants to boss everyone around for a few hours?"

In the back, he saw Rhumir raise his hand, only lowering it when Rufio smacked him upside the head.

"I'll do it," Gavin said.

Keeshiff looked to him gratefully, and yet with the gravity of knowing what a risk this could be for his friend.

Gavin made a shooing motion before Keeshiff could say anything. "Oh, don't flatter yourself—I have a lot of thoughts on reforming your government that I'm going to be trying to implement in the next hour."

Keeshiff looked unimpressed and replied, "Seeing how often the government is overthrown in Merimeethia, I fully expect to come back and find out at least three other people have been playing me." He turned back to Jahng. "I'm carrying her." He didn't care if he was ordering her. This was Astra, and he hadn't been just saying things when he'd told the sick princess that she was like a little sister.

Jahng's reaction was hard to read, but he didn't care. Not when she shrugged and said, "If you insist. Just come quickly."

And so with that, he found himself kneeling beside Astra. "We're getting you help. And I'm carrying you." His voice was firm. "Neither is optional."

She looked like she wanted to argue, but his tone must have convinced her that it wouldn't work. All she said was, "Alright."

Asher carefully aided Keeshiff in getting her ready and then picking her up. As tired as Keeshiff was from the long journey, his arms were still strong; he did not have much difficulty in holding her as they were led out of the room and towards the many stairs of the Orshian Tower. He tried not to linger in the doorway, pushing away that nagging fear that this would be the last time he saw his men.

Louko would come through.

Through the trapdoors, down the stairs, and into a long corridor, the little procession went. Jahng led them through a maze of plain, plaster hallways before stopping at one of the many doors.

"In here." She opened it, stepping back to let Keeshiff through first.

He stepped in and immediately went for the raised cot on the other side. As gently as he could, he set Astra down.

Asher was only a step behind him. "Tell me what you know," he instructed, already opening a tall cupboard to inspect what was at his disposal.

Keeshiff began explaining what had happened, from the days of riding to the ambush where Astra's Gift had lit up the whole camp. And then, of course, the two days of being chained to a cart.... He eyed Jahng, who still stood in the room, as well as the other man that had appeared. It was the one who had tried to help Astra before: Zhahn, his name had been.

"It seems to be a relapse," Keeshiff finished. "Or, I guess, more like she never healed in the first place."

"Mm." Asher did not pause his inspection, but Keeshiff could tell he was processing the story. He opened a cabinet full of colored vials and brushed over several, selecting one and holding it out to Keeshiff. "What does this one say?"

Oh, right, the labels were all in Nythrilian. Keeshiff took the small bottle, frowning over the word. "Er, auspicious? Maybe. Auspicious water?" He should have paid more attention to his tutor when he was younger.

"Give it to me." Jahng stepped forward and plucked the vial from his hand. "It says 'auminar tonic.'" She held it back out to Keeshiff.

"Perfect." Asher was already digging a cup out from one of the drawers. "Pour about one third of that vial in here, then fill the rest with water."

Keeshiff grabbed the cup and did as instructed. Meanwhile, Asher sat down near the bed.

"Astra," he called quietly. "Can you hear me?"

The slight rustle of sheets indicated a nod.

"Good. Alright. Now, as much as you can, I need you to tell me what you are feeling—no omissions," Asher ordered.

The splashing of the water Keeshiff poured from the jug nearly drowned out the raspy reply.

"I am just very tired. And everything aches. The worst of it is in my left side, below the ribs." The words were slow, as if each one took effort. "The pain is very sharp if I move, though more dull and aching when I am still. It hurts too much to touch."

Keeshiff finished stirring the mixture and carried the cup to Asher.

The physician took it as he said, "Alright. We'll take a look. First, I need you to drink this so that we can try and get your fever down."

"I have sent for more bandaging and supplies to be brought up. They should be here very shortly," Zhahn said.

Jahng quickly added, "Is there anything Zhahn or I can help with?"

"You could have not turned us in, for one." Keeshiff could care less about biting his tongue. But then he looked to Asher, wondering if there was anything that might help Astra. He needed to be careful, since Jahng was the only reason Astra was here and not dying in the Orshian Tower.

"Is there any way to get the red bronze removed?" Asher asked, ignoring Keeshiff's comment. "Louko says—and now I quite agree—that she does not heal as well with it on."

"On her wrists?" Jahng sounded doubtful, but when Asher nodded, she simply replied, "Give me a few moments," and disappeared.

Keeshiff wanted to ask the physician if Jahng would actually let her take it off, but he knew Asher would know nothing more than he did. He turned back to Astra, who was barely awake. "Hang in there, Shrimp."

The way Astra raised one eyebrow reminded him of how she had been before all this. "Shrimp?" Even faded as it was, her question was unimpressed. "That was the best you could do?"

He gave a weak laugh, "What? I'm bad at nicknames. I mean, you didn't think *I* came up with all of the knights' nicknames, did you?"

"You did come up with 'Grandfather,'" Asher grumbled, pulling out bandages and bottles of herbs. He motioned for Zhahn to help him with something, handing him a pestle and mortar before mimicking its use.

"Yes." Keeshiff gave a grin, if partly for Astra's sake. "I did, didn't I?" He knew Astra knew what he was doing...but he had to try anyway. If only Louko was here. If only they *weren't* here. If only...well, if only a *lot* of things hadn't happened. Perhaps chiefly that he had never let Louko go after Astra alone.

The sound of the door opening made Keeshiff jump and turn around to see Jahng return.

"Here," she said, holding out another pair of manacles. They looked nearly identical to the ones Astra already wore. "These are copper."

"A key to take these off would be helpful." Keeshiff's tone was dry as he regarded her carefully.

With a quick flick of her hand, Jahng produced the key. "Merimeethians have such short tempers."

"Yeah, well, when your friend is dying...you might understand." Keeshiff snatched it from her and quickly set about unlocking the manacles.

The moment the harsh metal left her skin, Astra's shoulders seemed to sag in relief. "Friends, eh?" He just barely heard her echo.

"Yes, friends." Keeshiff was firm. "So now you can't die."

Asher stepped in then, trading the old shackles for a wet, strongly-scented cloth. "Clean her wrists with this as best as you can," he said. "The last thing she needs is another infection."

Keeshiff was quick to obey, gently wiping her wrists as he addressed Jahng. "So are you just trying to let your conscience rest a little easier, or is there a different motive for all this?" He didn't like this. Why had she gone from, well, dragging them behind a cart to trying to perhaps save Astra from death?

"I haven't decided yet," came Jahng's blunt reply. "But I do know that I am not so willing to kill off children as my great uncle apparently is."

"Yeah, well...if you let her go back to Merimeethia, it will be worse," Keeshiff murmured, dread creeping in anew.

He saw the way Astra looked up at him, but she didn't say anything. Neither did Jahng.

Only after Keeshiff had finished his work and the new manacles had been locked in place did Jahng announce, "I have other work to look after. Zhahn, tell me as soon as there is any kind of diagnosis."

"As you wish, *Lieris* Jahng," Zhahn said with a bowed head.

Keeshiff snorted. *Lieris.* The highest rank of Nythrilian Hunters. "So, a nice little promotion, then?"

Jahng's chin raised ever so slightly. "Be careful of complaining over that which may help you later." With that, she exited the room and closed the door behind her.

The words rang a little longer than Keeshiff wished, and it didn't help when Zhahn commented, "You give her little credit."

Truly, her conscience was perhaps their best shot.

And with that in mind, he turned back to see how he could help Asher.

There was quiet for a while as Asher worked, and Keeshiff did his best to keep busy. He watched as Zhahn kept an eye on Astra's fever and then fetched things as needed.

It was no more than fifteen minutes, however, before Asher announced, "I think I know what the matter is."

The whole room stopped. Which, granted, wasn't much of a feat with only the four of them in it, but it still felt like a weight had settled. Or perhaps, a question. What was it...and could it be helped?

"She has something embedded in her abdomen, somehow. There's a fresh scar where a wound from the castle had healed, and it is very clearly infected." Asher did not seem certain as he explained. "Whatever is in there keeps fostering infection. I don't know how it ever healed over. Perhaps it's an Elvish thing or…I just don't know. How did I miss it?"

"It is not your fault," Astra was the first to say. She was pale, shivering, propped up in the bed. "The fact that I am alive at all is testimony of your work."

"Yes…" Asher's reply was not convincing. He looked troubled, starting to speak and then stopping. Finally, he sat down in a nearby chair. "If we do not remove it, the infection will doubtlessly reach your blood—assuming it hasn't already. If that happens, there is not much I can do." He rubbed the back of his neck.

Keeshiff assumed by his reluctance that there was some kind of catch. "Alright. So why don't we just do that?"

Asher looked to Astra, then straight at him. His hands settled in his lap. "In her current state, I don't think she could survive the ordeal of an open surgery. She is too weak already."

"I can procure some *kelosthmane.*" Zhahn's interjection perhaps would have made more sense to Keeshiff had he known what the word meant. Was it a Nythrilian one he had not heard of? He looked to Asher to judge his reaction.

Asher was already sitting up straighter. "*Kelosthmane*? How?"

"The king has trade with the south and procures it at great expense. It is to be used only for emergencies." Zhahn looked uneasy.

At this, Keeshiff chanced the question, "What is it, exactly?'

287

"Nothing I've ever used—your father's coffers weren't deep enough for that." Asher shook his head. "But if it is what it's said to be, it can put a patient in a deep sleep for over an hour. A deep enough sleep that not even an incision would wake them. Astra would feel nothing."

Astra shifted in the background.

"It will take a bit to get...I need to see if it is something Jahng can procure." He paused. "I'll know by tomorrow."

Tomorrow. That seemed so far away. "Is that too long to wait?" Keeshiff asked, fidgeting.

"We have little choice," Asher replied.

CHAPTER XVII

Louko:

"Show Jahng in, then." Ven sounded less than pleased as he addressed the servant, and Louko could more than sympathize, wondering if he would be able to control himself when she came in. Because right now, punching seemed to be the only good option he could think of.

The servant bowed and left. In another moment, the door opened again for Dia Jahng. She gave a tilt of her head and a thin greeting. "KingsHeir."

Louko barely moved before Ven grabbed his arm. "Dia Jahng. What can I do for you?" the lord asked.

Something possessed Louko to spit out the word, "*Snake.*" Perhaps it was the imprinted memory of his friends being forced to walk while bound by chains. Perhaps it was the panic on Mitheau's face when she'd thought she was going back in the cart.

Perhaps it was a lot of things.

Jahng narrowed her eyes but gave no response to the insult. Instead, she looked to Ven and said, "Your friend needs your help. I petitioned Dia Tzaro and had her moved out of the Orshian Tower, but the Merimeethian says the only way to help her is with *kelosthmane*. I..." She looked annoyed. "...I can't procure it alone. It's only for royal use, and Dia Tzaro would never allow it to be given to a prisoner."

Suspicion was quicker than hope, and Louko couldn't hold back his sarcasm when he pointed out, "Because you've cared *so* much."

"I have to say," Ven cut in, "my nephew does make a point, *Lieris* Jahng. This would be the perfect opportunity for you to...how can I put it...try and make a point to your great uncle?"

"If that were the case, I'm sure you could talk your way out of it." Jahng rolled her eyes and crossed her arms. "Besides, the princess is no use to anyone dead, and Dia Tzaro knows that as well as any. If you don't believe me, you can always talk to the physician and that irritating brother of yours." She gestured towards Louko. "I guess it doesn't matter to me what you choose. Either way, I've done my part."

Louko again made a move as if to go at her, but Ven's grip remained firm.

"So then, you are asking for my help, Jahng?" The amusement in his uncle's voice was as tangible as Louko's anger.

"No." The reply was a little too quick. "I'm saying you are the only chance that your nephew's little sweetheart has."

"Well, then." Ven did not appear pleased, and neither was Louko. Perhaps if it had been any other day, he would have taken a moment to comment on the "nephew's little sweetheart" thing, but he was a little busy freaking out at the moment.

Ven's tone was curt as he replied, "Thank you for the...information. If that is all, you can leave."

Jahng blinked. "Wait. That's it? No, no—I began this process, and I intend to see it through."

Louko's fist clenched, but a soft squeeze on the arm by his uncle warned against saying anything. He only acquiesced because Ven did, indeed, appear to have this more under control than it had appeared.

"My dear…" Ven's tone was collected. "It is pretentious of you to believe you *started* anything except this whole problem, and I do not need your help. I am quite capable of handling this all on my own. Your attempts to satisfy your own little conscience are sincerely appreciated and quite dutiful, but if you cannot put aside your ego, then I cannot and will not trust you with anything."

…Well, then.

It took Jahng a visible moment to even soak all that in. "Look." Her voice dropped. "No one told me she had been tortured or that she was *dying*. I didn't even know she would be there. I was ordered to capture a Drogan and her companion, and that's what I did." Then her defensiveness wavered. "But fine. My orders were wrong. Now I'm trying to set things right, and you seem quite intent on making that difficult. Just tell me what I have to do so we can get this over with."

Louko's own anger faded in the face of her small outburst, and he was the one who spoke first, this time. "Any help would be appreciated." He was surprised at the hoarseness with which he said it.

Judging by the look on her face, so was Jahng.

Ven just sighed. "Great. Now I'll have to put aside my ego, too." He didn't sound thrilled. "But I don't need you going around and getting your men involved if I'm not certain they're loyal to you—I need their names, first. Understood?"

Jahng looked displeased but nodded. "I'll draw up a list." Her folded arms returned to her side.

"Excellent. And I may interview as I deem necessary?"

Louko's stress returned as he wondered how long this was going to take, and what exactly his uncle's plan even was.

A pause and then another nod. "But we'll need to be quick," she said. "The physician seems to be in a hurry. The man I left with them said that they were worried over the delay. How do you plan to get it in time?"

"Oh, it won't be any problem. I'll have it sent up, promptly."

Well, didn't somebody sound smug, now.

"If you insist." Jahng had descended into monotone. "She's on the bottom floor of the west wing, third clinic room down. Make sure whoever drops it off has a good reason for being there." She softened. "And if you visit, just don't get caught."

"I never do," Ven replied.

Louko wondered exactly how much he didn't know about his uncle...and how much of that was a good thing, and how much a bad thing. Apparently, he would find out as his uncle found necessary.

When the pause lingered, Jahng finally seemed to get the point. "I suppose I should go draw up that list. Let me know as soon as you have something I can do. Until then, I'll keep stalling."

After a nod from Ven, Dia Jahng bowed and left.

It took Louko a couple minutes to process everything that had just happened, and when at last he did, all he could manage to figure out was that his uncle was up to...something. "So...you *are* going to help us, then?"

Ven sighed and turned to face his nephew, expression grim. "Yes, my boy. I will try everything in my power. And I'm not letting you out of my sight again, this time."

A long silence passed between the two before Louko raised his next question. "You have a plan?"

"Indeed, I do." A mischievous smile grew like a weed on his uncle's face as he explained, "I am going to stage the most spectacular coup of the century. One that even a Merimeethian could be proud of."

Louko was still wrapping his head around all of this. Three hours later, a detailed and extravagant plan, and he still wasn't sure he got it all. At least he now knew his uncle definitely *was* on their side. The extent to which he had already begun to undermine the king's throne was impressive.

And now, Louko was key to helping. Nythril was run by a council of lords, and the king could not be replaced by one of their own choice...but they could force him to step down early for the KingsHeir. And that was exactly what Ven was aiming to do.

But this was still not an easy task, full of all sorts of hearings and favors and evidence. Ven's complaint? Dia Tzaro was senile. It sounded ridiculous, but Ven assured Louko he could give a compelling case. After the way his uncle had handled things with Jahng and getting the medicine to Astra, Louko actually didn't doubt him. Not much, anyway.

"I still don't understand why anyone cares about my status," Louko announced as they stood in his uncle's study. All this lost prince nonsense...especially how his opinion somehow helped sway an entire group of lords from a country he hadn't stepped foot in since he was seven.

"You have your mother to thank for that." His uncle, arrayed in court finery, sat across the wide desk from him with some parchment in hand.

"I don't...understand." His chest tightened at the mention of the woman he would never know.

Ven looked up from the parchment. "Did no one ever tell you her story?"

Louko couldn't keep the self-disdain out of his voice as he replied, "I'm assuming you are not referring to the part where I killed her?"

His uncle blinked at him then slowly straightened. "*That's* what they told you?" He set the letter down as he shook his head emphatically. "Never leave anything to a Merimeethian," he muttered. "I think it's time to set the record straight and make sure you know the *whole* story—not whatever self-pitying nonsense Omath said."

Ven rested his elbows on the desk and folded his hands. His eyes softened. "Your mother and I were on our own from a younger age than most. Ravyen took up the responsibilities that our parents had once managed, even much of the running of our family estate. She was…" His voice grew thick, and he cleared his throat suddenly. "...intrepid. Stubborn. All admirable traits by Nythrilian standards, and she very quickly earned a stellar reputation for herself. She ended up petitioning the king for aid when running our estate needed a more experienced hand, and Dia Tzaro took a shine to her. Like a daughter he never had. I…" Ven trailed off for a moment, a displeased expression resting on his face. "Well, he saw me as a son. Tzaro was, in his defense, not as...old and displeasing as he is now. He was tolerable, even. Of course, Ravyen always brought out the best in everyone."

There was an almost whimsical expression paired with the last statement. Ven cleared his throat awkwardly and went on, "When she married one of the lords nearer the capital, Dia Tzaro himself approved." He gave a rueful sigh. "She left the estate to me and moved to be with her husband. I had only just received her letter announcing that she was expecting when I heard the news that her husband had died in a skirmish with southern forces."

Hearing someone talk of his mother was strange, and yet Louko found himself straining to hear more—even as his stomach knotted at already knowing the end of the tale.

Louko's uncle's eyes were no longer fixed on anything in particular. "Ravyen was supposed to come back to our estate, but before she could finish packing, this foreign dignitary paid a visit to the capital. It was the first time in memory that a Merimeethian ever made it so far into Nythril." Ven's hands grew taut. "I tried to talk her out of it, but Ravyen was immoveable once she had made up her mind. She wanted a father for her child, to be a mother to Omath's young son, and to attempt the impossible: uniting Nythril and Merimeethia. And worse...she claimed...they were in love." His smile was humorless. "It took some convincing to get Tzaro to agree, but Ravyen won her way. They returned to Merimeethia and were wed there. Your sister Mariah was born mere months later."

Ven looked tired as he sat back in his chair. "I visited a few times. Things seemed alright, but I noticed that Ravyen's health was not so strong as it had been. I couldn't tell if it was the ghastly weather or the result of childbearing, but I tried to talk her into getting out of Merimeethia more often. She wouldn't have any of it. And Omath refused to go against her—even for her own good." His uncle's shoulders drooped. "She should not have stayed. She should have gone elsewhere to recover. By the time you were born, it was too late."

He took a deep, shuddering breath. "I blamed Omath. In my anger, I did anything I could to bring home my sister's children and to keep Omath out of Nythril. In turn, Omath accused me of undoing in mere months what Ravyen had taken years to build. Dia Tzaro agreed. He was too busy fighting Drogans to want to fight Merimeethia, too. It wasn't until after that war ended that he finally agreed to back me." Ven finally looked up. "That was when you were about six. I wrote to your father demanding your return and expecting nothing. Instead, he wrote back and proposed a compromise: visits."

Louko's brow furrowed, but the memories were there. Of the visits. With...Tyron.

"To be forthright, I didn't plan on letting you go home." His uncle tilted his head with the admission. Then discomfort flitted across his face. "But, well, when I saw the way your, um, tutor took care of you, I thought that perhaps I was wrong about Omath after all."

A pit formed in Louko's stomach.

"I was not so fortunate," Ven said flatly. "I shouldn't have let you return. Not on that visit, nor the next. When Omath unexpectedly cancelled the third one, I wrote to your tutor directly. I received no reply. It was only through your letters that I heard about his departure." His uncle pressed his lips together, posture rigid once more. "So I went back to my lobbying. I made sure the whole nation knew of Ravyen, of her character and her attempt to tie Merimeethia and Nythril together, and then what it had cost her. Then I told them of her children, still trapped in that dreadful country that had killed my sister." He raised an eyebrow. "It was quite the tale, if I do say so myself. You and your sister became nearly things of legend. Of course, when Mariah so publicly disavowed Nythril and its people, I was sure my efforts were ruined. It turned out that her lack of loyalty only made yours shine all the brighter." Now his uncle's expression relaxed to something nearly mischievous. "I may have helped that along with tales of your prodigious intelligence and your many exploits in Litash. But in my defense, I never had to add to the truth: You have always provided plenty of material to work with."

Everything sort of spun for a moment as Louko struggled to digest everything. Half of him felt like it didn't really matter how anything had happened—it hadn't changed the outcome at all. But the other half of him...felt a strange sense of peace for knowing what had really happened. For knowing he'd been wanted. And for knowing that he could maybe be of some use.

This reminded him of why he had asked his uncle in the first place. "So you need me to be a witness?"

"Yes. The Lost Prince of Nythril should make a pretty case to the king's negligence of the mind." His uncle smiled. "But it will take several nobles some convincing. Jahng is to be there, though, as a noble. She will provide support, as will Dia Tzaro's advisor."

Louko raised an eyebrow, the last bit a newer piece of information. "Oh?" Ren Dhag? That man disgusted him, and the sentiment did nothing but again prick doubt about his uncle.

Ven sighed. "Please, have a little faith. That man is more disgusting than a half-dead hog and less loyal than one. But he seems to think I am going to do some favor for him when I am ruler over Nythril." He paused long enough to chuckle on some intimate joke that he apparently had just shared with himself. "What a stupid man."

There was a knock, then, and Ven's whole expression shifted. "Oh good, they finished in time."

Louko's brow furrowed. "Are we expecting someone?"

In reply, the door opened, revealing a servant with a brown paper package wrapped with a fine ribbon. Uncle Ven took it without a word, handing it to Louko as the servant ducked back out of the room.

"For you," Ven announced.

"Uh…" Louko uttered the sound as he stared skeptically at the package. "What is it?"

Clearing his throat awkwardly, Ven replied, "Your mother's favorite color."

The urge to take the package was as sudden as it was strong, and as carefully as if it were glass, Louko took it and loosened the ribbon. Folded and nestled in the thin paper was a coat. He'd never been much for finery, let alone fancy clothes, and yet the prince had an instant desire to put the thing on. It wasn't gaudy or overly ornate like so much of the court attire Louko had seen elsewhere. Instead, it favored the simple cut that so many Nythrilians wore. Its beautiful silver seemed to shine like starlight, the contrasting tones of darker silver embroidery curling all about the coat like billowing clouds. Louko stroked the red inner lining of the coat, enthralled for a moment.

It was like having a piece of his mother with him. Even more so than the library.

"Thank you," he whispered at last, sheepishly trying the coat on. A perfect fit, of course. Royals and their tailors.

Ven gave a cough. "Well, you need proper attire for addressing the Council of Lords. Say nothing of it. Now, we should get going. The carriage is waiting."

Louko knew not to press the matter, but he couldn't help but give a small, appreciative nod before following his uncle out of the room.

Together, they walked down the long, mosaic-paneled hall, comfortably silent in each other's company.

The carriage ride was not a long one, and yet it seemed like an eternity before they arrived at the large building—a lesser version of the city palace. The place was bustling with activity, and through a flurry of servants and footsteps, Louko and his uncle found themselves at last at the entrance to the courtroom, where they were promptly announced by the servants. No amount of coaching could prepare Louko for this, and all he could do was hope and try not to think of the way Astra was fighting for her life, possibly dying in some room without him there. It helped a little knowing Asher and Keeshiff were there—as Jahng had informed them—but not much. It was like Louko was dying with his friend, and yet, of *course*, he was as safe as could be. Always safe and coddled, it seemed of late.

But now, entering into the grand meeting room, Louko was forced to shove down such silly feelings and face the task ahead.

Well, right after a good gawk, anyway.

The hall was a round room, contrasting with the straight, paneled walls that created a strange blend of symmetry and elegantly straight, yet formidable lines. Unlike the throne room, blue and jade were nowhere to be seen, only thin gold strips where stone molding transitioned to the glossy wood of the walls. What was the most intriguing to Louko was that there were no raised platforms for the nobles to sit on. Instead, the room was littered with tables and chairs, each covered in gold tablecloths and cushions. It was more like some form of dining hall than a council room, and the noise raised by the plethora of men and women in the place aligned with such an idea. In fact, many were even being served what Louko guessed was lunch.

"Aelor Ven, you rogue!" An older man came up and clasped Louko's uncle on the shoulder, laughing as he greeted him.

Louko quickly looked to his uncle, expecting a look of disgust, and instead seeing the brilliant look of pleasantness.

"Lord Xo-Sha, thank you for coming." He returned the clasp on the shoulder.

"I assume it is for an urgent matter, seeing how the great Aelor Ven rarely pleads so for our convening." Another laugh sounded, and somehow rippled through the commotion of the room. "We all know how much you *love* meetings."

Louko's uncle gave a reserved chuckle—which, frankly was more than Louko had ever heard in public besides a slightly disdained snort—and replied, "Indeed...who are we missing?"

The young prince was thankful for the way in which Ven moved to business, again showing he seemed as concerned as Louko was over this.

"Lord Fael and Lady Dahj are, but that's no surprise. And then there's just Gi-Guoa and Ki-Song. But come, I have yet to be introduced to our lost prince, and this is an introduction I have long awaited." Lord Xo-Sha's genial eyes and greying—and rather pronounced—eyebrows turned their attention to Louko.

He had been quite happy to sit and observe and try to gain as much information through his uncle's interactions as possible. Several names sounded familiar between gossip and, well, Mariah. But still, he had only had his books, Ven's letters, and that short time before the ball to educate him on Nythrilian politics.

"Louko?" Ven's brow held concern, and apparently the young prince had missed something.

"Yes, sorry. Just…fascinated with everything," he murmured, quickly bowing his head to the Lord Xo-Sha. "It is a pleasure, my lord."

"Likewise, Prince Louko." The lord returned the bow in practiced fashion. "You are quite a legend here, especially after your close escape over the mountains. I think that, for once, I can speak for the whole Council of Lords when I say we will be glad to know you better."

Louko tried to manage some form of smile, not used to all the flattery. "Thank you."

"Well, shall we sit?" Ven clapped his hands and motioned over to the various tables and chairs.

Louko followed Ven through the rows until they reached their assigned spot. His uncle had already gone over how the seating was done by locality, so that each lord was next to his literal neighbors. That put them in between Lord Eren and Lord Hisor.

"May I call everyone's attention, please!" The unexpected, booming voice made Louko grip the table just to keep from jumping out of his seat.

The genial clamor of the room echoed into nothing.

"Lord Aelor Ven, KingsHeir, has called the Council of Lords into order, and thus will have the pleasure of opening with his official address." The man who was speaking was standing at a table across the room. He was not dressed like any of the other nobles, instead wearing simpler, longer robes.

This was a very different sort of atmosphere than Merimeethian court, and Louko felt more as if he was at some evening party than a serious and possibly life-altering meeting. Not that Louko had ever been invited to many evening parties.

"Thank you, Min." Uncle Ven assumed a tone that Louko could only describe as diplomatic: full-voiced and serious, yet comfortable and authoritative. "I have called you all here on a somewhat delicate manner. Not one, however, that should catch any of you by surprise."

Louko felt acutely uncomfortable as far too many sideways glances were thrown his way.

"All of us have known for some time that King Dia Tzaro has been declining in his advanced age. Out of respect for him and the wisdom of his years, we have all opted to remain quiet in these cases. And yet," Ven looked around the tables, gaze resting on a few of the lords in turn. "I don't think I am alone in observing the more drastic nature of these decisions. Think of Lady Sil's estate, Lord Vaizin's tenants, or the matter in the village of Fel."

A pause let everyone remember, and let Louko wonder what exactly had happened in all these situations.

"But I would not have called you all together simply over these old matters. No, I have called you over something that I believe to be far worse and far more pressing." Ven's tone darkened as he announced,

"King Dia Tzaro is threatening to deport my nephew, the lost son of my sister, Queen Ravyen: Prince Louko. And yes, back to the very country that killed his mother."

The strong reaction was flattering, really, and as much as Louko hated the now direct stares that shoved towards him like sympathetic and questioning daggers, he knew that his status with them was all that stood between Astra and Tyron.

"So I appeal to you all for help. I do not have the power to keep Louko safe—not by myself. And I can by no means send him back to Merimeethia." Ven sounded genuinely distressed by the fact. "I admit, I never expected such a low move on behalf of the king and so I don't know where to even start—much less what to do."

A mixture of murmuring and uneasy contemplation filled the air as Louko's uncle finished. It was all the young prince could do to not show how much he desired to scream amid it.

A lord seated across the room raised his voice to ask, "Ren Dhag, is this true?"

From somewhere near the front of the room, the advisor stood up. "Yes. The king has indeed been making deals with Merimeethia against even my heeding."

Louko forced himself not to glare at the man. He was helping them, and that was important. But Louko remembered all too well the *lack* of intercession Ren Dhag had given during the whole disaster.

Now there were quiet questions of "Is that even legal?" "How can he do that without the permission of the lords?" "How long has this been going on?"

Then someone stood up from two tables over, and Louko realized suddenly it was Dia Jahng. She looked like an entirely different person in the silk robes of a noblewoman.

Her gaze flitted over to where he sat and remained fixed there as she spoke. "I think, if I might be so bold, that it is time we hear from the lost prince, himself." There was no hostility in the request, nor in her eyes. Though this fact did not make meeting her gaze any more bearable. If not for the fact everyone was clearly focused on him, Louko definitely would have preferred staring at the tablecloth.

"I will second that," a lord to Louko's right made a motion with one hand.

Oh.

Carefully, Louko got up, taking a moment to breathe and better evaluate the large meeting hall. It was at this moment that Louko realized he had never spoken to such a large group before, let alone about something so critical as this. Even though Ven had gone over again and again what to say, the words still threatened to fly away in the stress of it all. Again, he tried to gauge the expressions of the lords and ladies that sat there waiting for him. They appeared expectant, a few skeptical, most rather intrigued.

Louko slowly grasped that he was not seen as Omath's son here. He was not the unwanted burden who'd fraternized with the murderer Tyron. No. Here...here, he was Ravyen's son, the lost prince of Nythril they had fought to reclaim. He found himself tugging at the sleeves of his coat, allowing its presence to comfort him.

And suddenly it hit him in full that while his father had seen Louko as a cheap replacement for his beloved wife, the people in this room—his uncle especially—saw him as a gift left behind. Not a burden. And as much as Astra had always tried to drill that into his idiotic, thick skull, Louko only now seemed to comprehend it. Here, in his mother's homeland, beside her brother, Louko felt more connected to her than he ever had. And through her, he found his voice.

"I will admit, I am not one for words." His voice rang loud and confident as he addressed the assembly. "And I am also no gossip—though apparently I am quite a topic of it."

There was a rumble of chuckles that eased the tension.

"But my uncle is telling the truth. And as such, I cannot help but fear for the safety of Nythril under King Dia Tzaro. I admit, it is partially under selfish motives...my brother and close friend are at this moment being prepared for the king to barter off to Merimeethia." He was banking on the disgust this knowledge would bring; Nythrilians did not *barter* with Merimeethians. "He tried to make Princess Astra and myself into his lackeys, forcing us to fetch his lost prisoners and threatening to send the Merimeethian refugees back to Steward Kaeden if we did not. He is in league with the steward and plans to benefit from a Merimeethian alliance by returning their alleged outlaws."

Now for the gamble that no one knew of Astra's exile: "As it is, he has placed Nythril on shaky ground with Litash by placing Princess Astra under arrest as well. If King Entrais were to find out...think of the repercussions."

Louko took a deep breath, steeling himself. "I will be forthright with you all: I barely escaped my father. I do not know what would have happened to me if he remained alive and in power. My brother—as unbelievable and detestable an idea as it may seem—was just as much a victim as I. King Omath was not kind, and Steward Kaeden is only worse. He was the one who killed Omath. And then he held me as a captive along with Princess Astra in the Merimeethian dungeons for *three weeks*. When we escaped, the only reason we made it back out of the country was because of Keeshiff. My brother brought me here, even though he knew he would not be well received, and he has shown himself honorable even in the face of capture—which Lieris Dia Jahng can verify." He nodded towards Jahng.

"Since King Dia Tzaro is making such outrageous deals with a murderer such as Steward Kaeden, and deals so dangerous and dishonorable to Nythrilians as these, I trust you can see why I am distressed. He has forced me away from what remains of my family and has laughed in my face with the utmost contempt. He does the same to all of your faces by hiding such deals from you. I beseech you: Please, do not let him send my brother and Princess Astra to their deaths. If not for the injustice of it, then for the knowledge that you will send yourselves into war with Litash...and lose me. If my brother goes, I will return with him—whatever fate awaits me." He sat down, feeling breathless and almost dizzy by the pummeling emotions that drove through him with every word.

The room was absolutely silent. Shock was painted on every face— even on those of the servants. The stunned lords and ladies all turned to each other with furrowed brows and quiet murmuring before one of them finally dared to raise their voice.

"Lieris Jahng, is this true? Has your great uncle really done all of this? Is Steward Kaeden really guilty of murder and holding the prince captive?"

Jahng nodded. "Yes. And I have confiscated correspondence between my great uncle and Steward Kaeden to prove several of these points. The letters are not pleasant to read."

The murmuring grew.

"Well," Lord Hisor, whom Louko was told rarely spoke at all unless it concerned books, scoffed. "That's entirely illegal according to nearly half of our bylaws. The king cannot initiate foreign trade without calling for a council, much less take prisoners from treatied countries."

"But it is clear that, unlike Lord Ven, the king cares little for our laws." Louko recognized the woman that spoke now as Lady Sil, having been given some descriptions by his uncle earlier. She was an easy one to recognize, if only for the scar running from her cheek to jawline.

Ven spoke again. "But how do we stop a man who will not listen to legality? How can we reason with him?"

Yes, this was definitely why Louko's uncle was a politician. Very clever.

"A gentle deposition seems in order." Jahng seemed the only one bold enough to say it out loud. "Within reason of Nythrilian law, of course," she added after the audible gasp.

"I agree," Lord Xo-Sha spoke up. "This madness must end."

Louko caught a brief smirk on his uncle's face, and it was followed by Ven asking, "Lord Hisor, what steps may we take in accordance with our laws?"

Of course, Louko and Ven both already knew exactly what steps they could take. That was why they were here.

The room's attention went to the bookish lord. "Well, if you want to fully depose him, there are a few ways to go about it...."

A GAME OF WITS

CHAPTER XVIII

Astra:

It had been two days since Asher had removed the piece of metal—a small shard of red bronze, apparently—from Astra's side. Thanks to the *kelosthmane*, she had not felt a thing. Even with the pain that came later, it was still a relief to have it out. She hadn't even noticed how much her body had been fighting the repressive metal until it was gone. Still, she had not missed the physician's tight-lipped expression when he changed her bandaging.

Yet it was Keeshiff who had caught her attention. He'd been there when she'd woken up and had since hardly left her side, sitting beside her like some fevered watchdog. In some ways, it was strange to have him there instead of Louko. And yet, his presence was familiar and reliable in a way that Astra did not quite understand. She only wished that Keeshiff could be with his brother instead of her; doubtless, Louko needed that support right now.

But their worry for Louko seemed best left as an unspoken mutuality. So Astra asked instead, "How are your men? Any word concerning Mitheau?"

"She's still in the dungeon. No one can see her," Keeshiff replied, quiet. "The men are hanging in there. Keeping spirits up." He paused. "How are you feeling?"

Still in the dungeon. Astra remembered the road here and how Mitheau had reacted to the prisoner's cart Jahng had put her in. Astra could not imagine what an underground dungeon would do to her. Or, perhaps even worse, Astra *could* imagine…. She suddenly remembered that Keeshiff had ended all that with a question.

"Oh, um, better, I think." She wondered how Louko was doing. He had been so panicked when the guards had dragged him away.

"He'll be alright, as long as you don't go dying on us, anyway," Keeshiff said, trying to sound casual and being very bad at it.

Astra looked down at her hands. They were resting in her lap, toying idly with a blanket. "Well, no matter what happens, at least he still has you."

Keeshiff let out a pent-up breath. "With all due respect, Astra, I think I blew that one a long time ago."

Looking up, Astra asked, "What do you mean?"

Keeshiff leaned forward in his seat, his elbows resting on his knees and his hands clasped together. He did not meet Astra's eyes. "I knew what living in Melye—what being trapped under our father—was doing to him…. After Tyron left all those years ago, it got so awful for him. And I justified my silence. I thought it would go better for him if I stayed uninvolved—that way, Father wouldn't punish Louko for 'turning me against him.' So, I wouldn't ever seek him out, but always let him stay if he tagged along when I was with the knights." Keeshiff was rigidly still as he spoke. "I told myself he just had to hold out until I became king, then it would be alright—then I could make it better. But then he stopped coming, and, being the imbecile I was, I didn't bother to try and find him. When Mariah rejected him, I told myself she'd been bad for him anyway;

she always made him follow her every whim, without a care for what he wanted. Then he ran away, and I told myself that was the end of it. Clearly, he'd gone to Nythril and would be fine. That was, until I turned up in Litash to help you and your brother...."

Astra felt heartsick. She remembered the terse reunion and had never understood it in full 'til now.

"...and he was there. I had to bring him back. I thought perhaps he would run off in the final battle so I wouldn't find him and be obliged to drag him home...but he didn't." Keeshiff's frustration played out on his expression, quickly followed by disgust. "So I justified it again; I told myself Father would accept him better now that he had fought valiantly in The War. Of course, he didn't."

Louko had been loyal to the end, staying to fight with her and Ent rather than securing his own future.

"Father got worse, and then Louko made that stupid deal with him...and I just...left it." Keeshiff swallowed. "I was a coward who told himself it was more important to not get disinherited. I was..." His cheeks reddened. "...I was slowly planning to get Father out of the way. I was trying to get out and get the respect of our countrymen and convince them Father was the brute I knew he was. But all that did was leave Louko alone with Father. I don't know why I ever thought Louko would last. I suppose that's why I thought he killed Father...because that's more or less what I was trying to do. Only I wasn't brave enough to just out and do it, and I was...angry at the thought that I'd forced Louko to it. But I should have known better than to take my time after he'd made that deal with Father." His voice petered off into nothing.

Keeshiff...had been planning to depose Omath? All that time? And to think that she had once considered him to be spineless. But one detail seemed more pressing than even a coup: "What deal?" Astra was nearly afraid to ask.

"Oh." She was sure she'd never seen Keeshiff look more ashamed. "Astra, I don't want to upset you...you're already so ill...it doesn't matter now, anyway, I guess. Omath's dead."

"And yet it still seems to bother you," was Astra's quiet observation.

He rubbed the back of his neck, sighing. His reply was equally quiet. "It does."

"Then I believe it still matters."

"You will hate me even more, I'm afraid...but I suppose it's only fair." Keeshiff looked to where Asher was pretending to be busy with his supplies as he listened in. He took a deep breath and said, "When Louko and I returned home after The War, Father was upset. Really. Upset." Keeshiff shuddered, and Astra felt her stomach twist in apprehension. "And, of course, I didn't do anything. Father was ready to put Louko under lock and key and constant supervision, paranoid he'd make off to Nythril and start a war or something. Well, Louko was summoned to talk to Father about it, and I, uh, listened in. Louko promised never to try and leave again on his word of honor, as long as Father would at least let him have some privacy in the house. And I guess that wouldn't mean much to most anyone else...but Louko *never* promises anything. And when he does...it's never broken. He signed his own death warrant. He wasn't allowed to leave the palace—let alone go into the city—without Father's permission. That's why he actually went to that stupid, stuffy ball where he met you again and brought you back. Father actually asked him to go, and I think he thought perhaps it was a small gesture of kindness. But apparently it was just to go and fetch you."

Astra felt so entirely wretched. To think of Louko signing his life away, of not even saying a word of complaint when he came to Litash, of suffering in silence for so many years…. But he was not the only one. And as awful as Astra felt for what he'd endured and for her own role in it all, that was secondary in this moment.

"Keeshiff, that makes me hate you no more than it made Louko hate you," she said. "And by that, I mean not at all."

Keeshiff looked anguished. "But he should. And you should. Didn't you hear what I did? I left him. I *abandoned* him, Astra. He is the best thing that has ever happened to our family besides his mother, and I let him wither away."

"I did no better." Astra wished it wasn't true. "I did nothing to stop his return. And I left again right before your father was killed. But as wrong as all of that was, how much worse would it be if I withdrew now because of it? Then he would only be more alone." She tried to think of how to say this: "I think the one who needs to hear all of this isn't me but Louko. Because like it or not, we both know he is loyal to the bitter end. And so he will be with you. You cannot undo the past, but you have been given this second chance for the future: You can still be the brother he needs."

"I don't know how, Astra. And now I might never get the chance to figure it out, anyway." The statement was said with no small amount of despair. Keeshiff seemed to catch himself, adding, "But *you* are the ill one. And have never harmed Louko by any means. I don't know how in Eatris we got into this, sorry."

"Don't be sorry," Astra said as firmly as she could. "But please don't carry this in silence the way he did. All that will do is keep both of you trapped. And what is more frightening: telling him and having it over with or bearing it for the rest of your life?"

Unexpectedly, Keeshiff chuckled. He shook his head in seeming amazement as he sat back, looking more at ease than he had in a long while. "I see why he loves you."

Astra blinked at him. Then her brow furrowed. "I'm sorry?"

"Oh, sorry. Nothing." Keeshiff was grinning now—in a way that actually looked quite like his younger brother.

Astra was wildly confused. She looked to Asher for interpretation, but he feigned innocence as if he had somehow not been eavesdropping in the tiny space.

"Keeshiff is at least right in one regard: You are still quite ill and need to rest." Asher came back towards the bed. "I think you have been sitting up long enough."

Astra looked between them with narrowed eyes, but she couldn't quite recall what it was that she had been asking about. The comment she remembered didn't make any sense now that she thought about it. Maybe she really was just tired....

"Alright," she finally consented.

"I should leave you and check on the men, anyway..." Keeshiff said, hesitantly getting up. Jahng had left a guard to escort Keeshiff back whenever needed, with false pretenses at the ready.

Waiting until Asher had helped her back into a reclined position, Astra gave the same reply as always: "Alright. Stay safe."

And as always, Keeshiff nodded. "Just so long as you stay alive."

With that, he left.

"Time for you to hold to your end of the deal," Asher said, fetching a glass of his usual bitter concoction.

Astra drank obediently but allowed herself the comment, "Believe it or not, I am actually trying."

Asher took the empty glass back to the cabinet. She just barely heard him murmur, "Could've fooled me."

What piece next, what piece next.... The white queen must return to the white king, the white knight must stay behind, and the pawn will press ever forward. But what does that mean for the black pieces?

A knock sounds at the study door and sends my thoughts tumbling.

"Enter," I call.

Julyn does so, bearing an armful of parchment all bound up with a string. "The courier from Litash has arrived, sir."

"Ah, thank you, Julyn." I clear a space on my crowded desk and he sets the bundle down. "Please make sure that the courier is well fed and roomed for the night. I will have some letters for him to take when he departs."

"Of course, sir." The chamberlain bows his head. "Will there be anything else?"

I shake my head, itching to reach for the letters but pasting on a smile instead. "That was all. Thank you."

As soon as Julyn shuts the door, I reach for the bundle and undo the string. I sort through quickly until I spot the seal: a woven pattern, like the bands of a puzzle ring linked together. I pull the folded parchment from the rest and sit back down as I pop the seal.

Dear Brother,

I hope my letter finds you well. All is going smoothly here, but I do worry how you are getting on. Has our red-headed friend visited you yet? Her absence has been felt here in the city. It is even said that the Captain will go to join her. Perhaps I will ask him to bring me back some of that Nythrilian tea you like.

Your sister,
-T

So Entrais has sent the Captain of the Guard to Nythril. An interesting choice. I would have picked Matthes over Soletuph. But no matter. I turn to the chess boards that sit near the window and slide the white castle forward towards its ebony counterpart. I muse over the boards a moment then return to my desk. Tirzah will be expecting a reply.

Dear Sister…

The next day, Astra was sitting up again with The Game spread out on her lap. Keeshiff sat nearby, watching and offering ideas from time to time. Admittedly, he knew even less of the full rules than she did. But after last night's memory—which had apparently scared Asher out of his wits—Astra was determined to put the new information to use. Soletuph was coming to Nythril. The question was, when? She had no way of telling how long ago the memory was, and therefore, no way of knowing when Soletuph might show up. Then there was the matter of whether or not he'd even be able to find them.

The Game stopped when a knock came at the door. Astra looked up just in time to see Dia Jahng let herself in.

"How are you feeling, Princess?" she asked as she crossed the room to the bed, eyeing Keeshiff guardedly as she addressed Astra.

Keeshiff returned the skeptical look, and did not move from his chair.

"Glad to have the surgery over with," Astra replied quietly. She was still unsure of this newest ally.

Dia Jahng started to speak again, but Asher cut in.

"Actually," his voice was heavy. "That is something I had been hoping to speak to you about. I was going to send a message through one of your men if you did not come today."

"Oh?" Jahng's steel expression was traced with concern. "Did the procedure not go well?"

Astra looked to Asher, confused. He had seemed increasingly pessimistic since the surgery, but he hadn't said anything 'til now. She had presumed the mood to be the result of fatigue and their situation.

Indeed, Asher appeared very tired. "Oh, no, the surgery could not have gone better. But I'm beginning to believe that it came too late." He rubbed the back of his neck. The glance he gave towards Astra held sorrow and frustration in equal measure. "Her body is not healing itself the way it should. She is still fevered, her breathing is not what it should be, and her pulse is still too high. In short, she is not recovering from the infection. And I think, except perhaps some Elvish trick, that she will not do so."

Jahng looked visibly peeved. "You have got to be joking…."

Keeshiff, expression alarmed, straightened in his seat. "You mean she's going to *die*?"

"Is there any way to get word to her brother?" Asher asked Jahng. "Perhaps he could send someone."

Astra did not contribute to the conversation, feeling oddly detached from the scene around her. She thought of Louko. And she thought of her brother. If Soletuph had been sent out, then Ent must have been the one to do it.

"Not in time. We'd be talking weeks." Jahng ran her hand over her face in exasperation. "And we just got everyone to back us on a coup, too. Louko has quite a silver tongue hidden behind that mop of hair. You can't just *die* on us now, he's finally calmed down."

"Then there's got to be a way to get her out of here," Keeshiff insisted, desperation edging his voice. "Some way without anyone noticing. That way, we can still free the knights without losing her."

Jahng sighed. "Great. I'm going to have to get that Drogan girl, aren't I?" She looked very annoyed. "Let me speak with Ven and figure this out."

Keeshiff, still gripping the arms of his chair, gritted his teeth and didn't reply.

"Alright," Asher said. "But be quick. We don't have long. Even less if we need to move her."

It was strange to have others talking so animatedly right in front of her—about her no less—and to not say a word. But Astra found nothing to say.

"Understood." Jahng was staring at Astra again. Extending her hand, she offered up a piece of paper. "He asked me to give this to you."

Though Jahng did not give a name, Astra knew it came from Louko. She took it with numb fingers. "Thank you." She did not open it. She forced herself to refocus on the chess pieces still strewn across her coverlet. "Could you give him a message for me? Just tell him that Soletuph is the white castle on the left. He will understand what it means."

Jahng hesitated, confusion marking her brow. But she nodded and walked back towards the door. "If we are in such a hurry, I suppose I'd best get going. It is already almost nightfall, and there will be much to do before the day is out." She let out a terse sort of sigh, turning to Keeshiff. "You need to be back in the Orshian Tower before the evening meal. I should probably escort you back."

"I—" Keeshiff's eyes locked on Astra. His shoulders drooped as if remembering he was, at the end of the day, a prisoner. "Alright." With a sigh, he added, "Please rest," before following Jahng out.

Now alone except for Asher, Astra looked down at the note in her hand. She opened it and found herself simply studying the handwriting. She'd never seen Louko's script before. And yet, it was unmistakably and comfortingly his. Neat, calculated, and with a certain elegance to it.

Astra. Sorry I can't come. I haven't killed anybody yet—be proud. I hope you are keeping to the deal and staying alive. We're going to get you all out. I promise. Please don't die.

Your friend,
Louko

Astra reread the note twice. Suddenly, she wished there was some way to call Jahng back, to ask her not to tell Louko the news that Asher had given. She recalled Jahng's words—*he's finally calmed down.*

And then there was the last line. *Please don't die.* Astra's throat felt thick and her eyes stung as if Asher's announcement had only just set in. Or maybe, it had only just mattered. She recalled those days back during The War, when she had not expected to survive to see its end. By some twist of fate, she had. And now she was determined to survive this one, too.

She realized Asher was watching her, shades of concern and consternation in his features.

"He says things are going well on their end," Astra finally said, refolding the note.

"Well, considering how many plans they've managed to lay already…" Asher started to pack up the chess pieces, a sign that he wanted her to lay back down. "I'm sure they will manage to account for this newest twist." The physician said this more like he was trying to convince himself than his patient.

For Louko's sake, Astra hoped he was right either way.

Keeshiff:

Keeshiff couldn't shake the reality of it, even as he walked down the corridor and back to the dungeon door, his dread heavier than his footsteps. Things always managed to get worse every time he thought things were about to get better. It seemed to be a reoccurring problem that had plagued his family for decades, despite how hard they tried to change things. Now it was Astra who was getting the brunt of it.

The sound of Jahng clearing her throat snapped him back to the present. "So…are you close to her?" she asked in stilted Merimeethian.

"Yes. She's like a little sister to me." He gave a stiff shrug, chest tightening. "I don't know what I'll do if she doesn't make it."

They rounded a corner and reached the door to the Orshian Tower. Jahng exchanged a nod with the guard stationed there as he let them in. She said nothing else, and Keeshiff assumed that that was the end of the conversation. But then they reached the first stairwell and, after waiting for him to go up ahead of her, she asked, "Do you think that, um, such an event is likely?"

"Why do you care all of a sudden?" He turned on the curved stairs and looked back down at her. He tried to keep the bite out of his tone as he added, "You brought us all the way here, after all. Why pity us now?"

Jahng stopped, jaw taut as she looked away. The reaction was deeply familiar, and Keeshiff suddenly felt like he was watching himself. He knew exactly how it felt to swallow all his words. Hadn't he just done the very same thing with Astra?

"I am a hunter by trade; I have been sent after many fugitives over the years." Jahng spoke in a low voice, eyes still fixed on some distant object. "But never have I seen anyone care so much about what happens to the people I drag back here. Your friend was different. She was sick and under duress and not even armed...." The rigid set of her shoulders softened. "And yet, in the middle of all that, she was helping that Drogan girl—the very one she'd been sent to capture. Your friend could have turned her in, and my great uncle would have let you all go." Jahng met his gaze now. "So perhaps a better question is: Why did *she* care so much?"

"Because. It's who she is. She just...does that." Keeshiff stuffed his hands in his hole-ridden pockets, wondering if he was seeing the same seeds of doubt in Jahng he'd long seen in himself, or if he was just imagining things. He remembered the years of half-wishing to catch Louko in the hall...of hoping Louko wouldn't be found when he'd run away. "She just...she makes you realize how much you just stand by and watch. Because *she* never does—even if it gets her, you know—" He waved his hand for emphasis—"killed."

Jahng stood in silence, hands still perched on the rail of the stairs. He thought she would say more, but she clenched her teeth again and swallowed. Her stiff, military bearing resumed, and she gave a short gesture for him to continue up the stairway.

"Right. Prisoner. Silly me." Keeshiff grimaced as he obeyed, another step closer to the prison cell. Where the rest of his friends were kept. The ones that didn't get to come out and see the outside of the cell.

They climbed up the stairs which wound their way around the circular walls of the Orshian Tower. At each new floor, he waited as Jahng rapped on the trapdoor and the guard pulled it open for them. As they climbed up all five floors, Keeshiff began to mentally brace himself, knowing he'd have to give his men the bad news about Astra's conditions. There would be all the usual questions, the inquiries after Asher, the bad jokes in an attempt to act cheerful. And Keeshiff would have to keep his head up and remain their example. He knew that they looked to him, whether or not he deserved it.

They stopped on the top floor, where the last, thick door stood as the guard to his prison cell. Jahng rummaged through the key ring that the jailor had given her.

"How are your men holding up?" she asked.

"They are strong," Keeshiff replied, wondering again how that would change when they heard of the deteriorating situation.

Selecting the proper key, Jahng commented dryly, "A lot of strong men in one small room can still make for a difficult situation."

"That's...true," he murmured. "I'm not really sure what else I'm supposed to say, though. What difference does it make if they're holding up well or not? If any of us are?" He bit his tongue, desperate and exhausted and wishing he had the discipline to keep his mouth shut. He should be thankful Jahng was helping. He should be thankful that Louko at least was safe, or that Aelor Ven was trying to get them out of this mess. But Astra was still dying. Keeshiff's men were still in the Orshian Tower.

"Believe it or not—" Jahng slid the iron key into its slot and turned it with a heavy click—"I understand what it is to worry for one's men." She pulled on the dead bolt and turned to face him. "It is a heavy burden." With that, the woman pushed the door open and stood back.

He did not doubt her and yet, he had no idea what to say. Acknowledgement seemed too weighty a task. So instead, he walked through, mumbling some lame form of thanks. Yes...thanks for getting them all caught. Thanks for putting Astra in a position that could kill her. And thanks for actually bothering to try and rectify her mistake. Perhaps it was more than Keeshiff had ever done.

"How's Astra?" Gavin asked, before Keeshiff even had the door shut behind him.

Keeshiff heard the metallic sound of the key then the dull thud of the deadbolt. "She's alive...but Asher thinks the surgery was too late. She's feeling better, for now, though. They have to find out how to get her to Litash." Keeshiff realized how grim that sounded and tried to put on a better face for his men. He was better than this. "But Louko and Ven are almost ready for us, so it's going to be fine. Jahng is going to see if we can arrange an early getaway so Astra can be sent to King Entrais. Elvish medicine should patch her up." He remembered how uncertain Asher had sounded when he'd suggested the option. Plus, Astra was an outlaw. Even if they got her to Litash, would she receive the help she needed?

"Elvish medicine, eh?" Gavin shook his head. "In that case, I don't envy the princess her early escape at all. Not if it means putting up with some Elves in the process."

The mediocre delivery was only further weakened by the half-hearted chuckles that went around the stone room. Keeshiff knew that his men were putting on as much of a brave face as he was.

Still, all he could manage was a roll of his eyes as he went over and sat down against the wall. "How is everyone holding up here?" he asked, feeling guilty for his relative freedom in comparison to theirs. At any moment, one or all of them could be sent off to Tyron—a fate worse than death.

"Well..." Farian plopped down nearby. "We've come to a vote and decided to let Rhumir and Rufio fight to the death next time they go at it. And if no one loses, we'll help."

There were a few snorts around the room.

"Other than that, considering the food's not bad and they let us sleep, we're doing pretty good." Farian gave that younger-brother grin, even as Ivinon threw him a dirty look.

"But how are you?" Uncharacteristically, it was Lucian who spoke. He always had that way of seeming like he saw everything when he looked at you. "And how is Grandfather?"

Everyone knew how hard Asher had taken Astra's case.

"He is...on edge. I'm afraid of how he will take it if things go more awry." If Keeshiff was being completely honest, he wasn't sure how anyone would take it.

There was a heavy quiet before Gavin dispelled it. "And you?" He watched Keeshiff carefully.

"Oh, just enjoying not having to be waited on hand and foot." Keeshiff forced a laugh as he stretched out, folding his arms behind him for a pillow.

No one laughed with him. But it seemed they at least got the hint to leave things be for now. Both Farian and Gavin got up, the latter saying, "Get some rest. We'll save you some food if it comes when you're asleep."

He gave a weak, "Thanks," and tried to close his eyes.

It didn't work. All he saw was Astra's pale expression. Or Louko's panicked, wide-eyed terror as he was dragged from the Nythrilian throne room. Keeshiff sighed and opened his eyes again, wishing there was something he could do instead of just sit. That's all he seemed to do; sit and wait. Whether it was waiting for Louko to get fed up enough to leave Merimeethia, or for their father to die, or for them to get to Nythril...he just sat there and watched everyone else do the work. Sat so long that he'd let his own sister not only turn in Louko but Astra, too.

Mariah. Keeshiff didn't even want to think her name. And yet he couldn't help but think of how it was his fault—after all, he'd played right into her manipulations. Where was she now? Still safely in Merimeethia? He tried to tell himself he didn't care. Jahng was right—it was hard to feel responsible for others. But perhaps in Keeshiff's case, it was just because he let others take up the responsibility for him.

Quietly groaning in exasperation, he sat up, rubbing the back of his neck.

"Too tired to sleep, eh?" It was Grenedil, sitting a few yards to his right. The man looked as haggard as Keeshiff felt, but the prince noted that he no longer had bandaging wrapped around his leg.

"Something like that," Keeshiff mumbled. "How's your leg?"

Grenedil looked down with a shrug. "If nothing else, sitting here has been good for it." He looked back up, worry drawing his mouth into a thin line. "Has there been any word on Mitheau?"

Right. Grenedil seemed in a similar position to Keeshiff. Mitheau was a hunted race, and now she was in the capital of a country that hated her. "No. Sorry. I'll ask Jahng next time." He should have thought to ask. Of course, he had been way too self-involved to think of it. This was all such a mess.

Grenedil seemed to accept this but muttered under his breath, "No Drogan should ever be kept underground. And no child belongs in a cell." He shook his head, letting out a deep breath before asking, "What of Astra? How likely is it that she will get proper help in time?"

Keeshiff was quiet. He didn't want to say it out loud. That would just make it all too real. Instead, he settled for a stiff shrug.

"I see." Grenedil rubbed the side of his face before resting his hand on his chin. "If only there was a way to get word to Cyl," he said, seemingly to no one in particular.

"Cyl?" Keeshiff bothered to ask. There wasn't much else to do right now, anyway.

"The current Guard. The one that's gone missing." Grenedil sighed.

"Right. That thing." Keeshiff crossed his arms, still unsure he really bought the multiple worlds thing. Seemed like something Louko would dream up. "The one Astra's supposed to take over from or whatever." He was feeling more frustrated by the minute. How was it that every time they got into one mess, they found out that there was a bigger one?

With a slow nod and another sigh, Grenedil spoke in an undertone: "If she lives to see it."

The wince was instinctive. "Right. That." What would he do if she died? What would Louko do? Keeshiff swallowed hard at the last part; he had a horrible feeling that if Astra died, he'd lose not just her but his brother as well.

A GAME OF WITS

CHAPTER XIX

Louko:

"So…it went well, then?" Louko asked as he paced his room, trying to make sense of all of this.

Ven was standing by a window. "Yes. And could you please stop before you wear out the rug? I'm getting mildly dizzy."

With a great effort, Louko did just that. Where was Jahng? Louko couldn't bear to have to sit and wait to hear how the others were doing. This was all taking too long.

The knock on the door nearly startled him out of his skin.

"Yes?" his uncle called.

"Oh, I'm sorry, is now a bad time?" Jahng's voice, dry as ever, entered before she did.

Before she had even shut the door, Louko blurted out, "How is she?"

Jahng's brusque attitude faltered and Louko caught the way she looked to his uncle.

Oh no….

"Your physician thinks that the surgery came too late," she finally admitted. "He doesn't think she'll survive without some kind of Gifted treatment."

Louko felt as if the room was spinning. "*What*?" The word came out weaker than silence. What?! No, no, no, no. "I need to go see her—" No matter how many times he had gone through this, he couldn't seem to handle it any better. Astra. Couldn't. Die.

"Woah, Louko, take a deep breath." Uncle Ven had caught him by the arm to steady him. When he seemed sure Louko wouldn't keel over, Ven looked to Jahng. "How long do we have to work with?"

Louko tried to pull away. Wow, what a perfect little princeling he would be if he fainted.

"Not long," Jahng replied. "I don't think we can wait to get her out. The problem is, if we plan an escape, we can't get all of them out. And, if I'm correct, your takeover won't happen in time to keep Dia Tzaro from shipping Prince Keeshiff back to Merimeethia in retaliation. Which he would definitely do if his prize prisoner suddenly vanished."

She'd hardly finished speaking when there came a knock on the door.

Louko jumped, every muscle aching with tension.

"I gave specific orders not to be disturbed." He barely registered his uncle's grumble.

What if someone had found out? What if....

A servant poked his head, scanning the room before locking onto Louko. The man's eyes were bright green....

Louko couldn't breathe, legs giving out as he felt like this stupid nightmare was getting even worse.

"Louko, what's—" Ven's attention was taken away as he noticed the servant in the room.

The man stepped in, eyes still trained on Louko. "*Where is she?*" He spoke Litashian.

"It—it—it's…" Louko couldn't get a word out. It was Tyron. Tyron was here and he was going to get Astra. "Someone get him!" He finally came to his senses, stepping back as he pointed a finger at the servant. Those green eyes, just like Kaeden.

Jahng moved first, pulling her sword and stepping in front of Louko and Ven.

Tyron reacted likewise, except that he stepped back instead of pressing forward. He kept his sword level as he seemed to quickly analyze the situation. *"I'm just here for Astra,"* he said evenly.

Louko's terror was suspended by the strange shift in the man's proportions. The hair grew longer and unkept, the sandy blond just about the polar opposite of Tyron's black hair. The body was sturdier, shorter, and his eyes did not hold the dark circles that Tyron's always had.

"S-S-Soletuph?" Louko had not seen the Ethian Guard since the ball in Litash that had started this whole mess, and it took him a moment to gather himself. Fear returned. "Wait. Prove it. How would you even be here?" Louko still couldn't move.

"Oh, wonderful, a shape-shifter in my home. What else could possibly go wrong?" Ven's dry comment intruded upon the moment.

"Sorry to crash the party, but I don't speak Nythrilian," came Soletuph's monotone. *"But I'd happily threaten you all in Litashian if it means you'll tell me where Astra is."*

"How do I know you're really Soletuph?" Louko switched to Litashian, unconvinced but no longer shaking with the uncontrollable terror of before. The man's behavior was certainly that of Soletuph.

"Soletuph...." Jahng said the name slowly, glancing back towards Louko. She did not lower her blade. "Wait, Astra mentioned a Soletuph. She said he was the white castle and that you'd know what that meant."

"*How do I know you're really Louko? The Louko I knew never called me by my actual name.*" Soletuph rolled his eyes. "*But fine, if you want proof, I can always whoop you in a sword match like Ent did that time you insulted Astra.*"

Louko might have been more embarrassed if not for the fact that no one had known about that. No one except Entrais and Soletuph. Not even Astra...and definitely not Tyron. Louko's fears deflated and he ran right at Soletuph, grabbing hold of him in a fierce hug. "*Soletuph! It's really you. Thank the Creator, what on Eatris are you doing here?!*"

"Sure. Hug the maniac shifter with a sword but punch me in the face when I save you. I understand," Uncle Ven grumbled from nearby.

"*Uh,*" Soletuph seemed far more put off by the hug than he had been by Jahng pulling a weapon on him. He disentangled himself and regarded Louko with near alarm. "*Ent sent me when Astra's letters stopped. What...*" He was still looking Louko up and down. "*...happened?*"

"*Entrais sent you?*" Louko could have cried with relief. What had Jahng said? Astra needed Gifting to heal...oh. "*You need to take Astra back to Litash now. She's dying. I thought we'd saved her but she's dying and nothing's working and—*"

"*What?*" Soletuph sheathed his sword and took Louko by the shoulders. "*Slow down. Where is she?*"

"*I do not relish being talked around.*" Louko had forgotten his uncle could speak the trade language.

"*This is a friend of Astra's, Uncle.*" Louko turned around to face his rather perturbed uncle. "*He's here to help.*"

"*So where is she?*" Soletuph repeated.

Louko's throat felt suddenly too thick to get words out of.

Ven replied for him. "*In the halls below the Orshian Tower. It's the palace prison. She was brought to a physician's ward there, and we are working on getting her and the others out.*"

Soletuph's expression was grave as he looked up at Ven. "*And you say she is dying?*"

"*Yes.*" Again it was Ven. Louko found himself once more an observer, unable to register that what was happening was real. Astra was dying. *Dying,* dying.

"*So we need to get her home. How long does she have?*" Soletuph asked.

Ven turned to Jahng and repeated the question in Nythrilian.

"A week, the physician said," she replied, still eyeing the shape-shifter.

Louko just stared at her. "W-wait, that soon?" Panic swelled again. That was. That was so little time. Only a *week*?!

When Ven relayed this to Soletuph, the Ethian let out a long breath. "*I can't get her back that quickly. It's not possible.*"

"*Wh-what—no, there has to be a way to get her back. Can't you shift into a dragon or something and fly her over?*" Louko blurted out.

"*I can't hold something that large for three days straight.*" Soletuph shook his head. "*Even if I could, I'm guessing she wouldn't be able to stay on. We'll have to find another way.*"

Louko was hyperventilating. This was seeming more impossible by the minute.

"What's happening?" Jahng broke in. "What's wrong?"

Ven explained the issue. "He can't maintain a different shape long enough to get Astra back to Litash."

Jahng paused. "So, what about that little Drogan? They can hold their shape indefinitely."

Oh. Louko blinked. "O-oh, that could work. Mitheau could probably do it—and she needs out of Nythril, anyway." He shuddered at the reminder of her terror at being shoved in a cage.

"*I can't understand you.*" Soletuph sounded annoyed.

Louko threw up his hands. "*Well, either I speak to you and she can't understand me, or I speak to her and you can't understand me! And right now, she has a little bit more understanding about what's going on.*" The constant switching of languages was enough to make Louko's head explode.

Soletuph raised an eyebrow and gave no reply.

"It could work...so long as she's willing." Ven went back to the subject at hand. "But we still have the problem of what to do about Keeshiff and his knights. It will be another ten days before I am on the throne—eight at the very best."

"How long could we make Astra's disappearance go unnoticed?" Louko was tapping his finger.

Jahng shook her head. "A day, if you're lucky. The king's physician checks in every morning."

Louko turned back to Soletuph. "*Do you think you could shift and play Astra for a few days?*"

"*Not really, no. Shifters have their limits, and one of them is eye color. You can't change our soul or whatever nonsense that's about. Her eyes are way too distinct, and mine...very green. I can't speak Nythrilian, anyway. We wouldn't be able to get away with it. And if I get caught, Ent would be blamed.*"

Desperation swelled with the knowledge that Astra would not make it eight days. Louko didn't like what he was about to say, and yet the words spilled out regardless of his feelings on the subject. "So what if we smuggled her and Mitheau out with Soletuph's help, then provided Keeshiff and the rest with weapons and supplies to barricade themselves in their cell until we get Dia Tzaro off that stupid throne?"

Uncle Ven seemed nearly taken aback by the idea. But then his hand went to his chin in thought.

From behind him, Soletuph sighed in a show of thinning patience.

"Could they really hold up that long?" Jahng asked dubiously.

"If anyone could, Keeshiff and his men would be it. Of course, I wouldn't dream of doing this without his consent." Louko wavered at the possibility of sending his brother to such a slow and terrible death. "He held his own during The War, and if they have Asher with them with medical supplies to tend anything—and plenty of food and water…." What in Eatris was Louko doing? This was a ridiculous idea that put his own brother at risk. How could he talk of lives so cheaply? His tongue felt filthy amid the calm tone it used.

Jahng and Ven traded roles, the former now assessing him curiously and the other folding his hands behind his back.

"As crazy as it seems, it just might work," his uncle said. "After all, the Orshian Tower was built to be impenetrable except for its single entrance. And considering its builders were trying to keep people in and not get them out, it ought to be easily defensible."

"Will the Council Ezai take issue with them defending it by force?" asked Jahng.

Ven made a shooing gesture with one hand. "If I am king by then, I'm sure I can talk them into a full pardon."

"*I'm assuming that everyone is discussing the plan?*" Soletuph asked with thinly veiled impatience.

Oh. Right. Louko turned to him and tried to sum it up as best he could.

The Ethian's expression sobered. "*How many men does your brother have?*"

Louko thought a moment. "*Ten...if we count Rhumir and Grenedil.*"

"*Hmm.*" Soletuph seemed to size Louko up yet again. "*Not the best odds.*"

How helpful of him to—

"*Leave me with them. You take Astra to Litash.*"

"*Wait. What?*" Louko furrowed his brow, confused. Soletuph had been so protective of Astra only a moment ago.

He was aware of both Jahng and Ven watching him.

Soletuph gave a half-shrug. "*You said the dragon-shifter is a girl, so I'm guessing she is only big enough to carry two at the most.*" His voice was that of a school-master giving a lecture. "*Your brother is short-handed and needs someone who knows how to withstand a siege.*" His tone quieted. "*And you have been the only one who has taken care of Astra. That leaves you more qualified than me to take her home.*"

Louko stood there awkwardly, guilt mixed in with a selfish relief. "*Alright,*" was all he said.

Uncle Ven cleared his throat to get Louko's attention. "Do you think this is the best plan, then?" He kept watching Soletuph from the corner of his eye.

"Best is an overstatement…" Louko realized he'd probably run his hand through his hair twenty times. What was he doing? What was he doing? *What was he doing?!* But if they didn't do something…they'd lose Astra. But what if they lost Keeshiff and everyone else instead? Astra wouldn't be able to live with herself.

"But I want to see Keeshiff." His voice was firm, knowing what was at stake. If Keeshiff agreed to this, he might die. And Louko would never see him again.

Uncle Ven must've understood because he turned to Jahng. "How quickly can we make that happen?"

"I go back this evening. I can make everything ready—if your shape-shifter helps, it should be easy to get weapons past the guards—and we can bring Louko with us," Jahng replied.

Louko didn't like this. Everyone knew Keeshiff would say yes, and that fact made him wonder if they were even asking him at all. He felt trapped in a corner where he had to choose between his brother and his best friend, and he didn't like it. And yet, what other choice did they have?

"*I have one request,*" Soletuph broke in, strangely quiet. "*I want to see her before you leave.*"

The dungeon door closed behind Louko, and he found himself standing in the center of the large cell. Jahng was watching the door, leaving Louko to face his brother and the others alone. He still wasn't sure how he was going to say this….

"Louko? What are you doing here?" Keeshiff got up from a cot near the wall. He crossed the distance between them quickly, taking stock of

Louko as he did so. "You look...different." His brother stopped a few feet away, looking suddenly awkward. He jammed his hands in his pockets as if he didn't know what to do with them.

Louko was confused but didn't dwell on it. "I'm here to talk out a plan. How are you all holding up?" He scanned his brother intently, trying to decide for himself even as he asked the question.

"The only thing we're suffering from is boredom." Keeshiff glanced sideways at his men with what was almost a chuckle. "But I'm guessing you didn't come up here just to hear us complain. What's happening?"

"Jahng told us what Asher said. Uncle Ven is in the process of deposing the king, but it won't be official for another week at least. Astra doesn't have that kind of time...so we were thinking of breaking Mitheau out and sending Astra to Entrais for Elvish treatment. But that would mean they'd try and take you all.... We thought, well, I suggested that we ask Soletuph—er, he's here, by the way—to supply you with food, water, and weapons, and you could hold off the Nythrilian soldiers until my uncle gets on the throne. It could speed up the process—they know you all are wrongfully imprisoned...but you might not...." Louko couldn't bear to finish. "It's a lot to ask. And a big gamble. I don't want to gamble with you, Keeshiff."

A lot of unfamiliar emotions flitted across Keeshiff's face. "You said you made this plan?" he asked. But he didn't wait for an answer. He turned to his knights and called, "Hear that, men? Who's ready to actually work for a living?"

A general cheer went up around the room.

Keeshiff turned back to Louko with a grin. "Oh, don't look so worried. Fighting is what we do. And to be honest, I think everyone here will be glad to do something after being useless for so long." His smile faded into something more sincere, and he looked towards the corner where Grenedil was. "I'm guessing there's no chance at springing him out, first?"

Louko ran his hands through his hair. "I don't think so...the only reason we can get anyone out is because Mitheau can...well...fly...and she can only hold two people. Well. Maybe he could go with Astra, instead." It felt so wrong for him to go, now. As if he were running away.

"Don't worry about me," Grenedil said. "So long as you watch after Mitheau, I will stay and see this through."

Keeshiff gave a grateful nod in his direction before addressing Louko again. "Besides, Astra needs you."

There was a knot forming in Louko's stomach. "Are you sure? I don't...I don't want to run away. I don't want to leave you." To his possible death, no less.

"Louko, you are the most loyal person I know." Keeshiff softened. "And the bravest. I know you would be right here with me if you could. But I have my men here, and Astra has no one. Go with her. Take care of her, and when this is over, I'll meet you in Litash."

Louko was rather shocked at the statement as a whole, and could only find a choked, "Okay." Keeshiff had never been so open, and honestly, the words struck deeper than the young prince ever could have imagined. Perhaps it was because they were words he had yearned his whole life to hear. Perhaps it was Keeshiff's statement about knowing Louko would be by his side if he could. Perhaps it was everything.

A knock came on the door, signaling that time was up. Louko took a reluctant step back, only to hesitate when Keeshiff started to speak.

Only, Keeshiff didn't say anything. Indecision warred openly on his face. Then he seemed to give up. "Oh, whatever," he muttered as he stepped forward and...and...and wrapped Louko in a hug.

"Oh. Um." Louko's unintelligible replies were lost as he found himself gripping his brother with equal fierceness, as if a fresh glass of water had been given him after a lifetime in the desert.

"You know I love you, right?" Keeshiff whispered.

Louko's throat tightened. "Yeah. I, uh, love you, too." he whispered back hoarsely, the words almost a novel phenomenon. Finally, Louko let go, stepping back and rubbing the back of his neck. "Yeah. Don't die or anything," he murmured like an idiot.

"You either," Keeshiff said, making Louko feel a little better. At least he wasn't any more awkward than Keeshiff was.

The knock at the door came again, this time more urgently.

"I have to go." Louko turned back towards the door. "You all stay safe, please." And with that, knocked on the door for Jahng to open it up.

He only hoped this wouldn't be the last time he ever saw Keeshiff.

Keeshiff:

Keeshiff watched until the door shut entirely, separating him from his brother with a resounding thud.

The sound hadn't even died away before the chuckling began.

"I love you, too, *Keeshiff*," Gavin snickered.

"Oh, shut it." Keeshiff turned around, face burning. But he didn't regret his words, and he didn't miss the odd sort of pride in his men's eyes. He knew they only joked to show they understood. "We have work to do if we plan to hold off in here for more than a week."

The laughter faded, only to be replaced with another sort of amusement.

"Don't think I've ever heard of defending a prison cell." Rufio's comment summed up all their thoughts.

"Well, to its credit, it's probably one of the best places we've been in the last couple months," Coryn jested as he got up. "So, then, we should be getting weapons...what else can we do? There isn't much furniture in here to barricade."

Coryn was unfortunately correct. "We'll have to hope that Jahng brings us something for the door," Keeshiff mused. "I'm guessing she won't be able to help us with the windows."

The windows lined the very top of the round, stone room. They were quite wide but very short; not escapable but enough to get an arrow through.

"Hm...if we can get some thick wood...." Lucian appeared in deep thought. "But I guess we won't know what she'll bring us until she comes."

They had been debating on different tactics for a couple of hours before the guards brought dinner. It was more food than usual, so, after everyone had taken what they needed, the extra was wrapped and hidden beneath the straw. The empty dishes were left by the door as usual.

They all milled around a while more, listening for footsteps or the telltale jangle of keys. Nothing. They were just starting to give up and settle down for the night when Lucian stood up abruptly.

"Do you hear that?"

Everyone froze, listening intently.

Keeshiff heard what he thought was simply the wind against the Orshian Tower walls. But then it grew louder, harsher, scraping with more force than any wind could.

"*Mind your heads,*" a voice called from...outside the window? And that voice...was definitely not human.

Before Keeshiff could even warn the others, something dropped from the narrow opening and fell to the floor with a metallic clatter.

Slowly, Keeshiff went forward, picking up what turned out to be a rucksack of...weapons? Keeshiff looked up to find two cat-like green eyes peering through the slim window. The prince jumped and swallowed a surprised shout.

"*More on the way. Be ready,*" the voice came again. The green eyes vanished with the faint scabbling sound of claws on stone.

In a flash, Keeshiff recalled Louko mentioning Soletuph. Wasn't that one of Entrais's men? One of the shape-shifters?

Keeshiff turned around and found all the knights gawking at him. "Uh." He scratched the back of his neck. "I think that was...Soletuph." He noted several alarmed expressions from his companions. Right. Many hadn't been to Litash before. "He's a, uh, shape-shifter. The one Louko mentioned." It still wasn't natural. Keeshiff couldn't help but shudder upon remembering the cat-like eyes. How did anyone live in peace in Litash?

Coryn stepped up, eyes on the sack in Keeshiff's hand. "Are those swords? Ha. I don't know who this So-Tough is, but I like him already."

A few more trips from Soletuph, and before Keeshiff knew it, they had a good supply of weapons. Then came the food and water—things that would keep during a multi-day siege. Finally, the green eyes appeared one last time, glaring a moment through the crevice before morphing into something small enough to slither through the crack. A moment later and a man suddenly stood in the gloom of the dungeon.

"Am...am I the only one not alright with this?" Farian said after a gasp.

Soletuph raised an eyebrow and turned to Keeshiff. "*I figured you could use a little more help. Ever been on the bad side of siege?*" he asked.

Well, unless he counted the time he'd barricaded himself in his own room at twelve...not really. "*No. I guess we were on the other end in Litash.*"

"*Yeah, well, unfortunately this end of it is much less fun.*" The shape-shifter was already surveying the room. "*They told me that Astra's disappearance will be known before midmorning. That gives us around nine hours to set up as much as possible and then rest while we can.*"

The next hour consisted of putting together the slats of wood that Soletuph had brought until they roughly resembled barricades. Then they turned to barring the windows with the leftover pieces.

"*Make sure that you don't wedge those in too tightly,*" Soletuph instructed. "*We'll have to pull them out to vent smoke if they try to burn us out.*"

With that comforting thought in mind, Keeshiff passed the word on to the knights.

They were just distributing the weapons when Rhumir, who had been posted on the door just to keep him out of the way, whispered, "Someone's coming!"

There was a rush to hide the weapons, but what did it matter? They had all these barricades sitting around the room!

"Quick," Keeshiff called in a harsh whisper. "Be prepared to take them."

"Don't get yourself all excited, it's just me." Jahng's unimpressed greeting filtered through the door, and a moment later, the huntress was standing in the entryway.

"Is something the matter?" Keeshiff's brow furrowed. Why was she here?

Jahng held up a bag. "The medical supplies took longer to get than expected. Couldn't get them to your shifting friend in time."

Right. Medicine. Keeshiff gulped. He'd been fortunate enough for all his men to make it alive so far, but how long would that last? "Thank you," he managed to mumble.

With a terse nod, she handed the bag over. Then she hesitated, looking around the room at all of the knights. She cleared her throat. "I am sorry about this." She met Keeshiff's eyes, even in the dimness of the cell. "I truly am. If I could go back, I would have acted differently. I hope that you and your men survive my mistake."

Keeshiff's shoulders dropped. "Thank you. You have already done more than enough. We are in your debt." He gave a deep bow. "I've made my fair share of mistakes, anyway. I'm hardly one to judge."

Maybe it was just him, maybe it was the lack of light, but Keeshiff was pretty sure that he saw Jahng's brow furrow as if in confusion. She opened her mouth to speak, only for her lips to hang open in a wordless expression. Then she regathered herself and held out the bag again.

This time, Keeshiff took it.

"I hope to see you on the other side," Jahng said. She bowed in the same fashion he had and then strode out the door.

A GAME OF WITS

CHAPTER XX

Astra:

Astra had never seen Asher so nervous. The physician had been discreetly packing away tonics, powders, and all with the shakiest hands she'd ever seen. She wanted to ask what had him so scared. But she didn't know if she should. She wasn't sure she wanted to know.

Just when she was on the verge of giving in and asking, the door opened. She turned her head to see…

"…Soletuph?" This had to be a dream. Or another memory. Astra couldn't tell them apart anymore.

"Hey there, Slip." An uncharacteristically soft smile put a crack in the Ethian's hard exterior.

She tried to sit up, but her only success was in making the whole room spin. "How did you get here? Is this real?"

"Ent sent me after you didn't send your normal check in. It just took me a while to find you, since no one knew where you were." His smile faded. "And yes, this is real. Louko even...hugged me…. Tell him never to do that again, please." His face twisted in a grimace. "How are you feeling?"

Louko...was he alright? Astra couldn't remember where he was. "Better. Can you tell Ent for me? When you go home?"

Soletuph huffed and folded his arms in front of him, looking over her like some disappointed parent.

Then another familiar voice cut the air. "Why don't you tell him yourself? You're leaving tonight."

"Louko?" This time she managed to push herself upright, head swimming.

"Hey," He sat down next to her, instantly entwining his hand in hers. He looked so…. "Everything's alright, don't worry. We're just going to get you some help."

Astra didn't quite understand. "But what about the others?" This *had* to be a dream…. The fever gave everything such a strange feeling that it was hard to tell.

"Well, I'll leave you two to it, then." Soletuph sounded almost...pained? Then the austere facade returned. "I have a tower to climb and toys to deliver." And with that, the Ethian turned away, only hesitating a brief moment to say, "Be safe," before leaving the room.

"The others are fine, don't worry. Uncle is going to get them out by next week." Louko's voice sounded so certain...so sure. "Are you ready for me to carry you?"

Uncle...Ven. He was talking about Ven. "Where are we going?"

"Your brother's." Louko's reply was soft as his hand withdrew and he moved closer to wrap her in a blanket.

Ent? "But how?" She didn't try to stop him.

"Magic." Louko's voice had a tint of humor in it as he gently hoisted her from the bed. "Wow. I don't remember you being so heavy...gained weight?"

Astra tried to look at him. She couldn't make out very much. Was he...joking? "I told Asher he was making me eat too much," she murmured, letting her head sink back against his shoulder.

"Oh, I'm sure. If you look at him, you wonder if *he's* eating too much," Louko continued as he carefully walked her out of the room. "How are you feeling?" The question was more serious as they went, Asher following behind with the satchel he'd been so nervously packing.

"Tired." The word came out like a sigh. "You?"

She felt them going down stairs but was distracted by Louko's reply. "Ready to get you some proper help. And apparently not bad at politics...."

"What does that mean?" She shivered as she felt cool air wash over them.

"It means I just helped overthrow a king...guess I'm not such a bad Merimeethian after all." His reply held more humor.

Everything seemed so out of place. If this was a dream, it was a strange one. "Sounds like you've been much busier than me."

"Seeing as you've been busy *dying*, I doubt it."

Astra didn't quite know what to say to that. It didn't seem to matter, anyway, as Louko had slowed his gait and she could pick up hushed voices.

They continued down, Astra clinging to him as they slowed and sped through the murk around her. She could register nothing except the one carrying her and just barely the fact Asher was following. Then, after some dizzying time had passed, she registered a gentle breeze hitting her burning cheeks. They...they were outside? She wasn't quite sure she even remembered what they were doing. What had Louko said again?

"Oh dear, she looks worse than I thought," said another voice, strong and approaching quickly with the sound of footsteps against cobblestone.

"Yeah." She felt Louko vibrate as he replied. "Is Mitheau ready?"

"Yes. She's a little roughed up but ready and able, she said." It was Aelor Ven, Astra recognized at last.

The mention of Mitheau stirred her, dredging up memories of the silver-haired girl in the prison cart. "Mitheau is alright?" she asked as she tried to put all the pieces together.

"Yes, darling, don't worry." It was still Ven.

Astra could feel Louko's arms waver a little as he spoke. "Probably should get a move on then."

Darling? Astra didn't have time to question the word or its application to her before they started to move again. The pain always had a way of interrupting her thought process.

More footsteps, another voice—this one softer and female—and one last pause before Astra felt herself being lowered. Someone else was helping Louko, now, setting Astra on the back of a...oh, this wasn't a horse. This had feathers.

And as she was settled carefully on its back, it vibrated and rumbled in a low hum.

"You alright?" Louko's voice was still near her, and she thought she could see him standing beside her and what she was on.

Astra was fairly sure that she managed a nod.

Asher appeared beside Louko then, worry still wearing itself in creases on his face.

"Here," the physician said, holding out a satchel to Louko. "This is three days' worth of supplies for all of you. Medicine, too. Make sure Astra drinks some auminar whenever you stop for meals. If you are having trouble waking her for those, there are smelling salts in one of the pouches."

"Alright. Anything else?"

Asher faltered then shook his head. "I guess not," he said. He still looked so out of sorts. Then he put one hand on Louko's shoulder. "You always did take care of her. I have no doubts that you will do so now." And with that, he turned away.

"Thank you, Asher. For everything. If anyone has saved her, it's you," Louko called after him, voice soft—or was it just Astra's ringing ears?

Asher did not reply.

It was Ven who broke in: "You need to be on your way." Ven made to step back then sighed. He gave Louko a brief, close hug, then pulled away and brushed himself off. "Be safe. Write when you get there."

"Of course, Uncle." And with that, Louko carefully mounted up behind Astra, using his arms to help secure her as she swayed in feverish dizziness. "Hang in there," he whispered.

They took off without another word.

It was several minutes later before Astra had regained her breath enough to say, "Oh. We're going by Dragon."

Astra did not remember much after that. The world came in brief, hazy glimpses: Louko helping her drink from a waterskin; tree branches waving gently overhead; clouds speeding by as the wind tugged at her hair. Slowly, things began to make less sense. And Astra began to be less bothered by it. All at once, she would be a child again, playing in the mountain creek near her home and simply enjoying the cool water running over her fingers. Or she would be sitting in Ent's camp, the strong scent of cut pine and woodsmoke filtering through the night air. Or she would be riding Dannsair—just riding. Nowhere to go, nowhere to be, just free to roam the wide, green world.

The only thing that ever gave her pause were those glimpses of Louko. She could never understand why he looked so worried. Or why he kept calling her name....

Louko:

"How long will it take to fly over the forest?" Louko asked as they landed not far from the Nythrilian border, visible before them by the mountains in the distance. Astra was barely hanging on. She looked so pale, so very sick.

"Over?" Mitheau looked up from where she had been digging through their pack for rations. "You mean, through?"

"No. We don't have enough supplies for through—or enough time. She has less than a week at this rate." She was burning up...Louko forced himself to focus. "And she needs water. Could you toss the canteen?"

Mitheau pulled out the water, but now she looked uneasy and seemed to have forgotten the biscuit she'd taken out for herself. "Flying over might still be worse. There's a reason Grenedil and I were arguing about it.... No one ever does it—there's a lot of monsters in the Forest of Riddles that hunt flying prey. And she's too sick for us to go up to a safer altitude."

"I still need the canteen." Louko extended a hand, waiting until Mitheau collected herself enough to hand it over. After getting Astra to drink a little, Louko asked, "Aren't the monsters pretty much gone now, though? After The War—I mean...the really dangerous ones. What could be scarier than a Drogan?" Mitheau still seemed so shaken from her time in the Orshian Tower, and he couldn't blame her. He remembered his time back in the castle with Astra and couldn't help but shudder.

"Lots of things. Trust me," Mitheau mumbled. She looked back down at the biscuit in her hands. "But maybe you're right. Maybe the Forest is tamer than what all the tales say." She took a bite.

"Yeah." He looked back to Astra, who had once more slipped into unconsciousness. He turned back to Mitheau. "Are you...holding up alright?"

"Uh." Mitheau looked a little lost. She gave a little nod. "Yeah. I guess, I don't know...." She regathered herself. "I guess I was just thinking about Grenedil. Did your friends ever say how he was doing?"

"Not specifically, no. But I saw him when I went to meet my brother—his leg seemed better. I'm sure he'll be fine." *What a lie, Louko.* He couldn't even say if Keeshiff was going to be alright, let alone any of the others. Who was he kidding? Again, he turned to Astra. He couldn't even guarantee *she* would survive.

Mitheau paused, this time studying Louko. He saw her glance towards Astra. "I'm sure he will be," she finally said. "He's gotten out of much worse scrapes."

It was getting harder and harder to breathe. "Yeah." They'd be fine. Everyone would be fine...yeah. "Are you ready to go on?"

Cramming the rest of the biscuit in her mouth and then washing it down with a swig of water, Mitheau nodded. "Ready. Let's go."

The wind rushed over Louko as he clung to Mitheau, sheltering Astra as much as he could from the biting air. At least he didn't have to hold onto her so tightly, anymore. After dealing with the gusts of wind through the mountain ranges, they'd found it wise to tie Astra to Mitheau. It couldn't be comfortable for the young Drogan, but at least Astra wouldn't fall.

Louko, on the other hand….

Honestly, all things considered, he wasn't doing too terribly. It helped to grasp onto the rope, and while Louko definitely *hated* riding Dragons, he had unfortunately done it several times during The War. Astra was the one that had always liked flying. And now she wasn't awake to enjoy it. Something stuck in Louko's throat, and he wasn't sure if it was emotion...or another mouthful of bugs.

His attention wavered when he saw Mitheau craning her neck, silver head scanning the Forest below. Then she angled up as she beat her wings in a quicker rhythm. Wait—why were they gaining altitude?

"Astra won't be able to breathe!" Louko shouted, hoping the wind wouldn't whisk away the message. They'd talked about this! What was Mitheau thinking?!

In response, he received nothing more than a low rumble. Right, Mitheau couldn't speak Litashian in this form—but she could still understand it, so why wasn't she stopping?

That's when Louko realized that the rumble had not come from Mitheau.

And then came the shadow, blocking out the sun as it swallowed them in its darkness. Louko stared at what appeared to be a monolithic mesh of vines shooting up past them and into the sky. Mitheau dove sharply to the right, and Louko fought just to hold on. Then he noticed the scales. And as the thing fell back down...the teeth. This thing...this enormous thing...was the largest monster Louko had *ever* seen in his life. The teeth alone were each twice as tall as Louko. To say Mitheau was a toothpick next to it would have been an understatement.

"What is *that?!*" Louko screamed, not even caring that she couldn't reply.

Mitheau swerved again, pinning her wings and pitching them all forward at blinding speed.

Again the beast shot up, and Louko was barely able to look down at the forest in time to see the gigantic rows of teeth climbing hungrily for them. Mitheau rolled this time, and Louko yelped as he nearly lost his grip on the Drogan and the rope, legs flailing a moment in exposed air before Mitheau righted herself. Louko swiftly hooked his legs under some of the rope, ignoring the painful chafing and telling himself it would be better than becoming a splatter on the forest floor.

Well...if they didn't get eaten first.

Louko twisted around and saw the momentum of the green scales begin to slow. The beast was coming back down. "Climb, Mitheau, climb!"

He felt her sides heave with her panting breath, wings pounding furiously. But they weren't getting any higher.

Again the beast snapped, so close that some of the vines that were tangled around its scales scraped up against Louko's arm.

They couldn't keep doing this. Mitheau was too burdened to fly high enough out of the way, and this beast was keeping up with them even as Mitheau was desperately trying to fly out of range. And they were getting so close to the treetops now. Louko looked down, for the first time having enough time to really get a view of the giant beast hunting them. It had some sort of snake-like body, thicker than Mitheau was long, and longer than Louko could even register. It snaked through the tree boughs, seeming to bounce and weave in order to get momentum. The effect was chilling; it was as if the very forest was alive.

Louko gripped Mitheau as the behemoth again shot its ugly head towards them and gnashed its teeth, barely missing Mitheau's left wing. At least Louko was more prepared this time when she lurched sideways. But now he noticed their other problem: Every time she evaded the thing, she sank lower. There was no way they'd get out of its reach.

So there was only one other option.

"Mitheau! You've got to go lower!" It all clicked in an instant as Louko's eyes locked in on the weaving form of the beast. "Fly back! We need to get it tangled up!" If this worked, it wouldn't hold the beast forever, but enough for them to get far away.

There was a gravelly bellow of protest from up ahead and Louko barely registered it had come from Mitheau.

"It's our only chance!"

With a final grunt of objection, Mitheau folded her wings until they nearly covered both Louko and the unconscious Astra. The sudden dive sent Louko's stomach up somewhere into his throat. He squeezed his eyes shut and tried not to scream as Mitheau began to spin. All around them, he heard the crash and chaos of snapping branches.

Mitheau dodged, rolled, and wove around the monster's lunges for them, each time a closer call than the last. Not that Louko could fully pay attention. It was all he could do to keep himself from falling off, as well as make sure Astra did not come loose from her bindings.

The beast lunged its head at them once more, and this time Mitheau was too slow to dodge. But...the thing's teeth snapped just short of her tail.

"It's working!" Louko couldn't help but shout. "It's all tangled up—*run for it!*" Or, er, fly for it? Louko's panicked brain didn't care to think that one through.

He heard the groan of the trees as the monster fought against them, thrashing and snapping wildly. But the trees of the Forest of Riddles were much stronger here near the roots; they did not give out.

Mitheau pulled upwards, weaving through the thick foliage with as much speed as she could muster. Her breathing was ragged enough for Louko to hear even over the rush of wind.

And yet they flew on, Mitheau's muscles seeming to strain to the point of breaking. Louko risked freeing a hand to check Astra's pulse, almost startled that she hadn't stirred at all. She showed no signs of waking...but at least she was still alive.

"Let's try not to find another one of those?" Louko gave a weak laugh as he called up to the exhausted Mitheau.

There was an annoyed growl in reply.

Keeshiff:

Keeshiff had never dreaded a sunrise so much as he dreaded this one. He tried to remind himself it wouldn't be all bad; if all went according to plan, Astra and Louko would be clear of the city by now. But then, when had anything gone according to plan? He let out a deep breath and rolled onto his side, ignoring the sharp prodding of straw as he did so. He could just make out the lightening sky through the cracks in the stopped-up windows.

And oddly enough, his thoughts went to Mariah. As he remembered all those times when she'd claimed she was doing everything for him, Keeshiff could have scoffed. What if she saw him now? Lying in a prison cell, hungry and dirty, waiting to get up and fight a losing battle that would probably claim his life and all of his men's. Would she still believe her own lies?

These pointless thoughts were pushed aside when Keeshiff saw Soletuph stiffen and straighten. The Ethian had slept propped up against the door. Assuming that the shifter was somewhere around the age of Astra's brother, he couldn't be terribly older than Keeshiff. And yet the prince felt like an untried youth compared to the stone-faced Soletuph. It didn't help that Keeshiff and his men were all worn down to nothing while the Ethian was in fighting condition, complete with a patchwork of leather armor.

Soletuph heaved himself to his feet and Keeshiff sat up.

"*It's time,*" the former announced simply.

The two words made Keeshiff feel cold. He didn't spare it any thought, stretching his sore limbs and getting up. He went from knight to knight and woke each one quietly. His stomach twisted at the thought that, when they next took their rest, there might not be as many to wake again.

The groggy knights were a little slow to wake, but once food and water had made its way around, the grim remembrance of what lay ahead set in. Each man pulled on a padded gambeson—chainmail had been too heavy and bulky to bring up for everyone—and strapped on their weapons in silence.

"Alright." Keeshiff kept his voice to an undertone. "Remember: We want to avoid casualties on both sides. If we kill a bunch of Nythrilians, we won't show ourselves in a positive light to the council; aim to deflect or to wound."

"Right," Lucian grumbled. "And no getting caught. Again…."

Yeah. That.

With that grim thought in mind, everyone split up into their teams. Soletuph and Coryn took up position with Keeshiff at the door, blades close and at the ready. Keeshiff glanced back, waiting until each of the remaining knights had taken up their places at the barricades. These would be brought down and used to fortify every level they took. When there were two men at each ready to carry, Keeshiff grabbed the door handle and hoped that Jahng had remembered to sabotage the deadbolt.

"*Ready when you are,*" he said to Soletuph.

In response, the shifter gave a chilling smile and stepped back. His body seemed to lengthen and change, a strange metamorphosis from man to beast. It didn't matter that Keeshiff had seen a shape-shifter morph before; it was something he doubted he'd ever be comfortable with. Skin changed to scales, fingers to claws, and teeth to hideous fangs as Soletuph soon towered over them on all fours, a dark, scaly looking feline, with those cat-like green eyes and fangs that protruded out from his wide muzzle. Keeshiff could have been sure he saw the thing smiling.

The beast—er, Soletuph—shook his scaly body, grumbling in what Keeshiff could only guess was a signal he was ready. The prince braced himself, took a deep breath, and opened the door.

Soletuph charged forward with a roar that made Keeshiff's teeth rattle. The scream from the other side told Keeshiff that the ploy had been effective, and he rushed in just as the terrified guard fled through the trapdoor.

"Hurry! Before he locks it!"

Coryn reached it first, yanking on the heavy latch.

Soletuph ran by in Human form and dropped to his knees by the opening. "*Set*," he called.

Five.

Heartbeat thudding in his ears, Keeshiff looked back over his shoulder only briefly to make sure the others were managing with the barricades. Then he gripped his sword and plunged down the narrow stairwell.

A soldier stood over the trapdoor through which his comrade had just fled. He still had his pike in hand as he glanced up in wide-eyed shock. His jaw dropped and he scrambled to pull his weapon back into stance, but he was too late. Keeshiff let out a raw-throated yell as he swung his sword, shattering the wooden shaft of the soldier's pike.

The guard fumbled desperately for his sword, only to give up and flee through the already open trapdoor. Keeshiff did as Soletuph had, dropping to his knees and scanning the room below before waving Coryn through. "Set!"

Four.

Two down, three floors to go.

The third guard was more prepared, apparently joined by the guard they'd chased from the fourth floor. But after Coryn wrenched the first one's sword from his grip and Soletuph shattered the second one's pike, both abandoned the level.

Three.

Soletuph took point on the second floor now that their element of surprise was completely gone. The guards had regrouped and drawn their secondary weapons, the three of them ringing around the shape-shifter. Keeshiff leapt down the remaining stairs to help. Soletuph was faster. Growling, he settled into a fighting stance and sidestepped the first guard's spear. Then he grabbed the shaft, twisted it around, and slammed his other fist against the back of the man's helmet. The soldier was sent head first into the stone wall and collapsed without a sound, his limp form tumbling into the guard behind him.

The second soldier tripped over his friend, a pause which Soletuph used to swipe his legs out from under him. The man fell with a yelp and scrambled back on his hands and feet.

"The door!" Coryn, grappling with the third soldier, was the one who shouted.

Keeshiff looked down to see another guard had come up the stairs to reach for the trap door latch. Keeshiff practically dived to stop him, yanking the knife from his belt and jamming it between the door and the floor just as the soldier tried to shut it. There was a screeching sound as metal ground against metal. But the knife held. Keeshiff yanked the door back open and kicked the guard in the face, sending him sprawling down below.

Already halfway in, Keeshiff didn't bother to check the level. They had lost the element of surprise, and now only had speed on their side. He kept his dagger in one hand and his sword in the other and charged the two guards who were trying to help their companion up. One let go but didn't draw his sword like Keeshiff had expected. Too late did Keeshiff realize that it wasn't the door that the guard was running for...but the alarm signal.

Jahng had warned them of this—a huge metal gong that would alert an entire company of soldiers. So Keeshiff dropped his dagger and scooped up a fallen spear as he lurched forward. The soldier grabbed the wooden beater and raised it to strike the gong, but Keeshiff brought the butt of the spear down against his hand. There was a sickening crack and the man cried out as he dropped the beater.

And that's when Keeshiff realized three very important things: First, he was outnumbered three to one and cornered at that. Second, a fourth soldier was now on the stairs and using his full body weight to hold the door shut, cutting Keeshiff off from his only escape route. And third, the main door of the Orshian Tower had just opened and let in more guards.

Wonderful. The hall guard must have called for reinforcements.

One of the three soldiers already on this level rushed him, and Keeshiff was left in a dangerous game of evasion as he desperately tried to keep them from flanking him. Several blows followed in quick succession, and Keeshiff tried to deflect them while getting around them to the stairs. Of course, the problem there was the soldier still on the steps. He needed to get out of here.

Keeshiff ducked another offensive swipe and got past one of the soldier's defenses, slamming him in the stomach with the butt of his borrowed spear. This allowed enough time for him to get another couple steps back. He looked over to the stairs just in time to see Soletuph yanking the trap door and punching the other Nythrilian. The guard plummeted with a cry down the flight and into one of the others on the ground, temporarily disoriented.

"*Retreat!*" Soletuph shouted. "*There's too many!*"

Keeshiff didn't so much as blink; he dropped the spear and ran for it, leaping over the winded soldier on the ground and up the stairs. The other two men ran for him. A few more steps, and Keeshiff was close enough to grab hold of Soletuph's reaching hand, getting pulled up and through the trap door.

Then he felt it.

It was all Keeshiff could do to stifle the gasp as something sharp slid in along his left rib cage, and too late he realized one of the soldiers from below had jabbed their pike upward in a last-ditch effort to stop Keeshiff's retreat. Barely, the prince held onto Soletuph's hand as he was pulled up, and as soon as he was in the room, the Merimeethian prince staggered to the floor, gasping and desperately trying to stop the bleeding with his hand. It was numb...and yet no one had ever told Keeshiff numb could hurt this much.

Also...he couldn't breathe.

"Keeshiff!" Coryn's alarmed shout pierced the air with more aptitude than the pike had Keeshiff's side.

As the world temporarily blurred around him, Keeshiff felt someone grab his arm and help him over to the wall where he half sat, half fell down.

"We need something to stop the bleeding, quickly!"

"Great, just what we need. Idiot prince."

"Stupid tower."

Keeshiff felt something pressed to his side and gasped again, fighting the urge to withdraw and instead pressing his head further against the wall. Ack, Louko was going to kill him for this.

At last, his vision returned, and he found himself blinking away the fog and greeted by the faces of Coryn, Soletuph, and Rhumir as they all held various expressions of annoyance or concern. Rhumir was the one who had cleaned and bandaged his wound, it seemed.

"No severe damage. Probably cracked a rib, though." Rhumir gave the report with a shrug. "Could have been worse."

Keeshiff put one hand gingerly to his side as he sat up, wincing as he bit back a groan. "Could've been better," he grumbled back.

He looked around the room and tried to take stock. He saw the crude wooden barricades situated on top of the trapdoor, just as they'd planned. Another piece of plank was jammed in the gap where the trapdoor hinges were bolted to the stone floor.

"Any noise from down there yet?" Keeshiff asked.

Coryn shook his head. "Not besides the alarm being sounded. They must not be used to prisoners trying to take their Tower instead of leave it."

Keeshiff had a feeling that the quiet wouldn't last long. "Well, if they want to sit and twiddle their thumbs, I won't argue. Any delay helps us."

Even the short sentence left him feeling winded, and he tried to ignore the burning sensation in his ribs. "Is everyone else okay?"

"All of us? Yeah." Another voice entered, and Keeshiff saw Gavin come down the stairs. "The problem is that we've got *too* many who are doing well."

Keeshiff squinted up at him. *Huh*?

Gavin joined the little group, looking Keeshiff over with concern before explaining himself. "One of the guards got knocked out during the fight, and we couldn't get him out before they locked the door. We're stuck with him."

Great. Just great.

"I suppose at least Grenedil can be of more use, now," Gavin grumbled. Poor Grenedil had, unfortunately, still been too injured to take part in the battle. He could handle a blade well enough, but the whole 'rushing with the element of surprise' thing hadn't been an option when he was still limping.

Oh, wait. That kind of went for Keeshiff now, too, didn't it? He should have been more careful. They couldn't afford to be down men this soon into the siege, and yet here he was, the first to go.

"Well, if you're up to walking, let's get you back up to the cell so we can get some food in you," Coryn said. "We took a vote and no one wanted to carry you."

"I'm flattered." Keeshiff rolled his eyes. Any further comment was cut off by the sensation of getting stabbed all over again when Coryn and Gavin hauled him to his feet.

And now for the stairs. *Four levels to go....*

A GAME OF WITS

CHAPTER XXI

Louko:

Three days after apparently surviving what Mitheau said was a Vheil Esr—which apparently literally meant *Dragon eater*—they finally reached Silbyr, the capital of Litash. They had only stopped a handful of times, and only long enough for Mitheau to regain her strength. Astra still did not wake up.

It was all Louko could do not to panic.

Now, at the foot of a stony cliff, Louko untied Astra from Mitheau and pulled her from the Drogan's back. He laid her gently on the ground and tried not to notice how burning hot her skin was to the touch.

"You stay here with Astra. Keep to the tall grass," Louko whispered hoarsely to Mitheau.

The Drogan shifted back into human form, a look beyond weariness twisted in every line of her face. "Be quick," she whispered back.

Louko gave one last look at the limp Astra, then up at the palace far above that loomed over them like a mountain. Then he was off into the darkness in search of the door Soletuph had told him of. As the palace was built on an outcropping with many tunnels beneath, several doors were merely locked and bolted instead of guarded. Louko found the one with the circle carved overhead and unlocked it with the key Soletuph had given him. The blast of cool, musty air rushed to meet him as he ducked in. The damp, the cold, the stone—it summoned up unpleasant memories of the servants' passages in Melye. It was a relief to finally reach the palace itself, safely away from the closed-in spaces.

The halls were quiet, devoid of any sound besides sputtering torches. He glanced up and down before daring to step out and into the ornate corridor. If he was spotted, he was as good as done for. Soletuph had said there were very few soldiers Entrais trusted—which raised questions of its own for another time.

Desperately, he tried to keep constant tabs on the nearest place to duck into, making sure to stay close to the walls. Echoes of footsteps seemed to be everywhere, and Louko could hardly keep track of them all over the roaring in his ears. He had to find Entrais's study. That's where Soletuph had said the king would be. That's where he always was at night, apparently.

"Hey, you, what are you doing here...." The voice came from a corridor hall that Louko had just passed.

He didn't know what else to do; he ran for it.

Louko skidded down the halls, almost tripping over himself in his haste. But he didn't get far when something flew by him. A...bird? He didn't have time to register before a guard seemingly materialized in front of him, spear leveled towards Louko's chest as he screeched to a halt.

Stupid shape-shifters. Stupid Litash.

"I asked...what are you doing here?" The man finished his question just in time for his other companion to come up behind Louko. He was caught; surrounded.

The panic tightened like death's grip around his chest.

"I...I..." Louko remembered what Soletuph had told him to say if caught before finding Entrais. Hopefully these guards were loyal to the king. "I come with news regarding the stars."

The soldier's steely gaze flitted to his companion and back to Louko. His eyes narrowed. Then he lowered the spear. "Come with us."

Escorted on either side, Louko was rushed through the low-lit corridors.

Were they taking him to Entrais? Or the dungeon? It was all Louko could do to keep breathing as he was brought down the endless halls and up a set or two of stairs. They came to a large door that seemed a separation of the residential wing from the rest of the castle, and one of the guards gave a patterned knock on the wood.

The door opened, and a woman poked her head out the door.

Vaguely, Louko recognized her—one of the other Ethians. But Louko hadn't known this one well.

"He said he has a message for the king regarding the stars, my lady."

The woman stared at Louko long and hard. "Wait...Prince *Louko*? Quickly, come inside; I'll show you to Ent. Thank you, Gaspian. Return to your post."

Louko's panic subsided—to a degree—as the lady gently grabbed his arm and led him inside the large doors, which closed behind them.

"What are you doing here? You have news of Astra?" she whispered as they walked down the hall. Louko noted the way the woman appeared to look everywhere—as if anyone could be listening. But the hall was deserted, except for a guard posted at a door at the end of the hall. Entrais's study. They must have come up a different way than Soletuph's directions had given.

"She's here...She-she's dying. I need to see Entrais immediately—she's dying and we have to get her help, quickly."

The Ethian's eyes widened, and her jaw went slack. Then she set it and broke into a jog, leaving Louko to follow breathlessly behind. "Ascriot," she called, voice low and urgent. "Quick! Get Ent!"

The shadow of a man standing guard turned, knocked twice, then pushed the study door open.

Louko had just made it to the door as a looming figure came rushing out the door, hair unkempt and shadowed grey eyes showing clear evidence of weariness.

The eyes immediately set on Louko.

"Quick, Entrais, it's Astra. She's here and she needs medical attention," Louko blurted out before even really being able to fully realize the haggard figure standing in front of him was actually Entrais. He'd not seen the king since the ball and, in all honesty, he didn't look well.

"Rusie, wake Tallaman, quickly. Get Jade up, too. We'll bring Astra up to the room." He turned back to Louko, "Where's Astra?"

"At the foot of the cliff, near the door Soletuph told me to use," Louko wheezed.

Louko blinked, and suddenly both he and Entrais were standing alone in the dark fields below the castle. He only barely registered Entrais had used Gifting to transport them. What happened next was a flurry of stifled panic and whispers as Louko showed Entrais to Astra and Mitheau. Entrais cradled his little sister and, without a word, disappeared and left Mitheau and Louko alone in the field. Anxious minutes passed before the king returned. But before he could transport Louko and Mitheau back, the young Drogan took several steps back and called out, "No, no, no Gifting."

Louko vaguely remembered the way Mitheau had cried out in pain when Astra had used her Gifting, and through his own panicked thoughts was able to nod to Entrais and say, "Just send someone to get her. She's been through a lot."

Entrais nodded, and without a word, whisked Louko away with Gifting, back into the hall Louko had been in only moments before.

The prince wasn't sure if he was going to be sick or pass out. Maybe both.

Entrais swayed where he stood. "Come with me, I think they've got Tallaman up now." He was already walking down the hall. "You will need to tell me everything. But not until my uncle tells us how bad it is. So, no talking in the room until he says so, understood?"

Louko managed a nod.

He kept up as best he could behind the long stride of the king, and before long, Louko found himself in a room guarded by two Ethians. Inside was weirdly quiet. No one running around in a hurry, no bandages or bowls of water for disinfecting. Just Astra lying motionless on a bed, and a tall, blond-haired Elf kneeling at her side. Both of his hands were wrapped around hers.

Spotting them as they entered, a dark-haired woman got to her feet and came to greet them. Jade. Her gaze snagged on Louko, and her face showed surprise. Then her eyes moved on to Entrais. Not a word was said, only glances that seemed to shout a thousand questions.

"I can *hear* you all staring at each other. Would you shut up?" the Elf by Astra's bedside grumbled.

Oh. Yeah. Definitely Tallaman. *Him*, Louko remembered from The War.

"Sorry, Uncle," Entrais mumbled.

Louko slipped into a corner, watching everyone and trying hopelessly to try and get a grasp on how things were going. But the room was a void. Void of noise, void of movement, void of news on how Astra was. Just Tallaman concentrating and holding Astra's clammy hand.

Discreetly, Louko turned his gaze to Entrais, who was now standing beside his wife. His gaze was riveted on Astra, sleepless eyes almost as feverish as her sweating, limp form.

Louko forced himself to watch Entrais instead of Astra, knowing doing the latter would only cause the helplessness and panic to tighten their grip on him. He just wanted to be by her side—he didn't want her to be alone.

Minutes dragged on and still nothing happened. How long would it take? Louko dared not ask. He watched instead as Jade quietly reached out her hand to grab Entrais's, and the king gave a startled jerk as he pulled away.

"Ent! You aren't helping!" Tallaman growled without looking up.

Jade tried again, and Entrais only closed his eyes.

Louko felt so out of place. *Astra. Please. Please don't die*. It was such a sudden, horrible thought, but more than anything, Louko felt the emptiness—and the vacant place at his side where the sword Astra and Entrais had given him should be. It would have been the only thing he had of hers if she died. And Tyron had it. Tyron had taken it, just like he'd taken everything else.

In the windowless room, there was no way to tell how much time was passing. In such stifling silence, it did not seem to be passing at all.

Eventually, both Entrais and Jade sat down across the room from the bed.

And still there was nothing.

It felt like hours before Tallaman let out a deep breath and opened his eyes. He let go of Astra's hand, face now as ashen as his patient's as he staggered to his feet. Entrais was immediately up and reaching to steady him.

"Leave me be," Tallaman snapped, wrenching his arm away. "If you haven't noticed, you're a little too late to fix all this." He stumbled over to the table and poured himself a glass of water.

"Uncle…" came Jade's soft protest.

"Oh, come on." Tallaman slammed the glass down. "Not even you can deny that this is his fault—he *exiled* her, for goodness' sake. Sent her right back to the very death she barely escaped last time, while he sat here comfortably on his padded throne. How many times do you expect me to piece her back together?"

Louko blinked, eyes widening with the horror of that statement. H...had Tallaman *really* just said that? He looked to Jade and found her agape with the same shock.

"Yes, we have established this, Uncle. I'm aware. Now, is she going to live?" Entrais croaked, eyes again trained on Astra.

Tallaman picked up the glass again and took a deep draught. "I don't know," he muttered. "I could only do so much. If she wakes, I will have to do another round. The infection is deeply rooted. And it seems she was weak to begin with."

Louko couldn't breathe. "Can I...come and see her, now?" Everyone stared at him, as if remembering for the first time that the prince was there.

Right. Everyone still had absolutely no idea what had happened.

Entrais moved to the side and motioned for Louko to go sit in a chair by the bed. He turned back to Tallaman. "Will it matter if we talk in here?" His voice was nearly a whisper.

The Elf narrowed his eyes and muttered something under his breath. He turned away without actually answering.

Entrais sighed, then turned to Jade, who had seemed about to say something unflattering to Tallaman. "Why don't you go check and make sure their other friend is settled in without issue. The girl with the silver hair?"

Jade met her husband's eyes, but whatever she wanted to say remained inside. Instead, she simply said, "I'll be back soon. Don't do anything stupid until I get back." And with that, she left.

Soon, the only ones left in the room were Louko, Entrais, and Tallaman. Louko felt uneasy as he sat beside Astra.

"Why don't you tell me what happened?" Entrais asked from where he stood at the foot of the bed, both hands clutching the wood as if it was all that was keeping him both steady and calm.

Tallaman paid no attention, returning to Astra with a soaked cloth. He began to wipe her travel-stained skin.

As best as he could, Louko explained everything that had happened in the past months: Mariah's betrayal, the Nythrilian king, meeting Mitheau and Grenedil, and most importantly...Tyron. Louko hadn't thought Entrais's face could grow any paler, but he was unpleasantly surprised. When at last he had drawn a close to the horrible tale, Tallaman was the first to speak.

"You were in there...for *how* long?" His pale blue eyes bored into Louko's.

Louko shuddered. "I don't...I don't know. A couple weeks." He didn't want to think on it anymore. He turned back to Astra's still form. He found himself reaching for her hand, wincing at how cold it now felt. She could die. She could die, and he would be alone. So alone.

Keeshiff:

Day two, and their improvised barricade on the trapdoor had held despite the Nythrilians hammering away at it. Not that Keeshiff got to go see for himself. He stayed up in the cell with Grenedil, taking turns to watch the Nythrilian guard. After the man had woken up, the knights had brought him up to the top level and bound him hand and foot. He hadn't said a word, not in worry, and not in protest. He just sat in the corner and watched them as they went about their business.

"*Not sure why you don't just off him,*" Soletuph said in a monotone; his stony expression turned on their captive.

Already, there was the worry about having to spare food and water for an extra person. Soletuph had warned them that once the siege had begun, the Orshian Tower would be too closely watched for him to fetch more supplies.

"*Because we are nice. Unlike some of us.*" Keeshiff found the only way to keep the shape-shifter from going completely feral was to meet him head-on.

Soletuph kept his arms folded across his chest. "*'Nice' won't feed your men.*"

Keeshiff was unimpressed. "*But it will help Jahng stay on our side.*" Who needed food, anyway...right?

"*And it gives you a hostage.*"

Keeshiff and Soletuph both turned to look at Grenedil.

"*Just, you know, if it comes to it.*" Grenedil shrugged.

Soletuph raised an eyebrow but said nothing more.

Keeshiff was saved from having to do so when the cell door swung open, and Coryn and Lucian walked in. They had just swapped out door-watch duty with Ivinon and Farian.

"You know…" Coryn faked a yawn. "As nice as it is to sit here all day, I think I rather prefer a battle on the open field."

Lucian grunted. "Why? What's not to like about being fish in a barrel?"

"I thought *they* are supposed to be the fish in the barrel," Gavin called from where he'd been pretending to sleep in the straw. "After all, I'm the one shooting."

With a weak chuckle, Keeshiff broke in with, "Shut up, the lot of you. You all are making me hungry with this talk of fish."

Delnor, in charge of the rations, shook his head. "Oh, no, none of that. We haven't got enough food to be passing out snacks."

"Besides, Keeshiff," Rufio grinned. "You have been eating more than you've been fighting. Can't have you getting out of shape now over a little prick in the ribs."

Keeshiff summoned up a good glower. "Say that again and I'll have Gavin throw you down there as a peace offering."

"They might throw him back," Rhumir muttered, earning an elbow in the side from his brother.

Soletuph brought the conversation back to Litashian. "*I always thought it was just Louko who insisted on talking through entire battles; I hadn't realized it was a Merimeethian trait.*"

The reminder of Louko revived the heavy burden on Keeshiff's shoulders, but before he could come up with some attempt at a witty reply, there was the dull, faraway sound of something battering against the trapdoor four stories down.

The muted rhythm killed any humor in the room.

"*Guess that's my cue.*" Soletuph strode off towards the door.

Keeshiff watched him go, hoping his help wouldn't be needed. Hoping the barricade would hold.

Keeshiff jolted, pulling away from whoever it was that was shaking him awake.

"Keeshiff! Keeshiff!"

He registered Gavin's voice.

"Come on, wake up." Gavin shook him again. "We have a problem."

Keeshiff hauled himself to his feet. "What? What is it?"

The question was answered by the faint scent of wood smoke.

Oh, no.

"Fire. They're burning the trapdoor," Gavin panted. "Rufio's still down there."

Adrenaline outdid the pain in his ribs, and Keeshiff was now on high alert. What were they going to do? They couldn't spare the water, even if they'd had enough to douse it with.

Then he saw Soletuph pick up one of the rag-stuffed cots and race for the stairwell.

Aha! Keeshiff and Grenedil grabbed one and Coryn and Lucian another, the group of them hauling the beds down the stairs into the thickening smoke. The stairs grew harder and harder to navigate with their watering eyes and burning lungs.

They reached the second level, where Rufio was coughing, despite the sleeve he kept close to his face. He'd apparently thrown his coat over the trapdoor in a vain effort to smother the flames. Soletuph kicked the ragged thing aside and threw open the door as Keeshiff and the others dragged their burdens. Indeed, a fire had been built on the top stairs and was now hungrily licking up and into the open gap. Coryn and Lucian were the first to reach the opening, and threw down the cots atop the flames, the fuel for the fire getting smashed and scattered, even as the cots stifled the yet-young fire. Keeshiff and Grenedil followed suit, and soon all that was left of the fire was the thick aroma of smoke.

With the source out and the trapdoor bolted shut once more, the smog faded enough for them to see the extent of the damage. It wasn't good. Half of the trapdoor was charred and still smoking, half of their barricade with it.

And it would only be seconds before the soldiers who had set the fire would return from where they had retreated.

"Coryn, Lucian, grab those barricades and see if we can keep this thing closed!"

Too late: The metal head of an axe burst through the blackened remains of the door, sending it into splinters. Another strike followed before there was any way to stop it. Keeshiff leapt forward, taking up a piece of wood from their shattered barricade and jamming it down through the opening. There was a clatter as an axe dropped from someone's hands and down onto the many stone steps below.

Someone grabbed the collar of Keeshiff's shirt and yanked him back just before an arrow pierced upwards and nearly buried itself up Keeshiff's chin.

Soletuph.

But he only had time to give a quick nod of thanks before the first soldier emerged from the burnt entrance, *his* axe apparently still in hand.

"Back! Pull back to the next level!" Keeshiff called as loudly as he could. Between the breathlessness of adrenaline and the stabbing sensation in his side, that didn't mean much.

No one argued, all making a run for the stairs that led up to the next level. Lucian and Coryn took up the rear, as always. As much as Keeshiff wanted to help, he knew he wouldn't last a minute against the towering man with the axe, and so followed Grenedil and the others up to the third level.

"Where's Coryn and Lucian?" Farian asked, voice straining from within the cell

Keeshiff strained to see down the stairs, eyes still watering from the smoke. There was nothing to see aside from the steep steps. But there was the sound of clashing weapons, followed by shouts and the general unintelligible ringings of battle. Then Lucian seemed to explode up into the room out of nowhere.

"Closethedoorclosethedoorclosethedoor!" Coryn yelled in a flurry as he appeared just as quickly.

Keeshiff sprang to action only to double up in pain. It was Lucian who turned back to hoist Coryn up and out of the way, just as Grenedil slammed shut the trap door in an oncoming soldier's face.

They were all left panting on the floor, thankful for the temporary quiet from below. But Keeshiff knew better than to expect it to last.

A loud scraping noise made the prince turn his throbbing head, and he saw Soletuph dragging over a long shield that he'd taken from some Nythrilian. This was laid over the door before Soletuph motioned them back. And for good reason. He shifted and used the flaming breath of his borrowed shape to melt the metal shield until it joined to the trapdoor hinges.

Then the Ethian shifted back to his usual blond self. "*Is everyone alright?*" he asked.

Keeshiff looked around at his friends; Lucian had an arm wound, and Coryn bore the traces of blood on his forehead. Then he looked down at the now reinforced trapdoor. Another level lost. Another step closer to their shelter turning into a trap.

"*As alright as we can be, I suppose.*"

Keeshiff was exhausted. Worse, so were all of his men. After the Nythrilians had figured out their little tactic of burning through the doors, it hadn't taken them long to take the other levels. Not even Soletuph's trick could stop them forever. They'd been driven back to the top floor: their cell and the guard room just outside it. For now, the siege had entered yet another lull, and everyone was just waiting for the next wave. Everyone was trying to rest or eat, but the palpable fear in the room made it difficult.

It had been five days. Five days that had put eternity to shame. How were they ever going to last? Even as he knew he had to keep face for his men's courage, Keeshiff was failing to see how they would get through this. Gavin was out of crossbow bolts, Coryn had been dealt a wound to the leg and was now out of commission, and Ivinon had taken a shield to his head that had knocked him out cold. He'd woken up after a few minutes, only to be nearly incapacitated by extreme nausea and headaches. But they had to hold on—if only for Astra and Louko, who would never live with themselves if they failed. If they had survived the journey to Litash, anyway....

Across the room, Farian suddenly picked up his head. "Footsteps," he called in half-whisper.

Keeshiff's inhale was so deep it was as if it would be his last. Without a word, he grabbed his sword with his bloodied hands and hoisted himself to his feet. "Wake Soletuph and Lucian," he whispered, already heading for the guard room and the barricaded door.

If the Nythrilians got through this time, there was nowhere to go.

Farian was on his feet in seconds, nodding and darting off. Gavin, having woken to the noise, dragged himself up with the help of his sword. He joined Keeshiff at the door.

"Ready?" he asked as he hefted his blade into a starting position.

"Could do this in my sleep." Keeshiff forced a smile, fearing it looked more like a grimace.

The footsteps from the stairs grew louder.

Then they reached the door. He heard the pause. He and Gavin both gripped their weapons and waited for the smoke to fill the room. But it never came.

Instead, there was a quick, polite knock.

"Keeshiff? Are you still up there?"

The voice was so unexpected that it took Keeshiff a good thirty seconds to recognize it belonged to Louko's uncle.

"While I am impressed with your morale, really, I would appreciate it if you stopped making such ninnies out of my men." Yes. The droll sarcasm definitely belonged to the one and only...

"...Aelor Ven?" Keeshiff called back at last, having found his voice— however hoarse it was. "Is that you?"

"No. It's your conscience, telling you to find some manners and stop throwing a fit every time you're locked in your room. Now, I recommend you address me by my proper title if you would like to entertain the idea of being allowed out."

Keeshiff hesitated, glancing at Gavin. "And what title is that now, exactly?"

"I mean, *Ezai Ru* is the proper term, but I think you uncivilized Merimeethians usually just stick with 'king.'" Keeshiff could practically *hear* the smug look the man had to be carrying.

But he was too busy being relieved, his sword dropping from his now completely weakened grip.

"Come on," he croaked to his men. "Let's get this open."

CHAPTER XXII

<u>**Astra:**</u>

Astra bolted upright. *Where am I?* She didn't recognize this room, nor did she have any recollection of how she came to be here. Something to her left moved, and Astra instinctively drew away as an unfamiliar figure came into focus.

"Woah, woah, Astra, it's alright."

She snapped around, searching; she knew that voice.

And there was Louko, right by her bedside, looking as if he had just gotten to his feet. He had his hands out and palms up as if to calm her. Or to warn her.

Astra was not prepared for the onslaught that hit her. Pain drowned out every other sensation, racking her entire body and driving the breath from her lungs. She couldn't have screamed if she had wanted to.

Whether it was seconds or an eternity, Astra couldn't tell. But the bout subsided as suddenly as it had begun and she was left shaking, gasping for air. Only then did she register Louko's hand gripping hers.

"It's alright, Slip, stay down," another voice came from beyond Louko.

Astra jolted again then froze. She looked to Louko, simply because she could not process anything else.

"Shhh, you're safe. We're safe, it's alright. You got really sick…." She felt him place his other hand over hers.

"What happened?" she asked, finding her voice to be scratchy and soft. "Keeshiff, and the knights—your uncle...."

"They are still in Nythril, but everything will be fine." Louko continued to rub her hands. "You just need to get better, alright?"

"That's all very touching," an unmistakably disdainful tone cut through, and Astra finally pieced together who the blond figure to her left was. "But if you're done, I'd like to look over my…" He sighed. "...patient."

Astra couldn't yet process her uncle's voice, much less what had made him so irritable. Not that Tallaman had ever required much of a reason.

But then Louko started to let go of her hand to allow her uncle to move closer to her.

"Wait, wait." Astra clutched her friend's hand, still overwhelmed by her surroundings and the final figure in the room. "I can't..." breathe. That was the word.

"Finnnnne." Tallaman's word was drawn out almost longer than his sigh.

Louko's hand stopped trying to pull away and was accompanied by a quiet, "I'm still here."

"Sorry," she murmured, trying to take deeper breaths and steady herself. She was still shaking, sweating.

But Louko's voice was ever calm and patient. "You're fine, don't worry."

Not even thirty seconds had passed before Tallaman huffed again, and Astra swallowed hard.

"Alright," she scraped out.

"Now, I'm going to give you something to drink, and you are not going to choke me, or use Gifting to transport me out of the room, or choke me, or maim anyone in this room." Tallaman's voice was wry.

Astra had already accepted the cup before she started questioning the oddly specific instructions against choking. She glanced towards Louko in muted alarm.

His shrug was not exactly comforting, nor the sheepish smile.

Disconcerted, Astra turned her limited attention back to her cup. The liquid was faintly bitter, but she was thirsty enough that, if anything, she had to keep herself from drinking too quickly.

"Well, you seem pretty awake compared to...every other time you've awoken. Seems like you're taking the treatment well. Pity." Tallaman's pretended distance was dampened by the relief that even Astra could catch.

"So she'll make it?" Again, the voice that came from the background.

"Don't play stupid, *Ent*." Tallaman spat the name like an insult. Astra flinched. "You've been through this enough times yourself to know."

"Well, *I* haven't been through this, so I would like to know." Astra barely caught Louko's tense whisper.

Tallaman huffed. "Healing and medicine are not fields that yield yes or no answers. She will *probably* make a full recovery, but if anyone could prove me wrong, it would be Astra." He added under his breath, "Or her blockheaded brother."

Astra could no longer shy away from the third person in the room. She made herself look at him.

But no amount of willpower helped her find any words to say.

"Hey, Slip." Ent appeared to have caught her gaze, holding it steadily but gently.

Astra looked down.

It was so hard to process. It was all so strange. He looked...he looked the way he had back in The War. Thin, worn, tired. It had been a lifetime since she'd seen him last or so it seemed. So much had changed, so much so that Astra couldn't even recall how things had been before she'd left.

But she remembered The War.

Her voice was raspy as she replied, "Hello, Ent."

It had been three days since Astra had woken up—or so she was told. She had no way to mark the passage of time in her windowless room. It didn't help that she was rarely awake for more than a few hours straight. While her uncle's Gift of healing had driven out the infection and the fever with it, he could not undo all of the damage it had wrought. Astra was very weak and very tired. Even if she had been allowed to, she doubted she had the strength to leave her bed.

"You're looking better, at least." Louko had hardly left her side, always in his spot in the chair, and ever vigilant. But even as her condition had improved, he didn't seem any less concerned.

Astra had the feeling that it had more to do with his brother than her. "I do feel better," she replied. She thought of asking if there'd been any news of Keeshiff, then decided against it; Louko would have already told her if there was. "How is Mitheau doing?"

"Rested. A little less traumatized." She could tell he'd stopped before adding anything about worrying for Grenedil.

"That's a start." It was the most positive thing Astra could find to say. She fiddled idly with the edge of her blanket. "How are you holding up?"

He gave a weak show of optimism which did seem *partially* sincere. "I slept...in a bed. An actual, real bed. It was strange."

Sometimes, Astra forgot that Louko was not quite like her. He had not grown up in the conditions of war and want and poverty. Astra could scarcely remember any other kind of life. "Hopefully, that will be a more common occurrence from now on." She tried to smile.

"Yeah," he echoed.

The silence lingered, and Astra's attention wandered. She thought again of Mitheau, then of Keeshiff and his knights, Aelor Ven...Tyron.... Her gaze caught on the other chair near her bed, this one empty. Ent had visited a few times, sitting quietly and simply providing company. He had not offered any conversation, and Astra had been too afraid to initiate it. How could she even begin?

"How is Jade?" Astra asked abruptly. "And-and my brother."

Louko ran his hand through his hair. "Well. I mean...I think alright...." He winced. "I don't know. They are acting rather strange. I don't know." The last bit was said with an attempted shrug.

Fear pricked her. What was wrong? Was Ent still afraid of her? Did he not want her here? "What do you mean?" she asked.

"I, uh, I don't know. Entrais, he's, I don't know, things seem...tense between them?" He appeared extremely uncomfortable over all this. "Or maybe that's just me. I could be imagining it. They are probably all just worried."

Astra did not get the chance to ask further. A sound startled her out of her skin, and she twisted around to see the door open.

"Ah, you look at least half alive, today." Tallaman's voice cut the air as he walked briskly in, followed closely by Ent.

Trying to catch her breath, Astra murmured, "I suppose that is better than half dead."

"You *are* feeling better." The relief in Ent's voice was almost tinted with humor.

Tallaman grumbled something unintelligible, and came up to the bedside. Astra braced herself as he reached to feel her forehead then took her wrist.

"How is the nausea today? I see you've at least had the decency to keep it off the floor." Apparently satisfied with her pulse, Tallaman turned to his table and poured one of his tonics into a cup.

"Better," Astra replied, watching her brother take his usual seat.

"Good." Tallaman handed her the drink. "Now, take this and you'll feel even better, I'm sure."

As much as Astra would have liked to argue, she knew better than to doubt her uncle's abilities and took the cup without complaint. One would think she'd be used to this by now.

"Do you think you're feeling well enough to talk, Astra?" Ent asked hesitantly from his corner.

Astra opened her mouth to reply.

"Really, Ent? Already right to business?" Tallaman's immediate vehemence robbed Astra of her response. "You caused this whole mess—you might at least have the decency to let her recover before you start making the next one."

388

Astra stared dumbly at her uncle. And then at her brother.

Ent didn't even reply, expression taut and lips pressed into a thin line.

Was *this* what Louko was talking about?!

Tallaman turned back to Astra as if nothing had happened. He reached to take her cup, and Astra wrenched away.

"How *dare* you?" Her voice was low.

A moment of confusion flickered across Tallaman's face.

"You have no right to speak to him like that," Astra went on, only angered more by the way her uncle didn't seem to notice.

"Astra, he's just tired. You know better than to take it personally," Ent interjected quietly. "Be patient with him."

His defense only added to Astra's ire, but she kept her mouth shut. She should not allow herself to get so riled up. Not when she wasn't wearing red bronze. She bit her tongue and held the cup out to her uncle.

Tallaman raised an eyebrow but took it without a word.

"So she'll for sure be fine, then?" Louko asked in an obvious ploy to dissolve the tension.

"As fine as any seventeen-year-old brought within inches of her life can be," her uncle answered in a monotone. "But she will survive."

Astra's irritation was only lessened by the distraction. When had she turned seventeen? She glanced at her brother, who was rubbing his forehead. His other hand gripped the arm of his chair. She tried to recall what it was he'd wanted to talk about before Tallaman had cut him off but couldn't remember a specific subject. Should she ask? Or would something else be less likely to make her uncle lash out?

She settled for something safer. "So, when did I turn seventeen?"

"Oh. Um…" Ent looked confused. "Maybe two months ago? What's today, again?"

"What an organized king we have," Astra heard Tallaman mutter under his breath.

She bit her tongue until it hurt.

"I think today is the third day of Vel," Louko replied in slow uncertainty.

"Right," Ent mumbled. "Then two and a half months ago."

Astra tried to think of where she'd been two and a half months ago. That would have been around…never mind. "Oh. Well, I'll try to remember that next year."

Tallaman came back to the bedside with a bowl of broth. "If your brother hasn't managed to get you killed by then."

"What is *wrong* with you?!" Astra nearly took the bowl from his hands and doused him with it.

"Astra—" Ent's face was white.

"—No!" Astra was not going to sit and listen to this. "This is ridiculous. How *dare* he blame you?"

"How can you not? Ent was the one who exiled you, after all—even after what happened to you last time," Tallaman said thinly.

"Happened to me? *Me*? Have you already forgotten that Ent was there, too?" Astra's vision swirled with patches of color. "He has the same scars. And it wasn't his first time, either. But maybe you've forgotten, the same way you conveniently forgot your relation to him in those years that my mother wasn't around to remind you."

Even Tallaman was quiet in the face of this outburst. Ent's eyes were wide, and his hand was gripping the arm of his chair so tightly it looked as if the wood might crumble to ash at any second. Even Louko appeared alarmed.

"You are still recovering. I will...curb my tongue, if you wish, but I am allowed to have my opinions. And as my patient, I do not like the idea of you reliving this trauma just for informative purposes, Astra." Tallaman sounded someplace between angry and distressed.

Astra didn't care. "And yet no one had any qualms about questioning Ent the very second we escaped. What makes him so different? I don't care about your 'opinions'—I care that you abuse him to his face and then turn to me as if I want your kindness." She was shaking again, but now with her rage. "If I didn't know any better, I'd say it's only because I look like my mother, and he looks like my father—the one you tried to kill. No wonder our mother left—"

"Astra." It was funny how Ent didn't need to raise his voice to get everyone in the room to stop. He just had to speak louder than a whisper. But the torture in his tone was far worse. "Both of you, stop. Uncle, if you want to help, stop getting her angry. This is not about me, this is about the fact that *he* is alive after all, and despite anyone's efforts he has again gotten to Astra. We can agree on that. Now, please. Will you both just...stop?" He got up with a near unnatural jerk, and Astra only just caught the tremor in his hands before they were shoved into his pockets. "I will go fetch us some food."

Guilt twisted in Astra's stomach. It was enough to douse her temper. Not so much that it went out, but enough that she went back to biting her tongue.

Tallaman gave a terse nod, and Ent exited the room.

"Well." Her uncle turned away brusquely, setting the bowl he'd been holding back on the table. "I suppose if I'm not wanted, I will get out of the way. I will do my usual rounds in the evening."

Without even a look over his shoulder, Tallaman left. The slamming door echoed behind him.

Astra sat, still biting her tongue and gripping the blankets. A few minutes ticked by before she was able to get the single word out between her teeth: "Sorry."

"Oh, no, I was rooting for you all the way." Louko gave a nervous chuckle. "Are you alright, though? Or perhaps rather...do you want to talk about it? Can you still breathe?"

As irritatingly winded as she was, Astra was in no mood to admit it. "I just...." Her throat felt suddenly tight, and her voice was gravelly as she went on. "He has no right. He doesn't know what it's like. And Ent..." She swallowed. "Everyone always *conveniently* forgets that Ent does. Why do they pity me and pressure him? It's not right."

"I suppose not," Louko murmured, eyes seeming to unfocus in deep thought.

Tallaman had no idea what it was to be helpless, bound in red bronze and unable to defend himself. He had never been at the total mercy of someone who enjoyed other people's pain. Astra knew what that was like. The memory of it still made her breath catch and her chest hurt. And she knew Ent remembered it, too.

Once again, Astra pushed herself to her feet, steadied herself, then took another lap. It was one of those rare moments when she was alone, and she was determined to make the most of it. She needed to be in better shape if she was going to be ready to leave. Astra had the growing feeling that she wouldn't have much warning.

She kept up her laps, wishing again for windows. Maybe some scenery would pull her attention from the situation at hand. First, there was Keeshiff and Aelor Ven—still no news after almost two weeks of waiting. Louko never said a word, but Astra knew how distraught he was over leaving his brother in such a situation. And she could not help her guilt when she knew that she was the cause of it all.

Then there was Ent. Still quiet, calm, withdrawn. Louko had encouraged her to speak to him, but she hadn't found the chance—nor the courage. So, she kept waiting and kept taking her laps.

And playing The Game.

She and Louko had it down to twenty-eight possible endings. They were missing too many moves on Tyron's side to narrow it down any further. And they needed to know what happened in Nythril before they could even really settle on those twenty-eight options....

Astra tried to refocus. A quick break for water seemed the best way to do it. She crossed to the little stand in the corner, hefting the water pitcher and pouring herself a glass. She was pathetically proud of managing the heavy thing. Just as she raised the glass to her lips to taste her little victory, she caught movement and froze.

It took her a long moment to realize it was a mirror that had been hung above the water stand. It took her even longer to realize that the person depicted in it was none other than herself. The glass showed a girl with skeletal white hands clutching a cup, her pallid skin contrasted shockingly by the red hair that hung just past her chin. The face was gaunt with dark, sleepless circles casting shadows over the pallor. A deep, red scar traced its way from her brow to her cheek, as if to outline the haunted blue eyes.

Astra did not recognize this reflection.

In a near panic, she set the cup down and fumbled to pull the little tablecloth out from under the water pitcher. She cast this over the mirror and tucked it in so it would stay. Then she stood breathless, making sure the specter was gone.

She was going to be sick. All at once she felt twelve again, watching as they seared Tyron's coat of arms into her skin. She had been marked, *branded*, by the very person who had ravaged her home. This was somehow worse; she couldn't hide this one with a shirt sleeve. Her hair would grow back, her body would recover from illness, but the scar at her temple would remain on full display.

A knock came from the door, making Astra spin around. Quickly, she returned to her seat by the chess table even as she called, "Enter." She didn't want Louko to see her panicked.

The door opened, but Louko didn't come in—Ent did. He took only a few steps before stopping and furrowing his brow in a show of concern.

"Are you alright?" he asked. "You sound out of breath."

Astra nodded. "I was just practicing walking, is all. Tallaman gave me permission."

His gaze turned to the now covered mirror. "I see."

Swallowing, Astra tried to redirect his attention. "Is everything alright?"

Ent bit his lip, turning away. "I spoke with Louko," he said gently. "I think...there's been some miscommunication on my end."

"What do you mean?" Astra asked, confused. They hadn't spoken enough to miscommunicate.

394

"Louko said..." Entrais winced, a remarkable and swift catch in his otherwise expressionless demeanor. "...that you thought I sent you away and abandoned you...and that I did so because it was your fault. I don't want you to ever think that. It wasn't something you did, Astra. Really."

Oh. Louko had spoken to him? "No, it's alright—I always understood." Astra spoke quietly and honestly. She tried to match his calm, even if she did not understand his withdrawn manner. "You didn't abandon me. You did what you had to in order to keep me safe after I had made such a mess of things." Yes, Astra was good at messes. She'd already managed to make things worse with Tallaman—he hadn't spoken to her in the last three days and hadn't remained in the room long enough for her to apologize.

"What? No. No, it wasn't your fault, Astra." He came a little closer, now looking openly perplexed. "I sent you away to protect you, yes...but I had already been thinking of doing so. Yes, the events at The Court exacerbated things, but they had been asking to experiment on you for a long time...I had..." He stuttered to a temporary halt. "I had thought Tyron was in The Court. I was trying to get you away from him...but I only gave you to him instead. And for that, I truly am sorry."

Astra stared at him, lips parted in shock. "You thought he was *here*?" Her question was disbelieving at the thought of all the repercussions. "You thought you were sending me away so that you would face him alone?"

"What—no. I mean. Yes. I mean..." He grimaced. "It's a complicated situation." The way he said the last bit proved he knew it was a pitiful excuse.

The thought of him standing alone against Tyron made her dizzy. She only realized how hard she was gripping the arms of her chair when the edges started biting into her skin. "Since when did we start doing everything alone?" she asked, hoarse.

No matter how much he had done it lately, Ent's new habit of standing completely still was more unnerving than the way he had always paced. Shoulders sinking ever so slightly, he didn't say a word other than, "I'm sorry."

And so Astra asked the one question she had thought she was too afraid to ask. "Why?"

"I thought there was no other way. I didn't even...I didn't even tell Mother or Father what happened until after you left. Astra...things are not good in The Court." Still, Ent made no move.

Mother and Father hadn't known? Such a little detail. And yet Astra's throat felt thick and her eyes welled. She turned away just so he wouldn't see. Her parents hadn't known.... They hadn't turned her away. Or been too unbothered to even come to say goodbye. They simply hadn't known.

"You could have told me. I could have helped." Looking away hid her tears, but not the raspiness of her voice. "Or at least not made things worse like I did."

"Astra, this is not your fault." All of a sudden, Ent was kneeling in front of her the way he always used to, putting himself at her level as he gingerly rested one hand on her shoulder. "If I had known—if I'd taken a moment to see that was how you felt—I would have told you that the second it popped into your head."

"You've always looked after me and asked how I felt." Astra tried to wipe away the hot, stupid tears. She thought of how Louko had implored her to say everything. And though she didn't want to, his pleading gave her just enough courage. "I only wish I hadn't lost the right to do the same for you."

"No. No, no. Astra, it's not you, I promise. It's me." His tone was desperate.

"How?" She finally looked up at him. She saw the pain in Ent's eyes, and it only made hers that much sharper. "I don't understand. I don't even know for certain what happened. All I know is that-that after they used me against you, it was as if there was this wall. And we were on separate sides and there was no way to cross. And I couldn't blame you if you wanted me to stay on the other side."

"What? No. No, Astra, I didn't want you to stay on the other side." He let go of her shoulder, staring in horror. "This is what I have done to you?"

Astra didn't know how to take that. But she didn't know how to stop herself now that she had started. "I knew you had Jade, then, and our parents. I thought maybe you were leaning on them and that you didn't need me. So I didn't want to get in the way."

"No." His reply was quiet. "You're not someone who can be replaced."

Now feeling nearly embarrassed at her outburst, she was able to bring herself back. She looked down at her lap. If Ent hadn't told her parents of anything, if things really were so bad in the Court.... "But it's not just me, is it? You haven't been letting anyone help you." She looked up to watch his reaction. Perhaps this collected, withdrawn demeanor was a mask that he wore all the time now—not just around her.

It did not change other than a furrowed brow, and he opened his mouth to say something...but nothing came out. He turned away. "I am not as strong as you."

That had *never* been true. But just as Astra started to argue, a knock came at the door. Neither she nor Ent had time to answer before Tallaman came through.

"I'll leave before I start another fight," Ent whispered as his shoulders squared. "I love you, Slip. I'll stop by again later. I'm—be careful." He seemed to stop just short of some half-formed apology.

Astra winced. Yes, no more losing her temper. "I love you, too, Ent."

She barely finished the sentence before he vanished from the room, using Gifting to whisk himself away. Astra wondered if it had to do with Tallaman still being so near the door.

Tallaman opened his mouth, clearly unamused with Ent's abrupt exit, but then his eyes landed on Astra and he snapped his mouth shut. He instead walked over to where she was sitting and said, "Up and about, I see. Not surprised. You always liked pushing limits." His grumblings were a little more half-hearted than usual. It perhaps would have been imperceptible to anyone else, but Astra had been around her uncle enough to see the change.

Accepting her usual draught of tonic, Astra did not yet drink it. "Uncle, I wanted to apologize for the other day."

"No need to apologize." The way he grumbled out the words didn't exactly seem to back that up.

"I suppose that depends on what part you're referring to," Astra said quietly. "If you mean what I said, then, I suppose I am not quite sorry for that. But I am very sorry for the way that I said it."

His frown deepened. "You are not very good at apologizing," he mumbled tartly.

"And you're not very good with your bedside manner," Astra replied in kind. "But that gave me no excuse to be vindictive. A right thing can be said in the wrong way."

She couldn't tell if he was growling or sighing, but whatever it had been was followed by an, "I suppose."

Astra figured that that was the closest thing she would get to forgiveness. She drank the bitter tonic her uncle had given her, then held out the cup. He took it.

"Thank you," Astra said with sincerity.

"Mm" was all he gave in reply. But then he paused, adding, "You know, being disappointed in someone *isn't* the same as hating them."

He was speaking of Ent. "And yet ignoring someone is hardly love."

It could have been her imagination, but his shoulders seemed to sag ever so slightly. But he said no more, leaving the room and leaving her words echoing in the air.

Louko:

Normalcy felt so...foreign. Astra was better—*really* better. Walking. Alert. Safe. And still no note from Tyron. It felt almost terrifying to even think of the possibility that they'd at last outrun his plan.

But for how long? It didn't help that everyone here was acting so...odd—and besides the obvious "Astra isn't supposed to be here" problem. There was a more potent tension that hung in the air. Entrais alone had enough to fill a room, and Louko had carefully watched how the king seemed distant from almost everyone. Not just quiet. No...something else. He was almost afraid to ask what.

"You're really getting around, now," Louko commented dryly from his seat on Astra's bed. She was...pacing.

"Not as well as I had hoped," she replied, nearly breathless. She sat down again in one of the chairs beside their chess table. Louko saw the way her gaze drifted towards the marble pieces.

"It hasn't been that long, Astra. You're doing well." They'd still not been discovered, either. Which...somehow only made Louko more nervous. Entrais couldn't hide them here forever, could he? But still there had been no word from Nythril. What if his uncle hadn't been able to pull it off? What of Keeshiff?

Louko wasn't actually sure that Astra had heard him. Either way, she registered no reaction. Without looking up from the chess boards, she asked, "You said that your uncle said the coup would take eight days, correct? So word should come by next week?"

"Yes. Soon." Right? Louko was trying not to obsess over it.

Astra looked up, a nearly regretful look crossing her face. "I suppose it is a good thing we have not heard. If things had gone awry, Soletuph would have slipped out and returned by now. A shifter by himself can travel fast—especially now that he'll cut across the southern range instead of going up through Merimeethia and the Merym Pass like last time."

He ran his hand through his hair for the thousandth time. "Yeah. That's true."

"Your uncle seemed well enough liked. And he's no fool. Surely he would have a backup plan with some of the other lords, even if the situation did go sideways." Louko must *really* be acting nervous for Astra to go on this way.

Clearing his throat, he croaked out, "Yeah. You're right. I'm sure it will be fine," in an attempt to convince himself. Things just...never seemed to go their way.

Astra stood up again, leaning on the arm of the chair a moment to steady herself. Then she crossed the small room and sat down beside him. She took his hand. "From what you've said, you have proved a high enough cause for everyone to rally around. I don't think that even Dia Tzaro could change that."

Louko forced a smile. She was right, of course. And she was trying so hard. "Yeah." His laugh felt weak. "Though they couldn't even pronounce my name right. I suppose admiration is no substitute for knowing someone."

"Perhaps not," Astra murmured. Then she seemed to seize on the chance of a more harmless conversation. That was usually Louko's trick. "Why? What did they call you?"

He rolled his eyes. "Uh...what was it...Lu quo? Something weird like that. I guess they gave it their best shot."

Astra's expression scrunched up. "What did you say?"

"...Lu...Quo? Like. You know. They made my name almost two different words, and added a *qu* sound or whatever." He shrugged. "I guess it was close enough to the real thing. Maybe I'm just particular."

Astra's brow furrowed in thought. Then she asked out of nowhere, "Did your mother name you?"

"Uh..." Louko ran his hand through his hair. "I don't...really know? I mean. No one really *told* me. So. Why...?" Why was she acting so weird?

"Because 'Lu Quo' has meaning. It keeps drawing me back into Nythrilian," Astra explained softly.

"Wait. What? What does it mean?" Louko was suddenly hungry to know. He'd never known who had named him but, thinking of it now, why would Omath have bothered?

Louko had not seen Astra smile since before the day Dia Tzaro had sent them off to hunt Mitheau down. But now, the gentle curve of her lips seemed peaceful. "It translates to 'Little Healer.'"

Louko's brow furrowed as he processed what she had said. Little Healer? Nythrilian? His mother…. It pieced together as if the puzzle piece long stolen had finally been returned, and as Louko realized the small gesture of love left by his mother, he wanted to break down and cry and laugh at the same time. Which perhaps was stupid, seeing everything they'd been through.

"She must have loved you very much." Astra was still holding his hand. "And she must have had faith in what you would become; names are not bestowed lightly, and yours is no exception."

"Yeah," Louko replied sincerely. She must have.

Then the door opened suddenly, and Entrais entered full stride, stopping abruptly and looking at the pair. More specifically, their hands.

Louko self-consciously pulled away, cheeks burning. Then, recovering, he realized Entrais rarely entered without knocking. He swallowed hard before asking, "What? What is it?"

"Someone is here. She claims to know you? Says she has important information?"

Instantly, Louko was alert. "Where? Did they give a name?"

"No, but she knew you were here. I can show you to her?"

Who could it be? No one knew they were here, except Ven and those helping him—it had to be someone from Nythril. "Yes. Please." Louko managed to get the words out even as his heart threatened to lodge itself in his throat. He turned to Astra. "I'm sure everything's fine." It came out more like a question—a desperate plea for reassurance.

"I'm sure," Astra repeated, one hand going to his arm. "She must have news—we expected it soon, didn't we?"

"Yeah," he breathed. "It must be." He gave a wince of a smile, and then allowed Entrais to lead him out of the room and down the hall.

A few minutes of agonizing patience later, and the pair were standing outside a door.

"She's in here. I'll come in with you." Entrais' statement was simple and succinct. It wasn't an option.

With a deep breath, Louko grabbed hold of the door latch and pushed. The door seemed to have more weight than normal, and yet he pushed all the harder, stepping into the room to face whatever news had come regarding his brother.

He was not prepared for the face that met him.

"*You?!*" His face paled as he stood face to face with a nightmare, and if his feet had not been so glued to the floor, he might have been tempted to take a swing at the figure before him—unarmed or not.

Mariah's face twisted in apprehension as she held both her hands up. "Louko, please listen, it's impor—"

"—*What* are you doing here?! Do you have *any* idea what you've done? You're lucky I don't just run you through and give you the miserable end you deserve!"

She blinked in shock, but Louko couldn't care less.

"I don't understand." It was Entrais. "I assume I should restrain her, then?"

"No! Please. Just wait. You can lock me up, I don't care. But just hear me out, *please*!" Mariah gasped.

"I am *done* hearing your serpent's tongue," Louko spat. "Done! You hear me?"

"Then don't listen—read." She fumbled in her worn-out coat and pulled out a crumpled envelope. "I stole this from his study when I left. I saw him tuck it away in a secret drawer; it has to be something important."

Louko snatched the thing from her hands and tore the envelope open. But the moment he set eyes on the note inside, his entire body went rigid. He thrust the jumbled languages into Ent's hands with the breathless request: "Please, read it."

Brow knotted in confusion, Ent glanced towards Mariah and then down at the note in his hands. Then he began to read:

Mitheau joins Astra's group—White Pawn No. 3 forward one

Princess Astra and Prince Louko return to Litash—Black Bishop No. 1 forward/left two, blocks retreat of White Pawn No. 6

Black Pawn No. 5 forward one

Aelor Ven usurps Dia Tzaro—White Bishop No. 1 takes Black Castle No. 2

Chamberlain Julyn seized for aiding and abetting escaped princes, spying on behalf of Nythril. Julyn executed—Black Pawn No. 2 takes White Pawn No. 7

Princess Mariah flees to Litash—White Pawn No. 8 forward two

Black Queen forward two

White Bishop No. 2 forward/left two

Tyron knew. He was still one step ahead. And he knew where Astra was.

EPILOGUE

Tirzah:

"A letter for you, my lady." The courier bowed.

Tirzah's heart dropped at the sight of the black seal. She said nothing as she took the folded parchment and waved a hand in dismissal. Only once the messenger's footsteps had faded from the hall did she get up and cross to the window of her borrowed room. There she faltered a moment, gazing out over the palace gardens. Then she swallowed and broke the seal.

Dear Sister,

So kind of you to think of me and to send our red-headed friend my way. But I couldn't let you be apart for too long: She is already on her way back to you. Be sure to give her a week or two to rest before you call on her. I'm sure she will be tired after her travels. As for that tea, I'm afraid that our friend had quite forgotten it. Please ask her to pick it up next time she is back in Nythril. Surely that will be soon.

Your brother,

-T

Tirzah reread the letter twice before crossing to the fireplace. She tossed the letter and its envelope into the flames, and watched both dissolve to ash. The wax of the seal bubbled and dripped from one of the logs, collecting in a black pool at the bottom of the hearth.

Every time she got another letter, it seemed as if the ring on her right hand burned with the reminder of her sister. She was nearly glad Rhioa was not here to see either of them. But then again, if she was here, would it ever have come to this? Tirzah didn't know. The only thought she could register was the same one that had been ringing in her head for years:

Please let this work. Oh please, let this work.

Louko and Astra will return in Book 5

Next book in A Daughter's Ransom series:

TO TAKE A WORLD: THE LIVING STONE

Exhausted, disheartened, and defeated, Baey and her companions have somehow managed to make it to Alkemar.... Now an even more dangerous task looms before them, and an even more dangerous arrangement: they must split up.

Some must go to the heart of Rugo and find The Living Stone, braving a country infested with Skayla's violet-eyed lackeys. And what happens when their best allies seem to be part of the race Baeno has hated for so long?

Meanwhile, Baey and her mentor are left in Alkemar to try and form new alliances, while the former GhostMaker struggles to overcome his past and the memories that now haunt him. Will anyone else be able to look beyond his past and trust them?

About the A Daughter's Ransom series:

The TetraWorlds live in ignorance of each other's existence...

One fallen behind in a Medieval time of fantastic and dangerous creatures, another fallen asleep in the comfort of their Victorian age, and the last torn apart by its own Modern innovation. When a dark threat rises up against them—one so quiet that none know to stop it, a Guard from each world must be called to protect their planet's source. But what will happen when these worlds entwine?

About the authors:

NIAMH SCHMID:

Born in Clifton Park New York, Niamh is (unfortunately) a human being. She would much rather be off in some pretend world battling an ogre or taming a rabid pegasus, but instead is currently engaging in completing a bachelor's in Piano Performance. In her spare time she cares for her two mini ponies (or monsters), Freddie and Taffie, as well as her Dorkie (dachshund/yorkie mix) Tobie. She also loves to compose, collect stamps, and dabble in being a very mediocre artist.

REBECCA SCHMID:

Though many seem to miss the fact, Rebecca is actually *not* Niamh. She is a separate human being, who just so happens to also be from upstate New York, also be a pianist, also love animals and literature and art, also have the last name Schmid…. Oh well. Perhaps she's a lot like Niamh. Rebecca lives with her husband and horde of dogs, and spends her time practicing piano, maintaining too many hobbies, and drinking way too much coffee.